KU-096-262

THE BOOK OF SPECULATION

Erika Swyler, a graduate of New York University, is a writer and playwright whose work has appeared in literary journals and anthologies. Born and raised on Long Island's north shore, Erika learned to swim before she could walk, and happily spent all her money at travelling carnivals. She is also a baker and photographer.

700043366167

THE BOOK OF SPECULATION

SPECULATION

Erika Swyler

with illustrations by the author

CORVUS

First published in the United States in 2015 by St. Martin's Press.

First published in Great Britain in 2015 by Corvus,
an imprint of Atlantic Books Ltd.

This paperback edition published in Great Britain
in 2016 by Corvus.

Copyright © Erika Swyler, 2015

The moral right of Erika Swyler to be identified as the author of this work has been asserted by her in accordance with the Copyright, Designs and Patents Act of 1988.

All rights reserved. No part of this publication may be reproduced, stored in a retrieval system, or transmitted in any form or by any means, electronic, mechanical, photocopying, recording, or other-wise, without the prior permission of both the copyright owner and the above publisher of this book.

This novel is entirely a work of fiction. The names, characters and incidents portrayed in it are the work of the author's imagination. Any resemblance to actual persons, living or dead, events or localities, is entirely coincidental.

10 9 8 7 6 5 4 3 2 1

A CIP catalogue record for this book is available
from the British Library.

Paperback ISBN: 978 1 78239 764 9
OME ISBN: 978 1 78239 777 9
E-book ISBN: 978 1 78239 765 6

Printed and bound CPI Group (UK) Ltd, Croydon, CR0 4YY

Corvus
An imprint of Atlantic Books Ltd
Ormond House
26–27 Boswell Street
London
WC1N 3JZ

www.corvus-books.co.uk

For Mom. There are no words.

Acknowledgments

Books have an awful lot of working parts; what follows are the essentials.

My agent, Michelle Brower, fixed a mess and didn't flinch when I said I intended to hand bind the manuscripts myself. Before giving me good news, she advised me to sit down. She was correct in all things.

My editor, Hope Dellon, steered the book and me with such gentle cheer. She and St. Martin's Press have been nothing short of fantastic.

Much of this book was written in the Comsewogue and Brooklyn Public Libraries. Circus history is wild and hairy, and an excellent reason to work in a library. When unable to invent towns, I relied on the historical societies of Charlotte, North Carolina; New Castle, Delaware; and Burlington, New Jersey. Any faults are mine.

A long list of names should go here, but there are too many. This book would not be were it not for Rick Rofihe and Matt de la Peña. Stephanie Friedberg called in the middle of the night to yell a chapter number at me, letting me know I was on to something. Karen Swyler was instrumental in the way only a sibling can be.

Finally, Robert. Out of all the endless coffee, you are the best cup.

THE BOOK OF
SPECULATION

1

Perched on the bluff's edge, the house is in danger. Last night's storm tore land and churned water, littering the beach with bottles, seaweed, and horseshoe crab carapaces. The place where I've spent my entire life is unlikely to survive the fall storm season. The Long Island Sound is peppered with the remains of homes and lifetimes, all ground to sand in its greedy maw. It is a hunger.

Measures that should have been taken—bulkheads, terracing—weren't. My father's apathy left me to inherit an unfixable problem, one too costly for a librarian in Napawset. But we librarians are known for being resourceful.

I walk toward the wooden stairs that sprawl down the cliff and lean into the sand. I've been delinquent in breaking in my calluses this year and my feet hurt where stones chew at them. On the north shore few things are more essential than hard feet. My sister, Enola, and I used to run shoe-less in the summers until the pavement got so hot our toes sank into the tar. Outsiders can't walk these shores.

At the bottom of the steps Frank McAvoy waves to me before turning his gaze to the cliff. He has a skiff with him, a beautiful vessel that looks as if it's been carved from a single piece of wood. Frank is a boatwright and a good man who has known my family since before I was born. When he smiles his face breaks into the splotchy weathered lines of an Irishman with too many years in the sun. His eyebrows curl upward and disappear beneath the brim of an aging canvas hat he's never without. Had my father lived into his sixties he might have looked like Frank, with the same yellowed teeth, the reddish freckles.

To look at Frank is to remember me, young, crawling among wood set up for a bonfire, and his huge hand pulling me away from a toppling log. He summons memories of my father poised over a barbecue, grilling corn—the smell of charred husk and burning silk—while Frank regaled us with fishing stories. Frank lied hugely, obviously. My mother and his wife egged him on, their laughter frightening the gulls. Two people are now missing from the tab-leau. I look at Frank and see my parents; I imagine it's impossible for him to look at me and not see his departed friends.

"Looks like the storm hit you hard, Simon," he says.

"I know. I lost five feet." Five feet is an underestimate.

"I told your dad that he needed to get on that bulkhead, put in trees." The McAvoy property lies a few hundred yards west of my house, farther back from the water with a terraced and planted bluff that's designed to save Frank's house come hell or, literally, high water.

"Dad was never big on listening."

"No, he wasn't. Still, a patch or two on that bulkhead could have saved you a world of trouble."

"You know what he was like." The silence, the resignation.

Frank sucks air through his teeth, making a dry whistling sound. "I guess he thought he had more time to fix things."

"Probably," I say. Who knows what my father thought?

"The water's been coming up high the last couple years, though."

"I know. I can't let it go much longer. If you've got somebody you trust, I'd appreciate the name of a contractor."

"Absolutely. I can send someone your way." He scratches the back of his neck. "I won't lie, though, it won't be cheap."

"Nothing is anymore, is it?"

"No, I suppose not."

"I may wind up having to sell."

"I'd hate to see you do that." Frank's brow furrows, tugging his hat down.

"The property is worth something even if the house goes."

"Think on it some."

Frank knows my financial constraints. His daughter, Alice, also works at the library. Redheaded and pretty, Alice has her father's smile and a way with kids. She's better with people than I am, which is why she handles programming and I'm in reference. But we're not here about Alice, or the perilous state of my house. We're here to do what we've done for over a decade, setting buoys to cordon off a swimming area. The storm was strong enough to pull the buoys and their anchors ashore, leaving them a heap of rusted chains and orange rope braid, alive with barnacles. It's little wonder I lost land.

"Shall we?" I ask.

"Might as well. Day's not getting any younger."

I strip off my shirt, heft the chains and ropes over a shoulder, and begin the slow walk into the water.

"Sure you don't need a hand?" Frank asks. The skiff scrapes against the sand as he pushes it into the water.

"No thanks, I've got it." I could do it by myself, but it's safer to have Frank follow me. He isn't really here for me; he's here for the same reason I do this walk every year: to remember my mother, Paulina, who drowned in this water.

The Sound is icy for June, but once in I am whole and my feet curl around algae-covered rocks as if made to fit them. The anchor chains slow me, but Frank keeps pace, circling the oars. I walk until the water reaches my chest, then neck. Just before dipping under I exhale everything, then breathe in, like my mother taught me on a warm morning in late July, like I taught my sister.

The trick to holding your breath is to be thirsty.

"Out in a quick hard breath," my mother said, her voice soft just by my ear. In the shallow water her thick black hair flowed around us in rivers. I was five years old. She pressed my stomach until muscle sucked in, navel almost touching spine. She pushed hard, sharp fingernails pricking. "Now in, fast. Quick, quick, quick. Spread your ribs wide. Think wide." She breathed and her rib cage expanded, bird-thin bones splayed until her stomach was barrel-round. Her bathing suit was a bright white glare in the water. I squinted to watch it. She thumped a finger against my sternum. *Tap. Tap. Tap.* "You're breathing up, Simon. If you breathe up you'll drown. Up cuts off the space in your belly." A gentle touch. A little smile. My mother said to imagine you're thirsty, dried out and empty, and then drink the air. Stretch your bones and drink wide and deep. Once my stomach rounded to a fat drum she whispered, "Wonderful, *wonderful.* Now, we go under."

Now, I go under. Soft rays filter down around the shadow of Frank's boat. I hear her sometimes, drifting through the water, and glimpse her now and then, behind curtains of seaweed, black hair mingling with kelp.

My breath fractures into a fine mist over my skin.

Paulina, my mother, was a circus and carnival performer, fortuneteller, magician's assistant, and mermaid who made her living by holding her breath. She taught me to swim like a fish, and she made my father smile. She disappeared often. She would quit jobs or work two and three at once. She stayed in hotels just to try out other beds. My father, Daniel, was a machinist and her constant. He was at the house, smiling, waiting for her to return, waiting for her to call him *darling.*

Simon, darling. She called me that as well.

I was seven years old the day she walked into the water. I've tried to forget, but it's become my fondest memory of her. She left us in the morning after making breakfast. Hard-boiled eggs that had to be cracked on the side of a plate and peeled with fingernails, getting bits of shell underneath them. I cracked and peeled my sister's egg, cutting it into slivers for her toddler fingers. Dry toast and orange juice to accompany. The early hours of summer make shadows darker, faces fairer, and hollows all the more angular. Paulina was a beauty that morning, swanlike, someone who did not fit. Dad was at work at the plant. She was alone with us, watching, nodding as I cut Enola's egg.

"You're a good big brother, Simon. Look out for Enola. She'll want to run off on you. Promise you won't let her."

"I won't."

"You're a wonderful boy, aren't you? I never expected that. I didn't expect you at all."

The pendulum on the cuckoo clock ticked back and forth. She tapped a heel on the linoleum, keeping quiet time. Enola covered herself with egg and crumbs. I battled to eat and keep my sister clean.

After a while my mother stood and smoothed the front of her yellow summer skirt. "I'll see you later, Simon. Goodbye, Enola."

She kissed Enola's cheek and pressed her lips to the top of my head. She waved goodbye, smiled, and left for what I thought was work. How could I have known that goodbye meant goodbye? Hard thoughts are held in small words. When she looked at me that morning, she knew I would take care of Enola. She knew we could not follow. It was the only time she could go.

Not long after, while Alice McAvoy and I raced cars across her living room rug, my mother drowned herself in the Sound.

I lean into the water, pushing with my chest, digging in my toes. A few more feet and I drop an anchor with a muffled clang. I look at the boat's shadow. Frank is anxious. The oars slap the surface. What must it be like to breathe water? I imagine my mother's contorted face, but keep walking until I can set the other anchor, and then empty the air from my lungs and tread toward the shore, trying to stay on the bottom for as long as possible—a game Enola and I used to play. I swim only when it's too difficult to maintain the balance to walk, then my arms move in steady strokes, cutting the Sound like one of Frank's boats. When the water is just deep enough to cover my head, I touch back down to the bottom. What I do next is for Frank's benefit.

"Slowly, Simon," my mother told me. "Keep your eyes open, even when it stings. It hurts more coming out than going in, but keep them open. No blinking." Salt burns but she never blinked, not in the water, not when the air first hit her eyes. She was moving sculpture. "Don't breathe, not even when your nose is above. Breathe too quickly and you get a mouthful of salt. Wait," she said, holding the word out like a promise. "Wait until your mouth breaks the water, but breathe through your nose, or it looks like you're tired. You can never be tired. Then you smile." Though small-mouthed and thin-lipped, her smile stretched as wide as the water. She showed me how to bow properly: arms high, chest out, a crane taking flight. "Crowds love very small people and very tall ones. Don't bend at the waist like an actor; it cuts you off. Let them think you're taller than you are." She smiled at me around her raised arms, "And you're going to be very tall, Simon." A tight nod to an invisible audience. "Be gracious, too. Always gracious."

I don't bow, not for Frank. The last time I bowed was when I taught Enola and the salt stung our eyes so badly we looked like we'd been fighting. Still, I smile and take in a deep breath through my nose, let my ribs stretch and fill my gut.

"Thought I was going to have to go in after you," Frank calls.

"How long was I down?"

He eyes his watch with its cracked leather strap and expels a breath. "Nine minutes."

"Mom could do eleven." I shake the water from my hair, thumping twice to get it out of my ear.

"Never understood it," Frank mutters as he frees the oars from the locks. They clatter when he tosses them inside the skiff. There's a question neither of us asks: how long would it take for a breath-holder to drown?

When I throw on my shirt it's full of sand; a consequence of shore living, it's always in the hair, under the toenails, in the folds of the sheets.

Frank comes up behind me, puffing from dragging the boat.

"You should have let me help you with that."

He slaps my back. "If I don't push myself now and again I'll just get old."

We make small talk about things at the marina. He complains about the prevalence of fiberglass boats, we both wax poetic about *Windmill*, the racing sail he'd shared with my father. After Mom drowned, Dad sold the boat without explanation. It was cruel of him to do that to Frank, but I suppose Frank could have bought it outright if he'd wanted. We avoid talking about the house, though it's clear he's upset over the idea of selling it. I'd rather not sell either. Instead we exchange pleasantries about Alice. I say I'm keeping an eye out for her, though it's unnecessary.

"How's that sister of yours? She settled anywhere yet?"

"Not that I know of. To be honest, I don't know if she ever will."

Frank smiles a little. We both think it: Enola is restless like my mother.

"Still reading tarot cards?" he asks.

"She's getting by." She's taken up with a carnival. Once that's said, we've ticked off the requisite conversational boxes. We dry off and heft the skiff back up on the bulkhead.

"Are you heading up?" I ask. "I'll walk back with you."

"It's a nice day," he says. "Think I'll stay down here awhile." The ritual is done. We part ways once we've drowned our ghosts.

I take the steps back, avoiding the poison ivy that grows over the railings and runs rampant over the bluff—no one pulls it out; anything that anchors the sand is worth whatever evil it brings— and cut through the beach grass, toward home. Like many Napawset houses, mine is a true colonial, built in the late 1700s. A plaque from the historical society hung beside the front door until it blew away in a nor'easter a few years back. The Timothy Wabash house. With peeling white paint, four crooked windows, and a sloping step, the house's appearance marks prolonged negligence and a serious lack of funds.

On the faded green front step (have to get to that) a package props open the screen door. The deliveryman always leaves the door open though I've left countless notes not to; the last thing I need is to rehang a door on a house that hasn't been square since the day it was built. I haven't ordered anything and can't think of anyone who would send me something. Enola is rarely in one place long enough to mail more than a postcard. Even then they're usually blank.

The package is heavy, awkward, and addressed with the spidery scrawl of an elderly person—a style I'm familiar with, as the library's patrons are by and large an aging group. That reminds me, I need to talk to Janice about finding stretchable dollars in the library budget. Things might not be too bad if I can get a patch on the bulkhead. It wouldn't be a raise, a one-time bonus maybe, for years of service. The sender is no one I know, an M. Churchwarry in Iowa. I clear a stack of papers from the desk—a few articles on circus and carnivals, things I've collected over the years to keep abreast of my sister's life.

The box contains a good-sized book, carefully wrapped. Even before opening it, the musty, slightly acrid scent indicates old paper, wood, leather, and glue. It's enveloped in tissue and newsprint, and unwrapping reveals a dark leather binding covered with what would be intricate scrollwork had it not suffered substantial water damage. A small shock runs through me. It's very old, not a book to be handled with naked fingers, but seeing as it's already ruined, I give in to the quiet thrill of touching something with history. The edges of the undamaged paper are soft, gritty. The library's whaling collection lets me dabble in archival work and restoration, enough to say that the book feels to be at least from the 1800s. This is appointment reading, not a book you ship without warning. I shuffle my papers into two small stacks to support the volume—a poor substitute for the bookstands it deserves, but they'll do.

A letter is tucked inside the front cover, written in watery ink with the same shaky hand.

Dear Mr. Watson,

I came across this book at auction as part of a larger lot I purchased on speculation. The damage renders it *useless to me, but a name inside it —Verona Bonn—led me to believe it might be of interest to you or your family. It's a lovely book, and I hope that it finds a good home with you. Please don't hesitate to contact me if you have any questions that you feel I may be able to answer.*

It is signed by a Mr. Martin Churchwarry of Churchwarry & Son and includes a telephone number. A bookseller, specializing in used and antiquarian books.

Verona Bonn. What my grandmother's name would be doing inside this book is beyond me. A traveling performer like my mother, she would have had no place in her life for a book like this. With the edge of my finger, I turn a page. The paper nearly crackles with the effort. Must remember to grab gloves along with book stands. The inside page is filled with elaborate writing, an excessively ornamented copperplate with whimsical flourishes that make it barely legible. It appears to be an accounting book or journal of a Mr. Hermelius Peabody, related to something containing the words *portable* and *miracle*. Any other identifiers are obscured by water damage and Mr. Peabody's devotion to calligraphy. Skimming reveals sketches of women and men, buildings, and fanciful curved-roof wagons, all in brown. I never knew my grandmother. She passed away when my mother was a child, and my mother never spoke about her much. How this book connects to my grandmother is unclear, but it's interesting nonetheless.

I dial the number, ignoring the stutter indicating a message. It rings for an exceedingly long time before an answering machine picks up and a man's weathered voice states that I've reached

Churchwarry & Son Booksellers and instructs to leave the time and date in addition to a detailed message as to any specific volume I'm seeking. The handwriting didn't lie. This is an old man.

"Mr. Churchwarry, this is Simon Watson. I received a book from you. I'm not sure why you sent it, but I'm curious. It's June twentieth, just six o'clock. It's a fantastic specimen and I'd love to know more about it." I leave multiple numbers, cell, home, and library.

Across the street, Frank heads toward his workshop, a barn to the side of his property. A piece of wood tucked under his arm, a jig of some sort. I should have asked him for money, not a contractor. Workmen I can probably find, the money to do the work is an entirely different matter. I need a raise. Or a different job. Or both.

A blinking light catches my eye. Voice mail. Right. I punch in the numbers. The voice at the other end is not one I expect to hear.

"Hey, it's me. Shit. Do I call enough to be an *it's me*? I hope you have an *it's me*. That would be good. Anyway, it's me, Enola. I'm giving you a heads-up. I'm coming home in July. It would be good to see you, if you feel like being around. Actually, I want you to be around. So, I'm coming home in July, so you should be home. Okay? Bye."

I play it back again. She doesn't call enough to be an *it's me*. There's noise in the background, people talking, laughing, maybe even the sound of a carnival ride or two, but I might be imagining that. No dates, no number, just July. Enola doesn't work on a normal timeline; to her, leaving a month's window is reasonable. It's good to hear her voice, but also concerning. Enola hasn't called in more than two months and hasn't been home in six years, not since announcing that if she spent one more day in this house with me she'd die. It was a typical thing to say, but different in that we both knew she meant it, different because I'd spent the previous four years taking care of her after Dad died. Since then she's called from time to time, leaving rambling messages. Our conversations are brief and centered on needs. Two years ago she called, sick with the flu. I found her in a hotel in New Jersey, hugging a toilet. I stayed three days. She refused to come home.

She wants to visit. She can. I haven't touched her room since she left, hoping she'd come back, I suppose. I'd thought about turning it into a library, but there were always more immediate concerns, patching leaks, fixing electrical problems, replacing windows. Repurposing my long-gone sister's room wasn't a priority. Though perhaps it's convenient to think so.

The book sits by the phone, a tempting little mystery. I won't sleep tonight; I often don't. I'll be up, fixating. On the house, on my sister, on money. I trace the curve of a flourished *H* with my thumb. If this book is meant for me, best find out why.

2

The boy was born a bastard on a small tobacco farm in the rich-soiled Virginia hills. Had his birth been noted, it would have been in the 1780s, after a tobacco man could set his price for a hogshead barrel, but before he was swallowed up by all-consuming cotton. Little more than clapboard, his diminutive home was moss tipped and permanently shuttered against rain, flies, and the ever-present tang of tobacco from the drying shed.

His mother was the farmer's wife, strong-backed Eunice Oliver. His father was Lemuel Atkinson, an attractive young man and proprietor of a traveling medicine show. With little more than a soft endearment and the lure of a gentleman's supple hands, Eunice gained three bottles of Atkinson's Elixir and a pregnancy.

The farmer, William Oliver, had three children to his name already and did not look kindly upon a bastard. Once the boy was up, walking, and too large to survive on table scraps, Mr. Oliver led the child into the heart of the woods and left him to fate. Eunice cried mightily at having her son taken, but the boy remained silent. The boy's great misfortune was not that he was a bastard, but that he was mute.

He survived several years without words to explain them. In light the boy was hungry and fed himself however he could, picking berries with dirt-crusted hands; when he happened upon a farm, he stole from it on silent feet. A meat-drying house meant a night's shelter and weeks of food. In dark he slept wherever there was warmth. His days shrank, becoming only fog, mountains, and a thick of trees so full the world itself fell in. The boy disappeared into this place, and it was here that he first learned to vanish.

People may live for a century without discovering the secret of vanishing. The boy found it because he was free to listen to the ground humming, the subtle moving of soil, and the breathing of water—a whisper barely discernible over the sound of a heartbeat. Water was the key. If he listened to its depth and measure and matched his breath to it, slowing his heart until it barely thumped, his slight brown frame would fade into the surrounding world. Had any watched, they would have seen a grubby boy turn sideways and vanish into the trees, becoming like a grain of sand—impossible to differentiate from the larger shore. Hunger, his enduring companion, was all that kept him certain that he lived.

Vanishing eased his survival, enabling him to walk into smokehouses and eat until heat and fumes drove him out. He snatched bread from tables, clothing from trees and bushes where it dried, and stole whatever he could to quiet his body's demands.

Only once did he venture to the home that had abandoned him, when his memories of it had grown so vague he thought them imagined. He happened upon the gray house with the slanted roof and was shocked to find it real and not a remnant of a dream. He lifted the latch on a shutter just enough to peer through with a deep brown eye. This vantage showed the interior of a bedroom lit by what moonlight the ill-fitting shutters allowed.

A man and a woman slept on a straw mattress. The boy looked at the man's rough features, the stiff dark bristles jutting from his chin, and felt nothing. The woman lay on her side, brown hair spilling across the edge of her smock. Something woke in the boy, a flash of that hair brushing the back of his hand. He crept into the house, past a long table and the bed of a sleeping child, and slipped into the room where the woman and the man slept, his body remembering the way as though it had traveled it thousands of times. He gently lifted the bedsheet, slid beneath, and closed his eyes. The woman's smell was at once familiar, lye soap and curing tobacco, a scent that lived deep inside him that he'd forgotten. Her warmth made his chest stammer.

He fled before she woke.

He didn't see the woman rouse the man or hear her tell the man that she'd had the sensation of being watched, or that she'd dreamt of her son. The boy did not return to the house. He walked back into the woods, searching for other shelter, other food, and places that didn't make his skin burn.

On the banks of the muddy Dan River, not far from Boyd's Ferry, was the town of Catspaw, named for the shape of the valley in which it lay; it was colored the ochre of the river's loam and dusty with the tracks of horses and mules. The freshets that plagued Boyd's Ferry would later cause Catspaw to melt back into the hills, but at the time the settlement was burgeoning. The boy traveled the Dan's winding edge until he stumbled upon the town. It was frightening but filled with potential; washerwomen boiled large tubs of clothing, sloshing soap and wash water down to the river, men poled flat boats, and horses pulled wagons along the banks and up through the streets, each carrying women and men. The cacophonous jumble of water, people, and wagons terrified the boy. His eyes darted until they latched onto a woman's bright blue dress and watched as the heavy cloth swung back and forth. He hid behind a tree, covered his ears, and tried to slow his heartbeat, to listen to the breath of the river.

Then—a wondrous sound.

Heralded by a glorious voice, a troupe of traveling entertainers arrived. A mismatched collection of jugglers, acrobats, fortune-tellers, contortionists, and animals, the band was presided over by Hermelius H. Peabody, self-proclaimed visionary in entertainment and education, who thought the performers and animals (a counting pig deemed learned, a horse of miniature proportions, and a spitting llama) were instruments for improving minds and fattening his purse. On better days Peabody fancied himself professorial, on worse days townsfolk were unreceptive to enlightenment and ran him out of town. The pig wagon, with its freshly painted blue sides proudly declaring the animal's name, "Toby," bore scars from unfortunate run-ins with pitchforks.

The boy watched townspeople crowd a green and gold wagon as it rolled into the open central square. Close behind were several duller carts and carriages, some with round tops fashioned from large casks, painted every color in creation, each carrying a hodge-podge of people and animals. The wagons circled and women pulled children to their skirts to keep them from running too close to the wheels. The lead wagon was painted with writing so ornate it was near indecipherable; on it stood an impressive man in flamboyant attire—Peabody. Accustomed to lone traveling jugglers or musicians, the townsfolk had not encountered such a spectacle before.

Never had there been such a man as Hermelius Peabody and he was fond of saying so. Both his height and appearance commanded attention. His beard came to a twisted point that brushed his chest and pristine white hair hung to his shoulders, topped by a curly hat that flirted with disintegration; that it held together at all appeared an act of trickery. His belly blatantly taunted gravity; riding high and round, it dared his waistcoat's brass buttons to contain it and strained his red velvet jacket to its limit. Yet the most remarkable thing about Hermelius Peabody was his voice, resonating through the valley with a rich rumbling that grew from deep within his stomach.

"Ladies and gentlemen, you are indeed fortuitous!" He motioned to a lean man behind him. The man, who had a thick scar that tugged at the corner of his mouth, whispered into Peabody's ear. "Virginians," Peabody shouted. "Before you is the most amazing spectacle you shall ever see. From the East I bring you the greatest Orient contortionist!" A willowy girl scrambled onto a carriage roof, tucked a leg behind her head, and tipped forward to stand on one hand.

The boy was transfixed. He inched from behind his tree.

"From the heart of the Carpathians," Peabody shouted and lifted his arms to the sky, "shrouded in the depths of Slavic mysticism, raised by wolves and schooled in the ancient arts of fortune-telling, The Madame Ryzhkova." The crowd murmured as a stooped woman wrapped in a broadloom's worth of silk emerged from a curved-top wagon and extended a twisted hand.

Peabody's voice resonated with the wild part of the boy, crooning and soothing. He inched toward the spectators, toward the wagons, snaking between bodies until he found a spot behind a wheel to best view the white-haired man with the voice like a river. He crouched, balanced on the tips of his toes, listening, timing each breath to the man's.

"Once in a lifetime, ladies and gentlemen. When else will you see a man lift a grown horse using one arm alone? When else, I ask, will you next encounter a girl who can tie herself into a proper sailor's knot or a seer who will tell you what the Lord himself has destined for you? Never, fine ladies and gentlemen!" With a flurry of movement, the performers hopped back into their carts and wagons, rolled down thick canvas coverings, and pulled shut the doors. Peabody remained, pacing slowly, running a hand over his buttons. "Noon and dusk, ladies and gentlemen. Threepence a look and we'll happily accept Spanish notes. Noon and dusk!"

The crowd dispersed, returning to carting, washing, marketing, and the ins and outs of Catspawian life. The boy held his position at the cart. Peabody's sharp blue eyes turned to him.

"Boy," the voice intoned.

The boy fell backward and a whuff of breath left him. His body refused to heed the command to run.

"That is quite a fine trick you have," Peabody continued. "The vanishing, the popping in and out. What do you call it? Ephemeral, ephemerae, perhaps? We'll think of a word or mayhap invent one."

The boy did not understand the sounds tumbling from the man. *Boy* felt familiar, but the rest was a jumble of beautiful noise. He wanted to feel the material that wrapped around the man's stomach.

The man approached. "And what do we have here? You are a boy, yes? Yet you seem to be comprised of muck and sticks. Curious creature." He made a clucking sound. "What say you?" Peabody dropped a hand to the boy's shoulder. It had been months since the boy had encountered a person. Unused to touch, he shuddered under the weight and, doing what fear and instinct commanded, pissed himself.

"Damnation!" Peabody hopped back. "We'll need to rid you of that habit."

The boy blinked. A rasping sound escaped his lips.

Peabody's face softened, a twitch of his cheek betraying a smile. "Do not worry yourself, lad; we'll get along famously. In fact, I am relying upon it." He wrapped a hand around the boy's arm and pulled him to standing. "Come. Let's show you about."

Afraid but fascinated, the boy followed.

Peabody led him to the green and gold wagon where a neatly hinged door opened onto a well-appointed room with a desk, piles of books, a brass lantern, and all the makings of a comfortable home for a traveling man. The boy set foot inside.

Peabody looked him over. "You're dark enough to pass as a Mussulman or Turk. Here, chin up." He bent down, hooking a finger under the boy's jaw for a better view of him. The boy flinched. "No, you're too wild for that." Peabody sat heavily on a small three-legged chair. The boy wondered that it didn't break under the man's weight.

He watched the man think. The man's fingers were clean, nails trimmed. Different from the boy's. Though his size was frightening, there was gentleness to him, the crinkles around his eyes. The boy scurried close to the desk where the man sat, listening to his rumbling.

"We haven't done India before. India," Peabody said to himself. "Yes, an Indian savage, I think." He chuckled. "My new Wild Boy." He reached down as if to pat the boy's head, but paused. "Would you like to be a savage?" The boy did not respond. Peabody's brows lifted. "Can't you speak?"

The boy pressed his back to the wall. His skin felt itchy and tight. He stared at the intricate ties on the man's shoes and stretched his toes against the floor.

"No matter, lad. Yours will not be a speaking role." The corner of his mouth twisted. "More a disappearing act."

The boy reached to touch the man's shoes.

"Like those, do you?"

The boy pulled away.

Peabody frowned, an expression discernible by the turn of his moustache. His sharp eyes softened and he spoke quietly. "You've not been treated well. We'll fix that, boy. You'll stay the night, see if it settles you."

The boy was given a blanket from a trunk. It was scratchy, but he enjoyed rubbing it across his temple. He huddled against the man's desk, pulling the blanket around him. Once during the night the man left and the boy feared he'd been abandoned, but a short time later the man returned with bread. The boy tore into it. The man said nothing, but began scribbling in a book. Occasionally his hand would drift down to pull the blanket back over the boy's shoulder.

As sleep overtook him, the boy decided he would follow this man anywhere.

In the morning Peabody walked the boy through the circled wagons, keeping several paces ahead, and then waiting for him to follow. When they came to an imposing cage affixed to a dray wagon, Peabody stopped.

"I've thought on it. This will be yours; you're to be our Wild Boy."

The boy examined the cage, unaware of the other eyes that looked from their wagons, watching him. The floor was scattered with straw and wood shavings that kept it warm in the evenings—a good consideration, as the boy would be barefooted and naked. On the outside of the cage hung lavish velvet curtains that Peabody had liberated from his mother's drawing room. The curtains were weighted by chains—to close out the light, Peabody said—and rigged with pulleys. Peabody demonstrated how to surprise an audience by snapping them open the moment a Wild Boy defecated or committed an equally abhorrent act.

"It was the previous Wild Boy's, but we'll make it yours."

The boy took to the act. He enjoyed the cool metal against his skin, and the act allowed him to observe as much as he was observed. Faces gawked at him, and he stared back without fear. He tried to understand the rolls women wore their hair in, why their hips appeared larger than men's, and the strange ways that men groomed the hair on their faces. He jumped, crawled, scrambled, ate, and voided where and how he pleased. If he did not like a man, he could sneer and spit without repercussion, and would be rewarded for the privilege. He experienced the beginnings of ease.

Without the boy's knowledge, Peabody studied and tailored the act, learning the intricacies of the boy's disappearing, perhaps better than the boy himself understood. If he left the child in the cage for the length of a morning, the boy would crouch low to the floor, his breaths would become shallow until his chest barely moved, and then, quite suddenly, he would vanish. Peabody learned to slowly raise the curtain on the disappeared boy.

"Hush, fine people," he instructed, sotto voce. "No good can come from frightening a savage beast."

Lifting the curtain was enough to rouse the boy from dissipation. As spectators drew in close to what they presumed was an empty cage, the boy revealed himself. The abrupt appearance of a savage where there had been none made children shout; beyond that, the boy needed do little more than remain mute and naked to drive a crowd to frenzy. The boy found his new life pleasing. He discovered that if he made his penis bobble or flaunted his testicles, a prim woman or two might swoon, after which Peabody would draw the curtain and declare the act successful. He began searching for ways to frighten, hissing and snarling, letting spittle drip from his mouth. When Peabody patted his shoulder and pronounced, "Well done," the boy felt fullness in his stomach that was better than food.

Though the Wild Boy cage was his, the boy did not sleep in it. Beneath the sawdust and hay lay a hidden door; after the curtains were drawn he undid the latch and climbed into the dray's box bottom, where a wool blanket was stored for him; from there he made his way to Peabody's wagon, where a change of clothing was kept for the prized Wild Boy. Peabody would sit at the far end of the wagon chewing at his pipe while writing and sketching by lantern light, occasionally pausing to give a conspiratorial look.

"Excellent take, my boy," he'd say. "You've got a certain flair. Mayhap the best Wild Boy I've had. Did you see the missus faint?

Her skirts went over her head." His belly shook as he clapped the boy on the back. The boy understood that the man liked him. He'd begun to recall words from a time before the woods, words like *boy*, and *horse, bread,* and *water,* and that laughter was good. The more he listened to Peabody talk, the more language began to knit.

Peabody spoke differently to the boy, with a quieter voice than he used with others. The boy did not know that within short weeks of their acquaintance, Hermelius Peabody had begun to think of him as a son.

It began when Peabody did not want the boy to spend an unseasonably cool night in the Wild Boy cage. Perhaps the boy's thinness inspired pity, but Peabody decided offering the boy a warm place to sleep was a good business investment and would reflect well on his soul. The boy curled up on a straw-stuffed cushion, the same cushion on which Peabody's son, Zachary, had once slept. Something inside Peabody shifted. Zachary had set out years before to make his fortune, leaving Peabody proud but at a loss. He looked at the sleeping boy and realized his latest acquisition might fill that space. When the boy woke he was greeted by a pile of clothing that was to belong to him. The knee britches and long shirts were no simple castoffs; they had been Zachary's.

In the evenings, the boy sat on the floor of Peabody's wagon, listening, picking out names, places, acts. *Nat, Melina, Susanna, Benno, Meixel.* Peabody schooled him little in social niceties, as he deemed them useless, instructing instead in showmanship and confidence born of understanding an audience. At first the boy did not want to know about the people who looked at him through his bars; he was pleased that the cage kept them at a distance, but curiosity sprouted as Peabody made him watch other acts, the tumbler, the bending girl, and the strongman.

"Watch," he said. "Benno looks at the lady just so, draws her in, and now he'll pretend he's about to fall." The tumbler, balanced on a single hand, wobbled dangerously and a woman gasped. "He's in no more peril than you or I. He's done the same trick with that very wobble since I picked him up in Boston. We lure them in, boy, lure them and scare them a little. They like to be frightened. It's what they pay for." The boy began to understand that those who watched were *others*. The boy, Peabody, the performers were *we*.

Over a series of weeks, Peabody taught his Wild Boy the art of reading people. Prior to each evening's show he sat with the boy in the Wild Boy cage. Together they peeked through the heavy drapes and observed the crowd.

"That one there," Peabody whispered. "She clutches the hand of the man beside her—that one's half affright already. A single pounce in her direction and she'll have a fit." He chuckled, round cheeks spilling over white beard. "And the big man—puffed-looking fellow?" The boy's eyes darted to a man huge as an ox. "See if he won't try his hand against our strongman." He murmured something about using the second set of weights for the show.

The boy began to think of people as animals, each with their own temperament. Peabody was a bear, burly, protective, and predisposed to bellowing. Nat, the strongman, broad browed and quiet natured, was a cart horse. Benno, whom the boy had started to take meals with, possessed a goat's playfulness. The corded scar that pulled Benno's mouth downward when he spoke fascinated the boy. The fortune-teller was something stranger. Madame Ryzhkova was both birdlike and predatory. Despite great age, her movements were twitching and brisk. She looked at people as though they were prey, her eyes bearing the mark of hunger. Her voice stood the hair at his neck on end.

They were setting up camp after leaving a town called Rawlson when Peabody took the boy aside.

"You've done well by me." He tapped his hand lightly on the boy's back and pulled him away from sweeping the cage. "It's time I do well by you. We cannot continue calling you *boy* forever."

Peabody led him between the circled wagons to where a fire burned and members of the troupe took turns roasting rabbit and fish. Darkish men some might have called gypsies played dice; Susanna, the contortion girl, stretched and cracked her bones against a poplar tree, while Nat sat cross-legged, holding the miniature horse securely in his lap, stroking its stiff hair with a dark hand. Weeks prior the boy would have been frightened by them, but now as Peabody tugged him toward the gathering, he felt only curiosity.

Peabody took the boy under the shoulder and hoisted him high into the air, then set him firmly atop a tree stump near the fire.

"Friends and fellow miscreants." His silvery show voice stopped all movement. "We have tonight an arduous, yet joyful duty. A wonder has traveled among us in this Wild Boy." The troupe closed in around the fire. Wagons opened. Melina, the juggler with striking eyes, stepped down from her wagon. Meixel, the small blondish man who served as a trick rider, emerged from the woods covered in straw and spit from tending the llama. Ryzhkova's door creaked open. "This lad has earned his weight and is well on to making us wealthier. It is our duty to name him so that one day, my most esteemed friends, he will be master of all he surveys." The fire burst and threw sparks like stars into the night. "A strong name," Peabody said.

"Benjamin," called a voice.

"A true name."

"Peter."

"A name that carries importance," said Peabody. Inescapable, the voice buzzed inside the boy, tickling parts of his skull. He stared into the fire and felt his heartbeat rise.

"He is called Amos." Madame Ryzhkova spoke softly, but her words sliced. "Amos is a bearer of burdens, as will be this boy. Amos is a name that holds the world with strength and sorrows."

"Amos," said Peabody.

Amos, the boy thought. The seer's eyes glinted at him, two black beads. *Amos*. The sound was long and short, round and flat. It was his.

Meixel found his fiddle and played a bouncy melody that started Susanna dancing and brought about drinking and laughter. Amos watched and listened for a time, but slinked away once he could tell he'd been forgotten. He spent his naming night stretched across the mattress in Peabody's wagon. Silently he repeated this moniker, hearing each syllable as it had sounded on Madame Ryzhko-va's lips. *Amos,* he thought. *I am Amos.*

Late in the night Peabody returned to the wagon and sat down to sketch in his book. It was long hours before he extinguished his light. As he did so, he spared a glance over his shoulder to where the boy lay. "Good night, my boy. Dream well, Amos."

Amos smiled into the darkness.

3

I t's an absurd hour for a phone call, but the more absurd the hour, the more likely someone is to be home. Though the sun is barely up over the water, Martin Churchwarry sounds as though he's been awake for hours.

"Mr. Churchwarry? I'm so glad to reach you. This is Simon Watson. You sent me a book."

"Oh, Mr. Watson," he says. "I'm delighted to hear it arrived in one piece." He sounds excited, almost breathy. "It's rather fantastic, isn't it? I'm only sorry that I wasn't able to hang on to it myself, but Marie would have killed me if I'd brought home another stray."

"Absolutely," I say reflexively. After a brief pause, "I don't think I follow."

"It's the bookseller's occupational hazard. The

longer you're in business, the more the line between shop and home blurs. Oh, let's be honest. There isn't a line at all anymore, and Marie—my wife—won't tolerate me taking up any more space with books I can't sell but like the look of."

"I see."

"But you haven't called about my wife. I assume you have questions."

"Yes. Specifically where did you get it and why send it to me?"

"Of course, of course. I mentioned that I specialize in antiquarian books, yes? I'm a bit of a book hound, actually. I hunt down specific volumes for clients. Yours was part of a lot in a series of estate auctions. I wasn't there about it specifically, I was there for a lovely edition of *Moby-Dick*; a client of mine is a bit obsessed with it." There is a jovial bounce to his voice and I find myself picturing an elfin man. "There was a 1930 Lakeside Press edition in the lot I couldn't pass up. I was lucky enough to have the winning bid, but wound up with some twenty-odd other volumes in the process, nothing spectacular, but saleable things—Dickens, some Woolf— and then there was your book."

My book. I haven't thought of it that way, though its leather feels comfortable in my hands, right. "Whose estate?"

"A management company was in charge of the event. I tried to follow up with them about the book, but they weren't terribly forthcoming. If something has no provenance, their interest is generally low, and the lot it was part of was a mixed bag, more volume than quality. It belonged to a John Vermillion."

The name is unfamiliar. I know little of my family. Dad was the only child of older parents who died before I was born, and Mom didn't live long enough to tell me much of anything. "Why send it to me and not his family?"

"The name, Verona Bonn. Wonderful sounding. Half the charm in old books is the marks of living they acquire; the way the name was written seemed to imply ownership. It was too lovely to destroy or let rot any further, yet I couldn't keep it. So I did a bit of research on the name. A circus high diver—how extraordinary. I discovered a death notice, which led me to your mother, and in turn to you."

"I doubt it was my grandmother's," I say. "From what I know she lived out of a suitcase."

"Well, another family member's perhaps? Or maybe a fan of your grandmother's—people do love a good story."

Yes, a story. We are of course a good story. My hands slip and suddenly my coffee is on the kitchen floor, pooling in the cracked linoleum. I grab for a paper towel to mop it up and knock over the sugar canister. The old sour feeling settles in the center of my chest, a familiar sensation that comes with being the town tragedy. A mother who drowned herself, a father dead from grief, a young man raising his sister alone.

"Do you do this kind of thing often? Track down families of people who used to own your books?"

"More often than you'd think, Mr. Watson—Simon. May I call you Simon?"

Blood wells from the bottom of my foot, a dark red bloom mixes with the coffee and sugar. I must have stepped on a piece of the mug. "If you like."

"Wonderful. I just last year came across a lovely edition of Scott's *The Lady of the Lake*. It had a beautiful padded and embossed cloth binding. Inside there was a pressed violet that was forty years old if it was a day. A little piece of magic. The owner, Rebecca Willoughby, had written her name on the inside cover. Rebecca was deceased, of course, but I managed to find her niece, who was delighted to receive a book that her aunt had obviously treasured as a girl. She said it was a bit like meeting her aunt all over again. I'd hoped to have a similar experience with this book. Has it stirred anything at all?"

The conversation has jostled memories, but not pleasant ones. "You found me, so you must know my parents are dead."

There is an awkward cough. "I'm terribly sorry. I apologize if I've caused any unpleasantness."

"It's been a long time." I exhale. And the book is fascinating,

and somehow connected to someone with an interest in my grandmother.

"If you don't want it, I understand. I'd just ask that you send it
back to me rather than disposing of it—I'll happily pay the shipping. It's just such a pretty book, and so old. I suppose I can con-
vince Marie to let me keep one more."

The thought of disposing of something that has survived so much
is abhorrent. "No, I'll hang on to it. And I'm perfectly capable of
keeping it safe. Weirdly enough, you've sent it to the right person.
I'm a librarian. I work with archives."

"How perfectly apt." Churchwarry laughs, and I begin to understand some of his delight in passing books on. There's a certain
serendipity, a little light that's settled in my sternum.

He asks a favor of me, gently, as though expecting my refusal.
"Will you let me know if you find out why your grandmother's
name is in it? It's not important, of course, I just love to know my
books' history. A quirk of mine."

I will look into it, not because he's asked, but because I should.
Too much of my family has been lost to the haze of time and for-
getting. "I will," I assure him before hanging up.

My hands feel large and clumsy. I stick a Band-Aid to my foot,
shove on my shoes, and watch the sun climb over the water. I don't
mop up the coffee or the sugar mess. Later. An hour passes after
hanging up from Churchwarry and the unsettling conversation.
How I spend it, I can't say.

Closing the door requires an abrupt tug, surprising it into shutting,
another side effect of an aging house and slipping-away land. I'll
have to rehang it. Maybe Frank can angle it with a lathe. I toss the
book onto the passenger seat, then wince. It's a crime to abuse anything this old.

The drive to Grainger Library runs the long way through Napawset, through the three-block historic district, where all the houses are
from the Williams family—colonial boxes built by brothers who div-
vied up the town in 1694—curving around the harbor road, past the

marina and fiberglass boats Frank hates, winding through Port and the captains' houses that tourists call charming. Port is packed with cars lining up for the ferry to Connecticut, and the big boat, huge jaws open, is swallowing sedans and sports cars. The harbor road climbs a hill crowned by a monastery, then dips down, following the salt marsh before turning toward the center of the island and a flat stretch of land, in the middle of which is the Grainger.

Leslie and Christina at the circulation desk confirm I'm late. No one is ever in first thing in the morning and the children's reading groups don't start until ten o'clock, but the ignominy of lateness is still present as I walk past the director's office to my desk in reference. I hear the hollow thudding of Janice Kupferman's heels pacing her office. Yes, she saw me.

Sliding into my chair usually feels like coming home, but today it's troubled. I set the book on my desk and stare at it. I should start on grant applications, or the never-ending stream of purchasing requisitions that inevitably get denied. After a few attempts at a statement of need for an update to our electronic catalogs and reading lists, I find myself gazing at the reference stacks. The Grainger feels like mildew and has a mood of disrepair.

The library's mainstay is the whaling history archive. Though Napawset never saw much in the way of actual whaling, Philip Grainger, the library's founder, was a man obsessed. Upon his death he willed his entire collection of documents on whaling and Long Island to the library. Shipping records, art, nautical charts, market prices for whale oil and soaps, manifests—some sixty years of collecting housed in two large windowless rooms on the second floor. It's Janice's pet project and the source of our funding, though most of us wouldn't mind seeing it go.

Over by an ancient microfiche machine, Alice McAvoy restocks shelves. There's something hypnotic about her thick red braid. Not quite red—strawberry blond. I watch it sway, timing my breath to her hair. I can almost hear the gentle swish, almost disappear into the sound.

Alice turns toward the scratching rustle of a tweed suit headed in my direction. Janice Kupferman on the move.

"Simon? May I see you in my office for a minute?" Janice asks.

"Absolutely."

Janice's office is low ceilinged and fits her fireplug build, which leaves me distinctly out of place. Sitting in her office chair requires me to eat my knees.

"Sorry," she says, seeing my predicament. "There's never any money for furniture."

"It's fine. I'm used to it."

"Yes, I suppose you would be." A tired smile rounds the just-forming jowls that indicate passage through middle age. "How long have you worked here? Ten years, at least."

"Could be. I've lost track."

She sits across from me, putting three feet of wood-grain laminate desk between us. "I hate this," she says. Each word is punctuated with a head shake that makes her earrings jiggle—dolphins, hung by their tails, peeping under a precise brown bob. "I really hate this."

I'd sink into the chair but it's too cramped. I know what's coming. "Budget?"

"The town cut us this year. Badly. I'll try and fight them as much as I can, but—"

"Blood from a stone?"

At her nod, any hope of a bonus to fix the bulkhead dries up.

"There must be something, a grant somewhere we haven't gotten."

"I'll keep trying, but the realities are what they are." She doesn't need to say it. Recessions don't breed interest in whaling history. "I don't want to, but I may have to let someone go. It isn't personal; I'm having this talk with everyone, but provided the town doesn't budge, someone has to go."

Someone. It's no accident that she mentioned the years I've been here. Alice is the only one close to me as far as seniority and I have three years on her. Alice also does programming. Programming can't be replaced by an updated electronic catalog. "I understand."

"I'll do everything I can, Simon. Nothing is set, but it felt wrong not to let everyone know what's going on."

"Absolutely," I say. When I started at Grainger I thought Janice was priggish, but after years of watching her I know that the day I met her she was already beaten by cuts, grant denials, and begging. If she let two girls in circulation go she might save me or Alice, but the resigned look, even the way she stretches across the desk as if to reassure me, say that she won't fire two people to save one. Bulkheads, terracing, foundation repair, roof work. None of it will be possible. I need another way.

"I'll try," she says when I get up to leave. "Would you send Alice in?"

"Sure. You'll get the money, Janice. You always do." It's hollow. We both know it.

I don't need to tell Alice a thing. Janice's office walls aren't thick, and everything she heard is written on her face.

"I'm sure it's me," she says.

I force a smile. "I'm sure it's nobody." Janice's door closes with a heavy click.

Two women sit by the front windows, knitting. The tapping of their needles echoes through the stacks. Reference is still quiet. I am once more alone at my desk. I put in calls to Springhead and Moreland Libraries to see if cuts are hitting them as hard. They are, which is daunting. I call over to Liz Reed at North Isle. "Tell me something good, Liz."

"How good?"

"Discretionary dollars, or new pay lines."

"Don't talk like that, Simon. I'm a married woman." Though I chuckle, she knows it's serious. "Job hunting?"

"Not yet. There might still be a spontaneous nationwide interest in regional whaling history."

She doesn't laugh. "I can send you a link to a listserv site that might help. Just remember, we're not librarians; we're information professionals. You can use me as a reference."

"Thanks, Liz."

I hang up and wait for Liz's email. From the corner of the desk the book stares at me. An interesting object in itself, it appears to be both diary and account book for a traveling show. Peabody's

Portable Magic and Miracles, a whimsically ludicrous name. Why my grandmother's name is inscribed on a back page is a mystery. The early pages detail the running of the show, listing various towns, money made, and traveling routes. Elaborate handwriting makes the narrative sections a difficult read, but they center on the development of an act involving a mute boy, Amos. The last portion of the book is horribly damaged. The leather on the back is ruined and the ink on the last pages is a wash of brown, blue, and black—reduced to its base elements by chromatography and time. Thumbing through reveals a second owner; where the earlier pages were filled with sketches, the latter are neat, free of drawings and confined to lists of income, dates, and names. Then the water damage.

Janice's door clicks open and closed as she works her way through the entire staff. Marci, the children's librarian, has just gone in when I see it. There, in plain black letters, a name. *Bess Visser. Dead. July the 24th, 1816. Drowned.*

I know that name. Worse still, I know the date. The flinch is involuntary and almost painful. My mother drowned on July 24th.

"Simon?" Alice looks over my shoulder. Tired. Frank's daughter is a neatly put together woman. I know her too well to call her beautiful, though an upturned nose, sharp chin, and thoughtful eyes make her so. She's just Alice, which is everything and nothing, and awkward because I've seen her every day since I can remember. Unrealized or unrequited, choosing between the words doesn't change what Alice and I are, or that she is off-limits. Because of Frank. Because of my parents. I run my hand down my face. She sighs.

"Janice will find the money," I say.

"She always does," Alice says. "Trust in the archive."

"In the archive we trust. Liz at North Isle is sending over leads. Just in case."

"Just in case. Right." Her eyes land on the book and she traces her fingers across the cover. "This is really old."

"Someone sent it to me. I'm not sure why."

"Ah, a puzzle. You like puzzles."

I would agree, but the book feels different now that I've seen a familiar name. Drowned on July 24th, like my mother. It's a small piece of awfulness. "It's a little off. My grandmother's name is in it. I spoke with the guy who sent it. He's a bookseller, antiquarian type. Says he got it at auction. I don't know what to make of him."

"Did you run a search on him? This *is* a library; research wouldn't be unheard of." She leans against the desk. The subtle curve between her waist and hip is juxtaposed against the reference stacks. Alice in contrast to encyclopedias.

"I haven't had time. I walked in the door and then Janice . . . "

We're both quiet. It's difficult to breathe when the air is pungent with the stench of oncoming layoffs.

"Dinner. Take me to dinner," Alice says.

"Sorry?"

"I'll help. Give me the name of the guy who sent you the book and I'll check into him for you. In return, you buy me dinner. Not at the Pump House, either. I want to go somewhere nice with good wine. Today is terrible and I want to go out." She pushes back from the desk, bouncing on her toes.

"I promise I won't take you to the Pump House." For so many reasons. Because it's filled with blaring televisions, bloated people bent over stale beers, and because I worked there and ate enough shift meals that just the thought of the Pump House is nauseating.

"Perfect. Pick me up at seven so I can grab a shower first. What was his name?"

"Martin Churchwarry. Churchwarry and Son Booksellers. Iowa."

Alice's apartment is in Woodland Heights near what's left of a strawberry farm, and when I pull up she is waiting for me. I take her to La Mer because it's where you take women to dinner. It's on the water and at night the lights from Connecticut shine across the harbor like they're crying. The waiters have accents and things come with sauces—there may be a Saucier. Alice wears a short pink dress, cut for people to admire her legs. I do. At work she wears practical pants and flats made for bending, stretching, and the dust that comes with libraries. In high school I saw her legs in her field hockey skirt. They were good then; they're better now. Her hair is half pinned behind one ear, the rest loose down her back. This is not a date. This is Alice. She smiles when I tell her she looks nice, a slight twist of her mouth.

"You clean up well too," she says. Then the waiter appears and Alice orders a glass of wine. "Have no fear, I won't break your bank."

I laugh. It's hard not to watch her lips touch the glass. "Did you come up with anything on Churchwarry?"

"I barely got to start. The shop is a real thing. Churchwarry and Son specializes in antiquarian books. It seems like he's both the Churchwarry and the son. It's a solo operation. I couldn't find much on the man himself, though. Maybe he's lonely and reaching out."

I shrug. "Strange way of doing it. He didn't seem that lonely." He'd sounded cheerful, in fact. Absolutely alive.

"I wanted to dig a little more into his bookstore, but I had to help out in the kids' room."

"What happened to Marci?"

"She was crying in the bathroom after meeting with Janice."

We agree that we deserve drinks while we still have jobs to pay for them.

"You'll be fine, you know," she says. "You're the only one who can stomach reference."

"Maybe. But half my job can be done by a computer. Ever apply for a grant that could eliminate half of what you do?"

"No, but that's just because I don't do grants." She taps a nail against the rim of her glass. "The question is, have *you* applied for a grant that could eliminate half of what *I* do?"

"Never crossed my mind."

"See? And that's what will get you fired."

We finish our wine and order more. Soon, we're soft and smiling and talking about a Fourth of July and Frank nearly burning my father's hand off with a roman candle. Alice swears it was the other way around, that she remembers her mother wrapping Frank's hand with gauze. It's difficult to reconcile the girl who launched herself off swing sets with the woman in front of me. I think she's always had a boyfriend. Men from Rocky Point or Shoreham, vague people I never met. She might have one now. Our food arrives.

"My dad's worried about your house," she says, pushing a piece of asparagus around her plate. "I called him last week and he couldn't stop talking about it."

"I'm worried too," I say.

"I don't understand why you haven't sold it."

"There's a lot of history in it." My phone rings and Alice rolls her eyes. I promise to get rid of whoever it is, but when I pick up I know that I won't.

"It's me."

I mouth to Alice that it's my sister and she waves me off. The benefit to knowing someone your whole life is that you don't have to explain why certain calls must be answered. I excuse myself and go outside. "Hey. Where are you?"

"Some hole in the wall. Can you talk?" There's a clinking sound in the background—glass striking glass. I ask again where she is.

"I don't know. A mall parking lot. Does it matter?"

"Not really. You don't sound good. What's going on? I'm in the middle of dinner."

"I had a really bad reading," she says.

"What? The cards?"

"Yeah. I feel cagey and I want to talk to you. Can I talk to you?"

I look back in the window at Alice, sipping wine and eating. I catch her eye. She waves. "Yeah. For a little bit."

"Do you remember when I cut my legs? I don't know why I thought of it, but I was driving and my legs hurt and I needed to talk to you."

"Why?" For a moment I think my phone's gone dead. Three times I say her name before she answers.

"Remember? I slid down those rocks and you carried me. I must have been heavy."

"Not at all." I was thirteen and she was eight. She weighed nothing. "Do you need me to get you?" I could take her to a doctor, or a hotel, get her food, anything. "I'm with Alice, she can come too if you want." Provided she's still there when I get back.

"We were climbing on those boulders with barnacles all over them. Don't know why we did that. Were we looking for snails?"

"Yeah. Enola, should I come and pick you up?"

"No, no. I'll be fine. I had that bathing suit on, the black one with the pink dots. You were on the tall rock, Toaster. Stupid we called it that. I wanted to get to you."

Inside, Alice chats with a waiter, who laughs and flirts with her. My date—it is a date, isn't it?—continues without me.

"Yeah, I remember," I say. At low tide the rocks crawl with life—barnacles, seaweed, sand fleas, and snails. We were on all fours, balancing on ledges, hooking fingers into crevasses.

"My foot slipped on a patch of seaweed."

I remember the sound of her skin smacking the rocks, and reaching to grab her, but she was small and wet and my footing was bad. She slid all the way down.

"Enola? Can I call you back?"

She doesn't listen. "The barnacles shredded me and the fucking saltwater stung so bad I thought it was eating me. It was so sharp. Then I got dizzy and everything closed in."

"I saw you slip and the next thing I knew you were underwater."

"I sank all the way to the bottom. My feet even got stuck in the sand. I screamed and screamed, and then you were behind me. You got there so quick."

I grabbed her and felt the open skin on her legs. No, there had been no skin; bits and pieces of Enola hung from the rocks. I flipped her onto her belly and cradled her.

Alice looks out the window. I mouth *One minute.* She shrugs and drinks her wine.

"You carried me home," Enola says.

She didn't see the bloody trail we left in the sand. When I reached the house it felt empty though it wasn't. Dad was at the kitchen table with a newspaper, drinking from a cup of what had once been coffee. He didn't look up. I carried Enola to her room and dropped her, stomach down, on the bed, then rummaged through the medicine chest. Half of it was filled with Mom's prescriptions. Six years expired and Dad still kept them.

Barnacle cuts are a wonder of nature—so many different kinds of bacteria and no way to avoid infection.

"You put iodine on me, you fuck."

"I didn't know what to do."

I threw myself over her middle, holding her in place while she screamed. We stayed there for what felt like hours, me sprawled over Enola's back, Enola on the bed, Mom's medicine all over the bathroom floor, Dad in the kitchen nursing empty coffee cups.

"You were good to me, Simon," she says.

I did what I could. She sounds calmer than she did when she first called. "Are you sure you're okay?"

"Yeah. I just wanted to hear your voice. Sometimes you make me feel better."

"Okay." *Bess Visser.* I suddenly remember where I've seen that name. It was on a slip of yellow paper with two other names Mom had written down. I found it last year when I moved her dresser to patch a leak. The paper was hidden in the back of a drawer. Mom knew that name.

"Wait, did you say you were with Alice McAvoy?"

"Yes."

"Alice. Nice. I should go. See you in a few weeks."

"Enola?"

"Thanks." There's a click, and she's gone.

Back at the table, Alice has finished eating and paid the check. I must look bad because she immediately asks how I am. I tell her that Enola just needed to talk. She raises her eyebrows but says nothing. I make all the proper apologies but everything feels off. My feet feel off. When I walk Alice to the car, I notice she's listing. She mutters something about her heels and leans into my side, a comfortable weight.

"It isn't fair," she says after we're buckled in and driving back toward Woodland Heights. "You always looked after her. I know you did. Then she leaves and expects you to just drop everything when she calls." She seems prepped and ready to go on but stops herself with a sigh. "I'm sorry. I'm drunk."

I smile. "No, you're not. You're right, but it's just how things are."

"Well, it's shitty."

"Sometimes."

We linger in the doorway to her apartment. I apologize again and promise to pay her back for dinner. She says not to worry about it. Her skin blanches where her hand touches the door frame.

"I need coffee," she says. "Would you like coffee?" And then, because she's complained about my family for me, bought me dinner, worn a dress, because we may not have jobs in a few weeks, because of the way her eyes close when she says coffee, and because she's Alice and in that lives the difference, I take the risk and lean in. Her lips are soft, inviting. At this too, she's better than me, perfect.

Her bedroom is a mix of practical and whimsical. An imposing hardwood desk lines a wall. Clean, square shelves are filled with perfectly organized books and pictures. Near her window hangs a small mobile made of periwinkles, broken moon snails, and tiny horseshoe crab shells—the sort of thing only a beach girl could love. It suits her. The bed is another matter. A mountain of pillows, different fabrics, sizes, different shades of pink. I start to laugh, but then her hands are on my shoulders, pushing me back, and falling on it is wonderful.

There are snaps and wires, zippers, hooks, and then there is skin, and yes, the freckles on her breasts are every bit as intriguing as the ones by her navel, her neck, and between her thighs. And then there is breath and touching, tracing all the places we've hidden from each other. Accustomed to whispering, even our laughs feel hushed, secret. Her hand runs down my back.

"Hi," she says.

"Hi."

Then there is the taste and feel of our bodies.

Alice sleeps on her side with her knees almost to her chest. She's fallen asleep this way sunbathing on the beach since we were children. I lie awake, thinking about Enola's call, the book, the house, and my job. I can't keep the house if my job goes. Despite what I told Frank, I don't want to sell, not when my parents are in the walls. I need money. Time. I need to call Liz's leads. On the desk there is a photograph of Alice as a teenager, holding a giant bluefish. She's thirteen or so, back when she had bangs. Frank must have taken the picture. Though he's not in the photo, I can see him staring out at me from her grinning face. I should put my arm around her, but it feels a little strange. I slept with Frank's daughter.

"You awake?" She sounds drowsy, happy.

"No."

"Liar. I can feel you tapping your fingers on the headboard. You're such a twitcher."

"Sorry."

"You worrying?"

"No."

"You're the worst."

"I don't want to keep you up. You look nice when you're sleeping." She looks perfect.

She nuzzles her cheek into her pillow and cracks a dark brown eye at me. "Thanks. You know, you don't have to stay."

"I want to."

"I don't know if I'm ready to see your breakfast face. Go. It's okay."

"You sure?"

"Yeah. I know where you live."

I take the turn by the salt marsh hard and the Ford's wheels spin. Here's the heart-in-throat feeling I've been avoiding. I'm about to lose my job. And the house—I've slept with the daughter of the only person who might have been willing to lend me the money to fix it. I don't feel as badly about it as I should. I don't feel badly at all, which is worse.

Back in the house I know it's pointless to try to sleep. It doesn't take long to find the slip of paper—it's still in the dresser drawer.

There are three names on it: my grandmother's; a second, Celine Duvel; and there in round, wide cursive is Bess Visser. Alice was right. I can't resist a puzzle.

The light from Frank's porch is almost enough to fill the living room. He's hung up a horseshoe crab shell to dry on his porch railing. It swings a little in the breeze. I think of Alice, alone in bed, and wish I'd stayed.

I write the names in a notebook and set it on my desk. Tomorrow I'll dig up what I can on them. Then I list every name I've ever heard mentioned from my mother's family—a pitiful handful. I open the book. The pages fall to a detailed yet crude sketch of a tarot card, a tall white building on a dark background rent by lightning. Below the sketch, delicately penned letters name the card the Tower. From a window in the tower, a man leaps, falling to the waves and rocks below.

4

Hermelius Peabody's back was pressed against a wall shelf while his throat was half crushed by the forearm of a surprisingly strong Russian crone. His initial response to Madame Ryzhkova's request had been negative, but he was rapidly becoming amenable to her position.

"An apprentice?" He coughed. "Madame, Amos is the most profitable Wild Boy I've encountered, not to mention that he is without speech. How precisely would you work with him?"

Ryzhkova made a noise that fell between snarl and squawk. "We will work well. The cards say it will be so."

When Peabody protested, Madame Ryzhkova muttered a stream of Russian that sounded murderous.

He'd always been somewhat frightened of her. She had simply appeared one day in New York City as he'd staggered from an inn on the East River wharves. She'd stuck her hand out of an alleyway, addressed him by his proper name, and said she would travel with him because the cards had decreed it. Though Peabody did not trust her, he couldn't turn away someone with such a pronounced sense of theatricality. Within hours of installing her in a wagon, she'd transformed it into an exotic room of fabric, cushions, and scents that made the head spin. He was certain she knew her way around poisons; she'd once slipped a powder into his food after he'd refused to advance her wages toward a bolt of silk. "You cannot purchase what you have not yet earned," he'd said. She'd smiled, and at eight o'clock sharp his guts had twisted, curling him up like a pill bug. The next three days were spent sweating in his wagon, shaking, until Ryzhkova appeared.

"Fortunate for you I know how to take pain away," she'd said, shoving a handful of bitter ashes in his mouth. By sunset he was recovered. Peabody was no fool; Ryzhkova received her advance that very night.

Not three hours after Ryzhkova backed him against the wall, Peabody told Amos the way of it.

"My boy, it is time for you to move on to better things." He beamed at Amos, who sat on a footstool. Amos shifted nervously and turned his palm upward in question.

"Have no fear; you've not done anything wrong, Amos. You were in fact the best Wild Boy I've ever had. Therein lies the problem, you see?"

Amos did not.

"You are no longer a boy. To keep you a Wild Boy is to chain your potential." Peabody ran a hand through his beard in thought. "You'll find I've devised a most exciting opportunity. Madame Ryzhkova's taken a shine to you. I believe she has need for an apprentice."

Amos knew some of what Madame Ryzhkova did; her cards told

tales people paid handsomely to hear. But there was an insurmountable obstacle to the arrangement: apprentices spoke. He put his hand across his lips and shook his head.

Peabody gently took Amos's hand from his mouth. "It will be of no concern. I thought upon it and began to understand her reasoning: you will be a lure. I can think of few things more intriguing than a mute fortune-teller. Unspoken futures. You and she will find the way of it. Profits, my boy, just think of it! An abundance of profits." Peabody slapped his small desk, jostling the inkwell. He tried mightily to ignore the look of terror that crept across his protégé's face. "Come, now. Change is a wondrous thing. It was change that brought you to me."

Amos looked at the cushion where he spent his nights, wondering if that would change as well.

"I could never tell you to leave," Peabody said. "You may stay here as long as you wish. I would like that."

The transition was noted by a line in Peabody's book: *19 June 1794. Wild Boy promoted to Apprentice Seer.*

When Amos approached Madame Ryzhkova's wagon, she opened the door before he knocked. Her hair was pulled back from her forehead by a dark green scarf knotted at the base of her skull. She smiled broadly; he could not remember ever having seen her smile. He blinked.

"Amos. Come in. I have much to show you and we are already behind." She waved, and Amos observed her swollen, twisted thumb, how it turned sharply and bent away from the rest of her hand, and part of him latched on to this. He followed the crooked little woman into her lair and away from what he'd known.

Her wagon was surprisingly spare. There hung from its walls a few small paintings—swarthy men and an angelic young woman.

"My family," she said, noting the direction of his gaze. "Father," she pointed to a thickly bearded face. "Brothers." Two younger men with Ryzhkova's intense stare. "Katerina, my daughter," she gestured to the young woman. "My beautiful Katya."

The rest of the wagon held little beauty. Madame Ryzhkova slept on a rough mattress atop a traveling trunk. He imagined such a bed left her bones aching.

As if reading his thoughts, Ryzhkova said, "The seer is a blade. Too much softness dulls the mind. Silks and curtains are for guests." He must have jumped because she laughed, a sound like wind through grass. "Peabody, he likes too much comfort. Yes, it is good you came here before he made you dull. Now, sit. Listen."

Where Peabody's face was full, Madame Ryzhkova's was hollow, the skin pleated and rumpled. Her nose stood perpendicular to itself, a large protuberance turning its tip sharply downward. Her hair stuck out from beneath her scarf, iron wires pointing in all directions. Amos found her eyes fascinating; dark gray in color, he'd seen their like only in animals—the color of goats' eyes before they rammed.

She pulled an empty crate into the center of the wagon floor and motioned for Amos to sit beside it. On it she placed a lacquered black box adorned with pictures in brilliant oranges and reds, each outlined with gold. Amos was drawn to a caged bird whose long tail feathers curled around the box's edge.

"The firebird," Ryzhkova said. "You like him, yes? You'll like even better what is inside."

She opened the box and revealed what looked to be a deck of playing cards. The back of each card was inked a distinctive deep orange. "Watch. Listen," she said and tugged at an earlobe. She set the box on the floor and began turning the cards face up. Each flip of paper revealed a masterpiece—the tall figure of a woman holding a single sharp sword, the sun beating down on a field, a hand holding a star, all in meticulous detail. The old woman touched them with reverence.

When the crate was covered in cards she said, "I will tell you their names and you will learn their faces, how and where we set them. In this way we speak." She pointed to the pictures and explained them just as Peabody had once explained people. "Fool is fool because of blind happiness. He does not see misfortune." The card depicted a young man about to merrily walk off a cliff. "Pride before the fall. He is like a child. Like you." Ryzhkova smiled. He looked away from her cracked, yellowed teeth to the card and the little dog that pulled at the Fool's curled shoe.

"Dog means many things. Protector, enemy. It depends." She talked for hours as her bent hands drew lines and crosses over the symbols. Deep in the night, she patted the crate and chuckled at Amos. "You listen well. We will make good work. I see you yawn. The tired mind does not hear well. To bed with you." With a light kick to his shin, she shooed him from the wagon. "Tomorrow you will come again and I will teach."

Ryzhkova instructed after shows, by candlelight. Rich red and blue fabrics were left hanging if she was tired, making Amos's classroom a gentle chamber for watching, listening, and on occasion vanishing. Ryzhkova's rhythmic speech lulled him until he became part of the cards, falling into them and letting his body disappear. When this happened, she pounded her boot on the floor and shouted a single guttural word. Once he reappeared she smiled, slapped his hand, and started anew.

Amos began to learn. He grew to love the Fool, saturated with yellow and orange—he liked the dog, how it at the last moment pulled its master to safety. He became accustomed to Ryzhkova's voice; it reminded him of wind in trees and the days when he had run through forests. Over time he found that even when not in her presence her voice vibrated through him. On evenings between towns he watched Ryzhkova lay cards—a cross with a line down the side. Two cards set across each other, then one above and one below, one to the left and its mirror on the right. Four cards down the side. What was to come, what would affect it, what ruled at the moment, and the question's outcome. She did readings for unvoiced queries, answering blank nothings.

"Chariot," she said, and turned a card up on the makeshift table. A man on a throne, pulled by animals with human heads. Amos shifted, uncomfortable at the sight of the uncanny animal men. "Conquest and journey. Triumph. See? Man ruling over beast." She rubbed her knuckles through his hair and clucked at him as if he were her child. "Paired with this card, makes much good." She set another card at its side. "World, see?" She raised an arm as though gesturing to the sky. "Not the woman in center but all around the woman, yes?" He nodded, eyes focused on the dancing woman's bare form and her knowing expression.

Before and after lessons Ryzhkova cleared the wagon with a smoldering bushel of herbs that stank of horse sweat. "Smudge," she coughed. "This is how to clear with fire, how you keep cards clear. Clean." She wrote words in the air with smoke plumes. "It is not the cards that tell the future as much as the person holding them. Me, you, whoever asks the question." She tapped the herbs against the wagon's door, sending embers and ash tumbling. "People touch the cards, leave themselves behind. Dreams. Hope. All trapped inside the cards." When the room became oppressive she threw the door open and let in the night air. "You. Me. We have no need for dreams from others. Sometimes bad thoughts, bad ideas, get caught in them. You and I, we clear them. Clean, good cards." She tossed the burned herbs to a blackened spot on the floor and snuffed the embers with a boot heel. She patted his head and the boy and the animal inside him smiled.

She taught him how to bind his hair, giving him one of her silks, a beautiful cloth covered with complex purple and gold patterns. She first twisted his hair into a coil, then folded the silk around it and wound it about his head.

"Good for appearance."

His scalp ached, but in time the pain eased, and the effect was dramatic. He was transformed from a nut-brown boy easily mistaken for a savage into an elegant, foreign young man. Ryzhkova clapped in praise of her efforts. "Now you look a proper young man of fate and destiny." Under her watchful crinkling eyes he felt himself changing. Inexplicably he began to think of the little house and the brown-haired woman who had smelled so familiar.

Amos was a solitary creature. Too many eyes on him at once made him itch, and meals with the troupe were like being trapped in a game with unknown rules. He liked to while away rainy mornings paging through Peabody's book, tracing his fingers over sketches. When Ryzhkova was too tired to teach and shooed him from her wagon he spent his evenings with the small horse, a lovely animal called Sugar Nip, who was ruddy brown, but for a white blaze down her muzzle. She was perfect, except in that she was one eighth the size of what she should be and did not seem to know it. She snorted and stamped as well as any of the cart horses, but was quiet when Amos sat with her. When he hunkered in the straw and pressed his forehead to hers, he felt a warm calm. He enjoyed the quiet that came from combing her forelock, and snatched carrots and apples for her, tucking them deep into the pockets of his britches.

Three days after Ryzhkova bound his hair, she waved him off after a complex lesson on reversed cards. "To bed, boy. You make me weary."

Amos made his way to the wagon Sugar Nip shared with the animal known as *llama*. He dug through his pocket, searching for a radish he'd kept for her. He was running his hand around it when he walked into Benno. Startled, he gasped.

Benno laughed. "Did I surprise you, Amos? I'd thought that difficult to do." He leaned against the wagon, stretching so that inside his striped pantaloons his knees appeared to bend backward.

Amos shrugged then nodded. From time to time he'd sat beside Benno at meals and watched him perform, but he knew little about him other than that he was friendly, and seemed well liked among the women.

"Melina spied you leaving Madame Ryzhkova's wagon," he continued. Benno said the juggler's name with an approximation of a smile, as his scar held half his mouth fixed.

Amos warmed at the mention of Melina. He'd watched her too, from across a campfire and through the curtains of the Wild Boy cage as she kept spoons and knives, eggs and pins spinning in flight. She had curling red hair, a sweet face, and a supple way of moving.

"She claimed Madame had worked a change upon you. I quite agree." Benno tugged at his own brown hair, tied neatly with a piece of black ribbon. "Perhaps if I pull my hair up rather than down, Melina will look at me, too. Do you think?"

Amos's brows drew together and Benno chuckled. "Worry not. I laugh at myself, not you, my friend. Madame Ryzhkova has afforded you the opportunity to show you are fine of face, whereas I . . . " He shrugged and touched his scar.

Amos looked at the corded skin, how it made a perpetual grimace, then took Benno by the arm and led him into Sugar Nip's wagon. He gave Benno the radish to feed her and shared with him the simple peace that came from stroking the little horse's nose.

They passed an hour in silence, after which Benno said, "I had thought you merely interesting. I was mistaken. You are a friend."

He clapped Benno lightly on the back, as Peabody had done with him.

Ryzhkova began teaching Amos how to behave with her clients—most of whom were women. "History is a man," she said. "Future is a woman; that is why they come." When women came in, their skirts filled the front half of the wagon with yards of fabric; thick with sage smoke, tallow, and the warmth of three bodies, the space became a dreamlike sanctum. Amos noticed that people stammered when first speaking to Ryzhkova. He'd once felt that unease; Ryzhkova could be terrifying, but he'd learned that she was soft, too. She touched their hands during readings, a reassurance here, an encouragement there.

She urged specificity in questions and excruciating detail. "Truth brings more truth, yes?" Men asked mostly about their businesses, future harvests, or the identity of the fellow who stole a pig. Nearly all the women asked Madame Ryzhkova about love. Amos liked these readings best because Ryzhkova cooed, petted, and praised them. He pictured Melina's round cheeks, her quick hands, and wondered if she dreamt about love.

Once the women left, Ryzhkova cursed their idiocy. "Can she not see the man is sleeping with other man's wife? You see this card? Look, look." She jabbed a finger at the Ace of Cups, which sat firmly in the position ruling the present. "See the water?" Streams of water spilled from a cup held aloft by a mystical hand. "Information. Communication. Rivers of lies he tells." She laughed.

Amos enjoyed seeing her face move from sweet and kind to disgusted, all of which melted into tired laughter.

Months passed with Amos learning, listening, and at last turning cards for Ryzhkova, clearing them with herb smoke, and taking them from and returning them to their fascinating box. He ate meals with Benno, stole glances at Melina, and spent nights listening to Peabody tut over his books or the occasional correspondence he received from Zachary. Peabody remarked that Amos had begun to smile more. Amos shrugged.

"You've grown into your skin," Peabody said, peering over the top of a letter.

Amos nodded, but he felt empty, like he'd stretched but his insides had remained small. His dreams were scented with curing tobacco.

A year into Amos's apprenticeship the menagerie stopped on the banks of the Schuylkill as they ventured toward Philadelphia. The fog off the water hung heavy. Amos had been sitting on the hinged steps to Peabody's wagon, watching Nat haul water from the river in sloshing buckets, when Ryzhkova's gnarled hands curled around his and pulled him toward her wagon. Her knuckles crushed his fingers and he thought of chicken bones scattered around the fire after a meal.

"Come. It is time to learn who you are," she said. Amos could do little but follow. From across the wide circle of wagons, he caught Benno's eye. The acrobat winked. "I will read your cards, and after you'll be an apprentice no longer."

They had of late acquired two small stools in Croton, but Ryzhkova's stare told him to sit on the floor. She tapped his shoulder and urged him down. "More grounded." She patted the boards. "Good for cards."

She had draped the walls and ceiling with cloth as she would for their clients, but the portraits looked out from between the folds of fabric. She gestured to the paintings. "It is good for them to watch. I paint them from memory. Except Katerina. My Katya sat for me." Each portrait was illuminated with gold. "When my hand was steady, before the fingers bent."

Her eyes trapped him as she began the ritual of cleansing. She produced a bushel of herbs from an unseen apron pocket, lit them with a candle, and began making symbols in smoke.

"Today, you," she said. "To tell others what will be is to become part of fate." The popping of hips and back preceded her sitting. She winced, folded her legs, and faced him. He realized the cart must be uncomfortable for a woman of her years. "You must know your own fate to read the cards, so not to mix your tale with others'. You see?"

She smacked a card to the floor. The Page of Pentacles, a young man, dark in skin and hair, holding a single star, would represent Amos in the reading. "Smart, eh? Like you. Stubborn. Scared. Young body, old mind." She tapped the center of his forehead with a sharp fingernail before turning another card. She moved so quickly Amos could barely follow.

"Queen of Cups. Much water. Change. She dreams, yes? Rules over you." A fair-skinned woman, dark haired, light eyed. Ryzhkova's crooked fingers danced and twitched as she spoke. The wagon began to feel small, as though it could not contain them and his body might burst through it. Something was happening. Ryzhkova turned over a card and blanched. A dark card. Lightning cut across its background.

Her stooped spine jolted straight. Her eyes rolled back, unseeing. Amos reached for her and she clamped down on his wrist. A flat, strange voice flowed from her.

"Water comes, strangling what it touches as if made flesh. Father, mother, all will wither. You will wear and break until there is nothing. For you it will be as water cuts stone."

A whisper crawled up Amos's neck. He snatched his hand from Ryzhkova. She shrieked.

He jumped, feet skittering on the floor, then leaned in to look at the reading. Ryzhkova quickly covered the cards and cleared them away, muttering in a language that was a hypnotic mix of thumping and lilting. She folded the deck into a scarf and stuffed it back into the box, then closed her eyes and breathed. Amos could not say how much time passed before she moved again, before she said, "Strong future. Much change. Beware of women."

She departed, leaving him alone in the wagon.

A month passed. Ryzhkova made no mention of the reading, though she took to asking him to spend more time with her at the close of day. He did not pry.

In summer the roads through New Jersey flooded and the wagons became mired, slowing northward travel to the promised prosperity of the Hudson River Valley. Days of backbreaking pulling, pushing, and digging wore on the troupe. Amos and Benno were too tired to stand straight, and even Nat's strength was exhausted. By the time they reached the Hudson, Amos was unable keep his eyes open to study cards.

When his head drooped, Ryzhkova brushed his muddy cheek. "I would paint you," she whispered. "I would put your face with my family."

That night, Amos tried to sleep in Peabody's wagon but could not. His legs ached with restlessness and his mattress stuck him no matter which way he turned—odd, as it had not bothered him before. Racing thoughts plagued him, of the reading Ryzhkova had done, the seer's hands moving the cards around, of the dark one he'd seen only briefly. Its image refused to take shape. He'd sat through countless readings and had never seen Ryzhkova have such a spell. Perhaps she was ill. The thought troubled him. He opened the wagon door, silencing the hinge with his palm so as not to disturb Peabody. Peabody talked to himself, sketching and scrawling as he murmured the occasional comment about "impossible roadways." Amos smiled despite his disquiet.

Outside the sky flickered with heat lightning and balmy air made his limbs slow. He heard the snapping of a fire that others tended and watched their shadows trip from the flames, Susanna's cracking and twisting as she practiced contortions.

From the woods came movement.

A volley of electricity lit the night a bright purple, illuminating the campground with the harshness of midday. Were it not for the flash, he would not have seen the girl stumble from the trees, drenched, shivering, clothed in a nightdress that clung to her legs, dirty and sodden. She wore no shoes. Her feet were bloodied, and her black hair hung to her waist, riddled with knots and leaves. She was a convergence of angles and curves, light and dark. His feet hit the ground noiselessly as he moved toward her.

Peabody watched Amos leave the wagon and run toward the woods. He gazed in the direction the young man traveled and his eyes widened. Between fog, lightning, and moonlight, the girl looked utterly impossible. Had he not been a skeptical man well versed in fantastical embellishment, he would have thought her a wood sprite. He observed Amos running and could not help but smile. *20th May 1796. Hudson, past Croton. Spring lightning storm brings excellent potential and a woman of unsurpassed, most ethereal beauty.* He snuffed the candle he'd been working by and stood by the door to the wagon in hopeful observation. "Yes, dear boy, bring her to us."

From her doorway, Madame Ryzhkova saw the girl's pallid complexion, the ink-dark hair, that she was soaked to the bone. The storm was dry and the river lay in the other direction. Through the dirt, her skin shimmered as if made of water. No woman, no girl, looked as such. The girl was something Ryzhkova had not seen in long years, not since her father had gone missing. She'd left everything she'd known to flee from it. She would not say its name. To name such things was to give them power, and yet it was impossible to stop her mind from whispering.

5

Finding information on Verona Bonn has proven something of a snipe hunt. I started in the simple places, ancestry websites, public records, filling the time between book requests and cataloging with casual queries. But beyond a newspaper clipping of a svelte woman balanced on a diving platform, not much turns up. The deeper hunting lies locked beyond paywalls or affiliations with institutions. At the moment I don't have the cash lying around for a casual foray into genealogy. Like Mom, my grandmother seems to have worked under different names. Verona Bonn must have been her last incarnation, leaving little clue as to why someone would scrawl her name in the back of a very old book, a problematic book.

Save for the book, Peabody's Portable Magic and

Miracles has no record of existing, and I found no evidence of contemporaneous traveling troupes. Hermelius Peabody's particular breed of entertainment was frowned upon during the Revolution all the way until 1792, when John Bill Ricketts set up an arena in Philadelphia. Yet from what I can tell, Peabody performed, traveled, and profited as early as 1774.

Worse, the names in it are real.

A printout of a scanned newspaper page, the *Catskill Recorder,* July 26th, 1816, sits on my desk. It took three days of searching to find it, but now I've read it enough times that when I close my eyes the words float in negative.

> 24 July 1816. Bess Visser, entertainer, found drowned in the Hudson River ferry crossing at Fishkill, presumed to have tragically taken her own life. The lady is reported to have been distraught, suffered from bouts of sleeplessness and mania. She is survived by a daughter, Clara, age four.

July 24th, and not simply a drowning, a suicide, like my mother. The coincidence is too much. When my search for Clara Visser came up empty, I turned back to the book. There, in the back, just before the wash of ink, I found Clara Petrova.

It's this that has me calling Martin Churchwarry again.

"I thought you'd like to know what I've found."

"Fantastic. Was the book your grandmother's then?"

"No, nothing so direct. I did find other names in it, though, someone named Bess Visser and her daughter, Clara. My mother knew Bess's name, so there's a connection somehow. I can't imagine it's a common name." Something in me holds back about the dates of their suicides. It feels too personal to share. I offer this instead: "In a way I think you did give me a little piece of my family."

I can almost hear him smiling. "That's kind of you to say, Simon. Thank you. I'm just glad to know the book has found a good home."

"It's fascinating, honestly. I'd like to show it to my sister. The tarot sketches that are in it—my sister reads cards. My mother did as well. I wish I knew something more about them. The sketches are interesting. Different somehow." I think about Enola, how uncommunicative she can be, and I can't imagine her telling me anything. "You wouldn't happen to have any good texts on tarot, would you?"

"Cartomancy?" he says with a light laugh. "I'm sure I must have something around. There's always at least a little interest in the subject. Hang on a moment."

I hear him walking around, the subtle thump of slippered feet, followed shortly by the sound of claws scrabbling on hardwood and a muttered, "Down, Sheila." So, he keeps a dog in the shop. I imagine it's a beagle. Something about Churchwarry screams beagle. He descends a staircase, a subtle change in creaking boards. "Let's see. I don't typically keep a large occult section—my father was more a classics man—but it's never a bad idea to have a few volumes. Ah. Oh, here you are, you sneaky bastard. *The Tenets of the Oracle*. That's all I've got at the moment. Lovely edition. 1910."

I jot the title on an envelope and tuck it into my notebook. "Would you mind seeing if there's a particular card in it? That is, if you aren't busy."

"Oh, not at all. Marie will be delighted that I'm speaking with a customer." He chuckles and I can't help but imagine a long-suffering wife, with wispy gray hair and plump cheeks. I describe the card and listen to him flipping softly through pages.

"Yes, that's it. The sketch you described sounds very much like the Tower. The simple interpretation says that signifies abrupt change, probably violent." There is quiet muttering. "There's a much more detailed explanation, though it's beyond me. I don't know how helpful it will be as our book predates *The Tenets* by a century at least. You might look it up for yourself, though. *The Tenets* is a fairly common book—though my copy is splendid, should you be interested. Gilded edges. Embossed cover."

"Something tells me I can't afford your copy."

"And the longer I hang on to it, the less I can afford to keep it. The two-sided problem," he sighs.

"Lenders and sellers."

"Neither with a penny to rub together," he says, cheerfully. "I do enjoy talking to you, though. I hope you'll tell me if you find anything else."

"I will, Martin," I say, and am startled to realize that I mean it. But there is no more time for reflection. The library beckons.

I shower, shave. The face looking back at me is tired. Messy black hair, a nicked chin, red bumps rising from an old razor and humidity that never lets sweat dry. Alice kisses this face. We're having drinks at the Oaks tonight. There will be a band, a jazz quartet, I think—maybe funk? Music and drinks might make it a date, or two friends listening to music and having a drink. I press on my bleeding chin. Is this my breakfast face?

I grab the book and envelope. In the car, I stare back at the house. A gutter hangs precariously from the roof. When did that happen? I glance at the clock. I'll need to get my hands on some braces. Easy-enough fix.

Ruminating over leaks, roof rot, jazz or funk quartets, I arrive at the library. The girls in circulation won't look me in the eye. Marci turns away when I pass. The only greeting is an atmosphere of shame, which has a broad embrace.

I am losing my job.

A dignified man might go straight to Janice's office, but I'm not dignified. I need my desk. The last stand I can make is sitting in the chair that has so become a part of me.

Not five minutes pass before the thumping of heels on high-traffic carpet approaches. Janice wears a dark pink suit today, a ragged edge material that's too warm for July. Today's earrings are silver periwinkle shells.

"Simon?"

"Can we do this here, Janice?"

She looks uncomfortable, her eyes maybe even a little shiny. Tears?

"It's easier if we talk in my office."

"If it's all the same, I'd rather not walk by everyone again."

A small parting of the lips, an *ah*. "I understand. Absolutely."

She begins the speech detailing how hard she fought, how if there was a way to scrape by without letting me go she'd have found it. I can't listen, not even when she launches into how much she's enjoyed working with me, seeing me grow. Pretending to listen is a favorite mask that wears comfortably.

"Reference will suffer for it," she says.

Even if she means it, which she may, it rings of pity. There, by the periodicals, a thick red braid. Oh, hell. Alice gets to hear me get fired.

"I'm terribly sorry about this. There's just nothing else to do."

I hear myself agree to two weeks. Janice offers to make phone calls on my behalf. "Okay," I say. Now I'm thanking her for letting me go, which is its own humiliation.

Fixing a broken gutter is pointless when there's no money for the rest. With the passage of a few minutes both my homes are gone.

Janice is wrong; I've been here twelve years, not ten. Twelve years of solitary work—stacking, sorting, scanning, cataloging, researching, letter and grant writing, fund begging, and book repairing. I've become part of the papers. They were mine, twelve years of pages and volumes. Now I have a single book.

Alice walks toward me. We've been trying to stay apart at work. Libraries are hotbeds of gossip—everyone knew about Marci's husband's drinking almost before Marci did. We've been carefully professional, talking to each other only when we need things, when I want the schedule for a room, or when she wants visuals for a speaker, or has to reach something. How will anyone reach things when I'm gone? She rounds the 300s, her sensible brown pants brushing against an oversized volume. I see it: pity. It's in the tight set of the mouth. It's in the slightly lowered eyelids, which on Alice makes her eyelashes catch the light. It's a look that pairs with *I'm so, so sorry.* The second *so* is the kicker. The potential for a second *so* is horrible. She catches my eye. Mouths an *Are you okay?* I shrug, because what else can I do? She's by the photocopy machines when an older man taps her on the shoulder. Comfortable shoes, white socks, tissue-thin button-down, shorts, old man knees. Old men love Alice. Thank God for that. I can't talk to her just now, not until I've tried to do something. I pick up the phone and dial Millerston Library.

"Leslie? Hi. It's Simon Watson at Grainger."

Forty-five minutes later and I've spoken with or left messages for the directors at nearly every library from Babylon to Mattituck. Gina at Comsewogue was kind enough to tell me that Janice had called on my behalf.

"She's heartbroken. You'd think you were her son. We'd take you on if we could, but we're in the same crunch. The best I could offer would be volunteering until you could transition into part-time once the summer kids head back to school. It would be an insult."

Pinching the skin at the top of my nose may not change the situation, but the pain makes the conversation easier. It's worse with Laura at Outer Harbor.

"Wish I could help, but I'm looking for me. I talked to Janice two weeks ago hoping you guys had wiggle room. Don't you get funds for the whaling collection?"

"Not enough."

When I hang up, nothing's changed but the hour. A book club meets in the armchairs by the front windows and a group of kids climb the stairs. Books need lending, shelving, mending. I still need to finish the grant application for the digital catalog funds. That will continue without me. I start working through the website Liz Reed sent, sifting through links. The New York section is filled with jobs in the city—digital archivists, information system architects, whatever that means. Even if I knew what it meant, there's no way I could handle the commute. The Long Island jobs are slim, most calling for interns or budget wizards, of which I'm neither. At the bottom of the page is a small green box advertising a manuscript curator position with the Sanders-Beecher Archive, a specialty library in Savannah, Georgia. Clicking around takes me to the archive's website, which reveals a beautiful old columned building. Photos of the inside show gorgeous dark wood shelves—walnut or cherry?—and rooms filled floor to ceiling with leather-bound books. A brief paragraph describes Sanders-Beecher as an archive with "a personal approach to broader history." They lay claim to volumes from Georgia's first printing press, diaries from early settlers, and a museum affiliation. I glance up at the whaling collection—a static snapshot of Philip Grainger's obsession crammed into two sterile rooms. Something about Sanders-Beecher feels warm and alive. Maybe it's the romance of distance causing rose-tinted longing. The miles between here and Savannah make the position more wish than reality, particularly when I've got the house to think of. And Enola coming home.

"Hey." Alice drops a stack of broken-backed books on my desk. She leans on them, petting the spines. Her nails are short and carefully filed; mine are chewed to the point of no longer being fingernails. Her pity comes with a sigh, and it's all right. I want a little pity.

"Hey," I answer.

"I'm sorry it wasn't me."

"Nice of you to say, but you don't have to lie."

"Okay," she says. "I'm glad it wasn't me but I'm sorry it was you. Better?"

"Better."

"Tonight's my treat, okay? As much as you want to drink, whatever. You can get sloppy, crash at my place, and I won't tell anyone."

I don't even know what I'd drink. "What do you drink when you're let go?"

"Rye, I think?"

"That sounds awful."

She smiles. "Sounds about right." We stay like this. Printers whir, copiers whine, fingers tap at keyboards. "You bring that book everywhere. Why?"

I don't exactly know. The notes and the sketches feel vaguely familiar. Then there's the drowning, and why my mother knew Bess Visser's name, and the oddness about the twenty-fourth; it's becoming an itch. "The guy who sent it to me might be right. I'm pretty sure it has to do with my family."

Alice casts an eye toward the clock above the computer bank.

Eleven o'clock. She needs to start setting up for a speaker soon. Don Buchman on salt marsh birds. She stretches. "You can't find family in a book, Simon."

I shrug. "You can't fix me with platitudes, Alice."

"No, you're unfixable," she replies. A soft chuckle—hers, mine. A curve of the lips. She grabs my hand and we both squeeze. "Is there anything I can do?"

Maybe it's because Alice said it, maybe it's because Enola hasn't shown up, but I want to find my family, in this book or elsewhere, and figure out what happened to us. "Would you mind doing a little more digging? I'm looking for anything you can turn up on two women, Verona Bonn and Celine Duvel. I've hit a roadblock."

"I was thinking something more along the lines of leaving early, but okay, sure. I'll check out your future dates for you."

"It's not like that—they're relatives. There's just something I'm curious about. I think they might fit into a pattern."

She arches a brow. "Care to enlighten me?"

"It's nothing really. I just need a project. You know me, I'm better with a project."

"I know."

The morning is lost to taping bindings and polishing grant language. At lunch I email résumés. For the hell of it I send one to Sanders-Beecher, even one to a museum in Texas. The beauty of electronic applications is the fantasy—thousands of miles disappear with a click. Then I'm helping a little girl named Lucinda find a book in the folklore section. It's a book on selkies, one that's thick, with a green buckram cover. I remember pulling strings from the binding years ago. Not far from selkies is a smaller book with a melancholy spine. Fairy tales—Russian folk stories, legends and poems from the Baltic. Mom read to me from it. I've got no more right to it than anyone else, but I tuck it under my arm and wander back through the stacks. I need one more book.

The library's copy of *The Tenets of the Oracle* has a simple red cloth binding, not embossed like Churchwarry's. It's a newer edition filled with art nouveau illustrations and seems less an informative text than an homage to mysticism. Churchwarry was right.

The drawing of the card in my book seems to be an archetypical rendering of the Tower card, though it's rougher than the picture in *The Tenets,* and has a lone man falling instead of two men crashing into waves. *The Tenets'* illustrations are beautiful, delicate—but not like those in my book. It's a signifier of change, and is just as likely to mark a new beginning as it does an end. A fitting card to study for the freshly jobless. I snag an hour or so in storage to page through it. Storage was my realm, a room with musty cabinets of materials not accessed frequently enough to earn a place on the shelves. Colonial printing history, animal husbandry, forgotten biographies. Someone else will have to run back here. By the time I leave storage and return to my desk, Alice has left a small stack of newspaper articles, photocopies, and printouts. On top of the pile is a call slip with her tight, slanted script.

S— Some info on your names. What's with the paywall on this stuff? Should I be concerned you're looking into dead women? P.S. My dad called. Gutter's falling off your place. Let's get you drunk. Pick me up at 8:00. —A

I sandwich the papers between the books and leave. Walking out the door feels almost like swimming, and I barely recognize the wire lawn sculpture I've hated since it appeared five years ago. I toss the stolen books onto the passenger seat along with Peabody's. I have two weeks to give Janice, but I won't go back. In my family we don't prolong goodbyes.

I speed the entire drive home. When the car bottoms out on the dip by the harbor I laugh.

The reality of how close the house is to the cliff sinks in when I pull into the driveway. Instead of sitting down with Alice's printouts or cleaning up for a night out at the Oaks, I attack the roof.

I hammer and wrestle the twisted metal back into the semblance of a working gutter. The brackets and screws are still attached, as though the roof itself shifted. An hour's worth of hammering and bending and shredding my hands, and the gutter is ready to be reattached to the eave. The wood splinters under the first screw. I adjust, try again, but it gives way once more, sending a chunk careening to the ground. Third and fourth attempts only loosen shingles and further disintegrate the eave. The gutter falls, beginning an outline around a soon-to-be-dead house. The roof is rotting. This is something I should have known to fix years ago, should have known needed maintaining, but no one told me. I was left a house and a sister, with no instructions on either. And the cliff creeps closer.

We used to run down it, Enola and I, feet sinking deep. Her hand in mine, we pulled each other to the shore, gape-mouthed and howling. Each leap had us falling, counting seconds before we touched ground. Knees bent we'd land, the earth catching us and giving way, sliding down to the sea. Each step chewed at the houses around us, mine.

I would take every one of those steps back.

I let the gutter lie. Hop over it to go up the step, tug the damned door that never opens. Into the living room. Pick up the phone. Call Alice.

"It's me."

"You skipped out," she says. It's hard to tell how she feels about that.

"I'm sorry," I say, to be safe. "Do you mind if I come by early? Is that okay? I can't be here right now."

6

It had been long years since the house in Krommeskill had known a baby. It was a place of clouds, hidden in the Hudson's haze and ruled by the strict and righteous hand of Sarah Visser—Grandmother Visser.

The trouble with Evangeline started long before Amos saw her in a lightning field. The trouble was that she'd been born.

"Naught is right with you," Grandmother Visser said upon examining Evangeline. "But I shall fix you." Her heavy cheeks shook. The baby was peculiar. She stared at those who held her from eyes like her father's, a strange man who'd tapped at her mother's window on nights when mist came off the river. Eyes colored like copper and dead dandelions, eyes in which Grandmother Visser saw her daughter's fall from grace.

Amelia Visser, the child's mother, was sixteen when the man visited her window. He breathed otherness, and a secret light burned inside him, spilling out when he spoke. His skin had a faint yellow hue like brass or gold, his hair was sooty black, his features were both boy and man, and infinitely interesting to Amelia.

The rapping sound had been gentle. Amelia drew back the curtain on those eyes the color of weathered metal. She opened the window.

His voice, a warm humming. "I've seen you at the river. May I watch you swim on the morrow?" Softness can compel, a voice can mesmerize, as did this man's quiet lilt.

Amelia felt him when she swam—in the tall grass and shadows of the woods, in the water itself because it tickled and made her skin come alive. Upon returning from the river Amelia discovered a strange shell left on her windowsill, a gift from the man. Smooth and hard with a sharp tail and spiny legs that ended in claws she dared not touch. She caressed the shell's fragile dome. It was curved and shaped like a horse's shoe. She left her window open with the drapes thrown wide. When her mother asked her why, Amelia answered, "For the brass-skinned man with the copper eyes," and had the backs of her hands switched for fibbing.

A kiss on the cheek was followed by a kiss on the lips, until what was wild in the man bled into Amelia. Her eyes became feral, her laughter uncontrolled, and her temper impossible. Her belly grew full.

Her mother nailed the window shut.

In months a sharp pain grew in Amelia's stomach. With the pain came blood. With blood came fear, with fear came loneliness—from loneliness came a most remarkable thing: a daughter.

When Evangeline suckled she drew life from her mother along with the milk, growing fat and round while Amelia wasted. She became drawn, waxen, and cried tears enough to wash the linens. She rose from her bed only once a day and would not let the baby from her side. In Evangeline's eyes Amelia saw the man who had visited her until summer had burned into fall.

Though Amelia withered from pining, Grandmother Visser saw only the price of sin and her negligence. She saw the face of a seducing man smiling out of a child and swore to teach the sin from Evangeline, to raise her better than she had her daughter. While Amelia lay dying and Evangeline's eyes were closed like a new chick, Grandmother Visser took the baby.

"I will wash you of the stain," she said, her voice clipped by abrupt Dutch English. Her broad bosom was covered by the stiff black wool of mourning—the modest attire she'd chosen to wear since the long-ago death of her husband, Johannes Visser, a good and righteous man. The cloth chafed Evangeline's skin, but she slept on until shocked by frigid washtub water.

"I myself shall baptize you."

Evangeline cried, but was silenced by wash water. Grandmother Visser held the infant's head and murmured prayers, rocking. With each verse she pushed Evangeline's head further below the murky surface.

"We repent our sins and fear new sin's approach, we clean ourselves in grace's water."

She pried Evangeline's mouth open with a finger, for the root of sin dwelled in the heart and the belly. Water flooded in—enough to drown.

"We are nothing save what grace allows us, vessels to be filled in the holy river."

The baby began to drink, swallowing as if to breathe, then closed her lips around her grandmother's finger and began to suckle. It was the suckling that touched Grandmother Visser, making her remember how she'd once loved holding Amelia to her breast. She lifted the child from the water.

Evangeline smiled around her grandmother's finger, unaware she'd survived drowning.

On her deathbed Amelia shone with sweat, hair stuck to her skin, framing her in darkness. To Sarah Visser, her daughter glowed like angels.

"I will raise the girl as if she were my own flesh," she promised. Then Amelia was gone.

Sarah Visser read to Evangeline from a tattered Bible, sang hymns to her, and ensured the first names the girl knew were the Apostles. Days began with prayer before sunrise, followed by tending to the hens and goats, hours in the kitchen learning to cook like a proper Dutch wife, prayer, laundering, cleaning, and spinning. Each day was constructed so that there could be no rest, only devotion and the tasks of a righteous woman.

Grandmother Visser loved Evangeline; though she feared the sin that made the girl, the willful part of her soul praised God for the chance to begin anew.

Evangeline grew from a biddable child into a young woman with a face like a cat, eyes large like dinner plates, and black hair that tumbled to her knees. Despite Grandmother Visser's vigilance, the river called, begging her to run and dive into its waters.

To keep her from running, Grandmother Visser took Evangeline's shoes and extended prayers until the candles burned out. Evangeline would lay abed until her grandmother left, then climb out the window, drop to the ground, and breathe in the night. She'd run through the garden, uncaring if stones scraped her feet. She'd run to the water, until its cold slickness greeted her and the restlessness that clawed her let down. She did not know her mother had walked these steps to meet her father.

Grandmother Visser discovered Evangeline's bloodied feet and remembered Amelia as if she'd died just days before. She began to lace Evangeline in stays so tight she could not breathe well enough to run.

"Good women do not run; they take measured steps, for sin lies in carelessness." She pulled the laces until the boning became a prison.

Evangeline tore them open with a letter opener, her lungs spreading wider with the snap of each cord. Then she fled to the river. No matter the way it flowed, if she followed, the water would take her away.

Evangeline's meetings with Will Aben spurred change in her

heart. Will, the miller's son, said that Evangeline's mother had taken up with a traveler who'd stolen her soul. Will's father had told him that once the man departed, her mother had grown so thin she'd vanished into the bedsheets and had blown away like dust.

Evangeline did not believe someone might die of heartache.

She was sixteen when they began to speak. Will was a young man of seventeen, strong in back, with hair so light it appeared colorless, and a charming smile despite a broken tooth. Evangeline sought Will to speak of things other than staving off sin and what Good Women did. Will, too, snuck away. Fascinated by the Visser girl and her wild eyes, he left the mill house to meet her, but he was not so practiced at stealth as Evangeline.

In late spring Dora Aben woke to the squeal of the mill gate opening. She watched from a window as Will walked to the river to meet the Visser girl. Still in her night rail, covered by a heavy dressing gown, she left the house. Once faced with his mother's ire, Will fled. Dora Aben took Evangeline's hand, grabbed a fistful of her hair, and dragged her to the Visser house. Dora pounded until the door opened, then promptly informed Sarah Visser that her granddaughter was a slattern set on seducing her son.

Grandmother Visser paid no mind to Evangeline's pleas, or that she'd long disliked Dora Aben and thought her prone to idleness and blasphemy. What she saw standing in the doorway was that despite the years she'd spent loving Evangeline, teaching, and correcting her sins, the girl's belly would grow as round as Amelia's had. She grabbed Evangeline's hair from Dora Aben's clenched fingers.

Sarah pulled her granddaughter into the kitchen, bent her across the farm table, and held her down by pressing her full weight onto Evangeline's back. Then she reached for the spoon. Sarah's hands bore scars from where her own mother had smacked her knuckles with a long-handled cooking spoon each time she'd dropped an egg, showed willfulness or a slovenly nature. She'd been lenient with Amelia, so much so that it had cost her her life. As Evangeline kicked beneath her, Grandmother Visser grabbed the heavy spoon from where it hung on the wall, waiting to again meet flesh in anger.

"Deliver me from the will of the flesh." Her arm swung back, a tight-drawn string, and with a snap descended.

Spoon hit skin and Evangeline writhed. Redness rose, raw and stinging. Welts blossomed as she was smacked for the river, smacked for Will Aben, smacked for her mother and the father she'd never known. Smacked for the pine needles stuck in her hair. Smacked for the dirt under her nails. Smacked for her bloodied feet.

Struggling to cover her face, Evangeline did not see her grandmother's tears, her sadness, or her fear.

Smacked for each broken lace. Smacked for scaring the hens so they wouldn't lay. Smacked for crawling out the window. Smacked for being unclean. Each blow ended with begging the Lord's forgiveness for lacking the strength to hone the girl into the steel that makes a faithful woman.

Sarah Visser was tired from the loss of her husband, her daughter, and from raising and loving a wanton child. While Evangeline had grown, Sarah had decayed. Her hair had grayed, her braid loops as thin as rats' tails, her face had widened, and her fire was doused under fat and wrinkles. Her arm grew weak, her breathing ragged.

Evangeline's hand flew out. Burning and wild, she wrenched the spoon from her grandmother. Force moved within her, filling her mouth with the taste of wash water. The spoon felt solid in her hand, as though part of her. She pushed the old woman forward, knocked her feet from under her, and drove Grandmother Visser to the floor they'd scrubbed and swept that morning. Evangeline's arm lifted. The implement struck down so strong, so quick, she could not believe that she had done it. And then she could not stop.

Grandmother Visser wailed. The spoon smacked her mouth. Evangeline's arm flew, whipping again and again as if driven by holy fire.

She did not hear her grandmother beg, "Stop, stop, precious thing, please."

Evangeline's body rang, each sinew and joint remembering blackened knees from kneeling, bruised ribs from tightened stays, and the pain of being kept from the river.

The spoon buzzed and hummed, singing, calling for her to let loose the wild. A sickening thump sounded as a blow struck her grandmother's throat.

Grandmother Visser's eyes snapped open like a startled rabbit. The spoon dropped. Evangeline's grandmother's face reddened, tears pouring from it like a split cook pot. Panic awoke. Evangeline backed away from where her grandmother gasped for breath that would not come.

Grandmother Visser's belly rose and fell in spasms, and her face turned a deeper crimson. She stared at Evangeline, awed.

Evangeline struggled to sit her up. Apologies spouted from her with the same fervor that her grandmother had for prayer. Her grandmother tugged on Evangeline's arm until their knotted bodies came to rest against the woodstove. She rasped and wheezed. Evangeline patted her cheeks and begged her to breathe. Grandmother Visser's head lolled to the side. A lank braid fell across her chest.

Cradling her grandmother's shoulders, Evangeline began to rock. Sarah Visser took her granddaughter's hand.

Evangeline felt the moment life left her grandmother. What had been quick was no more. When Evangeline had been small, Grandmother Visser had taught her the basting stitch, blind catch stitch, and the featherstitch for seams. She remembered her grandmother's hands wrapped around hers, a bone thimble balanced on her finger, guiding the needle through muslin, and the fresh smell of her skin after kneading dough.

Warmth seeped from Grandmother Visser's body. Evangeline tried to take it into her own as she shivered against the iron stove. She wept. She'd thought her love for her grandmother tempered by anger, but it bit like a fresh lash.

The rooster crowed as dawn pinkened a crack in the kitchen door. With the sound came a single thought: *Run.*

She left by a window and ran out the barnyard, through the tall grass and into the pines. She followed deer paths through the trees. When her stomach threatened sickness, she pressed her thumb to a bruise until the pain became an ember that burned away all but the need to run. *Find the water, follow the river,* she thought. *All will be well.* She ran toward the river, to the Hudson that flowed away from the body of the woman who had raised her. She ran until her feet begged she rest. When thirsty, she drank from the river and it filled her and gave her life.

She followed the Hudson south toward she knew not what, only that it was away. *Eva, Angel, Eve, I am a killer,* she thought, and the words became her name.

Time and season ensured that Peabody's menagerie and the mute fortune-teller's apprentice moved northward. On this day, Peabody noted in the margins of his ledger that the goats gave sour milk.

7

There it is. No question. Drowned, July 24th, 1937.

Celine Duvel, aquatic performer with Cirque Marveau, found drowned Saturday in the waters off Ocean City, presumed to have taken her own life. Duvel is survived by a daughter, Verona Bonn. No service to be held.

It's a tiny notice in the *Daily Sentinel-Ledger,* but the ramifications are shattering, because next to it is a microfiche printout of Verona Bonn's obituary. The Diving Queen of Littles-Lightford Circus, my grandmother, drowned in a Maryland bay. July 24th, 1962. Survived by her daughter, Paulina. Two data points could be coincidence, but four?

Something is very wrong.

What began as a passing fascination with the book has turned into something darker, fueled by the startling discovery that the women in my family have a disturbing habit of not only dying young, but drowning on July 24th. The book's original owner was more focused on profiteering and potential routes than detailing the lineage of drowning women, and there are many names: Amos, Hermelius Peabody, a girl called Evangeline, Benno Koenig, a fortune-teller listed as Mme. Ryzhkova, and more, but relationships are not remarked upon so often as wages. Dates are noted somewhat haphazardly, and nowhere is there mention of July 24th being of particular significance. Peabody only made note of things that struck his fancy, and clearly didn't anticipate that more than two centuries later an unemployed librarian would be using this journal as a primary source.

Alice's research has paved the way somewhat. She's let me use her institutional ID from Stony Brook, which she was smart enough to not let lapse. It allows me access to records that I'd typically be barred from without a research request approval. It made sense to work backward, and so I started with my mother, the newspaper story with her picture at its top, sharp-faced with her unforgivingly black hair—an aloof beauty. Despite my memories and their flashes of warmth, the picture shows that my mother was not a happy woman. Not something on which I ever dwelled. It's brutal to realize that someone might find a life with you in it unbearable. And so I've filled my days with digging through public records, searching folded newspapers and magazine scraps, until now I find myself staring at the *Daily Sentinel-Ledger,* and an alarming pattern.

It's past ten. Alice should be in and already through the first layer of her to-do list. Now is when she usually pauses to reorganize her desk, puts the pens on the right side, taps her papers into a stack. I call.

"It's me," I say.

"Can't talk long. Circulation glitch. Nobody can find anything and stuff on the shelves is showing up as checked out. Books are missing."

I look at the two I stole. Were I a better person I might feel guilty. "Probably something with the bar code scanner."

"Or the catalog. Anyway, what's up?"

"Does it seem strange to you that I know almost nothing about my family?"

"Not really. Strange is relative with you guys. I mean, look at what your parents named your sister. Who does that to a kid?"

"I know." Once I learned about the atomic bomb I was never able to think of my parents or my sister in quite the same light. I asked Dad about it once. His response was that Mom had ideas about reclaiming painful things; that if something terrible was made out of a beautiful thing there was an obligation to restore beauty, to reinstate meaning. The attempt with my sister failed; she exists like an explosion. I never had the guts to ask about my name. "I found something weird, though, even for us. You know the women I had you look up? They died on the same date as my mom. Women in my family have a way of dying on July 24th."

There's a pause. She shifts the phone to her other shoulder. Papers slide. I can imagine her neatening her letter tray.

"I don't know," she says. "Melancholy streak? That kind of thing runs in families. Add in a little seasonal affective disorder and it might make for a good coincidence or two."

"Could be." But seasonal affective disorder strikes in winter when the light is low.

"Are you going stir crazy?"

"Not yet. I've got applications out. I'm calling people." The truth is that unemployment has a way of softening the mind and blending the hours together until the impetus to start at dawn fades into a listlessness that has me on the couch nearing noon. Having all the time in the world makes getting things done impossible. I've earned a rest; I've worked without breaks since I was sixteen—two weeks without work won't kill me, and yet somehow it feels like it will. I've peppered every library on the east end with emails and calls to let them know I'm on the market, and to remind them of any small favors I've done across the years. An assist with grant language, a suggestion on tools for a specific repair. Nothing yet. Silence is its own kind of tension. There's a directorship in Commack that could work—a little beyond me, yes, but there's hope. I sent my résumé over last week, separate from the bulk. Follow-up call scheduled for tomorrow.

"The IT guy is here," Alice says. "I need to go. Tonight at eight, right?"

"Right. Bye."

Hanging up from Alice leaves me feeling anxious and strangely useless. I need work. I find myself checking on the position in Georgia. Sanders-Beecher still has the job posted. I'm dialing the number almost before I realize it. A woman with a voice stiff and sweet like meringue answers. She identifies herself as Miss Anne. I give her my name and ask about the library and the curatorship.

"Oh, well, we're very small, Mr. Watson," she says. "We're devoted to what we call the region's personal sociology, but we like to think of ourselves like artists. It's our responsibility to take the materials we're given and make them into a painting. That's what our curators do."

"I can't vouch for my painting skills, but I can sort materials with the best."

She laughs. "Pardon me. I tend towards the flowery, and I so love Sanders-Beecher. It's a very special place."

"Clearly," I say, wishing I could add something smarter.

"We've got a draft of the Constitution, did you know? Not the actual one, but a beautiful fake. It's part of a wonderful collection on a local notorious forgery ring. The Georgia Historical Society has one of the real documents, but I do prefer ours." She pauses to clear her throat. "There is drudgery, though. We do get so very many donations. Everyone wants to feel important, and there are so many old families here. It's difficult to explain to someone that their grandmother's Woolworth's receipts aren't significant."

And suddenly I know what to say. "Unless they're receipts from the first purchase in the state's first store, or if you were looking to document typical household expenses during a specific period."

I can hear Miss Anne smile through the phone. "Oh, you just might paint, Mr. Watson. Where is it you said you're from?"

"I didn't."

Miss Anne is stunned but delighted that a man from New York would inquire about their little archive. Her delight breeds the urge to exaggerate my credentials. I promote myself to curator of the whaling archive. Before the call is over, Savannah becomes a reminder of places other than Napawset, other than Long Island. But other places don't have Alice. And Enola could come back to stay.

I'm hanging up when the sound of snapping wood cracks like a gunshot. I jump, sending papers flying, and take three, four, five heartbeats to calm myself. A walk down the hall finds pictures hanging crooked from their nails, but not the sound's source. Everything looks fine until I reach my parents' room.

A thin split cuts up the wall by Mom's dresser and runs all the way to the ceiling, straight as a stud. When I put my fingers to it the house groans as if in pain. I have a faded half memory of running toy trains across the floor in this room while my mother sang something in French. I don't remember the words, only that she was braiding her hair at the dresser. I should check the other bedrooms.

Enola's room is unchanged. Iodine-stained quilt, a hole in the wall by her bed, a desk full of pencils chewed down to the leads. My bedroom door barely opens; it's either swollen or the frame has jammed—no, it doesn't hang straight either. Hell. I hardly spend time in there. Might as well keep my stuff in the living room until it's fixed.

Three armloads of clothing from the dresser, a stack of books, two pillows, and the summer sheets make the living room both bedroom and office, and me a refugee in my house. There's nothing else for it—I have to call Frank. I'd rather not, but Alice wouldn't have said anything about us yet. I asked her to not tell him about my losing my job either, not when it's temporary, not when I know how protective Frank can be. Alice and I are still being careful. We still don't know what we are.

He picks up on the fifth ring and immediately starts in. "It's not good to let the gutters go this long, you know. All the water straight off the roof can undermine your foundation."

I almost blurt that I'm sleeping with his daughter. Excellent. Now when I talk to him, I'm going to remember her calf wrapped around my back.

"Yeah. I messed around with them a little, but it's not straight-forward. It looks like the eave needs work too. I think the house is settling. A crack opened up in the wall in my parents' room."

He lets out a low whistle.

"I'll get someone over soon, but I was hoping you might know how to patch it."

"Something tells me this isn't patch territory."

"I know, I need to hire somebody." Out the front window the Sound is rough and high with whitecaps, a blue so angry it spits.

"Simon, I hate to see the place like this. You need to keep up on stuff, you're damned close to the water. Houses don't take care of themselves."

It's the condescension that gets me, as though I can't see my own house, as if I haven't been hanging off the roof or fixing leaks. Houses don't take care of themselves, but they do need money. "I'm well aware."

"Are you all right?" he asks.

"Just tired. Maybe you can send somebody to check out the house? I don't know where to start." I glance down at Peabody's book. It's opened to a detailed half-page drawing of a tarot card. The Devil sketched in brown, dressed as a courtier, cloven hoofs sticking out of pantaloons, a curling beard. Smiling, in each hand he holds a chain—leashes around the necks of a man and woman.

The Tenets of the Oracle has the card's meaning not as simple evil, but secrets, a lack of knowledge, or unknowing bondage. The Devil in *The Tenets* is dark and frightening. The one in my book looks more like a fun kind of guy, somebody you'd like to have a beer with. It's Peabody's interpretation of Madame Ryzhkova's card, but it raises the question—who was the person with such an interesting view of evil? It might be helpful to look into her, into the other names that pop up. Koenig, Meixel. The more complete the picture of the world, the more easily I'll be able to see patterns, spot their roots. I trace the end of the Devil's tail.

Frank says, "I've got a guy. I'll see if he has time this week. Listen, I'm sorry if I yelled, it's just that your folks loved that place."

I'd believe him, except my father never lifted a finger on it after Mom died.

"I know." I'm thanking him when I hear tires on gravel. They belong to a familiar rusted blue Oldsmobile. This is the sound of Enola coming home.

When the car door opens I'm already in the driveway. She falls out of the driver's seat, a jumble of loosely held together bones. I hold my arms out and she flies into me. For a second it's good, really good, and I pick her up, squeeze her. She reeks of the road and something stronger. She kicks, clipping my shin. Still, it's good to hug her again.

"Simon, you look like shit." Her words slip into each other.

"You smell like a brewery."

"Happens sometimes." Her laugh doesn't sound like it comes from her body. She wiggles free.

"You drove like this?"

"Apparently." She turns slowly, surveying the house, sniffing the air. "So, can I come in, or do I have to stand out here all day?"

"Sure. It's your house too." As though I've been keeping it for her. "Did you eat?" I look her over, taking her in. Her clothing hangs from her. A long hippie skirt, a huge hoodie—probably a man's—a T-shirt poking out from underneath, moth holes in the fabric. Under this stuff is my sister.

She shrugs, jerks the screen door open, and then slams it behind her. It's just me and the car and whatever she's left behind. I search for her things among heaps of fast food containers, soda bottles, and beer cans. The floor is covered with matchbooks from bars up and down the coast. Burned out lightbulbs are wedged in the backseat. No bags.

"Where's your stuff?" I yell.

"Trunk. Don't worry about it. Didn't bring much," she calls back.

"Not staying long?" I shut the car door and head inside.

"Don't know."

I hear her swear, followed by a tearing sound. Inside I find her standing over Peabody's book, ripping the sketch I'd just been looking at to shreds.

"Stop it. Why would you do that?" I shout. She flinches and scraps of paper float to the floor. "Do you even know how old that is?"

"Why would you keep that open? You can't leave things like that lying around." Her eyes narrow.

"You can't rip up whatever you feel like. That's mine."

"Where did you even get that book? Who has this shit?" Home a few minutes and we're already at each other. No wonder she left.

"A bookseller gave it to me." The second I say it, I realize it sounds odd. People don't give away books like this.

"Of course. Obviously." She flops down hard onto the gray couch and a dust cloud wafts from the pillows. "You're going to have to explain. Are you screwing people for books now?"

"No."

"That's a shame," she says.

I tell her about the package and my conversations with Churchwarry. I mention Bess Visser's name, that Mom knew it also.

She stares at me, suddenly sober. After a long silence she says, "I don't trust him." She pulls her knees to her chest, arms around her shins. On her wrist is a small blue tattoo I haven't seen before. A tiny bird.

"He's harmless. Actually, he's pretty entertaining."

"You're gullible as hell. What does he want from you?"

I look around. I've no money. I have nothing. "He's just an eccentric. Maybe a little lonely."

"Are you? Lonely?" she asks. "He got to you about Mom. You're fixated on her and it makes you an easy mark." She's dug her hands into the pockets of her hoodie. They're working, twisting the fabric and pulling at something inside. "She's dead, you know, not hiding in a book."

"It's hard not to be concerned. That book pointed out something fairly significant: the women in this family have a disturbing way of dying young."

Her lip twitches with the beginning of a grimace.

I say nothing about the 24th. There are lines I can't cross with Enola, and I'm edging close to one. "Don't you want to know why? If there is a why?"

"Not particularly," she says. "I'd rather just live."

"In a carnival. And I'm the one obsessed with Mom."

We glare at each other. She looks away first, picking at her sleeve. It's difficult seeing her when she's been gone so long. She could walk away again, right now, and I couldn't stop her.

"How've you been?" I ask.

"Hungry." She stomps off to the kitchen, a flurry of disjointed movement, feet slapping against chipped linoleum. Slamming drawers. "You've got fuck all in here. What do you eat?"

"Left-hand cabinet. Same as before. Third shelf."

More rummaging. "Ramen? Jesus. What did I even come back here for?"

"I did wonder."

"And why is all your crap in the living room? Wait, why are you home? Shouldn't you be working?"

"Budget cuts." Two deadweight words. I haven't had to say them yet, not to anyone that's mattered.

"No librarians on a weekday?"

"No more me. I was let go."

Just like that her arms are around me again, clinging, like when she was little and wanted me to carry her, like she needs me. "They're idiots."

"They're broke."

"Only you would make excuses for someone firing you."

Maybe. "Your turn."

"My turn, what?" She lets go and heads back to the kitchen, returning with a ramen cake.

"You know why I'm home. Why are you?"

"I wanted to see you. It's been a while." It has. It's hard to look at Enola without thinking of her tossing a backpack into the same car, leaving me. "You should come with me," she says, breaking off a chunk of dried noodles and popping it into her mouth. "You're out of a job. The carnival I'm with, Rose's, it's nice. Thom Rose likes me; he'd find something for you to do."

"I'm a librarian."

"Ex-librarian." That shouldn't hurt as much as it does. "You're a swimmer, too. You could do the dunk tank no problem." But she's not thinking about dunk tanks. She flops down on the couch again, crunching on the noodles.

"They've got a swimmer."

"Nope. That was your thing with Mom. I read cards."

As though I didn't show her everything that Mom showed me. How to empty your air and stretch your ribs, when to let the water weigh you down, when to smile. I remember her being little, in a polka-dot bathing suit, black hair floating all around her just like Mom's, smiling at me from the water while I counted. *Eighty-nine Mississippi, ninety Mississippi.* "I've got some leads. I have applications out and I'm calling a headhunter tomorrow. I'll make it work."

"It'd be fun if you came with me. I worry about you alone in the house." She looks around, taking in each crack, every hole that's developed since she left. "I miss you sometimes."

I sit on the floor, she stays on the couch, but a little of us slips together. "You scared me when you called. Something about a bad reading?"

"I don't want to talk about it." She picks at the arm of the couch, wiggling a little finger into a hole in the worn fabric. "Why's your stuff in the front room?"

"It's easier. The computer's out here. It's good for job hunting."

"The air smells funny. Did it always smell like this?"

"How is it supposed to smell?" It used to smell like coffee and cooking with a little bit of the ocean mixed in. She drops to the floor next to me in a smooth slump, an effortless fall. She picks up an escaped paper, absently bending the edge back and forth, scoring it with her thumbnail. *Circus Ephemera,* 1981. A small excerpt about high divers, one that briefly mentions my grandmother. She rolls the edge between a thumb and forefinger, like a European with a cigarette.

"Stop it. Did you come home just to mess with my stuff?"

"Don't look at me like that. It's been forever." She starts to say something else but chooses not to. Instead she says, "I talked to Frank. He says the house might go over."

"You called Frank? Why would you call Frank?"

"To let him know I was coming by. I thought it'd be good to see him. Is it true?"

"About the house? I don't know. Maybe."

"You should come with me." She reaches over and tugs a book from my desk. *Legends and Poems of the Baltic.* Peter Bolokhovskis, the book Mom read to me. She bends the spine wide, almost breaking it.

"Leave that, okay? That book is hard to find." And stolen.

She drops it on the couch and it falls open to a picture of a man leaning against a tree by a river. I remember the story. The man is seduced by a water spirit, Rusalka, I think. Half-souled spirits of children and virgin women who died unbaptized. Every culture has water spirits, mermaids, selkies, nixies. In America we don't name them.

"I'm sorry I left the way I did," she says.

"Okay."

"I know you were trying."

"Thanks."

She puts her arms around me, her head on my shoulder. We stay this way, looking at the walls, looking anywhere but at each other. She nudges in the direction of a book. "Do me a favor?"

"Sure."

"Read me that. I used to like it when you read to me. Nobody does it once you grow up."

It's from the Bolokhovskis. She wants me to read *Eglė.* I do. Slowly, the way Mom used to, unraveling the story of the farmer's daughter who would become Queen of the Serpents, and her children who were turned into trembling trees. All folktales have a price. Enola listens silently, pressing her forehead to my shoulder, letting me remember her.

Later, when the sun has set, I shift to work the blood back into a pins and needles foot. She says, "It was a long drive and my head is killing me. I need sleep."

I muss her hair with my knuckles. It mats up in soft, spiky black chunks. I want to ask why she cut it, but don't. "Your bedroom's the same. Haven't touched it."

She shuffles down the hallway. The door squeaks open. "Couldn't you at least get a new quilt?" No good nights for us.

I'm squinting at a bad photocopy when headlights make the room suddenly bright. I look at the clock. Nine-thirty. I was supposed to be at Alice's at eight. Yes, that's her car, and yes, that's her walking up the driveway. Jeans and a T-shirt, hair down. I look around. My things are everywhere, clothing, papers, books, noodle wrappers. *Shit.*

I head her off at the front step, leaning against the house, my back on the shingles. It would be good to ask her inside, but her apartment is clean, adult, and has a pillow-mountain bed.

"I completely forgot. I'm so sorry."

She twirls her keys in her hand, then smacks them against her hip. "You say that a lot."

"I mean it. Five minutes and I'll be ready to go."

"Whose car is that?" She nods at the Olds.

"Enola's. She came home today. We were talking and the time got away from me."

"She's here?" She crosses her arms over her waist, rocking back and forth on her toes. I don't know what Alice thinks of Enola, not really. Whatever she knows of her is from a long time ago, or from what I've said. *Obnoxious, selfish, immature, insane, waste.* I probably said that, probably to Alice. "I should say hi," she says. A look toward the window. I tell her Enola's asleep. She raises an eyebrow. "Do you not want me to come in?"

"No. Yes. She really is asleep. I want you to come in, but I'm embarrassed because the place is a wreck, my stuff is everywhere, and I already fucked up tonight."

She smiles. For a second I do too.

"Okay." Then she's past me, barging in before I can stop her.

In the middle of the living room Alice turns a slow circle, like she's surveying a gallery. Her flip-flops grind sand into the floor. We take it in, the papers, the clothing, the cracks and loose floorboards. I chew my fingers.

"Wow," she says.

"I know. I'd offer you somewhere to sit, but it'll have to be the kitchen."

"No, no. That's okay." She looks down the hallway. There are three doors, one has my sister, one isn't fit for me or a guest, and the other belongs to the dead. We would have to curl up on the couch with my books and clothing. "At work you were always so neat."

"Escapism?"

She laughs a little. Thank God. I suggest going back to her place. "I only need five minutes."

She says not to worry about it. "Enola's here. You guys should spend time together."

And then she's on the front step and there's a perfunctory kiss. Because she's seen the house or because her parents are across the street? Their porch light is still on. I say I'm sorry again, and this time she takes my hand, giving my fingers a squeeze. There's a perfect spot between her finger and thumb that's been made smooth and tough by a fishing rod. A spark runs between us and we hold on for an extra minute.

"Just call next time, okay?"

"Okay," I say.

I stay outside long after her car is gone.

I email a résumé for a video archive position. Out of my range, but worth a shot. Blue Point sent a message back. Position filled, of course. I listen to the water against the cliff, and let my mind run with thoughts of Alice, of the house falling in the water, of all those drowned women. I try for a while, but sleep won't come. I give up trying and read.

Later I hear a quiet flicking sound coming from Enola's room, the gentle slide of paper over paper. I look in. "Hey. You're awake."

She sits cross-legged, hunched in the center of her room. Her body sways slightly, as if in prayer. Lines of tarot cards spread across the floor, face up. She lays out six rows, each with six cards, quickly like a blackjack dealer. The cards move like a river. No sooner does she set the last card than she scoops the entire spread in one hand, shuffles, and begins to turn a new series on the floor.

"Enola?"

She doesn't answer. She's practicing. She doesn't need to; her movements are ballet. The deck is heavily worn, the backs faded, dull and yellow. They might have been orange once, maybe red, but are now a suggestion with ragged sides. Old paper, the kind that shouldn't be in this humidity. It's difficult to see, but the faces look bold, rough, possibly hand painted. She clears the spread away again, methodical. I watch as she repeats the sequence, shuffling, turning, shuffling. It's unseeing, compulsive.

I call her name again. She doesn't hear. Doesn't see me.

I pull the door closed. I'm in the living room looking at *The Tenets of the Oracle* when I remember. I've seen someone deal cards like that before—late at night on our square, metal-edged kitchen table, my father begging her to stop, to come to bed. She continued laying cards, swaying in her chair. The cards skimmed and swished. "Paulina," he whispered. "Please."

Something is wrong with Enola.

I take the phone outside. The night is warm and wet. He answers on the sixth ring.

"Simon? Heavens, it's late."

"I'm sorry," I say.

"No, just one moment." I hear him excusing himself and the gentle mumbling of a woman's voice, presumably his wife. A few shuffled steps and a door opening and closing. "What is it?"

"I found something."

"Something what?"

"It's about my family. I think some of them are in the book, like you thought. But there's more: they die. Of course they die, everybody dies, but they die young, *very* young. There's multiple generations—they drown. Every single woman." There is silence on the other end. I hear waves, cicadas, the blood in my ears. "Martin? You know about my mother. Her suicide."

"She drowned," he says after a pause.

"So did my grandmother, and her mother, and so on."

"I—oh." Little more than a dry whuff of breath.

"My sister came home today. She's acting like my mother."

After a short moment he says, "I'd imagine that could be disturbing, in light of your recent reading. I apologize for that."

And because it is before dawn, because the wee hours make the improbable believable, because of the names, because of the drowned, I say, "I'm not a believer in curses. I like facts."

A quiet swallowing sound, a thousand miles of telephone lines away. "Of course," he says quickly. "And when presented with a certain evidence, investigation wouldn't be unwarranted."

"It's seasonal affective disorder, most likely. Low serotonin levels."

"In all likelihood," he concurs.

"All the same, I'd like to find the start—the cause, if there is one. In case there's anything I can do."

"Of course, of course."

"Provided there's anything that needs to be done," I say.

Churchwarry agrees. I can feel us both dancing around something, each other, waiting for the other to take the lead. "If you think I might be helpful . . . ," he begins.

"How long have you been in business?"

"My father opened the shop as a young man, so quite some time."

"So you have contacts who might be amenable to finding some hard-to-find material?"

He coughs. "Simon, I tend to be the man people turn to when they need to find the impossible. Anything you need I'd be more than happy to assist you with. I'd consider it a bit of an adventure. Kismet," he says, though there's little joy to the word.

There are too many places to start—the book's original owner, Hermelius Peabody, how he may have been related to Bess Visser, Ryzhkova and the tarot cards, and what a wild boy has to do with any of it. "I think I need to know something about curses," I say.

In the background, Enola's cards flick against her fingers, a soft *snick* with each turn.

It's July 14th. I have ten days.

8

The heart of an aquatic act is torture—to drown without drowning—but Evangeline tolerated it. When the mute young man brought her before Hermelius Peabody, she knew it would not be without consequences, but the young man's eyes had been so warm that when he took her hand she followed.

Used to the plain dress and people of Krommeskill, Evangeline found Peabody's manner and appearance shocking. She could not decide on which thing to stare at—his excessive attire, the garish wagon interior, or the young man whose hair was bound in purple cloth so dark it bordered on black.

"We are fortuitous! A stunning specimen, aren't you?" Peabody burred and rolled. He surveyed her from tip to toe, and under this perusal her feet felt rooted to the floorboards. In the back of the wagon, the young man sat on a clever little bed that unfolded from a wall. His gaze tracked her too, but she found it reassuring.

"Evangeline, you say? A refined sounding name. Yes, you'll keep it." He jabbed the end of a quill against a leather-bound book before inclining his head toward the wagon's other occupant. "You've already met our Amos."

"I have."

The older man paced, a feat that required him to crouch slightly and caused his velvet-clad elbow to brush her arm. "You have the look of someone who has been running."

"No, sir," she replied.

"Pish. You're a terrible liar." He laughed, bouncing his stomach. "Even I have run from time to time. Have you any family?"

"None to speak of."

A grin peeked from under his moustache. "Excellent. We are all orphans here. Take this fine young man." He gestured toward Amos. "No relations at all. Mute as well, poor lad. Myself? My own mother is many years gone, may the Blessed Lord keep her." He executed a practiced flourish.

So, the young man was a mute. She remembered his touch as being kind, his palms rough as a farmhand's. He watched with passive curiosity.

"And what do you do, my dear?" Peabody asked.

"Do?"

"We all must do something. While it would be lovely to have you, we are, to state it crudely, a business." His tongue lingered on the word. "Each must pull his weight. Myself," he drawled, "I run the day-to-day, plan the routes, speak when speaking is needed, and manage what profits we might have. Amos is our fortune-teller's apprentice and occasional Wild Man."

A flush crept across the silent face. Amos's eyes flicked to his bare, dirt-covered feet.

"Though I am charitable, it is beyond my capabilities to take on one without earning potential. And so, lovely child, what is it that you *do*?"

I kill. I am a killer. She bit her lip and thought of what Grand-mother Visser said about her long-ago baptism, what she had dis-covered in the river's cold heart. "I hold my breath. What I mean to say is that I swim."

A white eyebrow arched beneath the brim of a curled hat. "Many swim."

"To be precise, sir, I cannot be drowned."

A twitch of a smile. "Excellent." He marked something down in a book. "Good that you are pretty," he murmured. "Undrown-able Beauty, a mermaid—most wonderful. Very well, the young man will help see to your arrangements. We cannot simply turn you away."

Well into the night, Peabody sketched the myriad ways to dis-play a mermaid. It would not do to have her simply hold her breath; he'd require a vessel that held a good amount of water, but was small enough for transport—a variation on a hogshead barrel, though comparatively squat, and not as large as the casks used in ferment-ing wine. He fancied it should be able to be taken apart, hoops and staves collapsed, in case the girl was not what she promised. He scribbled until his last candle left him in darkness.

After a private juggling exhibition by Melina helped negotiate a favorable price, Peabody enlisted the services of a Scottish coo-per in Tarrytown. The completed tub was simple. It was a pretty piece of work with hammer-marked hoops around perfectly locked staves, wide to hold enough water to swim, yet low enough that a standing man could see into its depths.

While camped and waiting for the tub's completion, Peabody had Benno set to work on building a series of small benches that could hold a group of ten. With Amos's help, Benno repurposed costume trunks and a washtub to make sturdy risers.

During an afternoon of hammering and cobbling, Benno re-marked in passing, "The mermaid girl is quite striking. I have seen you looking at her."

Amos nodded. Curls of wood peeled away as Benno chiseled a joint.

"Not near as comely as Melina, but pretty."

Amos braced a board and tilted his head. He'd hardly spared a thought for Melina since Evangeline had arrived.

"You are hopeful she will remain with us."

A knot tied itself in Amos's chest, an emotion he had no name for. He shrugged.

"Best not pine until we see how long she means to stay. Susanna, though. Think how she bends!"

Amos kept his eyes on the board, unwilling to answer his friend. Not thinking on Evangeline was impossible.

The tub was filled a bucket at a time by the troupe save for Peabody and Madame Ryzhkova, whose hands and back would not bear the work. Peabody oversaw the labor, delegating and directing, while he honed what would become Evangeline's introduction.

She was a mermaid from long-sunk Atlantis, a miracle of mystic seas and secrets. In an unusual splurge, Peabody commissioned a sign painter to create placards depicting Evangeline with a long tail fin.

She expressed concern that people would be upset that she possessed no such appendage. Peabody replied, "You are beautiful. All else matters little, so long as you hold your breath and perform aquatic feats." He insisted she wear a white gown that billowed around her when she descended into the tub.

The first part was painless, swimming tricks mostly, her backstroke was made sinuous by the lines of the wet gown and her blueblack hair. As she paused to smile and wave Peabody would ramble about the mysteries of her origin. Then he slashed the air, slapped the tub, and bellowed, "Dive!"

She pushed out her breath and sank to the bottom of the tub, her skirts trailing above while Peabody talked, his voice vibrating through the water. He encouraged the audience to count if they could and began a long, dark monologue.

"Tortures and horrors of the deep, fine ladies and gentle souls. This poor creature, this slip of a girl, she braves them! And would you survive?" Here he pointed a finger to the smallest boy in the crowd. "Fine lad, would *you* survive?"

Beneath the surface Evangeline was alone with the water and fear. When she closed her eyes, she imagined Grandmother Visser's bruised lips asking why she'd done it. As the water pressed against her stomach and rib cage, caressing her, it felt like her grandmother's hands, her voice, begging. *Please.*

Eternities after the act's start, Peabody rapped his hand against the side of the tub, signaling Evangeline to rise. She spread her arms so that her sleeves hung like wings, and floated up, the crown of her head breaking the surface, then her eyes, slowly opening. She smiled the showman's smile Peabody had taught her. Once her shoulders were above the water, she breathed. When she filled her lungs, the dress clung so that she rose like a Venus from the waves. At first the men's leers brought shame, but routine blunted its bite.

Two pairs of eyes always watched her; one belonged to a scarred man, the other to a silent one.

When they traveled the mud roads between towns the tub doubled as her bed; turned on its side and lined with a straw mattress it made suitable shelter, and an oilcloth over the front kept out wind and rain, affording her a small amount of privacy. She fastened hooks to the outside of the staves for a curtain Melina had given her, and fashioned the tub into an intimate sort of room.

Though she did not mean to, she found herself watching the mute fortune-teller. He had a fascinating animal quickness and was helpful to a fault, but she often caught him staring. His eyes would flit away, but something about him left her feeling exposed, as if he knew her secret. He would bring her blankets to cover places where stiff straw poked through her mattress and made sure cracks in the tub were properly sealed with pitch, running his fingers along the staves to check for shifting. He stayed until she pulled the oilcloth tightly over the head of the tub and told him gently, "Good night, Amos."

She did not know that he lingered until he was certain she slept. She knew only quiet contentment as she pulled the cloth down each night. She began to wonder if he had a voice what it might sound like. Peabody said Amos was mute but had never said why; perhaps he'd been badly injured. She wondered if he could make any sounds at all, and how he told fortunes while voiceless.

While Amos dreamt the dreams of a wild boy—of marshes teeming with animals, of soft mosses to sleep on, of the pleasures of cold rivers on the skin, of a lovely woman in the water, hair spread around her like blowing grass—Evangeline's nights were darker. She dreamt of crawling from the gray house in Krommeskill, knees bloodied and caked with mud and pine needles. Always her grandmother followed, face purpled, begging for mercy and salvation. *Why? Why? I loved you so.*

The troupe had left Philadelphia for New Castle's pointed brick houses when the sky shattered and sheets of rain threatened to flood the menagerie. The small horse kicked and bucked inside her wagon, the llama screamed like a wounded child. Fearing that any attempt at progress would mire them, Peabody ordered the wagons to halt until the rain passed. Nighttime broke into thick heat that forced everyone to their beds. The air hung heavy with thunderheads and the sky became a weight that held Evangeline down as her grandmother once had. She slept the disquieted sleep of the guilty.

It began with the dream of running, the bloodied knees and gasping for air. It ended with falling, forced to the kitchen floor by her grandmother's palm against her throat, prying her lips open, pouring pitcher after pitcher of scalding water down. Boiling water overflowed her mouth, burned her gut, filling the empty places that guilt had carved.

Her cry carried through the camp, startling those nearby. Amos awoke, his body shooting into a crouch. He sniffed the air and listened. The echo brushed his skin with an electric snap. He leapt from his bed in Peabody's wagon, threw back the velvet curtain, and followed the sound.

Toes sinking into soft ground, he crept to her upended tub. Tentative hands peeled back oilcloth and curtain. Wide eyes peered through. In the curved tub bottom she thrashed and kicked, not the woman he watched rise from the water but an animal caught in a trap. He listened. She panted. No, she choked. She couldn't breathe, was tossing, was not right, was afraid.

He climbed in beside her, fingers grazing her cheek. He pressed a hand to her shoulder and felt a pull. *Come here.* He shook her gently, surprised by the softness of her skin and how cool she was despite the heat.

Evangeline's eyes opened. She jerked away, knocking her body heavily against the tub's boards, her mouth working but making no sound. Amos understood. There was too much sound, it couldn't leave all at once. She shuddered against the wall.

He touched her collarbone. Her arms went around him and he noticed a deep red welt on her shoulder from the staves. It was a fascinating thing. He traced the edges, circling with his fingertips. A mottled, dark spot against her skin, a flush gone too deep—how could a bruise be so lovely? He tried to take her from the bed, away from the dream. He tugged her hand but she held tighter and cried more. Water ran from her eyes. He didn't understand why, but it made him need to hold to her. When he tried to put her down, to coax her back to sleep, she would not move. She felt like something warm that wouldn't take shape in his head, a fuzzy memory, something from before, when he'd been small.

He thought they would lie down, that he would curl up on the mattress with the very soft girl with the bumpy knees and the pretty bruise. She slept. Yes, Evangeline could sleep. Amos decided he would stay awake. Just in case. She was very scared and soft like duck's down.

Desperate to empty the space of stale air and bad spirits, Madame Ryzhkova had opened her wagon door and looked across the rain-soaked clearing. Then she'd heard the scream. A shiver at the base of her neck, the cold a woman feels when the dead speak her name. She'd heard the sound before, had traveled oceans to escape it. She'd closed her eyes quickly, only to summon the image of a man's pale hand with familiar square fingertips disappearing below the surface of a frigid stream. When she'd opened her eyes again she saw the shadow of her apprentice running. To where the drowning girl slept. Ryzhkova's lip curled. She spat to keep from saying it, but the name would not be contained. *"Rusalka."*

In the first light of morning, Peabody found them together, a bundle of tired bodies, half buried in straw from a torn mattress. Amos's arm curved tightly around the wing of Evangeline's shoulder; his fingers brushed an ugly bruise. They made an oddly joined puzzle, but the pieces fit in the right craggy places. It had been years since he'd felt longing like the boy did, at least ten since his wife had passed. He wanted to pat the boy on his head, to muss his hair a little, but thought it best not to wake them. He quietly pulled the oilcloth down, then patted himself on the back at his good fortune. A future filled with wonderful children—Wild Boys and mermaids, fortune-tellers and dancers—profitable beauties, all.

9

JULY 15TH

The sound of shuffling paper wakes me. Enola is up, at my desk, and thumbing through my notebook, her hair sleep-flattened on one side. The front door is cracked and the wind off the beach is sharp with salt. I yawn. Without looking she points to the floor, where a steaming cup sits. We both know better than to talk before coffee.

It's terrible coffee, burned, but not having to make it myself makes it delicious. She tips the chair back and drinks her own cup.

"Thanks."

"I looked at your notebook," she says.

"I noticed. I'd appreciate it if you didn't go through my things."

"Those names, the women—they're relatives?"

"Best I can tell. You know circus people. It's hard

to figure out who anybody really is." Names have a way of changing as people disappear into shows and new anonymous lives, drifting in and out with the wind.

"They've all drowned."

Something in her voice makes me say, "My sources are a little spotty."

She gnaws a little on her lip. "You think they're suicides, don't you?"

"Maybe, maybe not. Alice thinks so." It would be hard to rationalize such a string of deaths any other way, but something about the list doesn't feel rational. "Some might have been accidents."

"I can tell when you're lying, you know. Your left hand twitches." Enola puts a foot up on the desk. Her clothing is rumpled, slept-in, and her skirt hangs on her like a sheet. She starts to chew on her thumb, then slaps her hand, as if in punishment. "This started with the book, didn't it?"

"It's a puzzle. I like puzzles." Does my hand twitch? Seeing Enola acting like Mom—there are nine days. To what? Now Enola is very much alive, vital. I'm missing something. Could it be tied to age? Mom was only thirty-two when she died. Her mother was younger, I think. Celine Duvel—hell. I'll have to check again.

"Okay then, keep lying." Enola stretches, popping every bone in her spine. "I want to go swimming. Get your bathing suit—unless you're scared I'm gonna sink, or maybe you think you are." She smirks, as if she can tell my stomach just clenched.

We take the steps down. Horseshoe crabs dot the edge of the water, shining stones with devils' tails.

"Oh, it's blue! No jellyfish," she says, putting her foot in the water. "Nice. I just hate the damned horseshoe crabs." She's looking for a clear path to deeper water, but there are a lot of crabs.

"They're harmless. Won't even pinch you."

"They just look like they're up to something." Then she's out in the water, running forward, splashing and diving. I dash in after her. We gasp, grinning at the cold and then she dips her head under, a tuft of hair bobbing above the waves. Though the salt burns, I keep my eyes open. Enola's are closed and her face is bunched like a drawstring. I start counting, out of habit, maybe curiosity. How long can she hold? How long can I? One Mississippi. Two Mississippi. Enola paddles small circles, diving deeper. I follow. Eight Mississippi.

Simon.

Part of her is here, a whisper of our mother in the water—half wish, half fear. Of course she'd be here now that Enola's home. I grab my sister's hand and it's cold, slick like a fish. I pull her toward me. Her eyes open. I'm heavy enough to hold us both down at the bottom; otherwise Enola might float away like driftwood. She sees me counting five-second increments on my fingers and shakes her head. I squeeze her arm. Forty Mississippi.

Simon.

Enola squirms, legs jerking hard, pulling me sideways. Forceful, quick, we shoot to the surface.

"Jesus, Simon!" she splutters. "Do you know how long it's been since I've done that? Fuck drowning, you're gonna kill me."

Murder. There's always the question of murder, though that wasn't a possibility with Mom. No chance.

"You're not even winded." I thump the water from my ears. "You could always hold longer than me."

"Well, it's been a while." She looks a little gray.

We throw our clothes on over wet bathing suits. Enola says it's good to have salt drying on her skin. "Feels like summer," she says. We walk toward West Beach, near the jetties. I watch the bumps of her spine, too thin; she's always been skinny, but never painfully so. When we run out of beach we climb the bulkheads.

"I thought I heard something when we were under. Did you hear anything?" I ask.

"How the hell can you hear anything with water in your ears?"

"Never mind."

Sand spills through the wood where a section of bulkhead has given way, and broken pilings lean into the Sound. Without discussion we start climbing the cliff, our feet burrowing into sand and dirt.

She's breathing hard halfway up. "Dad would kill us for this," she pants.

"Probably."

He caught us once. We'd been running the cliff and were making our way up for another pass when he appeared at the edge. He grabbed us with hands so strong that days later his fingerprints ghosted my arm, reminding me I had a father. He dragged us back to the house, me by my collar and Enola by her pants. Her feet never touched the ground. I hated him a little.

At the top of the bluff we look out. A shell of a house tilts over the cliff's edge, the back wall torn off. The remnants drifted away in the last hurricane.

Enola says, "That's the Murphys', right?" It is the Murphys' and she could tell if she really looked and saw their refrigerator resting against the buckled siding and Mrs. Murphy's dining table overturned, its legs long gone.

"The last of the porch went over two years ago." Somewhere across the Sound, Connecticut kids make bonfires out of the porch where we sat with Jimmy Murphy, drinking lemonade.

"Then you've got, what, two years? Three?"

"Depends." It's not unheard of for a shore property to lose ten feet a year, depending on storms and the upkeep of the bluff. It's been worse since the hurricane, and the Murphys' place going over didn't do mine any favors. Once their bulkhead went, water cut behind mine, eating away at both sides of the last barrier between me and the Sound. Between winter storms, nor'easters, a hurricane, who knows?

"Do you have money to fix it?"

"Not right now." I'll need a loan. Without a job, getting one will be nearly impossible, and the job hunt is glacially slow. I could ask Frank for money. My chances of success there might be better; money toward saving my house is money toward saving his, and this was my father's house, and that's important to Frank. But for Alice. It's one thing to take money from Frank; taking money from Alice's father is different. I should ask her, but best to try the Napawset Historical Society first; they could make it a cause, landmark it. I look over to see Enola swaying softly, matching the waves.

"You should come with me." She sounds strangely urgent.

"Why?"

"What's left here?" she says.

"The house. I can't just leave it." At times it feels like our parents are still in it, in the walls, and someone needs to see them through to its end. I'm as rootless now as I'll ever be, but here I know what roads to take when the water's up, where everyone is based on the tide, who's a summer person, who lives here. Here my hard feet make sense. And Enola knows to come back here.

"Just come."

"I wouldn't know what to do and I wouldn't know anybody."

"You'd figure it out and you'd know me," she says.

"That hasn't always worked out so well."

She makes a face, then sighs. "You'd be okay. I'd help you." Her hand disappears into the skirt pocket and I can hear a soft shuffling.

"I saw you up last night," I say. Her hands stop moving. "What's going on with the cards?"

"They're just being weird."

When I press her about it, she pounces on me and rubs my hair with her knuckles, hard, burning my scalp. We both start laughing. She tickles my sides and I squirm to get free. An Indian burn ends everything when I twist her forearm until she howls and smacks me upside the head, stopping things as quickly as they started. We fall on the grass. For a second we're right again.

"You had Alice over last night," she says, gasping.

"I thought you were asleep."

"What's with you and her?"

"I don't know," I say. And I don't, not really, but I want to protect this old new thing between us.

"I like her. She's too good for you." She breaks off a piece of beach grass, puts it between her teeth and chews. "You'd like Rose's," she says. "It's the carnival that came around when we were kids. It's a family business."

"How'd you wind up with them?"

"A friend I met reading cards in Atlantic City. He'd worked with Rose's before and introduced me. I read Thom Rose's cards, we talked and wound up clicking. It's good travel and a steady gig through the summers. The money's not so bad."

"Did you mention Mom?"

"I'm not an idiot. What, I'm not going to say that my mother worked the circuit? That's probably why he hired me. He'd take you on if you wanted."

"And what would I do?"

"Don't be stupid."

My understanding of carnivals is esoteric. Here is the reality, my knock-kneed sister with the wild eyes, asking me to run away. It would scratch the itch that's always wondered what Mom was like before Dad. "Is it like it used to be?"

"Pretty much," she says. "A little bigger, more rides now, more games. The sideshow's changed, more acts, fewer bouncers." She sees my confusion. "Jars, the stuff in jars. Never mind, you don't want to know."

Things preserved in formaldehyde, animals and otherwise. I remember standing inside a too-hot-to-breathe tent, fingers glued together by sweat, staring at a milky white pickled shark with two heads, one at each end. "You like it?"

"Sure."

"You didn't sound great when you called. And you look tired."

"It's not great all the time," she says. "But what is? Eating crap, getting sick, shitting my brains out." She stretches an arm over her head. Her shoulder makes a loud popping sound. "I got really sick last year outside of Philly. I go into a bookstore because they clean those bathrooms. I'm in there sick like I'm dying—guts rolling around, staring at the floor trying not to pass out and I see these yellow shoes sticking out in the stall next to me. The lady figures out I can see her feet so she pulls them back, like I'm not supposed to know she's there. Like, if she picks up her feet she can forget she's hearing my shit hit the water. You don't deal with stuff like that. You've got a house. You've always got your own toilet." She scratches the back of her neck. The bird tattoo on her wrist flutters. "But most of the time it's good. Thom would love you."

"Why do you want me to go so badly?"

"Maybe I miss you," she says.

"I missed you too." I did. I always do. Could I go? Pile my stuff in the car, drive down a highway, following a line of trailers, campers, spend days and nights in a chlorinated dunk tank, and come back in six months, dirty, gaunt, and lonely. No, not now. We're just shy of the 24th and Enola's here. It feels too coincidental. "Why'd you come home now?"

"Rose's was coming by anyway. I asked Thom if I could take time to see you. I thought maybe we could talk." We watch waves grind sand until mosquitoes start in at us. She smacks one. "I do love you some." Some. It's what she's always said, but the way she says it is better than if she'd said she loves me wholly. Those years we were alone, maybe I didn't do so badly. We pick our way through brush and poison ivy to the path leading to the house. Her hands slip back into her skirt pocket and I hear the slide of paper against paper.

A beaten-up yellow car sits in our driveway—not hers. A lean form stands by it, arm propped on the hood. The figure could not be more striking. Serpentine and crawling with unknown potential.

Enola breathes deep like a diver, shrieks, and takes off running. "Doyle!" Unrestrained joy. Then she's in this person's arms, looping her legs around his body. Her shoulders block his face. All I can see are two skinny—tattooed—arms around her waist.

He twirls around, back to me, and she is up against his car. I jog over. Without looking, Enola says, "This is my brother, Simon."

"Hey. Heard a lot about you. Don't worry, it's all good." A voice made of casual and surf. His hands stay on my sister's hips. He spares no glance my way, allowing me to stare at a line of tattoos that creep up the side of his neck, over his shaved head, ending in dark green tentacles that wind along his jaw.

"Simon, this is Doyle."

I say I'm delighted to meet him. I'm not sure what else I say, because I can't stop staring. Nobody gets a tattoo like this unless they're actively courting gawkers. The ink slithers as he talks, tentacles writhing over skin. I feel sick. They pull apart.

"Long drive," he says and stretches, sleeves sliding up to reveal more ink, more tentacles. Does it cover his entire body?

"I didn't know you were coming," she says.

He nuzzles her neck, unmindful of my presence, and mumbles something about needing to "siphon the python" and heads into the house. Enola trails behind him, almost skipping. I catch up and put a hand on her shoulder, stopping her short.

"Who is he?"

"Told you. Doyle."

"And what is a Doyle?"

"A Doyle is a guy who drove a really long way because I told him I was going to see my brother. Be nice," she says and follows him. Over her shoulder she adds, "We fuck." There are few things with more visceral power than the sudden awareness that your sister has sex. The image of tentacled arms is too much. It is a full five minutes before I can go inside.

Doyle is sprawled across my sofa, my bed. I pull my chair into the middle of the room and sit in front of him. Yes, there are tentacles crawling up his arms and face. I can see the fine lines of each elliptical sucker. Enola shuffles pots around in the kitchen. For the moment Doyle and I are alone. There's a shiftiness to his pointed features. If I turned on the lights he'd skitter behind the couch.

"Wild place you got, man. Wild," he says. "Your house is pretty much hanging off the cliff."

"Erosion. It's a problem around here," I say. *We fuck,* she said. This thing copulates with my sister.

"Yeah, yeah. That's right," he laughs. A lazy half wheeze. "I'm shit at remembering stuff like that." He makes a twitching gesture. His hand is also covered with tattoos. Squid? Octopi? "Slept through earth science."

"So you and my sister."

"Yeah. She's a down chick, you know? Real cool."

I stare.

Enola returns with a box of cookies I'd forgotten about. She flops on the couch, draping herself over Doyle. Neither minds that they're in my bed. She feeds him a stale cookie and asks if we're getting along. Of course we are. Just beautifully.

"How did the two of you meet?"

"In Atlantic City, on the Boardwalk," she says. So this is the one.

"Yeah. She had her cards out and I thought, man, that's a sweet little bird."

He might not see the murder in me but Enola does. She puts her arm around his shoulders and the pale underside of her wrist attaches itself to his tattoo's suction cups. I ask what he does.

"I'm the Electric Boy." The lightbulbs in the back of her car begin to make sense.

"What exactly is the Electric Boy?" I lean back in my chair, almost tipping it. I know what's coming.

Enola cuts him off before he can answer. "You know, the Human Lightbulb?"

I nod. It's a static electricity act, pedestrian really, the sort of thing that's popped up since the discovery of electric current. Sometimes it's a deferral of current trick with a hidden metal plate; that's how they work electric chair acts. Nothing special.

"Doyle can light a hundred-watt bulb with his mouth and three in each hand," she says.

That is different. "Impressive."

"He does contact juggling with the bulbs while they're lit. It's crazy beautiful."

"Uh-huh." A tentacle-covered man juggling lightbulbs sounds gorgeous.

"I'll show you. Little Bird, where do you keep the bulbs?" He starts to get up but Enola shakes her head.

"Don't bother," she says. Doyle looks at her. "You can show him later, okay? You didn't bring beer by any chance, did you? Simon's got fuck all and I could kill for a beer."

"Sure thing," he says. He oozes from the room.

Enola leans forward, hands on her knees, and I spot the tattoo on her wrist again. A little bird. Jesus. "Quit being a bastard and pretend you like him. For me, okay?"

"I'm not being a bastard, I'm being your brother."

"Well, that's new," she snaps. It's true. I've been a parent, not a brother.

"I'm just concerned, okay? I know nothing about him." Or her, for that matter.

"For once, can you just be a little nice?"

"I'll try."

Doyle lopes back in, six-pack in hand. "Want one?"

"Sure, thanks." His tattooed finger pops open a can, and all I can think about is having needles so close to the nail bed. He catches me staring, so I ask, "That hurt?"

"Like a sonofabitch." He smiles and clicks his teeth together.

"Good beer," I say. It tastes like warm piss.

We drink in relative silence, which is me being nice. After another drink they begin chattering to each other. Names are tossed around—friends, cities, towns. She giggles, a different person from the one I saw last night. I glance over at the book. I'm missing something.

Neither minds when I flip through a few pages. Later, Enola drags him out to the bluffs to watch the sun brush the water. I am left alone with my books.

At some point music drifts in and I look out the window to see the moon and the dome light from her car. The driveway is bathed in blue and they're dancing. She is frenzied motion, elbows flinging, hips shimmying, dancing and detonating. Sweat covers her, eating moonlight as she sidles against him. Doyle flows over her as if held together by a thin layer of ink. The car shakes with bass vibration. A slower song comes on and they mesh their skin, fingers entwined. They've ceased to know I'm here. Like they never knew.

Alice answers the phone, sleepy, soft-sounding. "Hey. What's up?"

"Do you want to go out? Are you up for a drink? I need a drink."

She yawns and I hear the pop of her jaw on the receiver. "I've got work tomorrow." There's a small silence between us before she says a quick, "Sorry. That came out wrong. What's up?"

"Nothing. Just a little stir-crazy, I guess. Enola's boyfriend showed up. Too many people in a small house." Never mind that four of us once rattled around here.

"And here I was hoping you'd say you miss me."

I do. I miss her walking up the library steps. I miss her writing the program schedule on a white board and the curl of her lower-case g. I miss the Alice I don't see anymore. "Sorry. I'm just off. It's weird seeing my sister's mating dance."

"I've never felt so lucky to be an only child." She yawns again and I know I should let her go. "Tomorrow, okay?" she says. "I promise."

"Sure, sure." Then she's gone. I could have told her about the money, how much I need, but I'm not there yet. Close, but not yet. I turn my computer on and dash off an email to Liz Reed, asking if the situation at North Isle's changed at all, that part time would be fine if that's all there is. My inbox is empty but for a lone response to an application. The interlibrary coordinator position at Commack has been filled internally. I scroll through the listserv again, looking for changes, new positions. I think of things to call myself—Information Specialist, Information Technician, Information Resource Manager—I can be anything a job wants me to be. Eventually words blur and there's sand behind my eyelids.

I wake not with the sun but with a light in the window that pulses like a heartbeat. Doyle is in the driveway, a moving shadow except for his hands, which are lit by two forty-watt lightbulbs. He spins the bulbs, balancing them, passing them over the backs of his hands in smooth waves. The rolling incandescence illuminates small portions of the tattoo, a diver shining a lamp into darkness. Tentacles curl and ripple. A flash of light, movement, then gone. The lights roll across his chest, his face briefly visible in their glow. White teeth. Then black. The light moves, Doyle extends, dances. The undulating light passes across my sister, leaning against the car. Watching.

He's performing. For her.

I watch until it feels like spying, then close the window shade. Light leaks through. I go back to the book, to my notebook and the names. It's time to do a little math. Verona Bonn was born in 1935, making her twenty-seven when she drowned. Her mother,

Celine Duvel, died in 1937, when Verona was two—the same age as Enola when Mom died. Celine's obituary doesn't list a date of birth. A short amount of digging on the computer turns up a marriage license between a Celine Trammel and Jack Duvel. Her date of birth is February 13th, 1912; that's twenty-five years old when she died. Young, but not the same age as my mother or grandmother. No, there's something different.

The telephone rings. It's Churchwarry.

"I hope I didn't wake you," he says. We both know he hasn't, but I make polite assurances.

"No, it's fine. What's the matter?"

"Nights and an old dog. Sheila can't make it through a night without a walk anymore and Marie has declared that my duty. These days once I'm up, I'm up."

I understand the feeling.

"I found a book that I think you might find useful. I was wondering what might be the best way to get it to you? It's rather heavy."

"Overnight it."

10

The mermaid's shifting woke Amos from dreamless sleep. Frayed thumping filled his chest as he recalled her frightened eyes, how he'd held her, and the deep satisfaction of touching another skin to skin. Evangeline blinked, eyes dim with sleep and morning. He brushed her hair from her shoulder and smiled, an expression that felt stretched and unfamiliar. He pressed his fingers to the curve of her collarbone then to his own.

Evangeline shrieked and scrambled from the tub, knocking Amos back and jarring his bones against the slats. She fled, skirts trailing behind.

He waited. She would come back, if only because there was nowhere to go. Though Peabody and Ryzhkova's schooling had imparted a loosely civilized veneer, his patience remained weak. A quarter hour's time had him searching. Finding her wasn't difficult; humidity made the ground soft so that each step left a perfect impression, the curve of her instep, a divot from the ball of her foot. He followed her steps as he had so many deer paths.

He found her under an elm, crying and crumpled like discarded cloth. So much water from one woman, as if she held a lake inside; his animal heart knew that he and she were made of different things. He waved in greeting, but her head remained tucked against her knees. He wanted to call out, to see how her name felt on his lips. To show he meant no harm, he tipped his head and lightly touched her shoulder.

She brushed him away. "Go. Please."

He sat beside her. She rocked, cried, and refused to face him. He wrapped his arms around her, light enough to pull away in case she struck him. She gasped and it sounded like a breaking river.

Meixel cooed to the horses after rowdy towns, Peabody sang when writing, and Benno hummed when fixing axles—Amos wanted these things for himself. He held Evangeline, pressed his forehead to her shoulder, and matched his breath to the rise and fall of her sobs. From his throat came keening like bullfrog rattling and squealing wagons; sound, but not voice. Startled, he snapped his jaw closed and hid his face.

"Is that your voice?" A soft question.

He shook his head, pressing his lips together until they hurt.

"You made a sound. I heard."

He shook his head; it was all he could do but not nearly enough.

"From sound comes speech," she said.

He wanted it to be true, but knew his tongue to be unwilling, and his mind unable to fathom summoning sound, or how to make it pleasing. He shut his eyes against an unfamiliar sting.

Evangeline began to extricate herself from his arms. "We can't stay like this," she said. "I think it best I go, lest we be seen. Neither of us need mention what happened."

He wanted her to stay until his breath felt right again, but she wiped her eyes and stood. Before leaving she paused, a curious expression crossing her face. "You must stop looking after me, Amos. No one need look after me."

He watched her weave through the trees toward the wagons, and the burning in his gut intensified; he had felt the sensation before—shame. He tried to slow his heart and feel its place in the air, but peace did not come. Frustrated, he attempted a shout, but produced no sound. He had to speak. Hours slipped by while he worked the problem until the answer appeared as an image: the Fool.

He sprinted toward the wagons. In chance moments his feet settled into Evangeline's footprints and her warmth seeped into him.

Stealing the cards wasn't difficult. Harsh swearing from Peabody's wagon told Amos that Ryzhkova was settling her accounts. Departing a town required Peabody's review of the run's expenses and earnings. All finances were handled in the menagerie master's wagon, and Ryzhkova kept as tight a fist on her money as Peabody. The cards were unwatched.

Amos dug through scarves, sage bundles, and trinkets until he found the box. Once, when they'd been stuck inside during a storm, Ryzhkova had told him the story of the painting on its lid, of Ivan Tsarevich pulling the tail feather of the Firebird, of water that restored the bodies of dead men and water that would bring their bodies back to life. When his fingers touched the cards his skin hummed.

He crouched in the corner, his hands tripping frantically through the deck, searching for a specific picture whose meaning he knew well. Ryzhkova had taught him to smile when turning it over, how women's eyes grew soft when it appeared in their fortunes, and that if he held a woman's hand after revealing this card, the woman would pay him more. He tucked the card into his scarf, put the rest of the deck into his pocket, and went to seek Evangeline, only to run directly into Peabody, exiting his wagon and looking ruffled.

"Expanding horizons, Amos. Options as wide as the sea," he said, as though continuing a prior discussion. He smacked Amos on the back, jostling him. "As with the girl there, ah yes, My Lady

Mermaid. An excellent match. Well chosen, my boy." Peabody patted his belly and murmured something. Amos caught the words *delicious bit*. Madame Ryzhkova peered from the wagon door. He tensed and focused on Peabody.

Peabody leaned and spoke next to Amos's ear. "A piece of advice. A touch of chivalry would serve you. A little less wild fellow." He gestured vaguely in the direction of Amos's genitals, then ducked back into his wagon.

Evangeline was buckling the lid to a linen trunk when Amos found her. Nearby, Benno stretched, sitting splay-legged, touching both hands to a pointed foot, talking to her. Benno's scar nearly vanished when he laughed. Evangeline smiled. Amos approached the pair and their conversation trickled into silence. Evangeline started to speak, but Amos raised his palm. *Stop. Please.* He removed the card from his scarf and pressed it into her hand, cat quick, barely touching her.

A small line formed between her eyebrows. Had he been wrong? He waited for her to turn the card, held his breath as she flipped it to reveal a pretty drawing of an angelic presence watching over two figures—a man and woman in a state of undress, frozen in the moment before running to embrace. He watched her flush blossom.

Benno glanced between them. He cleared his throat. "Three never get on so well as two. We will talk later, yes, Amos?" He bowed to Evangeline. "Good afternoon."

Amos did not acknowledge his friend. The card drew all his focus. At its bottom, Ryzhkova's script spelled out *The Lovers*.

Amos was ignorant, but Evangeline was not; Grandmother Visser had made her learn letters and a bit of ciphering, which kept Peabody from robbing her blind and allowed her to read the words. Her color darkened further. Amos touched a hand to his chest, then to hers before touching the card, his fingers coming to rest between the naked figures.

"Certainly not," she said.

He brought the card to his chest. She chewed on her lip, but did not stop him when he pressed his other palm to her heart.

"Please go," she whispered. "I'm sorry, but please go."

Amos took the card from her, his face on fire, and ran, stumbling toward Sugar Nip's cart. The image was clear. Ryzhkova had explained one of its meanings as a destined love, guided by benevolent fate. He knew they'd been led to one another. He'd done something wrong.

A day's travel found the menagerie in New Castle, where houses were brick rather than wood—red clay dug from the Pennsylvania hills. The sturdy structures seemed at odds with transient wagons, but Peabody insisted that bricks meant money, particularly so close to Philadelphia. Benno laughed at this while he and Amos unhooked wagons. "Bricks mean broken masonry. All the more rocks to stone us."

The horses were fed and watered. Meixel walked the llama on the outside of town to avoid onlookers. Nat took Sugar Nip into one arm and carried the small horse to the river, while Amos and Benno swept out the animal wagons. Clothing and costumes were shaken and hung out to breathe. Evangeline's tub was checked for leaks, and righted for the arduous process of filling it. While they stretched, cleaned, and stashed away the loose ends of days on the road, Peabody made rounds with his book, surveying the performers as to any needs that might be filled within town—Susanna had worn through her slippers, Melina wanted knives to practice with, Nat needed a sack of buckwheat to sleep on for his sore back—and what cut of the take each would earn. Amos received a fraction of Ryzhkova's pay, but the amount did not matter, as Ryzhkova dressed him and Peabody provided for him from his own purchases. He needed little, but what he desired seemed increasingly impossible.

Ryzhkova was in a rush to take clients. She had Amos hook the silks inside her wagon almost immediately upon arrival. "Quickly, quickly," she said. "Town is full of questions. We must answer."

Amos was not pleased. After his exchange with Evangeline, he'd hoped to assist in setting up the water act, and to apologize. He looked out from the wagon to the line of performers shuttling water. Benno walked alone, a bucket in each hand. For the second time in as many days, Amos wished to be in his place. Instead he prepared for hours of listening and card turning. Long before the tub was finished being filled, he'd had to don his fortune-teller robes, while Peabody drummed up business from taverns and shops lining the Strand. One after another, the inquisitive knocked at the wagon door until the line of those seeking Ryzhkova's advice wound past the wagons.

They were more talkative than people from farther north, whispering of trysts, thievery, jealousy, and greed. But, as with the northerners, after an hour or two of listening the voices blended into a single aching demand. Amos tried to recall the shape of Evangeline's mouth, if she had smiled at all when he'd shown her the card. Ryzhkova clucked with appropriate sympathy, laughed when needed, and patted hands. When the time came for answers, she signaled for Amos.

"Young man will show the cards, yes? He has gift, hears fates." She used her most motherly voice to whisper, "Is why he does not speak. Hears terrible, terrible things." Ryzhkova's accent was at its thickest when speaking to customers. Showmanship, Amos thought; not so large as Peabody's, but there it was. "Secrets," she said. "They travel to his hand, see? His hand alone makes the cards speak." The clients watched Amos as if seeing their secrets in his veins.

"Much change. The man here, you see? He is Page. There is obstacle between you and your desire. Ah, I see." Her singsong voice would have been soothing were Amos not distracted. He'd picked the wrong card; he could have chosen the World, to ask Evangeline to look for possibility, but its meaning was less direct. He'd intended to be clear and instead he suffered for it.

"Three of Swords in past. Poor thing. Heart has broken," Ryzhkova told a mousy woman.

Three blades piercing a brilliant red heart. An apt image, Amos thought.

Ryzhkova comforted with her ruined hands, touching wrists, calming fears, speaking of future love. Whoever opened her door was told all would be well. It wasn't true. Amos had seen the cards.

Well into the night, after the last client scurried away, Ryzhkova pulled the drape closed on her cart and shut the door. Amos stood to leave, but she stopped him. "Very important, Amos." Her eyes were dark with warning. "You must know when to tell truth and when not." She searched for words. "More money sometimes means less truth. They pay us well," she shrugged, "we lie a little. Sit with me."

He sat in a corner and folded his legs, the wood biting into his bare ankles, and watched as Ryzhkova began the lengthy process of unwinding her head scarf. Her hair slid down from the crown of her head, a coarse gray and white rope. Never having seen it out of the scarf, he was surprised at its length. It fell nearly to her waist. He briefly wondered what Madame Ryzhkova had once looked like. He glanced at the portrait of her daughter, searching for similarities that time hadn't erased.

"I will teach you something," she said. "Before we begin, you must know you cannot trick me. Only truth between us, yes? No lies. Not for we who tell fortune." She smacked her palm on the top of a small stool. "You took my cards, yes?"

He nodded.

She laughed. "Good, good. You understand. Do not do this again."

It was something he could not promise. He remained still.

Ryzhkova inched toward the barrel where the cards lay, still spread from the last client. She leaned over them and gestured for Amos to do the same. The cart felt smaller and warmer than it had moments before. A single candle provided light. Over their heads the portraits of her relatives flickered in light and shadows, their eyes laughing at him. "I will not trick you. No lies for us. But," she said, raising a gnarled finger, "I will teach you how."

Until then Amos's life had been one of unwavering honesty. When he sat with Ryzhkova and watched her fingers play over the cards, he did not know what it meant to lie or that soon he would lie to the very woman teaching him the art of deception.

She showed him how to slip a card into the edge of his sleeve, how to stash one in his scarf, how to reverse a card to change its meaning, all of it too quick for the untrained eye to see. His first attempts were fumbling, clumsy, and sent her into fits of laughter. Hours of quick turns and pocketing, subtle flips and slides later, Ryzhkova grabbed his sleeve.

"You showed my cards to the girl, didn't you?"

A subtle tic, a twitch of his left hand betrayed him. Anger flared in Ryzhkova's eyes, then went dead. He had the sudden thought that a strong wind might blow her away like ash.

"You must not see her."

He raised a hand to protest, but she continued.

"She is beautiful, yes. But she is not like you, not like me. Look at her. She is half a soul, hungry for another. You stay with this girl," she spat the word, "and she will drown you."

He shook his head fiercely.

"She will not mean to. She thinks only of love, not the price. She knows only want. That is the way of Rusalki. Drowned girls." Her voice hitched. "They lure a man, play with him, dance with him until he dies. They drag him into water, not knowing he will perish. When he is dead they grieve. In grief, they look for another to comfort them, and so they go on. Leave her to another boy, to one who is not mine."

Amos's stomach lurched. He could not tell Ryzhkova what he'd seen when he'd held Evangeline, or how it had been she who had pushed him away. His teeth dug into his cheek until he tasted blood.

"I say this to protect you. Because I have seen. Because I love you, like my son." Her boot hit the table. A card bounced. The Page of Cups, a dark-haired boy with an overflowing goblet. "The girl, she may not know, but she will drink your soul. She cannot help it. Half a soul will kill to be whole." She struck her hands against the card box, bent thumb standing in defiance, shaking with fear and threat. "You will not lie to me. You do not see her."

11

I have a week. The book is a beautifully broken window with an obstructed view of what is killing us, and something is definitely killing us. It isn't just my family's endemic sadness. Yesterday I found a newspaper photograph of my grandmother two days before her death. She's young, an angel in an Esther Williams swimsuit, smiling so brightly it hurt. Genuine happiness, then nothing. Enola is home, falling into trances with tarot cards.

But I'm alive in the water. The bottom swarms with horseshoe crabs. They've been here more than a week now, far longer than their mating season. Could be global warming. It's warmer this summer, and the tides are vacillating to where at low tide I can walk out to the rocks with my feet dry. Joblessness is setting in and each day there is more plaster on the floor. A crab shuffles across my foot. Claws grab and release.

Lavinia Collins drowned in 1876, in Bridgeport, the land of Barnum. If I looked across the water I could see where she died. Born on February 3rd, 1846, to Clara Petrova, daughter of the drowned Bess Visser. Lavinia was dead by thirty. Everything after her birth is in the damaged pages, gone in a wash of spoiled ink and paper. Not a hint of foul play. Last night Churchwarry brought up the Flying Wallendas. Wire walkers, a circus family dating back four hundred years, with a string of falls and accidents tragic enough to be called a curse. Falling wire walkers live in the same world as drowning mermaids. A package arrived this morning, wonderfully musty, with a small note from Churchwarry.

I expect this returned, though there is no rush. I'd let you keep it, but I suspect neither of us can afford that. Marie would shout at me until my ears fell off. It's rather rare.

A heavy volume, *Binding Charms and Defixione* has an almost sinister look to it, a thick black leather binding, title embossed but not gilded, the pages soft with years of oil from fingertips of the curious. I touched it and felt almost the same shiver I had when touching the book—our book. I'll sit with it once my head is clear.

Something grabs my hair and yanks from the roots. A rush of air blinds me. I jerk to the side and a hand clamps around my arm. I try to wrench free, but the water makes me slow. The grip is tight. The fingers release my hair and grab my other arm. My gut spasms and the last of my breath is in front of me. Arms lock under my shoulders. I pull, but they don't move. Fight hits my tongue, bitter. I kick. The light grows wider and brighter as I'm dragged upward.

I choke, struggling to get free, pulled backward, stomach to the sky, water pouring into me. The arms slip higher, crush my neck, block my airway. I claw. Can't breathe. Can't spit the water out. Blackness slides in. Speckled shadows move until there is only dark. I flail. Try to break free. Breathe. *Breathe.*

Shit, we are cursed.

I'm on my back, a sand flea gnawing on my shoulder. Something on the outer edge of my hearing. A voice. A hand slaps my face. Eyes open. A head blocks the sun, shadows swallowing features. Not shadows—a tattoo. Doyle.

"Hey, guy. You okay? I squeezed harder than I thought. Really sorry."

I launch at him. I pop up fast, but am unsteady.

Tentacled fingers wrap around my fist, inches from his face. He holds it, turning my hand, as if examining the blue of each vein. He says something; it sounds like "Ease up, Bro."

"Are you trying to kill me?" I spit. Swing with my left hand. He brushes it away.

"The fuck?" he says. "You were drowning." He's unruffled, like we're talking over a beer. I push, but he twists my elbow behind my back. "Dude, you do not want to hit me." He locks me in a bear hug. "Chill, man," he says. "You're just freaked. No air. Makes your head all wonky." He's not even breathing hard.

From up the cliff, a shriek. Enola. The stairs—it takes a full minute to run them and the pounding means she's already started. I struggle, but it's just fighting shame. A single punch. I couldn't even get in a single punch.

"Dude, I saw you go under. I yelled but you didn't hear. You were down way too long, man."

"I was fine."

When Enola reaches us she smacks Doyle on the shoulder. "Let him go." He drops his hold, and she squeezes me tight. I can feel her panting, shaking against me. "Are you all right? What happened?"

"Your boyfriend tried to kill me." She lets me go so quickly I lose my balance, and then she's hitting—not hard, but if she stays at it long enough I'll have a dead arm.

"He did not. He wouldn't do that." The rest is high-pitched squealing. I grab her arms and hold them at her sides. Doyle stands a few feet back. I can feel him smiling.

"Easy, Little Bird," he says.

She is the opposite of easy. I am not easy. We will never at any point be easy.

Once she realizes I have no intention of letting her go, she sinks her teeth into my shoulder. I shout and she scoots free to look Doyle over for bruises. He mumbles, "I'm good."

I check my shoulder. There are white half-moon marks from Enola's teeth. "I swear he strangled me," I say.

She turns on Doyle, fists ready.

"He was drowning, I pulled him up." Hands in the air, innocent.

"Don't be stupid. My brother doesn't drown."

In spite of myself, I grin. "That's what I told him."

"He's a swimmer," she says. "He can hold his breath a really long time."

"Ten minutes long?" He makes a whistling sound with his teeth.

"Ten minutes?" Accusations all around.

"He tried to choke me."

"Doyle's a pacifist." This is the most ridiculous thing I've heard her say. "I told him to come get you. There's a contractor at the house. Frank sent him. You need to talk to the guy."

We are on the stairs, Doyle climbing ahead of us with simian ease, when she taps my shoulder. "Been doing that a lot?"

"Getting choked by your boyfriends? No. You should come home more. Almost dying is fun."

"Ten minutes is dangerous even for you," she says.

I'd say that Doyle exaggerated, but I don't know how long I was down. Her hands twitch inside her pockets. I see a quick flash of a card with what looks like a leg with a hoof. The Devil? But not like the one in *The Tenets*. Enola tucks it away.

"Sure," I say.

The contractor is Pete Pelewski, a heavyset man with bushy salt-and-pepper hair. He wears a checked shirt and beaten-up tool belt, and writes with a carpenter's pencil, a trustworthy costume designed to lessen the blow. Nothing a contractor says comes without pain.

"A hundred and fifty thousand," he says. My gasp is audible, but he bulldozes forward. "That's the basic bulkhead repair and a start on a terrace. The house," he shakes his head. "The foundation's in bad shape. You'll need masons and landscapers to secure the bluff. I work with some guys. I won't have a full estimate until talking to them, but expect another hundred thousand. Bare minimum." He taps his pencil on his notes. "And you need to move fast. We've got to be able to get trucks on the beach, and the ground's got to be solid enough to support grading."

I'm saying appropriate things, asking how many trucks (four if the town will allow that many), how much time (weeks, months, depends on the trucks), can I live here while the work is done (until the foundation work starts), and now I'm shaking hands, asking for an estimate in writing, and exchanging pleasantries. *Isn't Frank great? Yes, wonderful; my family's oldest friend.*

And then Pete Pelewski is gone and I'm leaning on the kitchen wall, next to the key hooks. The wallpaper is stained with fingerprints, Dad's fingers, Mom's, mine, Enola's, touching the wall as we hung up our keys, for years and years.

Four, three, two, one.

"You need to ask Frank for money," Enola says from the kitchen table. She's in Mom's spot, where the string from a teabag would hang over her cup, swaying, as she clinked spoon against porcelain.

"I'll try the historical society, see if they have landmark restoration grants."

"Sounds like it'd take awhile," she says.

"I'm good at grants. It's what I do."

"Did," she says. "If you asked Frank he'd probably say yes."

"I'd rather not."

"Why?"

"Why do you care?" There are harsher things I could say, things I've compiled and archived, each with a catalog card.

"I don't know," she says. "Dad lived here. I lived here." Past tense.

"You don't anymore." The divots in the floor from the chair, those are mine. The stained quilt is hers. The clothing she didn't take. A one-eyed teddy bear. Things she left behind.

"It's still mine." She slides her hands into her pockets, shuffling the cards.

Fine, let's play direct. "What's with your cards? I see you playing with them and you tore that picture out of my book."

Doyle answers, "She's had some really bad readings lately. Messed-up kind of shit."

"Oh, for fuck's sake, Doyle." She stomps. Chair legs scrape linoleum. "I'm not talking about it. That means you don't get to talk about it." She yanks open the kitchen door and stalks into the backyard.

Doyle grimaces, dragging down the tip of a tentacle, shadows mixing with ink. "She's been touchy."

"For how long?"

"Couple months."

Shit. And I have a week. "Any reason?"

"She just says she's worried."

I sit in my chair, the one that faced Dad's. It will always be my father's table though it's been more than ten years since he died. I don't have to close my eyes to see him, where Doyle is, waiting—though he would never say it—for Mom to come back.

I was nineteen, Enola was fourteen, and his was the first dead body we ever saw. Eyes bloodshot, paused over a newspaper he'd never finish reading. Enola came home from school and found him. A stroke, a tiny vessel blocked then burst like a snapped string. He'd been dying since the day Mom left.

We didn't cry until after his body was removed.

She sat on the sofa with her knees in an inverted *V,* staring out at the water. From then on she would be the only other person to know how we grew up, how to cook a steak like Dad, how it felt when he knocked the backs of our heads, the only one who understood the loneliness.

"I hate you," she said.

"I know."

"I hated him." We looked at the walls. The first sign of a crack starting.

"Me too," I answered.

"What happens?" she asked.

In the dark I said, "I'll take care of you."

Doyle and I look out the window, but Enola isn't there. He chews on his thumb. I hadn't noticed before, but his fingers are like mine, gnawed to the hearts.

"She won't go far," I say. "There's nothing to do in Napawset." I should probably tell him that most relationships with my sister involve leaving. The tattoo makes it difficult to see him beyond elliptical suckers and hours of pain. "How old are you anyway?" I ask.

"Twenty-four."

I had thought him closer to my age, edging thirty, maybe older. "I have to ask what you're doing with my sister." I am careful not to say *intentions,* because it's fatherly.

"Whatever she wants for as long as she'll let me." A right answer to a question that had none. "What's with you and staying underwater so long?"

"It's a family thing. Our mom taught me. She did circus and carnivals for a while, too."

"Didn't she drown?"

"That was different."

Doyle shakes his head and octopi glide across his throat. "Man, I don't know. My family's all pipe fitters." He laughs and cracks his neck. Impossible as it should be, I'm starting to like him.

Creaking comes through the window, the sound of someone sitting down at a half-rotten picnic table. We both look. Enola is cross-legged on the table my father built, not the bench—never proper—facing away from us, bent-backed.

"I'm worried about her," Doyle says quietly. "She's getting a little strange on the cards."

"I'll talk to her."

"Okay, man."

The concrete on the back stoop is broken, so she hears me coming and picks up whatever cards were on the table. The paper looks tattered and yellow, very old, the colors faded. I can make out the shape of a skeletal arm, half worn away, before she snatches the cards and stuffs them in her hoodie. She twists around to look at me. I sit on one of the benches and feel the old wood sag under me.

"Is that a Marseille deck?" That's what's in *The Tenets*. I've seen Waite decks, too, illustrated in the 1900s. Delicate pictures. This is not that.

"No. And I'm not talking about it," she says.

"Sure."

She stretches her legs and leans back across the table. "Why did Dad build this? It's not like we ever ate outside."

"We did once or twice."

"Not after Mom died, right?"

"No." Everything stopped after Mom died. "Doyle's nice," I say.

She scrapes a small patch of lichen that's grown on the table. "He likes me. I know that's hard to do sometimes."

"You're not so terrible. He's weird-looking, though. Even for you."

"I know," she smiles. "It's kind of why I'm with him."

"Where do you guys travel?" I want her to talk. It's been so long since I've spent time with her that it feels good to listen to her. The thing I don't miss about the library is the silence—the middle of winter days when there's nothing to listen to but the hissing heaters, the hum of computers, and pages turning. Why did I never just pull Alice aside to talk?

"Winter last year Rose's went deep into Georgia. Cards can be slow there. Churchy people." She rolls her eyes. "The houses down there are gorgeous. You'd like them," she says. "I took a ghost tour of an old brick place on this river that feeds into the ocean. It's got oysters on each bank, piled up like ruffles on panties." She stretches slowly. "Never seen anything so pretty."

Manuscripts aren't so different from ruffles; both need a light touch. I think about the job in Savannah. This morning Liz sent an email saying that the Sanders-Beecher Archive called her for a reference. She chided me for laying it on too thick with them, but said she corroborated my credentials. I'd do the same for her. Liz and I have always understood each other. I look at my sister, Enola, who I don't understand at all. "What's your show like?"

"Basic. Boring. The carnival is what you'd think, mostly. Swings, whack-a-mole, everything. Freak show."

"Is that where Doyle is?"

"Yeah. There's a maze with a Cyclops lamb and bouncers. We've got taxidermy monkey babies made into Siamese twins. It's like stumbling across an enormous dog shit—you need to stare. I mean how the hell do you get monkey carcasses shipped to you?" She looks at the kitchen window, perhaps at Doyle. "We've got a swallower, Leo. Does swords and flames. He's okay and he's almost normal. Wife, kids, middle-aged spread. We've got a piercer, too, kind of an asshole, but he knows a lot about anatomy." She digs a bit of grime from under her fingernail. "He hangs cannonballs from his nipples, pokes needles through his arms, that sort of stuff. At night shows if you pay extra you can see him lift stuff with his dick. George—he's the fat man—handles the cash. Doyle works mostly nights."

It makes sense. "The lights play better in full dark, I guess."

"Yeah. In daylight he moves well, but it's different at night. You get why he did the tattoos. In the dark he's not really human. You see the bulbs but the light comes from him, like he's part stars, part water. You look and think maybe you could be on that skin, move like that, and light would come from you, too. Sometimes I think the ink holds the light in so I can look at him, like maybe he did it because he wanted me, someone like me, to see him."

She drags her fingers through her hair, scratching her scalp. I remember cutting out a chunk of her glue- and glitter-matted hair.

"He's really good. He's better than me," she says.

My phone buzzes in my pocket.

It's Alice; her voice is flat. "I need you to explain something."

"Hey, what's wrong?" I get up from the table and Enola follows, listening in. She mouths, *Alice?* I put up a hand, but she hangs over my shoulder.

"Why exactly would you steal from the library?"

"I'm sorry, what?"

"Don't apologize. Just explain. Marci saw you take books and told Janice. I just spent *half an hour* being lectured on theft of property as if I'm responsible for you. Because we're seeing each other. Everybody knows because there're no damn secrets in this place. What the hell were you thinking?"

"I don't know. Shit. I'll bring them back."

She's quiet for a minute.

"Are you still there?"

"You're not pissed that I still have my job, are you? Because that's going to be a problem."

"No. God, no. I'm sorry. I just, I needed the books and I didn't think." Enola is giving me the stink eye. "I'm sorry. If I knew you were going to get flak for it—"

"Quit apologizing. Just bring the books back."

The thought of going to the library after being fired is humiliating, let alone to return stolen materials. "I can bring them to you tonight."

"It'll look worse if I bring them in." A loud sigh. "Just take them to the library, okay? For me. Also, my dad's been bugging me about having dinner soon."

The implication is clear. Sitting across from Frank and Leah, holding Alice's hand underneath the table. I make a noncommittal grunt.

"Yeah, I know. It'll be weird, but we'll get through." She hangs up, which I suppose is good. Anything I could have said would have made things worse.

Enola's cackle is startling. "Holy shit," she says between gasps. "Ho-*ly* shit. I know why you won't ask Frank for money. You can't. You're fucking Alice."

12

Peabody had been right about New Castle. A trade hub, merchants and shippers came up from the river flush with money, and cattlemen tumbled in from Hares Corner, crowding the herringbone streets and Dutch squares. It had been the colony's capital before the war, but with the influx of British and battles around Philadelphia, those in government fled to Dover, leaving behind a city steeped in melancholy reminiscence—exactly the clientele to seek distraction from a troupe of traveling performers.

Amos and Ryzhkova worked day and night until the tide of patrons ebbed.

"Those who long to live in past dream just as much for the future," Ryzhkova said, sipping a mug of frothy beer Amos had procured. His mentor had a liking for the bitter drink. "They desire for past and future to be one." Her eyes grew soft and glassy, and it was not long before she reclined against the mattress and began to snore.

He tucked a blanket over Ryzhkova's shoulders and set the mug carefully aside so as not to wake her. They'd seen their final clients; for the moment he was without obligation. Evangeline's tub had been emptied for a morning departure. Amos recognized opportunity.

He did not think about the lie as he searched for the cards, or that the very act was breaking a promise. The card he hunted held a subtle meaning, one he hoped Evangeline would find less frightening than the Lovers. The Strength card. It bore the image of a beautiful woman whose hands rested on the head of a lion. The beast gazed at her in adoration, while she both caressed and subdued him. He pulled it from the deck and began to close the box when he thought better of it and took the Queen of Swords as well—a dark-haired straight-backed woman who bore some resemblance to Evangeline. Best to be thorough. She needed to understand.

In the days since uttering the rasping noise, he had tested his voice, only to find it incapable of producing a satisfactory sound. At first, Peabody was delighted with Amos's efforts and offered assistance after catching Amos croaking to himself behind the velvet drapes in his wagon. He sat across from Amos and explained the proper way to support sound, using all the stomach's muscles to push out the air. "Like a bellows to the fire," he said, patting his belly. Peabody's gut swelled and emptied, but when Amos tried to duplicate it, all that emerged was a rattling hiss, which practice did not improve. They tried humming, whistling, and buzzing the lips. Peabody was convinced that tightness in Amos's tongue kept him silent. "It's trapping the sound down in your chest." He demonstrated yawning and tongue rolling. Amos recalled the llama making the same expressions before spitting slime. Amos's tongue would not comply.

Peabody's enthusiasm for the project waned. "Practice, my boy.

THE BOOK OF SPECULATION · 133

Patience as well," he said before retiring one evening. He rubbed his eyes and hung his hat on a brass hook above his bed. The velvet pile had begun to wear from the brim, and Amos imagined that the inside of his throat looked much the same—raw, thin. "One does not learn an art in a day. Mustn't be discouraged," he said as he opened his book and began to note the day's events.

Ryzhkova's cards offered Amos his best chance to speak. Chosen cards in hand, he felt purpose rise inside him, stronger than hunger.

Unattended, Evangeline's tub was drying in preparation for sleep. Amos shimmied the two cards between the stave joints so that they stood on end, and pulled the oiled canvas down so that none but she would see what he had done. He then went to the small horse's wagon and sat in the doorway to wait for Evangeline's return. He regretted not having an apple for Sugar Nip, but she was content to have her nose stroked and didn't mind that he smelled of burned sage. He calmed his nervous hands by combing her mane.

A half an hour had passed when Benno approached Amos's hideout. New Castle had tired Benno; his normal bouncing gait was replaced by an old man's shambling. Amos often watched his friend work, flipping from feet to hands and back again in endless circles, walking around on fingertips, or supporting his entire weight with the knuckles of one hand.

Though Benno made it seem effortless, it was not. Benno lifted himself into the wagon to sit beside Amos, dangling his legs over the side.

"I think you occupy too much of your time with birdwatching," he said. A light accent squared each word, sharpened his vowels. The unscarred corner of Benno's mouth quirked into a smile.

Amos grinned. There was no way to explain that he was in the midst of a conversation with Evangeline, only she had yet to discover it. He motioned toward Benno's legs and pantomimed his aching walk.

A short whuff of breath. "Ah well, we aren't all as young as you. Also, for you every town is the same. For me?" He showed his hands, scraped and raw, with a fingernail black like a sunflower seed. "A brick street is not as nice as a dirt one."

Amos thought of Ryzhkova's warped fingers. His profession would have its own punishments. He twisted his thumb to show Benno.

"You have many years before that. That woman has three lifetimes on you, surely. Speaking of women," he continued, "Melina asks after you. Go to her. See if she'll share a wagon with you on the road." He patted Amos's shoulder gently. "Courage."

Amos shook his head.

"The Mermaid is not for you," he said softly. "Melina or Susanna are better suited, happy women. A quiet man needs a happy woman. Evangeline, she pulls sadness behind her like a cat does its tail."

Amos tapped Benno sharply on the arm, glancing at him from the corner of his eye. A short but telling gesture.

Benno nodded slightly. "I understand. Where I come from some would call her nixie—half fish, half woman." At Amos's quiet snort he continued, though more softly. "Silly, I know, but she plays with death, Amos. And she says nothing of where she came from. There is a thread," he said, tracing a spot on the wagon floor. "A line that runs between the living and the dead. It is thin and likes to break."

Amos busied his hands to show he didn't wish to speak any longer. They sat together and watched Nat heave clothing trunks onto a cart, thick muscles pumping, and Melina by the fire, soaking her sore hands in a pot filled with water and salts. Then Nat returned to his cart, and Susanna sat beside Melina and struck up a light conversation. After a time Benno climbed down from the wagon. "You are my friend and you are kind," he said quietly. "More than is good. I was taught to watch for gentle souls, as they've not the wit to look after themselves." For a moment his eyes took a serious cast, but it vanished quickly with his strange half-torn smile. "I talk too much. Forgive me," he said and began the painful walk to his wagon. "Be brave. Happy women are good for kind souls."

Amos waited.

She walked in from town carrying several small bottles in her skirt apron. He remembered her dress as being Susanna's, though the blue looked brighter on Evangeline. Her skin was pink from the journey and wisps of hair curled around her face; save for when she was underwater in her white dress, Amos had never seen her prettier. He smiled until she crossed the length of the camp, past where he sat, to knock at Nat's door. Nat answered, leaning out, and Amos strained to hear what was said. Evangeline handed the bottles to the big man—oils, liniments for an aching back. He'd seen Nat use them in the past; menthols, herb oils, sharp-smelling things rubbed hard into the skin. He watched them exchange pleasantries and a sourness gripped his stomach. Nat laughed and Amos forced himself to look away. Sugar Nip nudged his back but the touch brought no comfort.

He did not see Nat close his door, leaving Evangeline outside, nor her trip to her tub. He felt a fool for not having gone and removed the cards, returning them to Ryzhkova and declaring himself finished with them. He curled up against the clapboard wall, closing his eyes. He breathed deeply, listening to the evening around him, slowed his heartbeat and tried to disappear into the wagon walls. Even with his eyes squeezed shut he saw her handing a dark bottle to Nat, how their fingers had touched. His heart panged.

He heard his name. First by Ryzhkova's wagon, then Susanna's. Evangeline calling him. He heard Melina but could not hear the words. His name mixed with cracking from the fire. If he stayed with Sugar Nip she might not find him. He would steal the cards back. He was light with his fingers, still quiet on his feet, and if he moved quickly enough he wouldn't wake her.

But Evangeline would know. Sugar Nip chewed the end of his scarf and he brushed her away. He couldn't bear more days of hanging his head, knowing that she thought him ridiculous. He felt ill enough already. He heard Susanna speaking with Evangeline; she was close now. If he did nothing, she would see the cards as the rambling of a mad mute. The small horse nuzzled his arm. If he showed her, if he tried, she might understand. She did not have to love him, but she had to understand. He would be the lion.

He faced the wagon door and struck his fist against the boards. He rattled the door until he saw her turn, searching out the source of the noise. He waited and watched, legs folded, as they would be if he were reading cards. Evangeline spotted him, but her expression was one Peabody had not schooled him on. He saw the cards in her hand, the familiar orange backs, and wondered what it was he'd thought to gain from them.

"There you are," she said when she reached him. "Were you hiding from me?"

He shook his head and gestured to Sugar Nip.

"You're good with her. Friends, I would venture."

He shrugged, shifting uneasily.

Evangeline looked down to the cards in her hand. "Did you leave these for me?" Her voice was firm, but not unkind.

He nodded. Unable to meet her eyes, he stared instead at the Queen of Swords. His mouth was dry, his tongue leaden.

"I'm sorry," she said. "They're quite beautiful, but I cannot keep them. I'm certain Madame Ryzhkova would miss them." When Amos made no move to take the cards, she said, "I would not like to see her angry with you. She's rather terrifying." He remained still. "You've been kind to me," she ventured, bending to place the cards beside him.

He looked at the cards and saw their meanings, all the days and nights his fingers had spent touching them, learning them better than he knew himself. Amos laid his hand over hers, trapping the cards beneath. He shook his head.

"Amos, I won't keep them."

He gently took the cards from her, careful not to touch her again, lest he lose his nerve. Before she could leave, he raised the Queen of Swords, holding it for her to see. He pointed to the dark hair of the painted woman then touched the black of Evangeline's. Though he willed them not to, his fingers trembled. Her hair was as smooth as he remembered.

"I look like her to you?"

It was more than that, but he nodded. He showed her the second card, Strength. He pointed to the woman who held the lion subservient, tracing the finely painted hand with a fingertip. Steadier now. She had not run. He bit his cheek and then touched Evangeline's hand, brushing her knuckles. He showed her the orange brown of the lion's mane and pressed his hand to his chest.

"I don't understand." Still, she did not run. How glad he was that she did not run.

He set the card on the floor of the wagon and hopped to the ground. Evangeline jumped at his sudden movement. He held up his hand, open-palmed, gesturing for her to wait. She did. He dropped to his knees in the soft dirt before her, lifting his eyes to meet hers. He took her hands in his, then placed them on his head.

How long they stayed that way—silent, still—neither could have said.

When Evangeline took her hands away, he stood.

"You are the lion?"

He touched his forehead to her shoulder and she held him in the comforting way of women. "And I . . . "

When she stated her understanding, a simple *oh*, it little mattered. The gesture had already spoken.

Later, in the dark of the mermaid's empty tub, they unwound his hair from its binding. Evangeline marveled at its sleekness and color. Amos did not realize she found it beautiful; his thoughts were disjointed, so taken was he by the curve between her hip and waist; the sweet, salty taste of the skin on her wrist, the inside of her arm; the flutter of her pulse at the base of her neck. Where he had known bodies were made to hunger, to labor, to run and work, he had not known they were meant to feel such sensation from another. Where before he'd held her to comfort and to quiet, she now held him to sate and slake. He feared that he would cry out, would make the awful sound as he had in the woods but, mercifully, he stayed silent.

When it was done and they lay limp on the bedding, cradled by the tub's boards, Evangeline drew the sharp edge of a fingernail along his collarbone. How good it was that people, like houses, had frames and that those frames could be so beautiful. This thing they'd done, Will Aben had thought to do with her. Had she never spoken with Will, she would not know the man she lay with. *I am a killer.* When she shivered, his arm squeezed tight around her. *A killer who beds a lion.* She smiled. How strange it was that *cleave* had two such disparate meanings; she'd known to cut and tear, but now she knew to cling. She rested her cheek in the valley between his shoulder and chest.

Amos lay awake until light bled under the edge of the canvas. He swore his skin still burned from where she'd touched it—a pleasure so profound it dwarfed all else. Nearly. He smiled into Evangeline's hair, more pleased with life than he'd thought possible. He'd found a way to speak.

13

How long does approval take?"

On the other end Kath Canning sips tea. "Several months to a year. It needs to go through land use and zoning committees. You know the town."

She doesn't have to say it. "Slow."

"For the work you're talking about you need an environmental impact study."

"More money." I shift the phone to the other ear.

"I have to be honest with you. The historical society can help with landmarking, but we don't have the money you need. It's just me, Betty, and Les these days, and we're all volunteer. Your best bet is a loan."

"Thanks, Kath. I appreciate your time."

"Best of luck. The Timothy Wabash house was lovely."

Yes, it was. I hang up, more screwed than I was ten minutes ago.

Enola walks into the living room, rubbing some kind of goo into her hair that makes it stand up in chunks. We're going to the Mc-Avoys' for dinner. I suggested a restaurant, but Alice said Frank wouldn't hear of it. She broke the news last night at the Oaks, while grumbling into her gin.

"Dad went on about how Enola's hardly ever here and it's ridiculous that no one's cooked you a decent meal. Did he bother to ask my mother? No, he just assigns her cooking."

"Enola's boyfriend's with her." I grimaced down a gulp of rye. Definitely the drink of the recently fired.

Alice sighed. "Sure, fine. What's another person? Maybe he'll distract my dad."

"From what?"

She raised an eyebrow. "Mom said seven-thirty. Is that okay?"

I twisted the end of her braid around my finger, and gave it a tug. "Seven-thirty is fine."

As we said good night she said, "It's weird to not have you at work." It was almost an afterthought.

Frank is going to ask about Pelewski and the house. And find out his jobless neighbor is dating his daughter and needs a quarter million dollars.

Enola and I wait while Doyle shaves. She picks stuffing from the sofa, tossing it onto one of my shirts. She's been away so long that every change seems enormous, from her hair to her thinness, the trances, and the man who followed her here. When I came in last night she was dealing cards while Doyle snored on her bed. No, they're not a Marseille deck or a Waite deck. They're different, but familiar. I tried to get her attention, but she was engrossed.

"Enola, are you okay?"

A piece of foam flicks from the couch. "Yep. Are you?"

"Can I ask you something?"

"No, but you will anyway."

"Your cards look very old. My book—Churchwarry doesn't know much about it because it was part of a big lot, but it reminds me of your cards, they've got the same kind of wear. I was wondering where you got them."

"Maybe he just doesn't *want* to tell you about the book," she mutters. "The cards were Mom's."

The cards Mom was dealing when Dad begged her to stop. "I didn't know Dad gave them to you."

"He didn't. Frank did." She continues methodically divesting the couch of stuffing.

"Why would he have them?"

"You'd have to ask him. He gave them to me before I left." By left she means left me.

"When can I expect you to start stinking up the house?"

"What?"

"You burn sage to clean tarot cards, don't you?"

She rolls her eyes. "It's called smudging and you don't have to do it every time."

"But you do have to do it."

"These aren't work cards, they're my private deck. Cards kind of gather energy from people and build history. You talk to the cards and they talk to you. These I don't clear because we're talking."

A conversation with Mom's cards is disturbing.

"What do you talk about?"

"You," she says with a shark-toothed grin.

Doyle exits the bathroom, clean-shaven. Though it does little to improve his appearance, it reveals the shadow of what might have been a nice-looking young Midwestern man beneath the layers of ink.

"Hey, we ready?" Doyle asks. He looks back and forth as if sensing something off.

"Sure." Enola flings herself at him, dropping a loud kiss right over his ear.

"You told them you're bringing me, right?" Doyle asks. "You gave a little warning."

"About what? The McAvoys are nice," she says.

He looks at me, concern pulling the tentacles on his jaw downward. "People can be weird about the tattoos."

I think of everything Frank will hear tonight. "I'm sure you won't be a problem."

I follow them down the pebble driveway, across the street, to the McAvoy house. White-shingled, a picket fence and freshly painted porch, a plaque proclaiming it the homestead of Samuel L. Wabash, established 1763. In the yard is a swing set Dad helped build for Alice.

"Looks like my mom's place," Doyle says, sticking the tip of his tongue from the corner of his mouth.

The blinds snap down on one of the front windows. Frank's wife keeps a pair of binoculars on the windowsill, watching all the comings and goings. Leah probably told Frank the instant the gutter broke on my house.

Enola waits for us on the porch. For a moment there's terror in her eyes, then as Doyle approaches the look dissolves.

"Hey," I say to her.

"What?" she replies, the *what* that ends a conversation.

The door opens and Enola hugs Frank.

"Too long, Enola. It's been far too long," he says.

I wave to Leah, who hangs back in the living room. She smiles and politely says hello. She's never been quite as warm as Frank.

Frank's eyes land on Doyle. He blinks a few times before greeting him, gawking. To his credit, Doyle appears to not mind. The Electric Boy sticks out a hand to shake.

"Doyle Bartlett."

I never even asked his last name. I assumed that Doyle *was* his last name.

"Frank McAvoy. Pleasure to meet you." The handshake lasts too long. I clear my throat and Frank drops his hand. "No sense in standing around on the porch. Leah's almost got dinner ready," he says, scratching his sunburned nose, "and Alice is here."

"Great."

"Good to have all you kids under one roof," he says, and pats my shoulder. I follow him inside. It's like my house; couch against the far right living room wall, a kitchen off the back, the hall to the left that leads to the bedrooms—three of them—only Frank's house has gone right. The walls are pale yellow, free of cracks, and sprinkled with pictures of Alice. By the door is a photo from our high school graduation. Alice is in the back row, the tallest of the girls. She's in the kitchen, delaying the inevitable awkwardness, the amount of which even she doesn't fully understand. She waves at me, then spots Doyle. She mouths with library-perfect silent diction, *What* is *that*?

Dinner is formal. Leah's taken out the good china, which only makes the meal more uncomfortable. Enola picks at the lace tablecloth. The fancy silver is out, and we're drinking tap water from the crystal, which is out of place in Doyle's green and black hands.

Alice radiates nervousness, or maybe it's me. Leah sat us together and our knees touch. When I say hello, her lips tighten, but under the table she weaves our fingers. *Hi.* I remember the Alice of the graduation photo and how she used to giggle at the smallest things; that is not this person, and she isn't the smiling woman from the library, either. Here she's a daughter. She steals quick looks at Doyle and he catches her at it. She blushes and it's beautiful.

It's been a while since I've seen Leah, but unlike Frank she looks the same, still wearing her hair in a long red ponytail. She might dye it. Maybe she's softened, gotten a line or two, but she's still Leah and openly gaping at the tattooed man sitting across from her.

"It hurt to get them done," Doyle says. "They go everywhere. It's the worst when the needle is over bone, but after a while you kind of fade out and it's not so bad."

"Oh," Leah says, her mouth going round. "I didn't mean to stare."

"It's cool," he says. "You can't help it."

"Why so many?" she asks.

"It's sort of like a hobby, but kind of like addiction?" he says, voice tipping up as he cocks his head. "You think you're gonna get just one, but then one starts looking really good with another and before you know it you want every piece of you drawn on. I wish I had more space. Some people don't like their skin, you know?" He pops a piece of broccoli into his mouth, using his fingers. "I picked mine."

"I got stuck with mine," Leah replies. "Horrible. I burn to a crisp if I'm in the sun for five minutes."

"Guys like freckles," he says. "True story."

A slow smile crosses Leah's face. "I know." Soon she's laughing, in pleasant conversation with a tattooed Electric Boy. Enola chimes in now and again. Alice stays quiet but keeps brushing my hand. She hasn't brought us up. That should feel good; it doesn't.

"Did Pelewski come by?" Frank asks around a forkful of pot roast. "He said he would."

Enola's eyes flick in my direction. I set my silverware down. "Yes. He gave things a good once-over."

Alice looks at me.

"Contractor friend of mine," Frank says to Alice. To me, "He's a good guy. Did the roof last year. What did he tell you?"

There is no easy way to say it. Pulling the Band-Aid slowly is just as bad as tearing it off. "A hundred and fifty thousand. To start. Probably closer to two hundred fifty for everything."

Alice stiffens. There's a blue flower on the wallpaper just to the left of Frank's ear. I look at its petals. Talk to them.

"What?"

I repeat the figure. Leah and Doyle's conversation stops.

"That's not a repair; that's a goddamned mortgage," he says.

"I know."

"You don't have it."

"I called the historical society." Now is where I'm supposed to ask, but I can't. Not with Alice next to me. Her hand pulls away.

Frank drinks some water, chews a few more bites, and looks down at his plate. "Well, we can't just let it fall in." He puts his palms flat on the table, as if the decision is made. "I'll float you some money, enough to get started. Give me a day or two to get things in order."

From Leah comes a quiet, "Frank."

"Dad." I've never heard Alice hiss before.

"It's not right to just let it go. Paulina and Dan loved that house."

He wants to save the house for my parents, dead people. I should refuse, but I'm in no position. "I'll pay you back."

Alice pushes her chair out, smashing the leg into my foot. My knee hits the table and the gravy boat spills.

"I'll go make the coffee," she says, and disappears into the kitchen. Enola and Leah look at their napkins.

"I'll see if she needs help," I say.

I walk to the kitchen as Doyle tells Frank, "That's a huge thing, man. Huge. You're a real good guy."

Alice grinds coffee by the sink with a large hand grinder, a relic of a machine. Her fist moves in hard circles. The counter light flickers over the gentle curve of her arm as she cranks the handle. If it's possible to grind coffee sadly, this is what she's doing. Her shoulders slope and her movements have a weight that makes everything deliberate and painful. Her yellow blouse is stained with dampness under her arms and the hair at her nape curls with sweat. I know she tastes like sweet salt. I have an old memory of her in her green field hockey skirt, freckles peeking over shin guards and knee socks. I have a fresh memory of her in her bed, feet twisted in pink sheets, dimples at the base of her spine.

"Hey, are we okay?"

"You didn't tell me about the contractor. You didn't tell me anything. You talked to my dad, but not me." She continues grinding. "Were you planning on asking him for money?"

"No," but then I know I'm lying. "Not unless I had to."

"They don't have much. And I don't want you taking it."

"I know."

"I can't make him not offer, just like I can't stop him from doing any other stupid thing he wants to, but I can ask you not to take it."

"I'm sorry."

"You're always sorry." Alice measures out spoonfuls of coarse black grounds and heaps them into her mother's percolator.

"I didn't think he would offer." The counter is cold when I put my hands against it and lean next to her. I promise to pay it back, but know the words are empty when the amount dwarfs everything. If Frank pays, if he helps at all, he'll own me.

She says, "That isn't the point."

"You've seen the house. I don't have anything." With each word she feels further away.

"You know," she says, "you could leave here. Find a job somewhere else. Colleges have rare book rooms, D.C. has archives all over, museums." Her voice softens. "I could help."

"I've been looking," I say. "There's a manuscript curator position in Savannah. It's an interesting place, a specialty library with museum and historical society ties and everything. They've got a canoe trip diary from 1654 that describes the entire coast almost untouched. It's far, but—"

"Georgia," she says, establishing the miles in two syllables.

I can't ask if she would go, though I can see her bent over a book, curled up in the rumpled sheets in an apartment—ours. I can imagine waking up, her back pressed to me, without fear of a collapsing ceiling.

In the dining room Enola swears. A quick look shows her mopping up water. Too thin. Pale. Jumpy.

"It's my parents' house."

I can see Alice's spine stiffen. "I could say things, you know. I could say things so he wouldn't give you anything. I could tell him that you fucked me and nearly got me fired. He wouldn't give you a cent." She tamps down the grounds with a small weight. It makes a soft thudding sound. Threatening.

"You could."

"I won't," she says. She fills the percolator and plugs it in, and then she's beside me, her back to the window. "Because I've known you my whole life, and there are things you don't do to people you've known your whole life. Keep that in mind." The sides of our hands touch, the little fingers lining up in a row. "If you take his money, it's because I let you."

"I don't want to hurt you. I really am sorry."

"I'm not hurt," she says. "And I wish you wouldn't say that."

Her presence is like a heartbeat. I feel her skin on mine, electrons and molecules glance each other until pieces of her become me. I wish I could do dinner at La Mer again and not have picked up Enola's call. I wish I hadn't taken the books, that we'd never left her apartment, that I'd said something years ago. "You sat behind me in French class," I say. "Whenever I try to remember French I can hear you conjugating verbs. I hear you all the time." Her accent had been good. Madame Fournier used to make her recite in front of the class. *"Je suis. Tu es. Il est. Elle est. Nous sommes."*

"Stop," she says, shaking her head. "I like you, Simon, but I'd rather not look at you right now."

I pull my hand back from the counter. "Sorry. I just—"

"You're taking advantage of my father. He's never gotten over your parents. You have no idea of the years of stories I've listened to about Paulie and Dan, Dan and Paulie. You think about how they haunt your life; it never occurred to you that they haunt mine."

For the first time since we began talking, Alice looks at me. She's calm, matter of fact. "So when you take his money—because you will—just know that you're taking it from an old man who's fixated on his dead friends. You're asking a lot from me."

"I don't have a choice."

"You do. You can leave." She takes a deep breath. "I think maybe you should leave. Maybe I should. I thought—forget it."

The bubbling of the percolator fills the silence. I stare at the column of her neck; she holds herself so straight that she makes me feel warped.

"I'd like you to leave me alone now." She says it sweetly and that makes it worse.

I slink back to the dining room, where Enola is telling Leah about the animal tents at the Florida State Fair and Doyle, thankfully, is using his fork. Alice returns with the coffee as though nothing happened and the rest of the meal is unremarkable, except for my shame. Dinner is over when Leah sighs and clears the coffee cups. Alice rises to help and Doyle and Enola scoot for the door.

"Simon, stay," Frank says before I can leave. "Have a beer with me."

"No, no. I need to get back." I say, "I'll call you tomorrow," yet I wind up on the porch, holding a beer. Our shadows are framed by the silhouettes of horseshoe crabs drying on the railing.

"I don't feel right about taking your money, Frank."

"What else are you going to do? Can't let the place fall in." He takes a pull from his bottle. "You can pay it off like a loan."

I don't want to talk about money anymore. "Enola said you gave her my mom's tarot cards."

"Did I?" He scratches his head.

"Right before she left. You gave them to her."

"Ah, I remember. They weren't the sort of thing you'd expressed interest in. Enola came by, said she was traveling like your mom did." He drinks. I do the same. "It felt like giving them back to your mother."

"Why didn't my dad have them?"

"Paulina and I were close, I was just as much her friend as his. I knew her one day longer than your dad. I'm the reason they met." He taps his foot, *tap, tap, tap,* twitching out the story. "It was the hottest damned summer and nobody was taking boats out because the sun would bake you until your skin split. Her show was in town, I forget the name of it."

"Carnival Lareille."

"Lareille, that's right. Don't get old—you hit my age and you've forgotten more than you've ever learned." He drains his beer and looks across the street to where lights pulse in the front room of my house. Doyle at play. "I figured I'd have a drink, cool off on some of the rides, maybe meet a girl. I saw a line outside this tent where you could get your fortune told. I thought what the hell, and there she was. Prettiest girl I'd ever seen. Your mom, she was striking."

I've heard my father's side, how Frank had taken him to the show the next night, how that night Mom had been a mermaid in a glass tank, holding her breath for impossible lengths of time, how he loved her at first sight.

"What did she tell you?"

"That I'd find a good woman and that my life would settle, *even though you long to drift like a boat,* she said. She was good." He stands up, stretches his back, and sets his empty bottle on the porch railing. "Your mom gave me the cards before," he gestures to the water. "I guess it was her way of saying goodbye. Wish I'd known."

She'd told me goodbye and I hadn't known either. "Was she acting strange at all?"

Frank coughs. "Strange was relative with your mother. If she'd seemed different to me or your dad we would have tied her down to stop her." He looks at my beer and grunts, "Drink up. I'll show you the shop and we'll talk about you paying me back. I'd straight up give you money, but the wife would murder me if Alice didn't skin me first. Something going on with you two? She looked ready to kill you all night."

"Not that I know of." Not anymore. He steers me behind the house to the large barn that serves as his workshop.

I've looked at the workshop but have never been inside; it was off-limits growing up. The walls are lined with tools, vises, lathes, saws, and things I can't begin to know the purpose of. At the end of the barn are two drafting tables. Frank leans against one. In the heart of the room a boat's skeleton waits for its skin.

"Sloop?" I ask, shrugging at the frame.

"Too small for a sloop. A dory, or will be." He makes a note on a drawing. "You'll learn. You can work the money off with me, do some of the first part of the finishing, the first sealing coats, nothing detailed. If you do get a job you can work weekends."

Alice must have told him I was let go. I told her nothing about the house or the money—I broke more rules than she did—but still, it was my failing to disclose.

Behind the drafting table, just past his head, is the most extraordinary thing: a huge dark purple curtain that hangs the full length of the wall. By all appearances it's velvet. Something about it reminds me of sketches from the book. Curtains drawn over a cage, drapes on the inside of a wagon. "Where'd you get that?"

"What?"

"That's a theatrical curtain." At the bottom there's a chain to weigh it down and seal out light. "Seems out of place in a workshop." I look around the barn and see a series of small portraits in oval frames hanging in the open wall spaces. Relatives? There's something vaguely Slavic about them, the moustaches on the men, the curved shape of a young woman's brow.

"It keeps the glare off the drawings in the afternoon and shuts out drafts in the winter. Was in a box of stuff that belonged to my dad. The pictures were in there too."

"Family heirlooms, then."

He shrugs. "Guess so."

"Do you know anything about them?"

"Nope. I never really went in for heirloom stuff. Things are things, you know? I just like them. They make the place look a little nicer, keep it warm."

There's a knock on the barn door, Leah with more beer. I refuse but a bottle winds up in my hand. Leah leans in to kiss her husband's cheek and brush sawdust from his shoulder, gestures made soft by habit. Out one of the windows I can see the Sound all the way to the harbor. The lights from the ferry amble toward Middle Ground Light and eventually Connecticut. People spend their entire lives moving back and forth over the same water, moving but staying.

When my bottle thumps on the drafting table it startles the both of us. A wide sweat mark swipes across the drawing, blurring the ink. I look back up at the curtains. They couldn't be the same ones, of course. But they're striking, individual, but very familiar. My eyes come to rest on the oval-shaped painting of a bearded man. His gaze is unsettling. I should check in the book for him, just in case. If only to prove that I'm imagining things.

"The paintings, are they relatives?"

"Might be. Don't really know. Like I said, they were in a box with the curtains and some of my dad's things. They were probably my grandfather's. I think I remember seeing them at his place when I was a kid. He kind of liked to accumulate things."

The bearded man stares back at me, demanding I look at him, look for him. I'm sure I've seen that face staring out at me from a page. "Frank, I'm sorry. I need to go."

Enola and Doyle are lying on their backs in the sea grass by the bluff, looking at the stars. Enola has one hand behind her head, and the other tucked away in her pocket. The cards again. They don't notice when I walk past.

The book is on my desk, closed as I'd left it. I start at the beginning, methodically searching for sketches, here a drawing of a tiny horse, one of what looks to be a llama, and there, the frame of a skeleton—the very beginning of a tarot card. A note about shoes and boots, costuming, a wig—and there they are, the curtains—draped over what looks like an animal cage with a young boy sitting inside. Not ten pages after, sketches of a wagon interior, hung with small oval paintings. And after, yes, there is the painting of the bearded man—Peabody's rendition. I've seen the actual thing; it's more eastern, the book's sketch vaguely anglicized. An interpretation.

Churchwarry picks up and asks me to wait while he gets rid of someone on the other line. "Dante fanatic. Insufferable man. Thinks he's my only customer," he says. "Did you get *Binding Charms*?"

"Yes," I say, and thank him. "That isn't why I called, though. I just had the oddest experience. My next-door neighbor, who I've known my entire life, has things I've seen sketches of in the book."

"You sound terrible."

"I'm a little shaken, I just . . . " The words don't come.

"What things?" Churchwarry asks. I imagine him pacing the shop. I can hear him prop the door open so that his wife can call down if she needs him. He walks toward what I imagine is the back of the shop, where the shelves are fuller, heavy like the reference shelves at Grainger, and muffle the sound of our conversation.

"Theatrical curtains, portraits." I hear his chair pull back. Books being moved.

"One curtain looks very much like another, no?"

"They're the same curtains, Martin, I know it. And the portraits—faces don't change."

He pauses for a moment. "Did he say how he got them?"

"He said they were his father's, possibly his grandfather's. Who did you say you got the book from? Whose estate?"

"John Vermillion, if I remember correctly. I wouldn't put much stock in the name, though. As I recall from the rest of the auction, he was a consummate hoarder. There was no rhyme or reason to the lots. Quality books were butted up against ruined paperbacks. Pulp. A total nightmare. We were all bidding on pure speculation."

"I just—I found out that my mother gave away her things, like she meant to kill herself. I saw the curtains and the paintings he had—my neighbor. My mother, she gave things to him, to the neighbor, to Frank." It could be so simple. Suicide might run through my family with a genetic marker as clear as blue eyes. Simple and horrifying. Enola, on the lawn with her Electric Boy, carrying in her a thing I am powerless to stop.

"I'm sorry," he says quietly, and there is kindness in it. "I feel like I may have stirred a pot I shouldn't have."

My mouth fills with a coppery taste where I've bitten into my cheek, the sort of little wound that will swell for days. "It's too much. To know he had her things, and then to see those paintings and curtains from the book. They're the exact portraits. I need—" It takes a few tries before the right words surface. "I need to know *who* he is. He's someone."

"We're all someone," Churchwarry says. He means to calm me, but instead I feel a cold black fear.

"You should know that we die—*they* die—on July 24th. My mother, my grandmother, Cecile Duvel, Bess Visser. All of them, every single woman, drowned. Six days."

"Six days?"

"My sister, Martin. My sister."

A small gasp.

"Exactly."

"Is there anything I can do?" There is something different about his voice now. If I could put a name to it I'd say it has the ring of tenderness.

"You like research?" He makes no complaint when I ask him to find out everything he can about my neighbor's family. "Franklin McAvoy, his father, grandfather. I need to know why he's got these things." I give him names to look for—Peabody, Koenig, Ryzhkova or Ryzhkov (damned patronymics). There's a larger picture at work, something that ties Frank to the book, to my mother, to whatever it is that's killing us.

The next hours are spent under yellow lamplight. The portrait in particular bothers me. From the sketches it looks as though it hung inside Madame Ryzhkova's wagon. A small column of figures nearby details expenditures—silks, herbs, salt. A fortune-teller's tools. I have a sneaking suspicion that if Churchwarry starts tracing Frank's family and I start with Ryzhkova, our research will intersect. I turn on the computer and do a cursory search for Ryzhkova. The name pings back thousands of results. Shit. Of course it would be the *Smith* of Russian names. Too much information is just as bad as none at all. Dates should trim things down, 1700s, late. Region as well. Most coming into the colonies would likely have come in through New York City or Massachusetts, Boston particularly. Philadelphia might be a stretch. Though she might hate me at the moment, Alice is still quietly helping me. I log into the National Archives, punch her university ID, and begin searching for ship passenger manifests.

When I collapse under the screen's glow, I dream of walking along the bottom of the Great South Bay, or maybe it's Jessop's Neck, where the water is bathtub warm and the beach is lined with yellow jingle shells. The sand blooms with long leaves of seaweed that becomes hair, red and thick like Alice's. A horseshoe crab crawls on my foot, then to my leg, clinging. It's followed by more until I cannot see the water through the deluge of crabs. I wake, gasping.

Enola turned my computer off. In the quiet I hear her shuffling cards.

14

Their language was devised in secret, as it depended on stealing Ryzhkova's cards. Lessons took place with little warning after evening performances in smaller towns, during lulls that came with travel, and in early mornings or late into night while the menagerie slumbered, save for a restless few. After traveling days Ryzhkova slept heavily. The bumps and kicks of the roads left her so depleted that on occasion Amos placed a hand under her nose to assure himself that she still breathed. If the air was chilled, he pulled an extra shawl around her. This small looking-after dulled the guilt that came each time he stole the cards.

Amos would signal a lesson by leaving a card for Evangeline to find in her bedclothes, nestled in the tub staves, or buried among her hair combs. She would hide it in her sleeve, wearing it by her skin until she found him waiting for her behind the pig wagon, which was set away from camp. Amos's affinity for animals meant his spending time there aroused no suspicion. From there he took her into the trees, or down to the rivers the menagerie followed, to a branch that formed a perfect seat, or a group of rocks that would shelter them from prying eyes. When they met she wore a sackcloth dress that drew no attention. Amos took no such measures; he remembered how to walk silently and hide with stillness.

Through each bower, knoll, and bended branch, Evangeline grew to know him; things he'd loved while running free, secrets he'd learned—how green moss made a soft cushion, the chatter of river toads at tossed pebbles—each meeting was gilded with knowledge. Through cards and grass blade whistles, she began to love the silent man.

Lessons started in the same manner as readings, by identifying the participants. Evangeline was represented by the Queen of Swords, for her dark hair and fair skin. She understood the card for the woman's coloring alone and did not know its kinship with sadness and loss. He thought it best not to tell her, and yet he felt a loss weeping from her, one he longed to ease. For himself, he chose the Fool, for its friendly appearance, and because the little dog made Evangeline smile. Together, Queen and Fool named each member of the menagerie.

The Hermit was Peabody, an easy choice, as the card was an aged man with a lantern and flowing white beard. To the untrained eye the card meant a solitary figure or a wizened man, but Amos knew the Hermit was a guide, a protector, one who shares in experience— all things he thought about the man who had become his proxy father. They chose the Two of Pentacles for Melina—a man juggling two golden stars. For Susanna, the contortionist, Evangeline chose the Hanged Man, an upside-down figure dangling by his foot, his free leg bent at the knee. Amos could not tell her that the Hanged Man spoke of the connection between the material and the divine, or that it appeared to those who grieved or questioned faith. Perhaps it was fitting; Susanna was quiet—what did he know of her thoughts? For Benno he chose the Four of Cups. The cross-legged dark-haired man reminded him of his friend and his generosity, a man with drink enough to share with many.

Choosing the card for Ryzhkova was difficult. Evangeline spread the trumps across a dark shale flat, searching for an old woman. Something about Madame Ryzhkova brought her grandmother to mind and set her skin crawling. Though they were safe in a hollow near a riverbank, Evangeline still watched the trees, wondering what would befall Amos should they be discovered. She didn't fear for herself; the refrain that had followed her since Krommeskill wrapped around her as well as any blanket: *I am a killer.* She touched the card named the Magician. It was fitting—Ryzhkova practiced what some thought witchcraft.

Amos shook his head in dissent. Ryzhkova had called the Magician the breath of God. His teacher was many things, but the will of the divine wasn't one of them.

Evangeline studied the pinch around his mouth and the urgency in his hands. Unused to anything but his approval, she said, "Very well, teach me who she is."

His fingers paced, tips sliding across paper as they'd done thousands of times, waiting for the cards to sing to him, each a bird bearing messages, telling him what they were and who they were meant to be. When his longest finger glanced the right card he snatched it from the shale: the High Priestess.

"Don't be silly. That's a young woman, and with a cross as well! Madame Ryzhkova would never wear one. You'd do just as well to choose the Devil." She frowned and turned thoughtful. "Your teacher does not like me."

He tried to laugh—an ugly scraping—and blanched at the sound.

Evangeline smiled and touched her palm to his cheek. "Your voice is not so terrible. Only a little broken. I don't mind."

Amos blushed and returned his focus to the High Priestess. He removed two cards from the deck and set them by Evangeline's toes—the World, with its garland of leaves and sky blue as cornflowers, and above it he placed the Sun's benevolent face. He held the High Priestess between his fingers once more, then set it atop the other two, covering them with her stately robes.

"Above Heaven and Earth, is she?"

Though it was not the precise meaning he'd intended, it was close enough to the truth. He thought of Ryzhkova's wry laughter, the way she teased him, how she'd shown him to wrap his hair, and her poor, bent hands. Those were the hands that had touched his most often. Peabody cared for him, slapped his back, and schooled him in being both Wild Boy and man, but Ryzhkova had taught him most how to be human, how to care.

Ryzhkova was above Heaven and Earth. She had been his mother.

"This is how you see her?"

He smiled and nodded. He knew Evangeline feared her, cringing fear that makes bodies tight. It was because she did not know the countless hours he'd spent with Ryzhkova, her patience and the care she'd taken to ensure that he would be more than a Wild Boy. She didn't know it was Ryzhkova who'd given him his name. He took the card into his palm and touched it to his heart.

Evangeline placed her hand over his.

He grew bolder in his thievery.

As they traveled toward Burlington, driving rain forced their lessons indoors. Amos snuck Evangeline inside the wagon with Sugar Nip and the llama. With rain preventing travel and the troupe having taken to their rooms, they would be safe; Ryzhkova would assume he remained with Peabody, while Peabody would assume he stayed with Ryzhkova. Evangeline left the oilskin tight over her tub, inviting no guests or inquiry. Together they curled up in the straw that lined the wagon and closed their eyes, listening to the mix of breath and storm.

A hand knocked on Madame Ryzhkova's wagon. She was unaccustomed to speaking with the man who called; in truth she found him disturbing: he smiled through a mask.

"Is Amos here? I had hoped we'd pass the evening playing dice," he said. "He was not with Peabody, and so." Benno cocked his head and Ryzhkova sensed his movements, cultivated ease. "He is not with you?"

"Have you seen the girl?" she asked.

"Melina? With Susanna, mending dresses."

He knew exactly who she asked after. "The Mermaid," she said and squinted at the tumbler. He shifted uncomfortably on his feet.

"Ah," Benno said. She watched his features slide, detecting a hint of worry just before his measured words. "No matter. I shall find Nat, then. Unless you would like a game, Madame?"

"I will tell Amos you were here," she grunted. "Leave me."

Ryzhkova knew her cards were missing before opening the box. She felt the lingering energy of Amos's fingers on the lid, the heat that stayed in his wake. She looked at the space where the cards should have been and trembled, thinking of the Tower and a long-ago reading. Betrayal and a woman. She had not expected herself to be the betrayed. Her legs buckled and she sat heavily on the floor. "Yelena," she whispered, "you are a fool."

Rusalki did not leave their home waters. It was knowledge she had come by through sorrow. The girl was supposed to have vanished once Peabody steered the menagerie to follow a different river, yet somehow this one remained, stronger, wilier than others.

As a child, long before she dreamt up Madame Ryzhkova, when she had been just Yelena and thought only of weaving, she had watched through a window as a woman lured her father into their stream. Stepan, her father, had been burly and strong from working the fields, with a beard thick and black like bearskin but soft as down. She remembered tangling her fingers in it. Her three brothers were nearly grown and gone by the time she'd been born—off to fight, farm, and sail. She'd had her father to herself and she'd adored him. Yelena loved how he'd picked her up and swung her around as though she were nothing more than a grain sack. He'd called her *little dove* and told her that he loved her best, better than her brothers. "You are my crown," he'd said.

Then the woman came—the pale face in their stream.

Across a month she watched her father weaken and their fields go fallow, burning in the sun. Instead of working, Stepan had spent his days at the stream. Her mother threatened to poison the water and Stepan threatened to tie her to the stove. When Yelena asked to ride with him in the cart while he worked, he would not answer. When she stuffed his pockets with bread, he returned with it un-eaten.

Her mother began to pray.

Yelena watched him die. Through slender alder trees she'd seen the woman's luminous skin and laughing eyes, had seen her father reach toward the woman to embrace her. His hand, once so warm and strong, was thin and wasted. His dark bearded face disappeared into the woman's soot black hair. Yelena had called to him but her voice did not carry. She shook her mother, but her mother stayed rooted, praying. By the time Yelena reached the banks, her father had long since been dragged beneath the water.

Once Stepan was drowned, her mother moved quick and sharp as a switch, piling their possessions into a wagon and moving them to a distant village on the edge of a still black lake. Yelena had cried, not wanting to leave her father, knowing that he was in the stream. Her mother slapped the backs of Yelena's hands. "If we stay, waiting for your father, she will take away any man we love. Would you have her drown your brothers?" her mother had asked. Yelena considered; what was a lost brother or two if it brought her father back? "When she kills them their deaths will be on your head," her mother warned. Then Yelena understood. No river would be safe again, but other waters would not hold her father's face. When her mother died she left her homeland, crossed countries and an ocean to leave the woman in the river and her father behind. In this safe land she bore her daughter and baptized her quickly to anchor her soul. Now, a lifetime later, a woman from a new water was tempting the boy who had become her son.

She waited for the Rusalka by the tub where the woman slept by night and drowned herself by day. Madame Ryzhkova saw Evangeline, flushed and breathless, and feared that she'd already stolen life and youth from Amos.

Evangeline froze at the sight of Madame Ryzhkova. The woman stood in the downpour, her clothing soaked, her face consumed by fury. They had been discovered.

"Madame, you must return to your wagon. You'll catch your death." She moved to put her arms around Ryzhkova's shoulders.

"Do not touch me. You touch my Amos, you charm him and make him lie to me. I have seen what you do, your kind. You are a murderer, a soul thief—*Rusalka*." Ryzhkova fought the urge to shout, to scream, but years of reading fates taught her that words were most powerful when spoken gravely. "You will go. You will leave this place and my boy. You will take no more from me."

"Madame, I think you do not know your boy so well." Evangeline walked past Ryzhkova and began untying the tub's canvas.

She glanced back at the old woman. "Nor me." If her stomach heaved she forced it down. If her hands quaked, she squeezed them. "Go back to your bed, Madame. It would be a shame if you took ill. Amos would be heartbroken. I was when my grandmother died."

Evangeline did not allow her eyes to water until she'd pulled the canvas down, and then only when she held herself, knees to chest, to muffle the sound. Whether it was fear or anger, she could not say.

Unhindered by her wet skirts, Ryzhkova flew across the muddy ground to Peabody's wagon. When she threw open the door Peabody was bent over his ledger, carefully sketching the detail of a tentlike structure. The expanse of his stomach spilled over the small desk and obscured the writing at the bottom of the page. Startled by the unexpected arrival, his hand jumped, causing his plumed quill to scratch an ugly line through his sketch.

"Blast."

"The girl must go." Ryzhkova's voice cracked.

"What is this?" Peabody turned the three-legged stool he called his ciphering chair. He regarded Madame Ryzhkova with a raised eyebrow.

She shook with violence. "Mermaid, you call her. *Evangeline*. She is warping my boy, my Amos. She makes him lie to me." She smacked her palm firmly on Peabody's desk, further smudging the sketch.

"Evangeline?" Peabody twisted the end of his beard to a thoughtful point, then wound it around his thumb. "I agree she has our Amos in a knot. Love, Madame, is nothing to worry oneself with overmuch. With time it will right itself." He murmured something about the course of young love and returned to his ruined page. "Good for the profits, Madame. I see no harm at all. If you don't mind, I've correspondence I wish to read."

Ryzhkova's eyes narrowed in such a way that Peabody's levity died. "Stupid, stupid man. You love the boy, yes? You think of Amos like your son, like your Zachary?" Her voice rose. "She will kill him. Then what will you have? Money? No. You will have a dead son. And the girl? She will vanish into the river. No Amos, no mermaid—nothing."

"Madame."

"We must go away from the rivers. Away from water. You will turn her out and burn her things." Her hands bunched in her skirts.

"Here now," Peabody said, rising from his seat. "The girl's been a draw since the day she appeared. If she makes Amos happy I am of the inclination to keep her."

Ryzhkova charged forward, placing a knobbed finger on Peabody's chest, marking each word with a stab. "He, who I have shown my secrets, he who I have loved like *my* son. He has lied to me. She will drink him, drown him. It has already begun."

Peabody removed her finger from his waistcoat, pausing to right the pile. He attempted reason. "You might establish rules with him, perhaps. Give the boy latitude, a bit of forgiveness, Madame. Do remember that Amos was not always civilized. As for Evangeline," he continued, "you might do well to try and know her. The girl has been nothing but amicable. Amos is not alone; I believe most of our men are half in love with her."

"Tongue speaks, but head does not know," Ryzhkova sneered. "You brought her to us, you must send her away. Or I will leave. I will go to my Katya." Her smile was predatory. "I will take the boy with me. Without me, he has no work. No words. Without me, he is nothing. He will come."

The ire clouding Madame Ryzhkova's vision prevented her from seeing a hard look pass over Peabody's face. "My dear Madame," he said, "I believe you underestimate my concern for Amos. I am aware of both his strengths and his shortcomings. Though you named him, that does not give you claim. It was me whom he came to, I who first clothed him, from *my* son's possessions." He leaned close to Ryzhkova, using his size, until her back was pressed to the wagon's wall. "Be certain that the lad is valued most highly and I, as ever, intend to look after his interests, romantic or otherwise—they are aligned with my own. While it would be unpleasant to continue without your esteemed services, I have discovered over the years that I am an intrepid soul and would assuredly make do." He turned to take up his quill once more. "Madame, I find that I am no longer desirous of your presence."

Ryzhkova backed away, taking the awkward step down from the cart. As she walked to her wagon to wait for Amos, she remembered a piece of something she'd heard as a child, when she'd still been Yelena. To Peabody, the words she muttered sounded like a madwoman's gibberish; they were in fact the beginnings of a prayer, the prayer for deliverance her mother had whispered, rocking on her knees, while Stepan drowned.

15

W ake up."

I open my eyes to a pile of papers, some of which are stuck to my cheek, and Enola staring down at me.

I fell asleep at my desk, having spent the last day teaching myself about curses and searching for Ryzhkova. The National Archives were lacking in ship manifests pre-1800, but allowed me to track bibliographies that led to the New York Public Library's archives and manifests from 1600 on. Access is by appointment only. I put in a begging call, asking for professional courtesy, though I'm no longer in the profession. I mentioned that I'm from Grainger, which is still almost true, and that we'd happily lend some of the whaling archive in trade. I'm a liar now; it doesn't bother me as much as it might because five hours later

I had the name *Yelena Ryzhkova*. A name that stuck out as a woman traveling alone in the mid-1700s, and because that name was Russian on a ship full of Englishmen. Going on that name I was able to find a daughter, Katerina Ryzhkova. From there things became difficult to track. Understandable; a revolution might have triggered an immigrant's need to blend in and disappear. Genealogy sites have a way of making the eyes bleed, and so the rest of the day was spent on curses, hexes, and jinxed objects—printing articles, reading. Churchwarry's title, *Binding Charms and Defixione,* is detailed and beautiful, and I've half a mind to keep it. I won't, not when he's been so kind. I spent the evening on curse tablets—words etched into stone and dedicated to a god to pray for an enemy's demise. Interesting, but not immediately relevant, nothing to do with drowning or felling an entire matriarchal line. I moved to cursed jewels: the Hope Diamond, the Koh-I-Noor Diamond, the Delhi Purple Sapphire, things revolving around theft, homicide, and power. But there's nothing in the book about jewels or theft, no suggestion of foul play in anything about the drowned. Most modern curses seem to be centered on holy objects, murder, or robbery, none of which seem to be a factor in the drownings. In the heavy night hours I delved deep into the 130s, the occult, and jinxed places. Lake Ronkonkoma—all my life living on this island and I never knew that the lake in the middle of it is cursed.

"Simon." Enola stretches and pops her knuckles.

"So, Lake Ronkonkoma is haunted by the ghost of a Native American princess who drowns white guys." My voice is thick with morning.

She blinks. "What the fuck are you reading?"

"I honestly don't know." My head is exploding and my eyes feel like I spent hours in the wind. If it's possible to have a reading hangover, I have one. The desk clock reads 7:30; it's early for Enola. I spent years dragging her out of bed for school, wrestling her as she kicked and growled. It's possible she never went to sleep. "Why are you up?"

"There are horseshoe crabs all over the beach. Like crazy." She smacks both hands hard onto my shoulders, pushing me into the desk and tipping over books—Alice's books, the ones I should take back. I called her yesterday but she said she couldn't talk. She can't stay mad at me forever. Enola keeps jumping, and the floor squeaks with each bounce. "I went down to the water early. I thought I'd catch the tide when it was up," she says. "They're everywhere, just like before."

"You went down by yourself?"

"So? Doyle was beat and you were asleep."

It shouldn't worry me, but there's a new and persistent little fear. Not so little really. "Don't go down there alone."

"Stop parenting me. That doesn't work well for us." She rubs her feet against each other, sprinkling sand on the floor. She's right. Much as I tried to look after her, it did end with her leaving. "Did you call Alice? Apologies are a good thing."

I ignore her. "So, there're lots of crabs?"

"A ton. It's creepy. I thought they were dying out, but I guess not." There's the shuffling sound again—she's playing with the cards. She looks at me and it hurts. I can feel her searching for the old me, from before she left, before Dad died. He's in here somewhere.

"I remember you with horseshoes all over you," she says.

"Me too," I say, because it's what you say. It was during the last days of Dad, the summer before he died. I'd seen the horseshoe crabs first, when I was looking down from the cliff, and needed to show her. I waited for her in her room—even then she'd snuck out, needing to get away from him, from me too, I suppose—she'd been out stealing change from pay phones and the quarters jingled in her pockets.

It was too late at night to go by Dad's room, so I went through the window, folding up to squeeze over the sill, inching forward until my feet dropped to the ground. Enola followed. There'd been a tree then, a pine that had fallen in the winter and lay dead on the lawn. Ever the better criminal, she slid the screen closed to cover our escape.

We walked to the cliff, cutting through the yard's tall brush, my hand pulling hers, no space between. I was barefoot. I remember stiff stalks of beach grass poking my feet. Looking into the yielding blackness, we decided against taking the stairs. I offered to piggyback her. She was smaller then and I could easily lift her, barely had to hold her. I walked down the bluff and she shifted each time I sank into the sand.

At the shore we let the waves bury our feet. After a few minutes something began brushing against our legs. Enola bent down to feel, discovering what I already knew: a cold shell, smooth and hard with ridges on the edge, and two bumps just there. Horseshoe crabs. I told her to look up, out over the waterline. Across the beach it looked like hundreds of glossy rocks had lined up by the shore. Farther out, dark shapes moved beneath the water, rising and falling. Before then I'd only seen a handful alive or come across the dead on the beach, carapaces hollow like cicada skins. There must have been hundreds of crabs, thousands, knocking into one another, their tails smacking and working like blind men's canes.

Enola smiles and it wrinkles up her nose. I've missed that. "You told me they were old. Primordial. I remember wondering if they knew that everything around them had changed," she says.

"They must." From purposeless instincts, from the pieces of brick and asphalt they scurry around. They know because the giant sea monsters are gone. Only the crabs remain.

"I wanted to get Dad," she says.

"It would have just made him sadder." It wasn't long before the end for him, when he spent all his time at the kitchen table, staring at an empty seat, imagining the woman who once sat there.

"I know," Enola says. She's back on the couch, picking at the arm. "I stayed on the sand, but not you; you walked out, horseshoe crabs all around your feet, laughing like an idiot."

"You didn't come with me?"

Her eyebrows lift. "I thought you remembered everything. I stayed on the beach. Those things scared the crap out of me. But you, you walked right into the water with the crabs. They crawled all up your legs, climbing you like a tree. I don't think you thought for a second that you could get hurt, that they could just swallow you up." Just now she seems younger, like her fourteen-year-old self. "The whole time you were laughing I was on the beach thinking, fuck, if they pull him under, what am I gonna do?"

Maybe I do remember her on the beach, shouting, begging me to come back in. But it felt good to be in the water with living things all around me, crabs crawling over my feet, tiny pincers scratching and tickling, the touch of ancient things. But nothing climbed me, no. Nothing like that.

"You were half covered in horseshoe crabs, like you weren't all you anymore." The soft flicking sound of cards is alive in her skirt pocket. I can almost see her running her fingers around the edges. "It looked like they were coming to pull you away. Like Mom was coming to get you." A bridge, a fall, she tamps the deck in her palm. A card emerges—a man and a woman, nude?—and is quickly tucked away. The Lovers?

"They were mating. It happens every year."

"I know that now, asshole," she says. "I was just saying that I was worried about you. Fucking horseshoe crab whisperer."

Then Dad died and there were no more crabs or beach nights, just us alone, and after that—much later—Enola left. As soon as she could.

"Why did you leave?" I don't expect myself to ask it, am startled that I do. But it hurt. It had been just us for years; even before Dad died it had been the two of us.

"This house is a mausoleum," she says. She looks out the window, over to Frank's driveway. "A memorial to people who didn't love me enough to bother staying alive." She glances at me. "I know, I know. You were here and you still are. If anyone gets a medal for staying, it's you. Mom didn't bother; she offed herself before she knew me. What Dad did was almost worse. Did he spend a single second on us after she was gone? No. He didn't do anything but pretend to be alive until he wasn't."

"I understand being angry."

"You don't know what you looked like. I knew every table you waited, dish you washed, the hours at the library, at school, and that you did it for me."

"We both had to eat and live, it wasn't just for you." I remember being tired, yes. Long days, knowing that there was no choice but to do, to keep on doing. "Was it so bad?"

"It would have been easier without me," she says. "Don't bother saying it wouldn't. You could have sold the house and gone wherever you wanted, except that I was here. If I'd stayed you would have wanted me to go to school."

"Probably." She's smart. She should have gone.

"And you would have kept working like that. I couldn't watch you anymore, knowing I was doing it to you," she says. Her fingernails are scratching the couch fabric, digging and picking. "It was hard, Simon. Maybe you don't want to think about it, but it was. I was a burden and it isn't easy being deadweight. I really thought you'd leave after I did. I wanted you to."

It's too hard to say that I kept the house not just for Mom and Dad, but for her, in case she came back. I know now, fiercely, that I wanted her to come home. Where would she come back to if not this house? "If you hate the house so much, why do you care if I fix it?"

"You like it," she says. "I'm not entirely selfish, I promise."

Then there's guilt, and not a little of it either, because I have thought her selfish. Over dinner with Alice. I make coffee while ghosts of us walk the kitchen. My younger self, leaning on the counter, tired like a dead man; Enola, watchful and quiet, curled up in a chair, trying to disappear. I fill two mugs. Enola: cream, three sugars. Mine: black. I drink it while it's still hot enough to scald.

"Why do you think Dad left this place such a wreck?" she asks.

"Grief, I guess."

"The great excuse."

We stare at our coffee, much the way he did. "He told me things sometimes, when he could talk about her." It was a year before he could say her name, longer before he could talk to me without his eyes looking painful and red. "He said that when he first saw her, she was wearing a blue sequined fish tail and swimming in a tank. She put her hand up to the glass, smiled at him, and he knew that he would marry her."

It had been more than that. I remember the words and his sour coffee breath. *I saw her in the water and I believed her. I knew it was true, even if she didn't really have a tail, even though there's no such thing, she was a mermaid. My whole life before that moment I'd been in a locked room, and then all the doors opened.* And Frank had stood there, witnessing that moment of falling in love. Dad went back to the show every night for a week. "She did different things. The mermaid act, card reading. He saw her being sawed in half by a man so old he could barely lift the saw. She was in a box, hands out the sides, feet out the bottom, helping the guy move the blade."

Enola shrugs. "Boxes get banged up on the road, the saws bend, they get stuck. You know."

"I guess the act was going really wrong, but there was Mom, dismembering herself and smiling."

He talked to me before the sun was up, about the way her hair looked that night. The way she blushed. *Like a ripe peach.* How he'd ditched Frank with some friends from the marina and waited around for hours until the show shut down for the night. He'd lingered outside the magician's tent until he saw her in shorts and tennis shoes, her hair in a ponytail. *Like a normal girl.*

"He told her he'd come by every night, just for her, and that if she didn't go for a walk with him he'd spend the rest of his life wondering if she'd been real."

"Doesn't sound like Dad at all."

No, not the Dad Enola knew, but the one before, the memory who told stories about fish so big they'd swallow a little boy in a single gulp. Mom went walking with him. He took her down to the harbor and under the docks. I've done it myself when the tide is out and the air is sweet with the smell of ocean and the sound of boats pulling at their moorings. It's a rite of passage for Napawset boys to take girls down there, to lean against a piling and wrap their arms around them. That was the sort of thing my mother loved—rituals in place for years that never changed. She'd been used to living in trailers, RVs, hotel rooms. He hoped that the lure of a home would be strong.

"He promised Mom the house," I tell her.

"Well, he could have bothered to take care of it."

I shrug and drain the last of my coffee. "Maybe with her gone there was no reason to."

She smirks. She doesn't have to say it: we should have been reason enough. She stretches and shakes her head. "You fucked things up with Alice."

"I know."

She swirls the coffee around in her mug. "She'll forgive you, though. She just needs time."

"You think?" During dinner she'd seemed unbending, disgusted. It's hard to recover from disgust.

A shrugged shoulder. "Sure. If you want her to. But you can't take money from Frank."

"I don't really have a choice."

"You do, you just don't like making choices. It used to take you forty minutes to pick out a shirt."

"It's the house, not a shirt."

"Exactly. You could just come with me and Doyle, forget the house, and give Alice time to cool off."

"I can't do that, okay?"

"Fine. Suit yourself," she says. "Oh, I looked at your book some more."

"Tell me you didn't tear out any more pages."

Her eyes roll. "I bet you don't know what you have."

In point of fact, I don't. "I know it's old. The earliest date in it is 1774. It follows a circus—well, not exactly a circus since there wasn't really circus in America yet. It had multiple owners, I don't know how many. A lot of it is ruined."

"It's an owner's log. Thom let me see his. Circus masters, carnival guys, they all keep them. You put in everything that happens on a show, who signs on, who leaves, what they make, where you travel, dates, everything. It doesn't stay with one person; it stays with the show. Thom's book is from his father. He's got a case of books that go back to the sixties. His dad bought the show when the last owner retired to Sarasota. It helps you keep track of the important shit."

"I figured it was sort of a show history."

"It's kind of like a family Bible. Yours, though," she nudges the book. "That's weird. It's not supposed to be like a diary. Thom's isn't sketched up that way, either."

"It's old. There probably wasn't an established way of doing things."

She taps her fingers two at a time, pinkie and index then middle and ring. Dad did that too. "Maybe. Still, you shouldn't have that book. The way it's all ruined in the back it looks like it survived a flood or something. Maybe that's why it's not with the show or with the family."

"What do you mean?"

"Books like that aren't supposed to leave a show. It's all inside information, history kind of stuff. Valuable. If there was a flood or fire, though, maybe somebody left it behind." She chews her lip and I can hear the unspoken words. Its owners left in a hurry, or its owners died.

"It's with family, kind of. Mom's relatives are in it."

"It's just weird that you have it. You should send it back to that guy—I know you won't. You should also forget about the house and leave, but you won't do that, either." Her hand twitches, a quick jerking motion, half wave, half threatened slap. "Why does talking with you always end with me being pissed off? I'm gonna get Doyle. We should check in with work today. And," she adds as she stops down the hall, "you need to talk to Alice."

Doyle is on the bed in her room, cross-legged, and meditating. The tentacles on his neck ripple with each breath. Enola says his name and his eyes flutter open. "Hey, Little Bird. I heard you guys talking so I figured I'd just . . . " He pops his neck. "You guys should talk more, right? It's good when people talk. Brothers and sisters especially." He says this as though it's profound.

"Yeah. Sure," she says. "Thom's going to want us to come by. We should get going."

"Right. Gotta keep an eye on the work situation," he drawls. He says *sitchyation* and stretches, moving like a man who needs to scratch. "We should talk to Thom about your brother, yeah?"

She nods.

"I have some things lined up. I'll be fine," I say. Sanders-Beecher checking references is a good sign. And the half a job lined up with Frank might tide me over—if Alice forgives me.

"Whatever," she says.

Seeing Enola and Doyle in her room makes me realize how small it is, a child's room. She rummages under her bed, bones and sinew thrown together in jeans and a dirty paisley skirt. I've never understood women who wear skirts and pants at the same time. She stuffs her foot into her shoe, shoving it over a mangled backstay. I stare at her other naked foot. She scrunches the toes up, a habit to hide a deformity, a slight, fleshy webbing between each digit.

"When will you be back?"

"Not sure. Swing by if you feel like getting out." She looks around her room. "Hell if I know how you stand this place." Without looking at it, she points to a deep gouge in the wall. To Doyle she says, "I did that." She began digging that gouge after Dad died.

"Really?" His forehead wrinkles, scrunching the dark ink that crosses his scalp.

"I liked really picking at something hard, you know? When I was pissed off I'd dig at it with a quarter." I let her lie to him. She used to eat the chalky lumps of drywall. When I came home late I'd check on her and watch as she dug at the wall with her littlest finger and licked the dust.

Things were that bad. They must have been.

"You want us to bring you zeppole?" Enola asks as we walk back to the living room.

"Huh?"

"From the carnival. You used to like them. You should come. If it's a slow day and George is bored he might share his weed with us; the Fat Man gets good weed. You want?"

"Thanks, no."

"Suit yourself. Come by, though, okay?" Enola pulls hard at the door, bracing her foot against the wall, yanking until it pops open.

"Do you think Thom would talk to me about his book?"

Doyle slinks an arm around Enola's waist. Maybe it's the light, but she's so thin that if she turned sideways she might disappear. She isn't well.

"Stop it with the book stuff," she says. "I know you want to think it's something more, but maybe it's just that we're sad. Maybe Mom was unbearably sad. It doesn't have to be more than that. Being that sad is enough."

And then she walks away. Doyle looks over his shoulder at me as they head to his car. For a moment I think he'll say something, but he rests his hand on her hip and walks with her. As they're pulling away he leans from the window and shouts, "Dude, just come."

Two steps from my desk a crack rends the air; my left ankle rolls and my knee buckles. *Shit. Shit. Shit.* I'm shouting, falling. The floor gives way and the lower half of my leg is swallowed by breaking boards, wrenched and wrong. I crash onto my back, skull cracking against the floor. The quickest flash of memory—Mom, pressing her lips to a bump on my head after I smacked it against the corner of the coffee table.

I'm close enough to the couch to press my shoulders into it and leverage my weight. Shimmying the leg from the hole adds splinters to the pain. I shout to Enola, Doyle, but they're already gone. My calf is chewed up and my ankle is bloodied and twisted. A dust cloud makes the air dirty. Papers fall from my desk, floating like leaves.

I could just lie here, couldn't I? Just for a little while. I look down at the hole. It's a decent size, a fair amount of damage, I thought it would be foot-shaped but it's no specific shape. The disturbing part is that there's a noise, lapping waves from the void below the floor. I stare into the hole. Is that sand? It could be sand. There shouldn't be sand down there. I put my belly to the floor and peer down through the hole. That can't be sand. I stick my head into the blackness. Only it's not entirely black. Light is leaking in.

With Enola and Doyle gone I call Alice, hoping pain will breed sympathy.

"Please don't hang up."

"Tell me why I shouldn't," she says.

"Because my floor just broke, maybe my ankle, too. I'm stuck by the couch and I'm sorry."

I hear her closing a desk drawer and remember that she color codes her pens. "You made it to the phone just fine."

"It was on the floor."

"Fine," she says. And I learn the meaning of a long-suffering sigh.

If I was hoping for softness, the Alice who opens the door lacks it. She helps lift me onto the couch, arms under my shoulders, with the efficiency of an ER nurse.

"I'm sorry," I say.

"Yes, you are." Before she leaves she slings a bag over one shoulder. "I'll take those books now."

The Tenets of the Oracle. "You said it would look bad if you brought them back. I promise I'll do it. Just give me a day."

She chews on her bottom lip and though she's angry it's lovely, drawing attention to a dark freckle in the valley between lip and chin. "What's going on, Simon? I feel like you're not here anymore."

I tell her that it's Enola.

She sighs. "It always is."

"She likes you," I say. "She thinks you're good for me."

She leans against the door and though she's here, she's somewhere else, too. "It'd be nice if you were good for me," she says.

"I do want to leave here, eventually," I say. "I don't want to take the money."

"Good," she says absently. "Keep that elevated." And then she's out the door. I push up on my hands to watch her go. She's at her car when she calls, "I'll cool off. Eventually."

I wonder, just maybe, if she and Enola talk.

If Enola is right and there isn't a curse, if we are just a sad family, the sort that's chemically unable to stay alive, if we drown ourselves for that reason, then my sister just told me there's nothing I can do for her. That is not a possibility.

Near the desk is a color printout of a flyer, an excerpt from *H. W. Calvin's Guide to Entertainments for the Discerning Gentleman*—a guide to clubs, speakeasies, and brothels, a piece of propaganda from the burlesque days of Celine Duvel, before she became the Mermaid Girl of Cirque Marveau. A fine line sketch shows that Celine Duvel is one of us: dark hair, light skin, eyes like Enola.

Back at the book again I discover a twisted little secret. More torn pages. Enola has ripped out every single sketch of tarot cards, each one carefully scored and removed with a thumbnail. She lied to my face. Who does that to a book, defaces art like that? My sister, of course, systematically destroying things for reasons she won't say. I should have photocopied everything. I should have never left her alone with it, not after seeing her destroy that first page. I hadn't thought. Maybe we're just sad, she said, as though she is deeply sad.

Always women. Drowned women make a paper river on my desk. No mention of a single son. Lovers, bereaved husbands, aggrieved fathers abound, but a son? A brother? No, only me. I am an anomaly. While she continually shuffles cards and defaces my already damaged book. How did it become so ruined?

The phone rings. It's the man who sent me a book I shouldn't have, that he shouldn't have had, unless something terrible happened. It's not a coincidence that the women die on July 24th; there are too many names. I pick up the call.

"Simon? I hadn't heard from you. Have you had any success with *Binding Charms*? Is it helpful?"

"Yes, sort of. It's intense reading."

He hums agreement. "I know. I suspect that's why I haven't been able to sell it. It's a lovely volume, but dense is an understatement. However, it was the best thing I had on hand. I—well, I know what I said in the note but you can keep it if you like, if you find it useful."

Maybe it's the pain in my leg offering the right amount of distraction but pieces of what I read in *Binding Charms* slip together with something Enola said. "Martin, I think I've figured out something. Something very bad happened to the people who owned this book. I think there was a flood or an accident." I run a thumb across a water-ruined page. "Something bad enough that it could almost infect—is that the right word?—infect an object, or anyone who survived with a piece of it. I think this book survived something terrible, and that it's marked because of it. I think my family may be too, and that's what's killing us."

There's a quiet pause. "I've been thinking. There's a danger with books. Text often breeds a notion of infallibility. It's very easy for someone like you or me to get lost in an object, to accept certain ideas as fact without proper exploration. I think perhaps we've both done that a bit."

"I've spent twelve years of my life in reference doing nothing but properly exploring facts. I have obituaries—my mother's, my grandmother's, her grandmother's. I've gone all the way back to 1816. I have facts and reliable texts, enough that at this point for my sake—for my sister's sake—I think I've earned a little leeway to speculate."

A woman's voice is in the background. The much-spoken-of Marie. Churchwarry tells her that he'll be a minute. There's a warmth in his words, a warmth that says his house, his shop, his person, is filled with traces of her. Alice has left a tiny scrape of sand near the door, dusting from a sandal, but that is all.

"I'm sorry," Churchwarry says. "I suppose I expected a more cheerful outcome. In the past when I've gifted books to strangers it's always been a positive experience and even earned me a customer or two. I was hoping for a bit of happy providence and now I can't help thinking I've opened Pandora's box."

And I can't help but feel I've invited him into sadness, a genuinely nice man who knew nothing about drowning women and the tragedy that was growing up a Watson. "My family is a little dark," I say. "But even Pandora's box had hope."

16

Though Burlington, New Jersey, was bustling and an excellent place to restock, it was not expected to be a financial boon. "Friends," Peabody muttered while writing. "Fiscally responsible teetotalers. A difficult lot for any showman." Amos's brows raised in question. "The Quakers, my boy. Fine persons with whom to conduct business, but they do not indulge. How I wish purse strings were not so reliant upon the flow of liquor. You'll find your work with Madame Ryzhkova to be lighter here than you're accustomed. Perhaps you'll enjoy a rest. Spend a bit of time with our mermaid, yes?" In his book, next to Burlington, Peabody had written, *Witch trials here before war. Shall take care with Amos.*

Peabody's words proved accurate. For the first time in many months Amos was at loose ends. There was still work to be done, supplies to be purchased, horses to be reshod, smudge-charred cloth to be replaced, all of which Burlington could provide. Amos liked Burlington. A patchwork of buildings ran along High Street, some brick and peaked like New Castle, others wood with squared barnlike roofs. There was also a firehouse with a towering steeple almost like a church. A mix of people filled the streets; dark-skinned men walked freely here—Amos had even spied one working in a bakery. Wandering the town, he began to picture a small house, brick perhaps, with a chimney, and a bed that didn't rattle over wagon ruts, a place he might share.

He'd been helping Meixel haul feed sacks—a bit of white ribbon tucked away in his pocket for Evangeline—when Madame Ryzhkova snatched his ear and twisted it painfully. "Come," she barked. Amos's face turned hot at Meixel's laughter.

The seer pulled him into the wagon with such ferocity that he tore his pant leg on an exposed nail. As Ryzhkova berated him, he worried the frayed threads with his thumb, comparing their softness to Evangeline's hair.

The angrier Ryzhkova became, the harder it was to glean her meaning; she slipped into the other language, clunking syllables like falling rocks. He knew she railed about Evangeline. Ryzhkova waved the cards at him, disgust carving deep lines in her face. It was too much to see Evangeline and not touch her, not talk with her, but he'd known that they'd become reckless, and suspected they'd been seen trading kisses. Ryzhkova knew. Her skin grew mottled and purple, and Amos became afraid, for himself and for his teacher; bodies were not meant to work in such a way. He took her hand, brown fingers closing around the cards and her crooked knuckles.

At his touch Ryzhkova's voice dropped to a whisper. Amos felt the portraits watching, begging him to listen. When he looked in her eyes he found them tired and sad.

Amos had learned much from Evangeline, how a smile did not always mean happiness, that crying might mean sadness or joy, and that women could be much comforted by an embrace. He put his arms around Ryzhkova, resting his cheek by her breastbone in the curved space where women held their children.

She cried upon him, her words weaving an incantation. "My son." *My son, my son, my son.* She spoke of worry, how she could not bear another loss. She knew Evangeline was this thing, *Rusalka.* If he was a good boy, if he was smart as she knew him to be, he would listen. *My son, my son.* She told him his lies mattered little, but he must stay safe. She could forgive him anything except losing his life. *My son.* She'd read him in her cards, had known she'd find him, she'd given him the name meant for a son of her flesh.

When her breath came evenly, she took Amos's face in her hands. "You must leave her. My own father, one of them stole him from me. Monster. She will kill you."

When he frowned, she closed her eyes to block his denial. "You would laugh, smile. My Amos, your soul is so good she longs for it, but if you stay with her your end will be drowned in a river. She will find another as if you never were. If you do not break with her, you will die. She has killed. She will again. I see this." Her palms smoldered with the same unnamable thing that allowed her to touch the cards and see what would come to be.

"Your card," she croaked, "was the Tower. I saw it all that time ago. The girl will bring this on you. Same reading there is Devil. Not reversed, as you like him. Over and over I read cards for you. Never do they change. She, the girl, she is there in middle." She took the deck in her hands, and a card's worn edge called to her. She pressed the Queen of Swords to Amos's hand, reversed so that the dark-haired woman's eyes bored into him. A woman—Evangeline— bringing loss.

He shook his head, unbelieving. She had not seen how frightened Evangeline was that night she'd walked from the woods, or felt the desperation when she'd held on to him.

Little knots formed in Ryzhkova's brow. She pulled another card from the deck in the same blind manner. The Devil, upright, a sneer on his face. Without pause she drew a final card. The skeleton on horseback. Death.

"This is what I saw. Then the girl came. We can leave here," she said, touching his wrist. "We can go to my daughter. I will take you to her—a beautiful woman. Whole."

A fine sweat broke over him at the thought of leaving Evangeline. He wrested the cards from Ryzhkova and felt her painted relatives' condemning eyes. Even the pretty girl glared. He shuffled and let his fingertips slide until he felt a cold pricking beneath his fingernails. He pulled the card from the deck, revealing its broad bright face to his mentor. The Sun.

"Happiness, light," Ryzhkova shouted. "He speaks to me of happiness. I tell you the girl will be the end of you. Happiness, you tell me."

Amos searched again until he felt a card speak to his bones. The Hierophant—a powerful figure who ruled over alliances from a throne set between two pillars. A marriage.

"Bah," said Ryzhkova. "Do not say such a thing. Soulless cannot marry."

Amos remained intent, flying through the deck, turning card after card, painting the life he saw for himself, a life he dared imagine with a small house and Evangeline. The Wheel of Fortune, the Ten of Pentacles, the Ace of Cups, the Lovers, Two of Cups. Together they spoke of marriage, a love that spilled over so that all would be touched by it, as flows water.

The last image stabbed her, a man and woman, hands joined around a cup, pledging fidelity. She squinted and pointed her crooked finger at Amos. "You see what you want. You taint cards with your hope. You do not read future, you see wishes." Her hand, weighted by rings, bent-branch thumb pointed outward, slid the cards back into the deck. The ends of her yellowed fingernails made the cards move. Much time had passed since Amos had first witnessed Ryzhkova make the cards dance like butterflies, magic that amazed as much as frightened. Once the cards settled, Ryzhkova placed her hand against the stack and pressed until her knuckles turned white. She closed her eyes, her face wrinkling until her features became indiscernible, forced out three quick breaths, and began to murmur over the deck. Her body swayed like a candle flame.

Something had broken between them; a tie he'd not realized was tenuous.

She spread the cards across the bare crate, a wash of color against dull wood. Four remained uncannily face up. Amos fixed on the pictures that stared up at him, the Tower, Three of Swords, Death, the Devil.

"Just as before. You see? She will wear you, bleed you, as water cuts stone," she said, her voice a quiet ache. She repeated the ritual. Nine of Swords, a figure crying in anguish, blades looming over his head; Ten of Swords, a body, facedown by a river, run through with blades. The Tower. The Devil. Before she could clear the cards a third time, Amos took hold of her hands. He shook his head.

"Every time is same," she said.

He felt badly for her anxiousness, but what she asked was impossible. He held Ryzhkova's hands and thought of Evangeline's tapered fingers. He knew of no way to apologize, but would repair whatever he could. In time, he hoped the women would grow used to one another. He hoped, foolishly perhaps, but he'd always loved the Fool.

Amos shifted his weight to his knees, bones pressing hard into the wagon boards. He released Ryzhkova's hands and bent slowly forward, chest over thighs, until his forehead touched her tattered brown boots. Subservience, perhaps. Forgiveness, he hoped. He begged. He remained still, head at her feet, until she bid him rise with a firm tug at his shirt collar.

"Not this from you. You are my son, not a servant. Not a dog." She smiled and was once more the kindly woman she'd so often been with him. "Please. I forgive you, but you must leave her."

His fingers stiffened against the floor.

He had grown to a fair height in the years since joining the menagerie. At that moment he regretted his stature; he wished nothing more than to stand straight before this woman, but the low ceiling forced him to duck when he rose. He shook his head in refusal, but his stooped shoulders dampened the intended force. When he dropped down from the door and his feet touched grass, it seemed too late to stand properly.

He crept away in search of Evangeline. Like a dog, he thought. He found her preparing for the afternoon's show, floating in her tub, hair spread in the water, her dress pooling about her like a water lily. At his approach she pulled herself up on the tub's staves.

"Why are you crying?"

Ryzhkova had no energy to follow Amos. Her anger dissipated as quickly as it had risen, leaving her an empty sack. She dealt the cards again, watching for changes. Peabody was useless; he saw only money. The boy saw only beauty. She turned the cards again. With each reading came her father's face, floating in the stream, and Amos there beside him. She turned and turned until her fingers could no longer bear the touch.

She could not stay. To watch a father die had burned her, making her into the hardened woman she'd become, a woman who had parted with her daughter because she'd learned that to cling too tightly was to strangle. Yet Amos had crept beneath her skin. She had little life left in her; to watch a son die would break her.

Ryzhkova locked the wagon door and waited for night to fall, until the chattering voices that stayed up latest—Melina, Susanna, Meixel—had quieted. She unwrapped her scarf and filled it with her possessions: letters from her brothers, the paintings, coins, and a small brass pendulum on a silk thread with which to find water and tell fate. Her hair had grown long, white, and rough like a horsetail, far removed from the black softness it had been when she'd been Yelena. If she looked at her reflection, she knew she would see a stranger.

The camp was quiet. Only Benno was about, practicing short tumbling passes near the fire. Deep in concentration he gave no indication that he saw her. She moved quietly toward the dray that carried Evangeline's tub. Amos would be there; he would be unable to help it, not when he was so enchanted.

She found him, asleep, covered by a worn blanket, with his arms twined around the girl. His scarf had come loose and his hair escaped, reminding her of the untamed child she'd first known. She would kiss his forehead, run a hand down his cheek, but it would wake him. Or the girl. She had no longing to stare such a creature in the eye once more.

She whispered goodbye and called him by his name.

Ryzhkova returned to her wagon a final time to collect her belongings. She lit a tallow candle, one already burned low, and ran her hand over the box and the cards that had spoken so much. Taking them would leave nothing of her behind for him, and she wanted him to remember, to love her if he could, even just a little. She opened the lid to the box, looked at the cards that she'd inked so carefully, proud of their color. Perhaps, once the Rusalka pulled hard at his soul, perhaps he'd remember that she'd loved him and it would be enough.

She touched her hand to the paper, feeling Amos in it, and whispered a prayer for him. She said the words she would have said for her father. "Keep him safe. Give him family. Give him a home. Drive the Rusalka from him; that she will drown in sorrow deep enough to tremble through her blood. May the water take that blood and wash her and her line away. Let her not drown another man. Keep him safe."

Ryzhkova was accustomed to tarot with its layers of meaning, interpretations, and reversals, and how a picture might look one way but contain a contrary truth. Used to her silent apprentice, she had forgotten that language itself was as subtle and slippery as her cards, and that words contained hidden seeds that blossomed with a speaker's intent. A wish for safety meant nothing if the force behind it was a desire to kill. Though she spoke of love and protection, dread, grief, and anger bled through. Each word that fell from her tongue bound itself to paper with a small part of her soul, infusing the cards not with love as she thought, but with a hex burned strong and deep by fear. Buried in the heart of the deck, the Fool's eyes shut.

She closed the box.

A knot in her scarf fashioned it into a sack, easily carried on her shoulder. She blew out the candle and stepped from her wagon. She crossed the camp slowly, careful to not let the coins she carried jingle.

Benno watched as she passed his wagon. She did not understand him, laughing one minute, somber the next. But he watched over Amos as would a sibling. He was strong, like her brothers, but protective as they had not been. She nodded to him. The tumbler executed a small bow.

"You have sharp eyes, yes?" she asked.

"Always, Madame," he answered.

"Good. You will use them. Watch her. Keep him safe."

Confusion clouded Benno's face, but Ryzhkova said nothing more and continued past him. Soon she heard the soft thumping of Benno's palms against the ground as he practiced. Ryzhkova walked from the circle of the menagerie's wagons and disappeared into the darkened streets of Burlington.

17

JULY 21ST

Frank is on the front step, waiting for me to let him in. He's come to talk about the details of the money. Boat shoes, khaki shorts, a slightly frayed polo shirt, casual attire for what amounts to hours and blood. When I asked if we could postpone, he said, "We should deal with it quickly. It doesn't look like there's time to play around."

I let him in, leaning against the door; the ankle is more grotesque than yesterday, just a sprain, but painful nonetheless.

Frank's eyes go immediately to the hole. "Jesus, Simon. What happened?"

"The house attacked." There's a bump on my head where it hit the floor. If I touch it, pain spiders across my skull, and when I close my eyes there's a pulsing checkerboard. Frank says something and it sounds like he's two miles away.

"Looks like it," he says, pacing around, eyeing the hole. He crouches down, rubs a callused hand around it. "Shit." I can't remember if I've heard Frank swear before, but it sounds strange. We should talk about the money, I know, but there's something else.

"The curtains and the paintings you have in the barn, did my mother know about them? Did she ever touch them?" A trigger point for a curse may be hard to find, but if it's there, then there's a chance to break it. There is no stopping sadness. Sadness slips through the fingers.

Frank doesn't answer. He raps his knuckles against the floor, tapping and knocking in different areas. He mutters something. "What happened to this place? The outside's bad, we knew that, but the inside?" He stands with care, testing the boards. "Dry rot's all the way through."

"It's just a floor. Was my mom in the barn when she gave you her cards?"

"Just a floor? This is bad. Bad." His mouth snaps closed, bulldoggish. He walks the rest of the room, tracing the walls, tapping and listening. He stops at my desk, carefully avoiding the hole, and looks at the book, leafs through a few papers and casually slides them across the desk.

"I'd appreciate it if you don't touch that, it's very old," I say. "Delicate."

"Delicate." The word is a slap. "The floor is gone. Gone, Simon. Haven't you done anything? Why didn't you ask for help?"

"I did."

His hand starts pumping. "I need to get a few things. I'll be back," he grunts. "Don't touch anything, and for chrissakes, don't— just *don't*."

He slams the door. Plaster crumbles, leaving a dust shower in his wake. Inching back to the desk is a wobbling balancing trick, and when I get to the chair there's the distinct feeling that I'll be here for some time. My face itches. I rub it hard. Lack of sleep is taking its toll.

I spend the next hour and a half bouncing through genealogy websites. At last, a name pops up among a record of marriage ceremonies performed in a Philadelphia church. Among a column of names one sticks out, highlighted in yellow. At the sight of it I gasp. Ryzhkova. Katerina Ryzhkova was wed to a Benno Koenig. Madame Ryzhkova's daughter and the Koenig from the book. If there's one thing I've learned from my research it's that my parents were the exception, not the rule; circus performers tend to marry each other. I can hear Frank loading and unloading things from his truck, a beaten-up flatbed made of rust. He soon pulls out of the driveway, leaving me to work in silence. Their marriage leads me on a search for children, which does not disappoint. Within two years of marrying, the Koenigs had a daughter, Greta. Greta Koenig proves something of a dead end, turning up no records after 1824. In fact, the Koenigs seem to disappear. I dash off an email to Shoreham's reference librarian, asking Raina if she wouldn't mind searching for marriage or death records for Greta Koenig. She has a sweet spot for genealogy, her family being one of the oldest on the east end. On a whim I ask her to search for Greta Ryzhkova as well. Performers can be funny about names; if Ryzhkova was a bigger draw than Koenig, it's possible Greta went by her mother's name. I go back to the book. While the portraits almost certainly belonged to the fortune-teller Ryzhkova, the curtains have no purchase record; they appear only in drawings and notes on a cage for a Wild Boy. Nothing indicates how or why any of them would wind up in Frank's possession and there's no mention of what caused such substantial damage to the book. I'm missing things, in part due to Enola. All the cards. *The Tenets of the Oracle* should refresh my memory as to what she destroyed. But *The Tenets'* pictures are different, flatter somehow, and less sinister; they read like stained glass, whereas the pictures Enola ruined were a shattered mirror.

Frank returns, his truck rattling as it pulls into the gravel driveway. Before I can hobble to him, he's already set up a sawhorse on the beach grass that passes for my lawn. I get closer and hear a string of swears. He stops when he sees me. It's clearly an effort.

"I'll patch the hole so it's not gaping."

"Thanks," I say. "This may sound strange, but is any of your family Russian? The paintings in your—"

"Stop with that. Just stop," he says as he grabs a piece of plywood. "You're like a dog with a damned bone. I don't know about that stuff, we've just always had it."

I offer to help. He looks at my ankle. I limp back to the house and he stays outside. I'm glad he does. He kicks the sawhorse and swears again, then paces around his truck, picking out tools, putting them back, pausing to look at the house and judge the lean of it. I can't help but see Alice in him, the way she tips her head when looking at something high up in the stacks. If I don't take his money I might keep her, but then I'm letting the house go, all of it—Mom's laughter in the wallboards, the only place in the world I can picture my father. Where would I go? To Alice's? On to Savannah with its grand houses and grass rivers?

Frank drops to his knees, face low to the ground, eyeing the foundation. There's no need for a level—the interior of the house makes everything clear: no door hangs straight, none of the windows open and, surely as all the tables lean, the house will go over if nothing is done. It's rotting at its core.

I should have gone to the carnival with Enola. I should be watching her. Last night, she and Doyle staggered in closer to dawn than dusk. I heard him whisper in the rasp-voiced way that makes things louder. *He's fine, Little Bird. It was just a weird day. Get some sleep, okay?* They were gone before I woke. She left a note telling me to come by the carnival. Thom Rose wants to talk to me.

Frank walks into the house like it's his. He puts his hands on either side of the door, resting on Dad's palm prints, and it feels perverse. "How'd you let it get like this," he barks.

"It's been in bad shape for a while. Dad didn't do much maintenance."

He squeezes the back of his neck and tugs on the hair peeking out from under his hat. "I thought you were trying to keep the place up, but this? This is structural, the whole damned thing. You did *nothing*." He goes on about support beams and foundations, undermining. His color rises until he looks like a ripe plum. "I called the town. They're sending an inspector."

The knot on my head announces itself. "You did *what*? You know what will happen."

He nods. "Maybe."

The house will be declared uninhabitable and I'll be forced out. "Why would you do that?"

"You've got no money. You're borrowing off me and I've got to move fast or we'll lose her. I didn't know how much you'd let her go. Every day work's not done is a day closer to her collapsing. The town will condemn her and force a rehab. You'll have to leave, and then Pelewski can start on the structural work right away." *Her*, like the house is a woman. He surveys the room, the subtle bulge of buckling walls, the loose floorboards. "It's dangerous, too. You shouldn't be here," he says, but he's staring past me. There is no mention of when I could come back or if I ever could. His eyes are wet. Good god, is he crying?

"I won't take your money. I'll figure it out."

"I want you out of here," he says, his voice flat and even.

"Excuse me?"

"You heard me. If they need to, Enola and that Doyle kid can stay with us a few days." He rubs his forehead. He *is* crying, actually crying. "But I want you all out. Nobody stays here. It isn't safe."

"What gives you the fucking right?"

There should be silence or a moment of apology. There isn't.

"I've got the right." He scratches his splotchy neck. "I've got the right," he repeats. His eyes dart to the ceiling, the kitchen, the floor. "It's my house as much as it is yours. I bought this house for Paulina."

Through a thousand feet of water I ask, "What?"

"I bought this house for your mother."

It isn't true. Why would he lie? Dad promised my mother a house, this house, that's why we never left, never sold. It was his love letter. "Why?"

He moves to the couch, by the arm Enola picked bare. "I loved her." It's sincere, awful, like hearing she's dead all over again. He presses the heels of his hands to his eyes.

"You what?"

"I loved her. You don't remember, you were too young, but Paulina was so, so beautiful."

"Shut up." I remember.

"It's nothing you could understand. I just—" He coughs. "I met her first."

"What does that have to do with anything?" I don't recognize my voice.

"I brought him back to meet her. Had I known," he laughs bitterly. "Had I known. The night I met Paulina she read my cards. She read my palm, too. She held my hand."

Mom's thin fingers held in those square hands, those carpenter paws—her fingers that messed my hair—her fingernail tracing across his lifeline. "Stop it."

"Maybe you don't know because you're a quiet kid, but when a woman takes your hand like that and looks you in the eye, something changes inside you. I brought Dan with me because I had to show my best friend the woman I was going to be with."

My foot bounces, sending rhythmic stabbing pain up my leg. I can't stop it.

"I told her to come see me, that I was up early and she could find me at the dockmaster's in the harbor. She came by in the morning. The day after, too. She kept coming by, even after he saw her. Even after he told me he loved her, she kept coming by. I never should have brought him. You can't know what it is to stand in the middle of a crowd, watching the woman you love, watching your best friend fall in love with her." He talks to the floor, to his feet, unable to meet my eye.

"Did she know?"

"That I loved her?" He rubs his bulldog jowls and sad man splotches. "Yes."

"Dad bought her the house. He promised it to her."

"My grandfather left me money. Paulina wanted to settle down. She was sick of traveling; she'd been on the road her whole life, hadn't ever lived in a house. Maybe she didn't want me then, but I could give her that. So I gave him the money."

"He took it."

"I didn't want to lose him, either. He'd have followed her anywhere. She was like that; she could do that to a man."

I remember my father manning a folding grill, Leah and my mother sitting in beach chairs. Frank telling a story about kids running aground on a sandbar. Would anyone have noticed if his eyes lingered? "No. You don't buy a house for a friend."

"No," he says. "You don't."

There is the other half of the story, and he tells it like a drunken man. Mornings at the dockmaster's came with quick touches, kisses, things they'd meant to stop. That they did stop, eventually. "After a time," he says. He is kind in that he's not explicit. "She loved your dad, I know she did. I loved him too." So he began dating Leah, a teaching student at St. Joseph's, and married her. They all became friends. Of a sort.

"You slept with my mother."

"If you want me to apologize, I won't. I'm not sorry for knowing her." He gets up to pace and feel for cracks in the walls. He stops by a photograph of Enola in the water, in my mother's arms. "I took that picture." He starts in about how it was the end of June when the water gets warm but the jellyfish aren't out yet. "Paulina didn't want Enola to get stung, so she made me go in first, just to check. I'm not sorry for knowing you, either."

"Don't pretend you're my father." I see him wince. "You slept with her."

"Yes."

"How long did it go on? How long did you fuck under my father's nose?"

"Don't talk about her that way." A floorboard creaks.

"Was it before I was born? After? After Enola? How long? Months? Years?"

"A while," he says quietly.

"Am I?" We both know what I mean. Am I his.

"No."

"Enola?"

"No."

"Dates," I say. "I need to know the goddamned dates." I need to be sure.

"We stopped when Dan wanted kids. We were apart a year before she got pregnant with you. It wasn't me." His cheek twitches as if holding back a wince. "It was hard to look at her sometimes, hard enough knowing I was sharing her, but then she wanted his kids." And not Frank's. "It tore me up some, but I'd give her anything she wanted. When you were around two we started up again. On and off for about two years. Then she wanted another kid, a little girl. I guess she saw Alice and fell in love. She cut it off, said she was done. We hadn't been together in a year and a half before Enola." Here is a new awful part: all the time he wanted my mother, he had his wife, and they had Alice. Quiet, perfect Alice. They threw us together—was it to keep Leah occupied? Were we an intentional distraction? My gut hurts. For me, for her. Frank sits down again and reaches over as if to touch me, but he stops.

"Dates," I say.

"I don't have them." He's almost shouting. "I didn't write it down. It's not something—it's not the sort of thing I ever thought I'd have to explain to her son," he says. "You're his. Hell, you even chew your fingers the way he did. It was never a question. Your mom wouldn't let it be. No matter how much I wished you were mine sometimes."

"Stop lying." I'm up. My ankle shouts, but it fades into the rest of the noise. My teeth hurt. My veins hurt.

"I wouldn't lie about that. You're not mine, but I wished you were."

"Did she know you gave him the money?" He doesn't answer. "Did she know?"

"Yes," he says, at length. "It was the one thing I could give her. And it's gone to shit, Simon—"

"How much did you give him?" He looks at me blankly. "How much did the house cost?" We'd been family, all of us. Frank, who'd shared a boat with my father, gone sailing with the man whose wife he slept with. I've eaten at his table. Kissed and loved his daughter.

"Two hundred fifty thousand."

There is no apology in him, and that, of all things, is most repugnant. "And for how many years? How long were you two together?"

"Five years, on and off," he says.

Five years; 1,826 days. "If you look at it logically, that's fifty thousand a year to sleep with my mother. How many times a year do you figure?" His jaw clenches and his Adam's apple bobs. Still, no remorse. "Once a month would be around four thousand and change. Once a week would make it roughly a thousand. So, my mother was worth a thousand dollars a week to you. That's like keeping a family on the side, just for fucking."

His fist slams into the wall and an apple-sized hole devours it. He pulls his hand out, cradles his fingers, then examines the wall. He touches all around it, murmuring, apologizing—to the house, to my mother.

"Did my dad know?"

"We didn't tell him."

It's answer enough. "He knew."

"I used to watch her swim in the mornings. Even after," he says. He doesn't look at me. Can't. "That's when your dad figured it out. It was a little more than a year after Enola was born. He was coming down the steps and I was going up. He passed me and asked if Leah knew. I said there's nothing to know. There wasn't by then, hadn't been for a good couple of years. Next thing Paulina says he's looking to move you all upstate."

Away from anywhere that might be a good place for a man who works on boats.

"I loved her," Frank says, softly. "Every day even after I knew it couldn't continue, I loved Paulina. We stopped because I loved her, him too. Then she was gone." He pulls his hat from his head, crumpling it in his hands. "If you stay out of the house for a while, I can fix it up. I'll get Pete and we'll start working, but it isn't safe here now. You could get hurt. I loved you, too, you and Enola. It would have killed me if he took you all away."

Picture life over again. Picture the things I sometimes wished. Frank as my father. The family across the street would be strangers, people who occasionally got our mail by mistake, people we'd see as we took out our boat. But where is Alice? There would be no Alice.

Mom died. Dad sold the boat. We saw less of Frank, only when I was on the beach with Alice, or when Leah watched us. I'd thought grief had made Dad cut Frank out, but it was worse. My mother drowned and he cut ties with his best friend. It's a simple logic chain.

"Your money fixed nothing. All it ever did was break things. Us. The house went to hell because he wouldn't lift a finger on it. Not once. He didn't put a penny into it. He didn't care if the whole thing fell down because you bought this house to hold on to my mother." It's a crippled token of one man's love for another man's wife. Dad knew it. He must have sat at that kitchen table, praying it would collapse. "You killed him, too," I say. "It just took longer."

"Simon," he pleads.

"No, you don't get to say my name." I can't be here in this place that smells like varnish, sawdust, and carpenter's glue—like Frank.

I go to the car. I would run but my leg won't let me. Frank follows. He's talking, but I can't hear him through the car door. I don't care. I can barely feel my hands on the wheel. I pump them a few times to get the blood back in the fingers; stress causes both vasoconstriction and vasodilatation—a fact I picked up when helping a student with a term paper—this is vasoconstriction. Three pumps. Frank is at the car. He's broken, but not broken enough. I roll down the window. He puts his hands on the roof, hooking his thumbs into the interior, creeping inside.

"I'm sorry," he says. "You have no idea how much I wished you'd been my son."

"You never came by after he died," I tell him. "We had to go to you." My shame is that I could have loved him, despite everything, if he'd so much as tried.

"It was too much. With your dad and the house, and there was

Leah and Alice," he says. They hadn't been enough to stop him before. No, Alice and Leah were only concerns after, when Enola and I were difficult to love, not as convenient as the family he already had. The fruit is too ripe to not be picked. I feel myself smile, knowing I look insane. I throw the car into reverse, spinning the tires. Frank stands in the driveway, covering himself with his arms like he's naked.

Yes, Alice will be mad at me, but she is already. I lean out the window and yell, "I fucked your daughter. Go ahead and fix my goddamned house."

18

At dawn Amos woke, legs tired from dreams of chase. Evangeline lay beside him, a soft presence, warm with sleep. He looked toward Madame Ryzhkova's round-topped wagon and was gripped by unease. Once, he'd seen a man keel over dead while hefting a cask; the man's face had turned beetle-shell dark before he gasped and dropped like a stone. Ryzhkova's face had been a similar color the prior night. Her warnings were twisted and misguided, but she cared for him and it was rare enough to be cared for that it should not be taken lightly.

He climbed from the bed, moving slowly so as not to wake Evangeline, and crossed the camp to Ryzhkova's wagon to wait at the stairs by her door. She'd always known when he approached, teasing, "I can smell your unwashed hands coming near." When he sniffed himself she smiled and said, "Think you I would not know my own? I know when you seek me."

Amos waited until impatience demanded he knock. When there was no answer he turned the handle, only to find the door locked. A hard pit settled in his chest. Ryzhkova was dead and he had killed her. He ran to Benno's wagon and pounded on the door until flecks of yellow paint stuck to his hand. The acrobat opened the door in disarray, peering out through a crack. Behind him the shadowed form of another sprawled across a mattress. Benno stepped down and hastily closed the door behind him.

"What is this?" he muttered, rubbing a hand across his sleep-drunk face.

Amos took Benno's arm and dragged him down the steps and to Ryzhkova's wagon. He pulled the handle to show Benno that she would not answer.

"It is early yet, Amos, barely light."

Amos smacked the door with the heel of his hand, jarring the hinges until they clanked. Inside no one stirred, but Amos continued to knock, looking at Benno in desperation.

"Stop. You cannot work with bloodied hands." Benno took hold of Amos's shoulders, gripping tightly until, at last, he stilled. "I'll help. Wait here." Benno jogged off, reappearing a short time later with a small leather pouch. He bid Amos stand aside as he produced a series of thin brass strips. Amos looked on while Benno gently pushed the door until the lock caught.

"Where I am from it is necessary for a man to have skills that are not always looked upon kindly. On occasion they prove useful." Benno put an eye to the sliver of space between door and wagon frame and proceeded to slip two of the strips along the door's edge, wiggling them around the wood.

He was a thief, or had been. Though they'd traveled years together, Amos knew little about him, only that he was quick to smile and easy to be around. Amos watched him bend one of the brass pieces, molding it to the door. Then, a flick of his wrist and the lock was open.

"For you only do I do this." Benno returned his clever keys to the pouch. "Forgive me if I do not stay. I have another matter to attend to," he said, and hurried back to his wagon, pouch tucked against his side.

With a light push, Amos swung Ryzhkova's door open. What he found inside was confusing. The cart was stripped bare. The walls bore the faint outlines of where the portraits had hung. She was gone.

Amos staggered down the wagon steps and fled, running toward town. Burlington. She must have gone into Burlington; nothing else was near and she wouldn't venture to the river alone. He bit his tongue and the blood rose sharp with anxiousness. The road into town was not far behind Peabody's wagon; he could see chimney smoke from morning fires puffing into the sky and he ran toward that smoke, past the blacksmith and the butcher, and into the streets. The shops were not yet open, the inn was still dark, and the roads were empty save for a half-starved mongrel dog. The streets were so well traveled that searching for her footprints proved impossible. Madame Ryzhkova had vanished as if she had never been. His stomach rolled with a pain worse than hunger. He returned to camp, to Peabody's wagon.

Peabody lifted the latch and peered out, squinting. Hatless, his scalp glinted pink in the early morning light. He murmured a quick apology and fumbled at a side table before clapping on a curly brimmed hat. "What devil finds you awake? None with a soul is about at such an hour."

Amos gestured in the direction of Ryzhkova's empty wagon, but Peabody would have none of it.

"I am aware of what occurs in this menagerie. You quarreled with Madame Ryzhkova," he puffed. "She is a temperamental creature; I'm certain it is nothing that rest and a new town won't find the fixing of." His smile was cut short by a yawn.

Amos seized Peabody by the shirtsleeves and pulled him from his wagon despite his protestations. Heads poked out of doors, Meixel and Nat, Susanna. Evangeline woke. Benno stood on his steps and Melina appeared behind him, rubbing sleep from her eye.

By the time they reached Ryzhkova's wagon, Amos and Peabody had garnered an audience. Amos threw back the door to reveal the barren interior.

Peabody's face turned ashen. "My dear Amos, I am in terrible need of making apologies. I simply . . . " His worlds faltered. "Hell. She has done it. No, that is not right. Ah, Amos. I am sorry." He doffed his hat, touched it to his chest, and wandered to his wagon in a fugue. Amos lacked the will to follow. He sat on Ryzhkova's steps, dangling his legs and taking note of the air—something of old flowers in it, something like his teacher. He studied each dent on the steps she'd climbed for countless years, outlining the marks left by her boot heels.

Meixel came to him first, giving Amos's back a rough pat before walking to start the morning's fire. Nat, the strongman, inclined his head, and Melina squeezed his knee. Their touches did not feel like comfort, more like gifts for the departing.

Benno touched Amos's shoulder. "I do not pretend to understand why she is gone, but know that it is not for want of caring for you."

Amos flinched.

Evangeline waited, knowing that he would come to her in time. He would learn that she'd quarreled with Ryzhkova, that she was the reason Ryzhkova had left. She wondered if everything she touched would sour and die. *I am a killer.*

They were to leave that day, following the banks of the Rancocas, but they did not. Whether it was in hopes that Ryzhkova would return, or out of respect, Amos could not say.

"One day more or less shall make no difference to those who don't know to miss us," Peabody said.

Amos stayed inside her wagon, running his fingers over where she'd draped cloths and hung portraits, looking for the soot stains from burning sage. He kicked the straw-filled sack that served as her mattress and threw himself upon it, only to knock his head on a sharp corner. There, tucked away beneath the edge of her bed, lay Ryzhkova's card box.

She'd left them for him.

He lifted the lid and the orange backs smiled at him. He touched them to his chest, feeling their smoothness, feeling Ryzhkova in the paper, cackling, teasing and scolding, kissing his cheeks when he'd done well. Teaching. His heart both broke and mended; he would not be lost. He tucked the cards into his shirt and sought Peabody.

Peabody sat with his book, drawing thick black lines through a long column of figures and names. Near the bottom of the page he had begun a sketch, a wagon perhaps, too vague to yet tell. Upon seeing Amos he cleared his throat. "Apologies," he said. "Terrible. A great and terrible thing, but not your doing. I had recently conversed with the woman." He drew a small flourish in the air with his quill. "It was less than pleasant. We shall see the right of it, I promise."

Amos threw his arms around the man, embracing him.

Peabody coughed. "Yes, well. Quite right."

Amos pulled the deck from his shirt and nimbly moved through the cards. One following on top of another, he showed Peabody Cups for communication; Pages for a great journey; the High Priestess for her, Ryzhkova, and how they must find her; the Fool for himself, as it was his fault that she'd left.

Peabody's expression shuttered. He sat at his ciphering chair, looking every one of his years, and smiled with regret. "Darling boy, I cannot glean what you are trying to say."

Amos cried out, the sound an unnatural grunt. He searched for the Hermit and presented it to Peabody, pushing it to his chest, where buttons pulled at velvet.

"I am sorry," said Peabody, quieter than Amos had ever heard him. "Deeply sorry, but I've no idea what you mean." He set down his quill, capped the inkpot, and rested his hands on the bulge of his stomach. "I can try," he gently promised. "But I am old, it will take time." Seeing Amos's distress he said, "We've managed well enough, have we not?"

Amos began to weep. Peabody patted him, but his ministrations were of little solace. He let the young man curl up on the floor. For long helpless moments he watched as Amos quaked.

"She may yet return. We'll wait the night and sort out the season. If she does not, well, then we must adapt." He glanced at his ledger. Ryzhkova's loss would slow their money; they couldn't afford to keep a man without trade, no matter how much he liked him. He scratched his beard. The best thing for Amos would be to keep him valuable, to reevaluate him. Yes, Ryzhkova was gone, but where there was money lost there might also be money gained. He pondered a small sketch he'd done earlier of a horse.

"Did you know, Amos, that I was once a student of Philip Astley? When there was less of me I rode horses. In London, though I'm certain the name means nothing to you. I sat a fine seat. Astley was a marvelous man. Powerful voice. In my better moments I fancy myself like him; he taught one to swing from a saddle, stand atop it, and how to balance plates and teacups on one's fingertips while galloping about a ring. A fine time, surely." He paused to write a few lines. "But one cannot ride forever. I was vaulted over the front of a disagreeable brown mare—Finest Rosie was her name, though she was quite a tart; threw me flat on my back in the middle of the amphitheater with half of London looking on, kicked me in my stomach and back so I was never to ride again. It might have killed me, but I mended. A ship across the sea finds me here, in this place where they've never seen one such as Astley, or one such as me. It would be a lie to say that I don't miss riding, but in many ways this is better. Here I may be Astley, rather than his paler shadow. You see, my boy? I have adapted. As will you."

When Amos calmed, Peabody helped him to stand. He straightened Amos's shirt, picked the straw from his hair, and dusted his shoulders. He looked the boy up and down, eyed the soiled spots on his shirt, the frays in his pant legs—no gentleman, but passable. He gave Amos a solid grin that tipped his moustache.

"There now, young master. Powder or a wig would improve you, but we cannot make silk from flax. It strikes me that you are in need of comfort best provided by the fairer sex. Go to your lady. I've always found that the sorrow of a departure is best remedied with a greeting—onward to romance!" Peabody pushed the door open, ushered Amos through, and watched as he shuffled from the wagon. A mute fortune-teller was a draw when working with a partner; alone, therein lay difficulty. Without Ryzhkova the accounts wouldn't balance; he'd lost not one but two of the troupe. In the interim they could hang curtains in the Wild Boy cage, but the thought troubled Peabody; he could not place the moment when Amos had become his second son, but there it was. He thought of his time with Astley, and how it had not been his back that had pained him most, and for the first time in his long life, Hermelius Peabody felt old.

In the wagon with the small horse, Evangeline waited. "It is true then. Ryzhkova is gone," she said when he climbed in.

She'd been crying, he saw the redness in her eyes, the spots staining her cheeks. When she tried to embrace him he pulled away, reaching for the cards.

"At least she left you that," she said.

Amos did not listen; he was desperately tired of listening; he wished to speak. Working through the deck, he showed Evangeline card upon card, building thought from image. The Fool over and over again, the High Priestess, then the darker cards. Amos set them all before her, his life in mosaic, his thoughts, and more than before, his fears. Evangeline tried to keep pace, speaking his thoughts as she saw them, but he moved with furious speed. The pictures flashed, slid, and blurred until at length his hands slowed, and he began to repeat a sequence of cards, one she remembered. In the lesson he'd used two cards—one for him, one for her. Now he used just his, the Fool. He began matching it with another, the solitary old traveler that was the Hermit. No, not Peabody—how layered their language was—in the lesson he'd used the cards to ask, "Are we alone?" Now the variation.

She knew it. "Am I alone?"

He repeated. *Am I alone? Am I alone?*

She layered her fingers over his and touched her lips to his forehead. "I am here," she said. She repeated the words, but he did not hear. She searched for her card, the Queen of Swords, then for another with which to pair it—one they'd settled upon to mean home, place, wherever they dwelled. The Six of Cups. Children at play in front of their home. She placed her cards on the wagon boards, touching his in answer.

Am I alone?

I am here.

Am I alone?

I am your home.

19

JULY 21ST

In the carnival parking lot I shuffle the pieces, rearrange things until they line up. My father loved my mother, he told me so. Love at first sight. Enola is not sick; she's fine and we don't die. Except that we do.

The red and white awnings of Rose's Carnival crest over the lot next to the brick box that is the Napawset Fire Department. Inside are rides and ride jockeys, rigged games, a fun house with shifting floors and mirrors, a sideshow, and my sister. I've parked by the torn banner proclaiming this the "45th Annual Firemen's Carnival and Fair," the carnival Enola and I went to as kids; after all the money I spent trying to win her goldfish that died in a night, it's hers now, hers and Doyle's.

I hobble down the midway—a wide walkway of

trampled-down grass lined with booths, fried food, and blinking lights—in search of a card reader's booth. A man calls the tin horse races through a megaphone. Whack-a-mole, a shooting gallery, and the ring toss are manned by teenagers, or a peculiar breed of thin person with sunken cheeks—pockmarked and hungry, but intriguing. The air is heavy with kettle corn and cotton candy, and pop music blares. This is Enola's home. The grounds teem with sweating faces, and children dart between parents' legs. I can almost feel my father's hand gripping my shirt to keep me from running to the coin toss to try to win a live frog. I stumble, roll my bad ankle, and the pain tastes like metal.

Towering over the carnival is the swing ride—a classic model Chair-O-Plane, candy cane–striped yellow and purple, the top adorned with mirrored panels that catch the sun. I remember Dad buckling Enola into a seat. I remember sailing in the chair next to his, watching the wind plaster his hair to his forehead. Even then he hadn't smiled; he was too busy looking for a piece of Mom in the place where they'd met. The next year Enola and I went alone. Laughter streams from the swings as chains tighten and chairs ascend, careening in centrifugal grace. I limp to the end of the line. A higher vantage should help me find Enola.

It's a tight fit, my knees are almost in my mouth, but then we lift. I rise, spiraling outward, and see houses looking out from the walls of the town—a place where neighbors steal mothers in the night and drown them. At the top of the arc I can see the Sound beyond the rooflines that somehow contain my house—correction: Frank's house. The water is dull, not smooth as glass or angry and thrashing as in books. It's gray, calm, and dead. I hate it, hate that's hard like a shell. She drowned herself in a second-rate water.

I swing my foot, bend the ankle, and the sting feels pretend, just an idea of what pain is supposed to be. The carnival looks like a toy with a windup key. There, the concession with the pink lemonade. There, the Wheel of Fortune everybody plays though it's universally known to be rigged. Voices are fading shouts, laughter, cries at nothing.

Toward the back I see it, a purple tent with a line of people. Yes, that's her.

When we swing to the ground in loping waves, things are different. This is no grand carnival, but I would run away with it.

I need Enola. Three days left and I need her.

An enormous man in a Hawaiian shirt lumbers by; a scraggly braid dangles down his back like a possum tail; he heads toward a striped tent and ducks under a flap—the sideshow. This must be George the Fat Man, the one with the weed. I search around for Doyle, but he's nowhere.

I walk toward the small purple tent, past the shouting and the funnel cake, French fries, and zeppole, each with its own fry-oil perfume. The back of the grounds is marked by the Zipper, a rotating conveyer belt that whirls riders in spinning cages in the sky. I took Enola on it when she was too small; the lap bar didn't lock right and she knocked herself out. For weeks she had a goose egg with the dark purple imprint of waffled chain.

Dunk the Freak has a short line of people waiting to throw softballs. The Freak is a skinny guy in a dirty tank top who shouts that I throw like a girl. Behind him is Enola's tent—purple velour and duvetyn, spangled with gold moons and stars, hand painted. A sandwich sign leans against the tent corner, a picture of a hand floating over a crystal ball with the name *Madame Esmeralda* written in Gothic style.

Esmeralda. Really.

The interior is lit by a lamp covered in a red silk shawl. At a card table draped with paisley cloth, Enola is a child's idea of a fortune-teller—head wrapped in a purple scarf, gigantic gold hoops in her ears. She's got two clients, a couple of teenage girls; twin ponytails, blond and brown. And there is Doyle beside her, his tattooed hands slithering over the table.

Lifting the curtain lets in light, making the girls turn their heads. Doyle squints. Enola glares at me through rings of black eyeliner. In a thick accent she barks out, "Outside! Esmeralda will be with you."

"Enola, I—"

"You. Out. Now." She smacks her palm against the table. Doyle eases from his chair to usher me out.

"Five minutes, okay? Chill." He pulls the tent closed.

I push a fold of drape to the side, enough for a peephole, and watch as Enola rocks in her chair, speaking in a low voice to the ponytail girls, who huddle in close.

"You want to know of love, yes?" Enola asks. The blonde starts to speak, but is shushed by my sister's hand. "Not to me, darling." Dah*link*. "Tell the Painted Man," she says. "The Painted Man keep your secret. He hold your secret. I fix it. Future has two doors, yes? One to open, one to close. Painted Man closes." She touches a fingernail to a sucker on Doyle's forearm, then touches her chest. "Esmeralda opens."

It's crap, but there's something about her eyes; they're different, not hazel like Mom's, more black—someone else's. The blonde leans over and whispers in Doyle's ear, her ponytail brushing his arm, tentacle meeting tentacle. He nods and puts his hand over Enola's. There's something disturbing, something that reminds me of a notation: *Wild Boy promoted to apprentice fortune-teller.* I'm not looking at Enola, but Madame Ryzhkova, mixed with Mom, echoing through my sister's body.

Enola's eyes roll and her spine shoots out of its chronic slouch, pole straight. There is a blur, movement and slapping sounds as she lays the cards in a perfect Celtic cross. I recognize the spread from *The Tenets of the Oracle.* Ten cards. Two in the center, forming the cross, one above, one below, one to the left, and one to the right, then four cards dealt in rapid succession in a line up the side. I can see their faces. They're different from the ones in *The Tenets,* but common. A Waite-type deck, delicate, with pictures even I know. The girls angle their chairs, ponytails swinging like pendulums. When she sets the last card Enola's head falls back sharply, as if her neck has snapped. With perfect timing, Doyle snakes a hand around and tips her back up. Her eyelids flutter open and she bends over the cards.

"Yes, yes," she says. "Two of you love one man. Yes. Always same." She laughs; in another woman the sound would be sexual but in Enola it's carnivorous. "This one." She points a finger at the blonde. "She is one with force behind her. Always chase, this one is." The brown ponytail bobbles up and down. "This boy, he like a strong girl. See here? Swords. He like decision, confrontation." She waves her arms, an air of madness in the gesture. "You." She stares at the brown-haired girl. "You wait for scraps, yes? Second best for you always." A small giggle from the girls, a joyless ripple. "See the cups?" Enola continues. "Water. In this position is change, flowing. Communication. You talk to him, yes? She does not speak."

The girls crowd together like hens to grain, studying the cards. Abruptly Enola's voice falls away and her jaw goes slack. She stares through the girls, beyond the tent and into something I can't see. Her hands move, sightless birds navigating migratory patterns. A new arrangement overlays the old, six lines of six cards, each set atop the others. She turns and turns, and when she speaks again it is without trace of accent, without a glance at the cards; discarnate, the voice moves through her. I can see Death, the Devil, and the Tower, and a heart that's stabbed with swords.

"Losses will be borne. Death rising from below. Barrenness. Empty fields. There will be no children."

The tent begins to hum as gooseflesh rises to meet air. The girls squirm in their seats. One shivers. A flurry of silk streaks across the table as Enola grabs one of the girl's wrists.

"All around you those you love will wither. Mother, father, and down the line." Her words spill and Doyle pops up from his chair, cracking like a spark as he latches on to Enola, shaking her. She continues, "Your name dies with you and will never pass another's lips. For you it is as water cuts stone, you will wear until nothing is left." Doyle squeezes her shoulder but she is gone.

As water cuts stone.

The dark-haired girl tugs her friend's wrist from Enola's grasp. A tic in the neck, sand leaking from a bag and Enola folds in, her face so white as to be clear. Enola again, but less. Her eyes flick to my hiding spot, our gazes lock, and it chokes.

"Wrong card," she says. The accent is back. "Happens sometimes.

Many spirits walk these grounds." She pats her scarf, tucks in an escaped hair, and then glares at me. "Get out."

I snap the drape closed, a deep pain sprouting in the middle of my skull.

Doyle sticks his head outside. Peering from the tent he looks like a mounted trophy. He laughs, nervous and conspiratorial. "Bro, you gotta give it some space, man."

"Huh?"

"You're showing up in the cards. You're too close. Give her like—" He pauses. "Yeah, like, five minutes."

"I'm good here."

"No, dude," he says with a slow twist of his head. "You are seriously not good here. I've got it covered."

"I'm her brother. Let me—"

"That's my point; you're too close. You're making stuff murky." He scrunches his face up. "Let her ramp it down, okay?" His hand comes through the curtain. He pats me on the shoulder. "Go see Thom. We told him about you and he wants to talk to you. Seriously, go. Give us five, ten minutes. Okay? He's in the big RV with the birds on the side." His hand disappears and reemerges holding several crumpled dollars. He pushes the money into my palm and gives me a soft shove back. "Get food."

As I hobble away he asks what happened to my foot. "Pothole," I reply.

"Hey," he calls. "If you swing your right arm wider it'll help keep the weight off your ankle, yeah? Diagonals, man. Think diagonals." I don't want to, but as I walk toward the smell of fried dough I find that I'm swinging my arm wider.

Enola's face was wrong when she looked at me. The way her head snapped back, there was no control, no lie, just that voice. Something's very wrong. Drowning wrong. I need to talk to her, and maybe I do need to talk to Thom Rose.

The RV is, as Doyle said, past the rides on the back of the lot, huge and plastered with white silhouettes of ducks in flight. I lean against it, taking weight off my foot, and knock. A tiny bald man answers. He wears a checked shirt, shorts, and sandals. Deep wrinkles line his mouth. His eyes are framed by squint marks from a lifetime of driving into the sun. I don't know what I expected a carnival owner to look like, but he looks like someone's uncle.

"Are you Thom Rose?"

"Who wants to know?" His eyes narrow, and it looks as if I'm about to have a door slammed in my face. Then he grins suddenly and flings the door open. "You're Simon Watson, aren't you? Anybody ever tell you that you look just like your sister?"

The camper is filled with books and papers, what looks like piles of receipts and bills, an unmade bed, and a small kitchen that is surprisingly spotless. "Sit, sit," he says, pointing to a chair by a table that folds out from a wall. "Enola says you're looking for work."

Am I looking for work? Library work, but work. "Yeah, I am."

"She says you're a swimmer." He opens a can of soda, pours himself a glass and offers me one. "Talked you up a lot. Said you can hold your breath for ten minutes."

"Give or take."

He drinks his soda for a while, contemplating. A yellowed finger taps at the table as if searching for something, a pencil, a cigarette. "It's been a while since we've had any good athletics, but a breath-holder, a swimmer, that's a hard sell for a man. Not saying we can't do it, but it's always been a woman. Mermaids. Put a cute girl in a small bathing suit, lots of long hair, a little peek here and there."

"I know." My mother was a carnival striptease. "Enola thought you'd be interested, but I told her I didn't think it would work out."

"Oh, no. I *am* interested. It'll just take me a minute to figure out. Your sister's a good kid. If she's happier having you around and it doesn't cost me anything, I don't see why not. It's been a real long time since I've seen a swimmer. There are those Weeki Wachee girls down in Florida, but they're not the same. You don't need an air tube, do you?"

"No, sir." I *could* try it, maybe. Just for a little while, see what wandering feels like.

"Good. It's better that way, cleaner lines. We could rework the dunk tank, maybe. That damned kid's a pain in the ass anyway. Doesn't matter if he's a different kid, he's always a pain in the ass." He sucks on his teeth, then barrels on. "Best mermaid I ever saw was back when I was a kid. Gorgeous." He sketches the outline of her with his hands. "A diver, too. You don't dive, do you?"

I don't know. Maybe, but no, at the moment I don't dive. I tell him so.

"Shame. That'd be something," he says. "She'd jump into this glass tank—no splash at all—and stay under so long you'd figure she'd either died or grown gills. White bathing suit, built like the prow of a ship." He whistles. "My folks wouldn't let me have pin-ups. Verona Bonn was better than a pinup."

I hide my reaction. "I think I've heard of her. Any idea what happened to her?"

"Took up with a lion tamer, I think. Got pregnant. That'll put a mermaid out of a job fast."

Verona fell in love, had my mother, then drowned. Not so different from Mom, not so different from any of the other women. Each left a child behind, two in my mother's case.

"This may sound strange, but Enola mentioned you let her see some of your log books? A little while back someone sent me a manuscript that I think belonged to a carnival. I'd love to have something to compare it to."

Thom slides his chair back. His expression closes and he begins to play with an empty ashtray. "You don't show that sort of thing to anyone who's not family," he says.

So, Enola is family. "Of course. I understand. No harm meant." We resume a light conversation, discuss me taking on work until we can figure out an act. Ride jockeying, basic back breaking. I want to get back to Enola.

I am near the door when Thom says, "You aren't by any chance Paulina Tennen's kid, are you?"

I stop. "Why?"

"Ah, thought so. Your sister said her mom worked shows, but she wasn't real specific. You and your sister, you look so much like her it's uncanny. I ran across her a long time ago, back when my father was running things. I think she was working with a magician. She seemed real nice. Pretty, too. Hard to forget a face like that. You said somebody sent you a show book?"

I nod.

"That's odd. Unless it's got to do with your mom, one of her shows. Wasn't Lareille, was it?" I shake my head. "Thought not. As far as I knew Michel was still chugging along." He scratches his neck. "Any idea why they sent it to you?"

"He thought it might have belonged to a family member."

He chews his lip, showing a tobacco-stained tooth. "Books stay with a show. If one's just floating around out there loose, that most likely means a show went under."

The water-stained pages lend his words an unintended accuracy. If the show fell victim to a flood it could explain the Koenigs' disappearance as well. "It's pretty old," I say. "Filled with drawings. Lots of them of tarot cards."

Thom Rose grins. "And let me guess. Your sister won't tell you anything about 'em."

I shove my hands deep into my pockets. "Exactly."

He laughs drily. "Yeah, she's tight-lipped. Sorry, but you're shit out of luck with me. I don't know much about cards except that your sister does 'em right. I like her. Keeping her happy keeps the Electric Boy happy, and that's good for me. That kid's a gold mine." He opens the RV door and ushers me out. "Tell her I said I'll figure out how to take you on."

Limping back toward Enola I wonder what Thom would have said if I'd told him that Verona Bonn was my grandmother, that she and my mother both drowned. But tight-lipped runs in the family, among other things.

I'm about to go into Enola's tent when the ponytail girls rush out. The crowd swallows them in a sea of patterned shirts and sunburns.

"What just happened?" I ask, lifting the tent flap.

Enola turns on me fast. "What the hell do you think you're doing barging in on a reading? I don't go to your work and fuck stuff up. Oh, wait. That's right, you don't *have* a job. And what happened to your leg?"

"Floor trouble." I duck in. It's sweltering, with a vague smell of clove cigarettes. Doyle is folded up lotus style on the ground by the table, a glowing lightbulb rolling around his hand. The only sign of his unease is a slight brow pinch, pulling the tentacle ends tight across his cheeks. Enola grabs a bag from under the table, shoves her hand in, and pulls out a zeppole, dripping with fat and sugar. She stuffs her mouth, chipmunking it.

Around half-chewed bites she asks, "I thought you weren't coming. Why are you here?"

"You scared the hell out of those girls. And what's with the accent?" I ask.

"Quit answering questions with questions," she says and wipes the back of her neck. "Damn it's hot. I'm going to need a swim later. The accent's been part of the deal for a while."

"And him?" I nod to Doyle.

"Just a thing we're trying out," she says.

"Brings in more cash," he says, without opening his eyes.

"Adds to the mystery," she says.

"Those things you said to the girls? Does that add mystery too?"

"No idea what you're talking about." Angry silence.

"Frank had sex with Mom." The lightbulb stops twirling.

"Fuck," Enola says. I tell her what Frank told me, about how they met, how long they were together. About the house. Enola makes notches in the side of a card with her thumbnail. The Hanged Man, an inverted figure strung from a cross by his pointed foot, almost like St. Peter. Not the supple cards she keeps in her skirt pocket; these cards are stiff, with backs covered in fleurs-de-lis. "Shit. Well, that screws you and Alice. Fuck, wait. She's not our sister, is she?"

"No. *God,* no." I say. "Mom cut him off."

"Well, at least there's one damned thing she did right." She sneers and a small bead of sweat rolls from her lip.

"Little Bird," Doyle says.

"Give me a minute to process, okay," she mutters.

"He kicked us out of the house," I say.

"So, come with us. Did you talk to Thom?" She puts her feet up on the table. They're bare and dust clings to her toes. A sliver of light breaks in. "Out!" she yells. "Esmeralda is busy." The curtain flops shut. Doyle hops up from the ground to chase after the client. His flip-flops disappear beneath the drapes. Alone again, we stare at each other. "Well, shit." She chews a piece of skin by her thumbnail, the card almost touching her mouth. "I knew Frank had a thing with the house, but I never got why. Wow. That's gross." She's fidgety. She puts down the Hanged Man in favor of the entire deck, fanning, restacking, and flipping the cards over her knuckles. "I really am sorry about Alice. That makes everything weird. Are you going to tell her?"

I hadn't even considered it; it's an injury none of us needs. The last she saw of me was bruised and in a broken house. She wouldn't cry if I told her, that isn't like her, but would she slam a door on me? Absolutely. Would she look me in the eye after? "I don't know if it's for me to tell. I have things to figure out first."

"Right. Shit. Where are you going to stay? I'd offer but we're cramped." She shrugs.

"You have a place?" This is news.

"Doyle and I have a trailer that hooks to his car. We follow Rose's with it sometimes."

"Oh."

She shoots the deck between her hands in arcs. "It got to be a pain keeping his stuff in the car, lightbulbs were always breaking." She absently draws a line in the air. "We do a caravan kind of thing. We can probably figure something out for you."

I hadn't expected her to have a home. Not her—them, there is a *them*. I'd always pictured Enola as solitary, but she's perfectly paired. They pass cards back and forth like it's speaking. I have no such language, though the librarian I was had decimals, everything a classification. What would they be? The 400s for the language, 300s for the sociology, 900s for the history of her, us; though something about them begs for the 200s and religious fervor.

"Hey," she says. "You okay?"

"I found something strange. Mom died on July twenty-fourth, and so did her mother. Also, Thom saw our grandmother perform, which is weird, but that's not even the strange part." I'm rushing, but I don't care. "I went through the book Churchwarry sent me, and then a bunch of books and articles that Alice and I found, death registers, newspapers going back—way, way back. I went back until I could find names that were in the book. They die on the twenty-fourth, all the women, Mom's relatives. They all drowned and they drowned on July twenty-fourth."

She stops moving. "That's it. You think we're all going to drown, don't you?" She shakes her head. "That's twisted. That's you wanting to hear things, fucked-up things. You've been alone in that house for too damned long." She looks down at the table, at her hands, her cards. "You think we're like *her*."

"No," I say and hope that for one second she believes me.

"You're the worst bullshitter." Enola's chair tips forward and she sighs. "She just got sad, okay? Unbearably sad. I told you that book is messed up. Forget about it. Go get your stuff, come back here, and we'll set up a place for you tonight. Get the hell out of the house. If Frank wants it, let him have it; it's filled with dead people and it's going over." She reaches out to squeeze my hand, grinding the knuckles together. "Look, I'm sorry if I left you alone too long. I'm sorry, okay? Get your stuff. Bring it back here. *Don't* bring the book."

She looks so earnest, as if I am the problem, as though she didn't just scare the life out of two teenage girls. "What's going on with your cards?"

"Nothing," she says, too quickly. "It happens sometimes when somebody interrupts a reading. Messes up the vibe, taints it. Speaking of which," she waves a hand, "I need to clear the room."

"I went through the book. I saw what you did."

"What did I do?"

"You defaced it. You ripped out every single sketch of tarot cards and I want to know why."

"I'm not fighting with you." She adjusts her scarf and wipes at a black eyeliner smudge, making it either worse or better. We stare at each other.

Doyle slips back into the tent. He looks back and forth between us before slinking over to my sister. "Dude, you need to let it go."

His arms form a mass of dark octopi around her shoulders that looks like it could strangle. She puts her hand on his elbow and it's this simple touch that makes it clearer than any performance he's done for her, the miles he's driven, or whatever she might say about him—she loves him. They have a home, a life, and I'm outside it.

"Okay," I say.

"Get your things and come back. Promise? Get away from Frank," she says.

"Camp out in your car. I've done it, it's no big deal," Doyle says.

They take turns saying things about making a place for me, how everything will be fine. But I look at Enola and see the shimmering ghost of fear; she may lie to herself, lie for Doyle, but she heard me. She's frightened.

"I'll be by later," I say as I leave the tent. I need to figure out what to do about Alice. I need to call Churchwarry.

20

S *eer vanished. Possibly deceased. Reconfigura-*
tion requires additional sojourn in Burlington.
It was difficult to encompass the depth of
guilt Peabody felt at Ryzhkova's departure, if
only for the effect that it had on Amos.

Reluctant to leave it, her cart became Amos's home.
He had no wish to spend his days with Peabody, who
wore pity like one of his waistcoats. Worst of all was
sleep. Amos's dreams overflowed with visions of
Ryzhkova and her cards.

Having given up the search, they departed Burlington, passing the day in mud, rocks, wagon ruts, and
loneliness. That night he simply held Evangeline. In
the morning she moved all her possessions into the
wagon with Amos. When Evangeline's arms could
not comfort him, Amos concentrated on the trace

musk of burned sage, and imagined Ryzhkova haggling pay with Peabody or discussing stitch work with Susanna. Gradually he grew to understand the Three of Swords's pierced heart; Ryzhkova had broken him.

He spent more of his days with Sugar Nip, content to pass hours with a creature who didn't care whether he spoke or worked, or mourned. Kindness and food were Sugar Nip's currency, one he deeply understood. On a late evening, Amos went to the small horse's wagon to feed her wild onions, and found Benno already inside and scratching Sugar Nip's forelock. Startled, Amos nearly fell from the door, but Benno steadied him.

"Apologies, I did not mean to frighten. I was hoping to speak with you. Something weighs heavily upon me, something perhaps I should have told you." His voice was a whisper, and his eyes glinted in the shadows.

Sugar Nip snorted and stamped uneasily. Amos fed her the onions and crouched beside Benno, tilting his head in question.

"I saw something I believe I was not meant to. Evangeline. Before Madame Ryzhkova left, I witnessed them quarrel. I thought little of it at the time, but then Ryzhkova departed and I began to wonder."

Amos started.

"I say this out of care, and because you have been kind to me. Did you never wonder where Evangeline came from before she found us? She worries me. You know me now; I've shown you what I was. You trust me, I think. Can you say the same of her?" He put his hand on Amos's shoulder as if to steady him once more.

Amos felt bile rise. He spat into the straw.

Benno slid forward, poised on the lip of the door. "I think sometimes it is difficult to look after ourselves," he said, thoughtfully. "We look to friends to do it for us. But perhaps I am mistaken. I thought only to warn you and, selfishly, to ease my mind. I've done so. I ask only that you think on why she drowns herself." He rubbed his thumb over a scratched knuckle on his left hand. "And why Ryzhkova would leave." Benno hopped down, and left Amos to his thoughts.

It was an hour before Amos felt right enough to leave the wagon.

Peabody granted Amos an amount of time to sort himself out, but after two towns with Amos doing little more than cleaning up after the animals, Peabody pulled him aside. "Work, Amos." He sat Amos down by the accounts table and mussed his hair, which without the benefit of a head scarf had started to mat.

"Idleness is our enemy and never did fill a man's purse." At Amos's puzzled expression, he added, "Money has a way of changing one's outlook. We shall find you something. Enterprise, my boy. Nothing leavens the spirit like enterprise." Beneath the shade of his hat, Peabody's eyes were tired. Amos knew what would come.

The Wild Boy cage reappeared. Evangeline stood beside him when the velvet curtain was drawn back from the bars. She had only known Amos as the fortune-teller; he'd preferred it that way. He pulled his arm from hers.

Peabody touched a glove to the boy's shoulder. "For the moment, until we are able to confabulate a vocation for you."

"Is there truly nothing else?" Evangeline asked.

"Your water act is hardly fit for two," Peabody coughed. "As it were Amos remains a Wild Boy without compare. He was glorious. It may be enlightening for you to see him at the height of his powers. Quite the thing."

But desperation made the act fearsome. Women screamed and fainted more than they had before, and the troupe began to give Amos a wide berth. Money came as Peabody had promised, though the draw was less. "The joy has gone," Peabody said after the closing of a lean show. "The showmanship, my fine fellow, is not what it could be."

Amos agreed. Vanishing was the only part of the act that was tolerable. When he let his body listen to the breath of the world and fade away, in those precious moments the ache left him; it returned in the dark, when he held Evangeline tightly and remembered Benno's words.

After Amos was pelted with rotted fruit in Wellston, Peabody spoke to him while still in the cage. Amos drew a shirt over his head to cover his nakedness. Things that had once been delightful—

the cold iron bars, the straw against his skin—were now irksome; he missed the intimate work of a seer, and the privacy. He missed the language he used with his teacher, and being looked at without fear. Peabody sat beside him, an air of sorrow about him, unmindful of the sawdust and dirt that clung to his clothing. "I miss her as well. I find there is an emptiness." He tapped his chest near his heart. "Madame Ryzhkova had an excellent presence about her. But," he punctuated, pointing to the cage ceiling, "move on, we must."

Amos grimaced, but nodded. Everything about Peabody always seemed ready to burst, whereas his own insides seemed to be forever shrinking. He touched his cheek to Peabody's shoulder, then removed himself from the wagon, through the trapdoor, as he had when he'd been a child.

That night he buried his face in Evangeline's hair and she held him, knowing she had driven Ryzhkova off as surely as she'd murdered her grandmother.

Evangeline's stomach began to round. They did not speak of it until it could not be ignored.

"You must teach me," she said to Amos as they traveled south. She rested her head against his shirtsleeve. In one hand he held the reins of the horse pulling their wagon; with the other he traced Evangeline's neck. At her question his eyes strayed from the road.

"To read the tarot," she said. "We would make a handsome pair."

A wheel sent a stone spinning off into the brush. Roads were never easy except in more worn places outside of New York and Philadelphia, but Amos noted every pit and root now that each bump jostled the swell of Evangeline's belly. He shook his head. Ryzhkova lived in the cards, the last touches of her that he could not bring himself to clear away. Each time he held them he felt a bit of her old humor, the brush of her crooked thumb on his hand. They were too private to work with, too dear.

"Watching you play savage is unbearable." Evangeline shifted and began to search through the deck nestled between them on the seat board. "It isn't you. Perhaps when you were a boy, but not now. It's watching you dying," she said, showing him a card with an impaled man. "It kills me, too."

He looked back to the road, thinking of the things he'd meant to tell her: that he'd dreamt of leaving with her; that he wished to build them a house—have chickens, perhaps a dog, as he'd always liked them. He feared, too, that just as she had come in the night she would one day leave him. Perhaps it would be best if, like Peabody, they continued to move. He'd thought many times over Benno's words, but did not tell her of it. He could not ask her of her past, not when he knew nothing of his own.

Evangeline tapped the cards together and smacked them against Amos's leg, demanding an answer.

He pulled back on the braided leather, causing the horse to trip to a halt, and skated his fingers through the deck. Ahead, the yellow door of Benno's wagon disappeared into the trees. For a moment he thought to pair the card with another, but a tingling in his spine told him the one would be enough. He pressed Strength into Evangeline's palm.

She contemplated before saying, "I cannot swim much longer. Few will want to see the Atlantis Mermaid and her enormous stomach."

He squeezed her hand, pressing the card between them, heating it.

"Peabody has said as much. I must find other work during my confinement else my employ will end."

Amos swallowed. Peabody could not afford to lose two incomes in a season, and there would be another mouth to feed. He snapped the reins. The horse protested but began to move.

"It would be good to work with something that does not pain you," she said softly. "I think you wouldn't miss the shrieking and the stares, or the insects and the rain." She brushed an angry mosquito welt on Amos's wrist, and his flesh leaned into the scratching. "You looked well before. A fine man who I would like to see again."

He heard the longing in her voice and remembered how women sighed during card readings; Ryzhkova had said it was the sound of a spirit breaking.

"I believe I would take to it. I confess that I sometimes grow tired of water. It wears at me, like a river does its banks."

He nodded, but his face grew grim. Their language had been one of double meanings, a weakness of the cards. In giving her Strength, he'd hoped she might see it as comfort, that he would protect her. Abide and all will be well; he would learn to be happier, to take care of her. But she was breaking, and in so had sought an older meaning, one unique to them, from when he had knelt and placed his head in her hands, lion acquiescing to lady.

The wheels bounced and Evangeline tumbled toward the edge of the seat board. Amos caught her and pulled her to his side. Evangeline snuggled into the crook of his arm. After a time, her eyelids drifted closed, light blue veins showing through her skin. He would teach her tarot, if only to keep her with him. On a not-too-distant night they would come to the lesson that had brought him to Evangeline but had cost him Ryzhkova. A knot formed under his ribs. He dreaded the day when, sitting in Ryzhkova's wagon, he would teach her how to lie.

21

Have you come up with anything on Frank McAvoy's family?"

"Simon, is that you? Where are you? It sounds like a war zone."

"A carnival parking lot."

"Oh," he says.

"Did you get a chance to look into him at all? I've been trying to track down another name, the card reader, Ryzhkova. I think there's a chance that Frank might be a relation. The portraits in the book, the ones Frank has, I'm fairly certain they were hers. I did some digging on genealogy sites. Ryzhkova had a daughter, Katerina, who married one of the circus performers, Benno Koenig. I've hit a snag finding their children, but if you've started from the present and I'm working from the past, I think we'll meet up."

A group of boys shouts as they spill out of the carnival and into the lot. I cover my ear. Though some of the ride noise still filters through, it blocks enough sound that I can hear Churchwarry's breath hitch.

"I'm afraid I haven't gotten much done at all. A client took up a great deal of my time. I had to track down a title for his mother's birthday. *Green Jade for Laughter.* The closest copy is in Washington State in a library that wasn't keen to let it go."

"We're protective of our archives; they justify funding."

A dog barks in the background. Churchwarry shouts, "Down, Sheila!" followed by a scuffling noise. "Yes, well, they're certainly funded now. It was all terribly time-consuming."

A man passes by with a waddling little boy, sticky and screaming. I duck into my car hoping for more quiet. Inside isn't much better, but with the windows rolled up I can hear, though it's boiling inside and the phone slips on my cheek sweat. "I'm running out of time."

"Do you think perhaps you're too close to things?" he asks.

"It's my sister."

He clears his throat. "I've noticed the hours and frequency you've called and I can't help but wonder—I'm sorry there's no better way to ask, but are you still employed?" When I say nothing he continues. "I mean no offense, but I've known slow periods myself, long hours and financial strain do funny things to one's perspective."

My mouth goes dry. "My perspective is that I just saw my sister go into a trance and curse two teenage girls to a lifetime of misery, barrenness, and death. Also, I think I've just been offered a job as a carnival attraction, so I'm perfectly fine, thanks."

Churchwarry coughs. I recognize the sound of spluttering tea. He is of course the tea type.

"I—"

"I'm a breath-holder, a swimmer." Saying it to him is different than saying it to Thom Rose; it's shucking the mantle of librarian and announcing an intrinsic part of me. "So was my mother, so is my sister and all the women on my mother's side. Ten minutes, no breathing."

"Ten minutes?" he says.

"Ten minutes. That's how I know something's wrong, Churchwarry. We shouldn't drown at all, and definitely not so many of us."

He starts and stops a few times before asking, "Was it a bad thing that I sent you the book?"

"No." There's something else, though, something nagging at me. "A man I just spoke to, a carnival owner, thinks that the book being at auction means that the show went under. Some of the people in the book—Koenig and his family—there's no record of them after 1824."

There's a small silence while he thinks. I wait, peeling my arms from where they've stuck to the vinyl seat back.

"I don't know that I should be encouraging you," he says, though the tone in his voice says he's thinking more. "But the book is very damaged, and if the Koenigs were with the show . . . "

There's satisfaction. He's thinking what I am. "I'm thinking it was a flood. That could be where this all started."

"Maybe," he says. "If you have a year range it's a place to begin looking. Do you really think that a flood could be the cause?"

"I don't know," I say. "But my sister is pretty convinced I shouldn't have the book. I wanted to ask her about the tarot cards in it, but she ripped all the sketches of them."

"Really? Interesting. Symbols can be powerful triggers." He pauses. I plug my ear with a finger, straining to listen.

Churchwarry hasn't paused at all. My phone cut out. No connection, nothing but the brief memory of a window repair I had done in April, and falling behind on the phone bill. A repaired window on a house I'd just as soon fell off a cliff, a house I have to go back to in order to call Churchwarry.

The car flies over the dip in Buck Harbor Road, staying airborne for seconds. Enola took out the exhaust system here when she first learned to drive. When I pull into the driveway Frank's truck is still parked in it, its shadow huge. I could just ram it. I pull the emergency brake and cut the engine but don't get out. He's inside the house, his stark profile in the window.

I wait. A broken spring in the seat pokes my back, scratching a reminder of something. Three of Swords, a heart triple pierced. Eight of Swords, the man stabbed in the back, run straight through. I don't remember all the cards that were in the book and my sister eliminated any ability to check, but I'm sure some of them just appeared in her reading. Everything is getting mixed up. My mother moved back and forth between Frank and my father, and Frank has things I've seen in pages of my family history. Enola and Doyle are passing cards, sharing fates and futures, like ink bleeding down a wet page—the ruined end of a book.

A tap on the windshield. Small, pink, oval fingernails surrounded by dotted skin. Alice.

"What happened between you and my dad?" Little wisps of her hair escape her braid, giving her the curious look of being almost on fire. "I asked you to stay away from him. This is why I didn't want you taking his money. He's been in there for hours and says he won't come out until he talks to you. What did you say?" Her voice is high, tight.

I didn't say anything, he did the talking. No, that's a lie. I told him I'd fucked his daughter—but of all the sins spoken, that was the least. That was the one thing I did right. And now I know I won't tell her; it would kill a piece of her.

She crosses her arms over her stomach. "You didn't tell him, did you? You didn't tell him I slept with you." I glance back across the street. Leah is peeking out from a bent slat in a window shade. Our eyes meet and the blind snaps shut. Alice takes my silence as assent. "You did? Jesus. Why? That wasn't for you to say." The mix of anger and worry is striking on her. "Go talk to him," she says, softer now. "I can fix it later, but just get him out of the house. He's got high blood pressure. Being this upset isn't good for him."

She knows his blood pressure, his cholesterol, each arthritic joint. Things I never knew about my father, even after he was gone.

"I'm not taking money from your dad. I told him."

"What?"

"I don't want it. You're right; he's too wrapped up in my family. The money would make it worse and I don't want that. I'm letting the house go." I didn't know until I said it, but it's true. "Please don't be mad at me anymore."

"I don't want to be mad, but you keep doing things." She steps back from the car enough so that I can open the door. When I get out she asks, "Where are you going to go?"

"I don't know. I could go with Enola for a while. Her boss seems all right. I put in for the curator job in Savannah and they're calling my references. Liz can talk anyone into anything, so there's a chance."

"Oh," she says, and I wish it was more. She looks down at my ballooned ankle. "Foot any better?"

"Better is a range."

She laughs and I've never heard her more bitter. "Can you please get him out of there before he gets hurt?" She leans against the side of the car, khaki summer shorts riding up her thighs.

"Was he a good father?"

"Excuse me?" Her eyebrows pull together and the freckles between them kiss.

I repeat.

"Yes, he's a good father," she says. "Stubborn, but good."

"When you skinned your knee, did he put a Band-Aid on it?" I bandaged Enola's legs, pulled out splinters, not Dad. I've got scars on my shins, my knees, my hands, that Dad never touched or cleaned.

"Sure." She shifts her weight to one hip in that cockeyed stance that belongs only to women. "Can't you just get him? He won't come out and it's scaring the hell out of my mother. Whatever is going on with you two, it's not her fault, or mine."

"He was at graduation, right?"

"Yes," she says. She looks like she might cry, which makes me wonder if I know her at all. "Yes, he could be shitty and stubborn, and maybe a little obsessed, but he helped me sell Girl Scout cookies. Took me to the circus. He was fine. You know, you were there."

I was alongside her, watching, wanting to be taken with her. The McAvoys were my phantom limb.

Alice glances back to the house. "I don't know what he did that you're so pissed off about, but it doesn't matter; he's not talking to me and it's frightening. Get him out of your house. Please don't be mean to me right now, I can't take that." She's bright pink, blondish eyebrows standing out against her skin. Upturned nose. Small lips. Square jaw. An exact cross of Frank and Leah, and I'm making her cry.

I touch her hand. She doesn't pull away.

"I'm sorry. I can't promise that he won't try to fix the house, but I swear that's not because of me."

"Okay."

"I'm sorry," I say again.

"I know." She squeezes my hand, once, quickly, then lets go. It's enough.

I have to go in anyway. Frank is in my house with my books, like he's sitting in my veins. For Alice I'll get him, but only for her.

She follows me, but I stop her at the door. "You shouldn't come in."

"Don't say anything awful to him," she says. A tiny burst of envy runs through me—I want that defensiveness. She would wake me up if I had a nightmare; she's that sort of person. She wouldn't care about my breakfast face. She would learn to love my sister because I do. For that, I'll talk to Frank.

"Honestly, it's probably going to be the other way around, plus it's dangerous inside."

"What did he do?" she asks, quietly.

Telling her might make me better in her eyes. Or maybe it would break her. "He doesn't deserve you."

She looks across the street, to the window where her mother watches. "Maybe. But I decide who deserves me."

The front door is stuck and I have to kick it open, rolling all my weight onto the bad ankle. Alice grabs my arm and holds me steady. Her skin is warm against mine and I can almost feel the paper cuts from library books, a chipped nail, but then she is gone. Back to the McAvoy house. Back to Leah.

Frank is at my desk, where the book lies open on makeshift props.

"You're back. Good. I thought—" He shakes his head. "I don't know what I thought. But there's something you should see." He hops up from my chair.

I close the book. "Go home, Frank. Alice is worried."

He frowns. "Let's not talk about Alice."

"Why are you here?"

"I need to show you something." He pushes past me toward the door. Two steps down the porch and he's heading for the bluff. Alice and Leah watch anxiously from the McAvoys' porch. Dragging an ankle that feels like an anchor, I try to keep up. By the time I catch up, Frank is at the cliff's edge, where the grass breaks away into a tear of falling land. "Look." He nods toward the shore.

"What the hell?"

"Exactly," he says. "I meant to let you cool off, let us both cool off. We said some things we shouldn't have." He digs the toe of one boat shoe into the ground. "I was taking the Sunfish out for a sail, but I got to the cliff and saw them. Damndest thing. Then I remembered."

Not hundreds, thousands of smooth brown horseshoe crabs are on the shore. This isn't what Enola said, it's not like when we were kids; this is massive. They stretch across the Sound like cobblestones. They don't do this, not during the day, and never so many, piling on each other in strata, like oysters. Something else is different. "The buoys."

"Damndest thing," he repeats. The swimming area has drifted out, back and to the east, toward the power plant.

"They're pulling them out to sea." I start for the steps but Frank grabs my collar.

"Don't go rushing off. While I was waiting for you I looked through some of your books." He sees my reaction and grimaces. "You slept with my daughter. I'm pretty sure we're beyond personal boundaries."

"Touché." I would tear his house from shingles to foundation to find a single hair of my mother's, to take her back.

"I saw that list of names, the dates, some of what you've written. I couldn't make sense of all of it, but I figured something out. You're worried about Enola. You think she's like your mother. You think she's going to die."

"I don't know." The things he told me this morning showed me that I knew far less than I thought. "But I'm worried."

Frank draws in a breath and lets it out slowly. "She's different from Paulina, I can tell you—sweeter in some ways, but meaner, too. I don't know, I saw those names and then I saw this. The horseshoe crabs came like this a couple of days before Paulina died. Thousands of them. After she was gone a red tide came through and killed everything—crabs, fish, snails—all of it; the whole Sound looked like rust. I haven't seen horseshoe crabs like that again until now."

So this is why he collects them, why he dries their shells and hangs them from his porch, and why, perhaps accidentally, he taught his daughter to love them. "Why are you telling me this?"

"You're looking for patterns, right? I could see from what you wrote. I don't know if that's a pattern, but it's strange enough that I can't forget it, and seeing this many crabs again made me sick." We stare down at the writhing mass.

"About Alice . . ." I say, because I feel I should.

"She makes her own decisions," he mutters.

"She's worried about you. Go home, Frank."

"Okay," he says. "Okay, okay." He repeats the word until he's worn a rut into it, then walks back to his house and the women waiting for him. I should tell him that I haven't said anything to Alice, that I won't, but I still want him to suffer. I look back to the water.

The beach is packed not just with crabs, but people from the other houses on the cliff. There's Eleni Trakos, I recognize her by her steel-gray bun and leathery skin, tanned to her body by decades of topless sunbathing. There are her grandkids, Takis and the other one. Next to her is Gerry Lutz from up the street, Vic and the cul-de-sac people, Sharon, the Pinettis. They cluster like it's a crime scene, touching, whispering, talking.

Eleni and the grandkids have their toes right up to the edge. One of the kids picks a crab up by the tail and waves it around; the body arches at its hinged joints, exposed, blindly searching for footing, and flinging back and forth with each movement of its tail. I look at Eleni, then back up the beach to Gerry, Vic and Maggie Simms, Terry, Sharon and the other cul-de-sac people. It's rare to see them all together. Weddings, maybe. I think the last wedding was Wyatt's, Gerry's son, and that was three or four years ago. And funerals, yes, everyone shows up for funerals. I can recall them all wearing black—suits, dresses with matching jackets, shiny funeral shoes. Eleni with just rings, no necklace.

At Mom's service, Dad had been flanked by Frank and Gerry. Frank stood at my father's side, mourning her too. Leah stayed with Enola and me. She put me in a too-big suit from the Presbyterian Church. Enola wore a black hand-me-down dress from Alice.

John Stedbeck paces by the boulder where Enola skinned her legs. Nervous and lanky, he shouts into a cell phone, bending and straightening, holding his arm out to search for reception. I borrowed his suit for Dad's service. My father's gray suit had been too wide at the shoulders and too short in the legs. He wore the black in the casket.

Faye and Sharon snap photos, Faye crouching as far as her knees allow. They brought us fruit pies, both times. Ted Melnick brought us a basket of oranges and handed it to me while apologizing. Gerry and his wife gave us lasagna, which Enola ate all of as soon as the house was empty. Eleni gave us baklava. "For the sweet in the sorrow," she'd said. Though food poured from the doors and windows, though each of these people hugged us and begged us to *eat, eat, eat,* we tasted nothing.

The clicking and thumping of crab tails hangs in the air; a roiling wave, they clamber at the shore. The wind is full of crabs and the beach is filled with a funeral party.

Back in the house I try Churchwarry, but there's no answer. Next to my keyboard is *Legends and Poems of the Baltic,* the other book I must return. Why did Mom fill my head with stories of kings under the sea and women who danced men into streams? I log on to my computer to find a short email from Anne Landry at Sanders-Beecher Archive. They're still reviewing applicants, but would like to schedule a call at my convenience. There are questions about my willingness to move since they lack the capital to fund relocation. I tell her I'll call in the afternoon on the twenty-fifth. There's also a message from Blue Point. While they thank me for my interest, the previously listed position in reference has been eliminated due to budget restructuring.

In the middle of my inbox, hidden among the spam, is a message from Raina at Shoreham. She's found Greta Koenig—rather, Greta Ryzhkova. My hunch was right, only she didn't bear her mother's name for long. It seems that her mother remarried, and Greta took her stepfather's name. A Victor Mullins of New Orleans. In 1826. The Mullins name pings back a glut of hits. But why the remarriage? Katerina Ryzhkova was widowed. I flip through the book, running my fingers along the warped pages. Toward the middle, before the switch in handwriting, there is a delicate drawing of a boat—it looks like a rudimentary prototype of the kind of steamers that once crawled up and down rivers throughout the country.

I look up to see the light still on at the McAvoys', and Frank and Leah's silhouettes on their living room couch. This is how it's always been. I'd thought it had been Leah watching us, but it was me on the other side of the glass, wanting in.

Then I begin the hunt. A hunt for a flood between 1824 and 1826, the kind that might swallow a troupe of traveling performers, perhaps a floating circus. The kind that might have killed enough people to imbue any objects left behind with a spirit of loss deep enough to cause a curse. I know in my heart this is poor research. Wild chases go against the fundamentals of good research. But the book found its way to me, which works against all logic as well.

Hours pass before I discover it. In 1825, the Mississippi River floods, inundating New Orleans. Katerina Ryzhkova remarried in New Orleans. It fits geographically and with the timeline.

I catch sight of a small sketch on the page opposite the little steamer boat. I'd seen it before but it hadn't seemed important, just another absentminded doodle of a man prone to think through sketching. At the corner of a page, just above a quickly jotted note about oppressive heat and fog, is a delicate brown illustration of a horseshoe crab.

I shut the book and leave the house as quickly as my ankle allows. I need to get into the water, to clear my head. My foot and the stairs make for slow going. The bottom two steps have washed out, but someone installed a pool ladder on the bulkhead, so I'm able to tumble down. On the sand, crabs scramble around my feet and over each other. The tide has come up since the afternoon, hiding the thousands more horseshoes that lurk beneath. They seem to part, making way as I shuffle into the water.

Three deep breaths, in, out, in, out, in, out. One last deep sharp breath down, spreading the ribs wide, stretching each muscle and filling it with air, and then I am in the black relief of night swimming. Below is life, tails switching against shells, above is water, then sky—in the in-between there is only me. I swim farther into the dark.

I open my mouth for just a moment, tasting the salt.

There is a cycle at work. My mother knew her mother drowned. My grandmother must have known the same. They must have feared, like every member of the Wallenda family who takes to the wire knowing the specter of death is a breath of wind away, until the wire becomes a curse. A combination of thought and tragedy makes it so. *Binding Charms and Defixione,* that bulky text Churchwarry sent, puts the source of curses as the written word, intent manifested through language. Below crab tails smack against shells, conjuring the image of Peabody's drawing. The boat, too, followed so shortly by the water-damaged pages, as though the sketch itself called a flood. My stomach rolls with a cold undercurrent.

Curse tablets bore the names of their targets, sometimes little more. To name a thing is to set it apart—imbuing it with power, or steering it toward destruction. Bess Visser. Amos. Evangeline. Curse tablets were hidden, buried where they wouldn't be discovered until long after the charm had done its damage. A discovered tablet could be smashed, breaking the charm, just as burning letters can exorcise old lovers. The book hid itself, through flood, finding homes with people interested in books and old things, people who wouldn't dare destroy such an interesting piece of history. Until it found its way to me.

It's ready to be undone.

I let my breath out and sink down to the sand bed, dangling my feet until they touch the smooth top of a carapace. It shoots out from under me, slick, and unknowably old. For the first time in days I feel like smiling, and almost gasp in the salt. By the time I emerge from the water, shivering, dawn has crept up.

I know what to do.

22

Peabody was elated at the prospect of Evangeline's pursuit of fortune-telling; it solved the problem of Amos's employment and afforded him the opportunity to exercise his creative capabilities. He spent days and nights sketching, searching through chests, and confiscating any errant piece of cloth or bit of ornamentation from other wagons—an intricate piece of ironwork from Melina's door, a length of muslin Susanna had left out, a tin of silver dust that Nat had held onto from his days as a smith—all snatched, borrowed, wheedled, and cajoled away. He refurbished Ryzhkova's wagon in what he deemed the highest style. Blue, yellow, and white paint on the exterior, trimmed with flourishes and fleurs-de-lis. Swags of cloth were hung inside the door and the interior was painted an eggshell blue typically reserved for women's skirts. Peabody painted compasses and stars along the walls, and supplied cushions from his own wagon. When finished, he conceded that he'd transformed Ryzhkova's lair into a passable replica of an ostentatious French parlor. His book noted the change. A single line scratched through *Mme. Ryzhkova, svc. Occult,* under which was written *M. & Mme. Les Ferez, svc. Oracular.* Evangeline became *Apprentice Seer,* and next to Amos's name *Wild Boy* had been emphatically stricken and replaced with *Seer;* small changes that meant a wholly altered life for Amos and Evangeline. For purposes of record keeping they became Etienne and Cécile Les Ferez.

"Russians are passé," Peabody explained as he bestowed a costume trunk upon Amos. "*Les vêtements,*" he said, dropping the box. It thudded to the ground, sending curls of dust into the air. "Think, Amos, all this time you'd been sleeping atop your future. Costumes from my last trip to the Continent." When neither Amos nor Evangeline took his meaning he elaborated. "France, dear children." He shook out an age-stained floral scarf. "*La France.* The very height of civilization, fashion, and art!"

Amos balked when presented with the trunk brimming with stiff white fabric, lace and ruffles. Peabody cleared his throat. "Changes are difficult, but 'tis this or *déshabillé.* I understood you were not well pleased with being a savage." He sized a pelisse against Evangeline's increasing girth. "Most concealing, most concealing," he murmured. "The French are—how shall it be phrased? Accommodating to ladies of parturient condition."

The voluminous garb of a Gallic bohemian well disguised Evangeline's pregnancy when she sat, and she sat a great deal. In her new employment she found that, were it not for the occasional pain and sudden bouts of sickness, pregnancy was not the inconvenience she had feared, and that she liked some of the changes reading cards brought.

Peabody spoke at length on aristocratic attire, the elaborate coiffures, wigs, and powder. "Lice," he chuckled, "the fiends are rife with lice." Evangeline took on the task of dressing Amos's hair in the heavy ringlets Peabody stated were fashionable. Each night she used a fine wooden comb to part his hair into sections, twisting each into a corkscrew, which she then tied with cloth scraps. While she combed, she practiced her accent, pursing her lips. By evening's end her face grew tired from overuse and Amos looked like a dandelion. While Amos seemed at first embarrassed by the task, after a week's time she felt him longing for the quiet moments and the simple pleasure of having his hair brushed. She would sit on a chest while he sat cross-legged on the floor, bracketed by her thighs, and gave himself to her ministrations. She watched his breath slow with each pass of the comb. It was good to care for another.

On first inspection of Amos and Evangeline in full costume, Peabody could not contain his delight. "Elegance, my lovely things. You shall be the jewels of our menagerie. Monsieur et Madame Les Ferez, we shall teach the lowly and the unwashed about refinement, their futures, and *style*."

But first, Evangeline had to be taught the cards. She was a quick study, provided Amos did not grow frustrated with teaching, which required the use of exaggerated pantomime and steering Evangeline's questions in directions he could answer. During demonstrations of the spreads, positions, and meanings, he was prone to break into conversations without signaling when a lesson's discourse had ended. Evangeline suspected that he held back. She noticed that he hid particular cards when they appeared, changing their positions or removing them. A blur of brown skin, a blink of color, it was difficult to see what he'd done. He tucked away the darker cards— the Tower, the Devil, Death, but also Swords and more often Cups. He kept secrets from her, but she could raise no complaint, not while she carried her own shadows.

If he withheld a piece of trust, she felt justified in having private places. In early morning, while he slept, she would swim. Though she did not miss her act or the leering eyes, she longed for water. As Amos dreamt of tobacco drying sheds and rabbit holes, she slipped from his side to walk into the river and wrap her arms in it.

She'd strip the weighty clothing of Cécile Les Ferez and again become who she'd always been. She dove in, slicing through the reeds, plunging to the bottom to taste the sweet earth flavor of fresh water. If they were close to the ocean and the rivers were salt, she'd float on her back, studying the changing line of her stomach, watching water sluice over it. When the moon was up she looked for silver glints of scales and followed currents the fish rode. With life blooming inside her, the water answered her questions with a whispered *yes*, and part of her knew home. In a tidal river on the Virginia coast she encountered a peculiar creature that scuttled the riverbed. She held it up and examined the graceful curve of its shell, its neat spike of a tail, and spidery feet that kicked and scratched at the air as she cradled it in her palm. A wonder just for her, she thought. The flickering of a child inside her laughed.

Evangeline and Amos tried out their new selves in the town of Tanner's Ferry, a stop on the way to Charlotte, North Carolina. "Excellent Ladies and Gentlemen," Peabody's voice skated over the crowd. "By special request I bring to you from across the wide seas, from the elegant salons of Paris, the toast of high society, advisors to royalty," he said with a flourish of his arm. "Kingmakers they are, fine folk, seers of futures and fortune, Monsieur et Madame Les Ferez!"

Amos and Evangeline stood on the stairs of their wagon, stiff in mountains of petticoats and lace. The crowd searched them over with wonder and suspicion. Tanner's Ferry was little more than a meeting place where farmers hauled their crop for sale and shipment, an outpost to the larger world. The houses were compact, easily built and destroyed should the town need to fade into the woods come another revolution. The women were wives and daughters of local merchants, and their enrapt expressions let Amos know what the lay of the night would be. The girls were taken in by the costumes, having never encountered such extravagance. Amos understood. They would be swamped.

"Counsel to all the French houses," Peabody rumbled on, enjoying himself. "Their visions have guided the hands of the powerful. Esteemed friends, I bring the luxury and privilege of their cards and sight to you."

The glint had returned to Peabody's eyes. He was in excellent form, rolling his *rs* and gesticulating. Amos looked to Evangeline. A heavy stomacher covered her increasing belly. In the abundant gown, her hair curled and woven into a complex structure, she was not the mermaid or the birdlike girl who'd stumbled from the woods; she was a refined woman, the sort who shrieked and fainted at the sight of a Wild Boy. This was the woman who tied his hair, tugged his lace, and made him into a man none would suspect had been a professional savage. Inexplicably he missed her.

"Don't you find it strange," Evangeline whispered, "that Peabody seems none the worse for Ryzhkova's having left us? She traveled with him for years, but he has every appearance of thriving."

Listening to Peabody, Amos had begun to think the same. He should be pleased to see Peabody so happy, but found himself thinking of Ryzhkova's turned thumb, and how she warmed bricks in the campfire to later soothe its ache. He squeezed Evangeline's hand, making their fingers a tight basket.

"He takes such delight in us that one might think he contrived for her to go. Terrible to say, I know. Yet it would not surprise me."

From midday to evening, breathless young women and men asked of love, riches, and hope. He listened to Evangeline charm them with a lilting voice he assumed sounded French. He was unable to concentrate on a single reading. Things were moving around him, subtle shifting that left him ill at ease. He focused on the tarot. As they appeared, he plucked cards from the deck and tucked them in his cuffs, cards Evangeline had no business seeing.

After a difficult section of road thick with mud and overrun with brush, the menagerie rested along the Catawba before their approach to Charlotte. Amos practiced a six-line spread with Evangeline, working with the undealt cards from a prior cross. At the end of the fourth line Amos's left hand had darted out to snatch a card just as it had been turned. Evangeline grasped both the card and his fingers. "Why do you hide them from me?" she asked. "How am I to learn to do a proper reading if you insist upon taking all the interesting cards?" She saw he was troubled and had meant to be gentle, but he flushed and looked to the floor. "Please," she said. She turned his hand palm up to reveal the card. The Devil.

Amos did not know that secrets bred their own sort of uneasiness, or that when Evangeline pressed her belly to meet his back she was beset with dark thoughts. He wondered if Ryzhkova's anger with him lived in cards, corrupting and warping his words. He looked at his hand in Evangeline's, not much more than a filthy paw.

He put away the cards they'd been working with and began to speak in earnest. He showed Evangeline the High Priestess— Ryzhkova. He flipped, shuffled, and turned, telling her of Ryzhkova's worry and how he was afraid she'd left it in the cards. He laid himself, the Fool, atop Evangeline's hand, to show her he wished to protect her from what Ryzhkova had feared.

"The Devil is it?" She took the cards from Amos's hand and set the six-line spread they'd been practicing. The Devil landed soundly at the fourth row's finish. There could not have been a less auspicious position. The downward turn of her mouth told him that she knew. "There was a woman who believed me Devil possessed," she said. "And a woman I loved believed that the Devil might be beaten back with a wooden spoon." Her laugh was high and mirthless. "Anyone defeated by a spoon is not worth fearing. You've no need to hide things." She did not mention what became of the spoon or the Devil who had wielded it.

Amos nodded but did not agree.

Well into the night they were awoken by pounding at the cart. Amos cracked the door to find Benno, lit by the wavering flame of an oil lantern and scarcely recognizable. The tumbler's normally placid face was distorted by dread, the scar tugging his mouth tight.

"Get Evangeline," he said. "Please." When Amos made no move, he continued. "The river. It has turned foul, gone dead—everything. Your woman, she swims there at night while you sleep."

Amos blinked at this revelation. She'd managed to leave him without his knowing. Benno had been watching.

"I will say no more, it would only anger you. Please, get your woman."

Sleep rumpled and twisting her hair, Evangeline appeared behind Amos. "Hush. I will come."

They followed the flickering light of Benno's lamp through the bulrushes and cattails that ran to the water's edge. Amos held Evangeline's hand and kept her close, watching her steps as Benno's light ducked between reeds, vanishing and reappearing, blinking in the wind. How little he knew her. When they reached the riverbank the light stilled.

"I have seen you swim this river," Benno said. "Do you know anything of this?"

Decay weighted the night, making breathing difficult for the stench of it. Evangeline had swum the river that morning, reveling in its sweetness. The lamp cast a glow over where land met water. The shore shone in a wash of silver and the air buzzed thick with flies. Piled high at the river's edge were rows upon rows of fish, dead and dying, gills gasping. Their eyes were clouded, sinister opals. She covered her face to block the smell, stumbling from the reek.

"Or this thing. Have you ever seen its like?" Benno crouched to pick something up from the ground. A dark brown stonelike creature with a leathery shell and a tail like a switch. It twisted in his hands, knocking itself from side to side. "Wicked-looking devil, is it not?"

Her stomach lurched. Though larger and more disturbing, it was the same creature she'd found in the salt river in Virginia. "I've never seen such a thing before," she said.

Amos's arm went around her shoulders and she wondered if he could feel the cold that had rooted in her bones, if he could feel her lie.

"Of course you've not." Benno's words were heavy and sad. "But they line the banks now. Do you see them? Like demons from the water. You swim here. I have seen you as recent as this very morning," he said, dropping the strange creature to the sand. Hundreds like it filled the shore, burrowed underneath the dying fish, hidden among the stones.

"The water was clear when I swam," she said.

Benno's eyes roamed over Evangeline as if cataloging the parts that made her. His frown snapped into a flashing smile. "Of course. What could you have done? I thought you might have seen something; that is all. I'm sorry to have woken you." He glanced back at the river. "However, it is certain we must leave this place."

Amos watched the bodies thrash on the sand. He knew of no reason so many fish would throw themselves to the shore, only that it was a sign. The frantic flapping of gills and the erratic beats of failing hearts ran through him. Bad things awaited in Charlotte, things that could sour a river. They must depart, but if they continued to Charlotte, he could not say they would not be walking toward darkness. It was certain too that something had shifted between Evangeline and Benno, and he needed to shield her from the man who'd been his friend. He thought of the Ten of Swords—the stabbed man.

Benno had called the pointed little creature a devil, and Evangeline understood that she'd brought it to her. She squeezed Amos's hand, felt the soft skin on his knuckles. It was she who'd fouled the river. She thought of Amos's hidden cards and her stolen swims, that they might choke under their secrets until they gasped like the fish on the shore. She carried murder within her and it poisoned everything she touched. *I am a killer.*

23

It's kind of a weird request, but anything you can do would be appreciated."

I hear her pause, but Liz Reed is the consummate librarian, and dances the line between friend and acquaintance. "I tried to check it myself, but I'm locked out of Grainger's systems. Janice had my ID removed," I say.

"Kupferman locked you out?"

"I skipped out on my two weeks and held on to some materials a little longer than I should have."

Liz does not disappoint. "That's still rude of her. What do you need?"

"I want to check on something. It's a riverboat accident, a showboat sort of thing. I'm looking at 1825, New Orleans, when the Mississippi flooded. I'm looking for the name of the boat, shows, survivors—anything you can get."

"Okay, that's weirdly specific. Any particular reason?"

"Trying to impress a potential employer," I say.

"Sanders-Beecher putting you through the paces?"

"Something like that," I say. She asks if I've got a backup plan. "I may travel with my sister for a while. Oh, if you come up with anything call me at the house. My cell is out."

I'm thanking her when she asks, "Did something happen to Alice McAvoy?"

"No, why?"

"I spoke to her yesterday and she sounded awful. You two are close; has she said what's going on?"

"Nothing that I know of," I say. The lie feels square on my tongue. I thank her again, hang up, cross Liz Reed off my list, and move on. Raina at Shoreham and then Elisabeth Booker at Center are next on a list of five—all of whom I've helped find books, sat with through conferences, bemoaned budgets with, and commiserated with over the demise of the card catalog. They're relieved that I'm not still asking for a job. If I'm not looking it preserves the hope that work exists for people like us. An hour later I have a small army searching out Peabodys, and the descendants of Madame Ryzhkova's granddaughter, Greta Mullins. Tennen, Bonn, Duvel, Trammel, Petrova, Visser—in the end my bizarre family was not so difficult to track. Even in a sea of names a drowning mermaid has a way of standing out.

Soon I'll have more answers, but right now I know that Alice sounded terrible. And I'm the likely cause.

The lights are on at Frank's house. They never went off. Eventually the silhouettes moved, Leah first, then Frank much later; part of me hopes she broke whatever's left of his heart. No one has come in or out, though it's already midmorning. Alice could be in there with them. There was already a worn sadness to her when her hand touched mine as we leaned against the car.

I try Churchwarry, but there's heavy static on the line.

The book is open, spine cracked, abused in a way that no one with respect for paper should ever do. It's not quite a Gutenberg Bible, but something this old is meant to be carefully handled. Held by a bookbinder, sewn and glued. Board, leather, paper pricked to better take ink, scratched by quill, nib, even fingernails. Though it seems impossible to stumble on our past in what amounts to a hand-written journal, it feels right, a satisfying answer to a question I'd always wanted to ask. The book traveled from hand to hand, father to son it seems, until it was lost, surfacing again at Churchwarry's estate auction.

My family's drownings passed silently through generations. Was it because we wandered, because our footprints washed away? In the first cold hours spent underwater holding our breath, Enola and I knew we were different. Drowning is in our marrow. Our mother knew she was different. She found Bess Visser's name and knew that more than just her mother had drowned. In that moment of touching that cursed past, did she feel her own ending, drowning like those before her?

To break a curse you destroy the source. My recourse is to obliterate our history, all evidence that Enola and I are descendants of the extraordinary. The book is the only record of a family I will never know—a mute boy, a mermaid, fortune-tellers—and part of me will be lost with its destruction. Yet it's an incomplete record. There is no Celine Duvel or Verona Bonn in its pages. My mother's name belongs there too. Generations of drowning women and disappeared fortune-tellers are absent from its story. This fractured work, this cursed thing, is only part of us, just a beginning.

But it's a map.

I write everything I can, page by page, for hours, until my hand cramps. I shake it out and begin again. Names, dates, places, bits of lines Peabody found amusing. *"Simple is the lamb who makes the wolf its confessor."* Cities traveled to, New York, Philadelphia, New Castle, Burlington, Tanner's Ferry, Charlotte. Vissers, Ryzhkova, Koenig, and those whose names were not paired with a last—origins unknown. Any questions I have about copying the information are silenced by what I've read in *Binding Charms*. What makes a curse isn't the words themselves, but the will bound to them, intention married to ink and tragedy. A blister bursts in the cradle between my thumb and forefinger, a stinging drop of lymph falls, smearing a word. I can break the curse but preserve the history.

A car pulls into the driveway, followed by an insistent pounding recognizable by its annoyance.

"It's open."

Enola stomps in with Doyle behind her, a languorous presence. "I told you to come back. Where the hell have you been? I tried your cell but it's going to voice mail."

"It got shut off. Watch the floor." I gesture to the hole.

"Was that there the other night? What the hell happened?"

"Pothole," Doyle says, grinning.

Enola edges around the living room, eyes roaming the floor and walls. "I thought you didn't want to come back here. That's what we agreed. Thom said he's good to take you on when you're ready." She pauses by the picture of her and Mom, the picture Frank took. "You can't be here anymore. Get your stuff and come with us for a while. It'll be fun."

"Little Bird, what's a day's difference going to make? He can catch up to us." To me Doyle says, "We're heading to Croton for some of August before we swing down south again. Atlantic City for part of the fall, then down south." He leans up against the door and props his feet on the frame, worn boot heels showing this to be a favorite position.

She shoots him a look.

"I'll come with you," I say. "There's a curator job in Savannah I'm looking into. I just need to take care of something first."

"If it's about the book, it has to stop, Simon. You're scaring me. If it's about Frank and Mom—let it go. She's dead and there's nothing he can do to take it back." As if on cue, Frank's truck starts up. We watch it roll out of the driveway and down the street—to the marina, to the bar, to wherever sad men who've fucked their best friends' wives go.

"I think we should have a last bonfire before we go." The idea is so quick, so natural, it's almost brilliant. "Remember when we were little and we used to cook out?"

"No," she says. Doyle is up from his post at the door, rubbing his hands against her shoulders.

"It was great. Corn and hot dogs, burgers, lobsters, too. Dad and Frank would make a bonfire and let us toast marshmallows." The *us* who toasted marshmallows was Alice and me. Even then we had our shared and parallel lives, watching each other while flakes of charred sugar and cornstarch flew into the sky. "I want a last bonfire. I want one good memory here. We deserve a good memory."

"As if one bonfire could fix it," she says.

I picture Alice across that fire, Alice standing on my porch, furious, Alice at the restaurant waiting for me while I talked to Enola, Alice on a date with me, without *me*.

"Haven't I been here every time you've called? Haven't I always answered, even when it's three A.M. and you need me to drive somewhere to take care of you? Haven't I always? I carried you when you were bleeding. I patched you up and I waited for you to come back. Don't you know that's why I stayed? I thought you'd come back but you never did." Enola was never abandoned; I was. I have the right to guilt. "I want one last bonfire."

She shakes off Doyle's hands and flops down on the couch. The floor squeals and we all hold our breath to see if it will give out. It doesn't. I've got her; she's pissed off, nearly crying, and thinking of a hundred things to yell at me, but I have her. She looks at Doyle, then me. "Then you'll come with us?"

"Then I'll go with you."

"Fine."

"Cool, cool," Doyle murmurs.

"Good. Thank you," I say. I get up, test my weight on my ankle. The pain is still there, though duller than yesterday. "I want it to be perfect." I turn to Doyle. "I need you to help me get something."

Doyle and I stand outside Frank's workshop. Enola is inside with Frank's wife, having refused to participate in these activities. She's checking on Leah, to see how she's holding up and to keep her distracted. Once Leah let her in, Doyle and I went to the barn. He offered me his shoulder when my ankle threatened to roll. He has no objection to what we're about to do.

"I get it, man. Dude took a wrecking ball to your family so you want to torch a few of his things. I totally understand. It's okay."

In front of the workshop it's not okay. A large padlock hangs on the door latch, rusted and intimidating. Of course it's locked. Why would I think it wouldn't be locked?

"We need bolt cutters," I mutter.

The man next to me tilts his head, swings an arm back behind his neck and pops his shoulder in a gruesome cephalopodan spasm. "Nah," he says. "We're good. I got it. Hang on a second." He disappears for a few minutes, leaving me alone with the light-headedness that seems to accompany impending thievery. Eventually he comes loping back, empty-handed. "Car," he says, by way of explanation. I must look confused because he adds, "Paper clip," and pulls a large silver clip from the pocket of his baggy cargo shorts. "Always got a few."

Before I can respond he's already unbent the clip, straightening one end and leaving a large hook at the other, clearly something he's done before. He drops into a crouch below the lock, and begins to gently work the straight end of the clip inside. His tongue pokes from the corner of his mouth. He strokes the top of the lock, as if feeling for movement. Suddenly, he flicks his wrist and the lock twists open, pulling free. He spins the paperclip around on his finger and stuffs it back into his pants. "Haven't done it in a while, but you never really forget."

"Doyle, why do you know how to do that?"

A shrug, the tiniest movement of suckers at his brow. "I used to play around with stuff like that when I was a kid. Wanted to see what I could get into. Started out because I always forgot my keys. Figured it was a good idea to make it so I didn't need them." He opens the door.

"Did you ever steal the change out of pay phones?"

He winks and smiles broadly, enough to be charming. "Now

why would I do that?" Unlikely as it should be, my sister has found her perfect match.

Frank's workshop is littered with empty bottles, freshly accumulated since I was last here.

"I'll get the paintings. You work on the curtains."

We pile it all, portraits and fabric, onto the frame of the dory Frank was working on. It needs to be gone, everything that was drawn in the book, because it, too, is marked by tragedy, if not intent. I'm moving slowly, awkwardly, but Doyle manages the curtains with an acrobatic grace, jumping and tugging, flinging the fabric over his shoulders.

"You're freaking Enola out, you know," he says, tossing a length of curtain onto the boat's bones.

"I don't mean to."

"Yeah, I know. But just—I don't know. I'm worried about her a little, okay? She talked like you guys were really close. I thought her coming here and seeing you would make stuff better, but then you're not close and you're not so good either. This is making her worse."

"Worse how?" I stack the pictures on top of each other, bearded face upon bearded face, stern-looking people, vaguely Slavic.

"You saw," he says. "She doesn't do that, not to kids. She sometimes messes around with people who are assholes, but she never does a reading like that to kids. I've never heard her talk like that before."

I tell him not to worry, because it's all I can do. I'm not sure if I can explain how burning a few things will make everything better, or how much of this is hinged on hope. "Let's get this stuff to the beach. She may not remember it, but she loves bonfires. They're good for the soul."

Doyle carries the bulk of things down to the beach, where we heap it all on a flat stretch of bulkhead to keep it from being swarmed by horseshoe crabs. We stare down at the scrabbling throng.

"No worries," he says. "I'll find some wood and kindling and see what I can set up. You get Enola, I'll get this."

"Thanks."

"Hurry up. Smells like lightning." He bends over the bulkhead and pulls from it a piece of driftwood that was sandwiched in the space between the posts and the boards. The Electric Boy not only juggles lightbulbs, but he can pick locks and smell lightning. A bubble of laughter rises.

Enola is more than happy to be rescued. Frank told his wife everything, from the story about his palm being read, to how my mother brought him coffee each morning, and about the house. When Leah opened the door her face grayed at the sight of me and for a brief second I thought she'd be sick. I thought I might be sick as well.

"I'm sorry," I told her.

"For what?" Leah said. "It's not as though you did it."

"Are you okay?" I asked, because it's what you're supposed to ask, and following the prescribed motions is all we can do.

She laughed, loud and fierce. "I'll be fine," she said. "It's not like I didn't have other options. It's not like I don't have choices." She leaned against the door. "I could take him for everything, you know. I could kick him out. But right now, right now, I'd like to see what his back looks like after a week of sleeping in his workshop. Then, we'll see. Nobody loves you quite like someone who's sorry." She smiled and her eyes took on a hard edge. "We'll see."

For a moment I pictured Alice's straight back, grinding coffee, and Frank, curled inside the skeleton of the dory in the barn, sinking into the frame.

Then my sister appeared behind her and we left Leah alone.

"She spent last night and this morning finishing the wine," Enola says as we walk down the drive. "I don't mean a bottle either. She finished *all* their wine. I'm surprised she isn't dead."

"It looks like Frank did some of that too. The barn was filled with bottles. Was Alice in there?"

"No."

"Good."

"This sucks," she says softly. "I loved them. I mean, didn't you want to be their kid even just a little bit, even just once?"

"Sure," I say. "Once in a while. Couldn't help it." But then, maybe being us wouldn't have been quite so terrible were it not for Frank. "Leah will be fine," I say.

"She's tough," Enola answers. Then after a while: "Did you get what you came for?"

I nod. "Doyle picked the lock on Frank's barn. Did you know your boyfriend is a thief?"

"We've all got to be something," she says.

Dusk has fallen and Doyle appears to have been right—thunderheads are pushing in from the west. We'd best get moving. I tell Enola that I'll meet her down on the beach; I need to swing back to the house to get something.

Climbing down the ladder rungs to the beach is difficult with the book and a bottle of lighter fluid under my arm. It would be easier to drop everything down, but the book would be mobbed by crabs, and the last thing I need is to have the thing get so damp it won't burn.

And maybe I want to hang on to it a little longer, this last piece of us.

Once you've held a book and really loved it, you forever remember the feel of it, its specific weight, the way it sits in your hand. My thumb knows the grain of this book's leather, the dry dust of red rot that's crept up its spine, each waving leaf of every page that holds a little secret or one of Peabody's flourishes. A librarian remembers the particular scent of glue and dust, and if we're so lucky—and I was—the smell of parchment, a quiet tanginess, softer than wood pulp or cotton rag. We would bury ourselves in books until flesh and paper became one and ink and blood at last ran together. So maybe my hand does clench too tightly to the spine. I may never again hold another book this old, or one with such a whisper of me in it.

But on the beach stands my sister. She is not in my books, and what kind of man would choose words that are already written over what might still be? When I carried her, her legs torn open, part of her flowed into me, and who would I be if I could not part with this beautiful thing for the person to whom I promised, "I will take care of you." I said always. Even if it meant hurting me.

I dig my good foot into the sand for balance.

Doyle has made a driftwood tepee, under which the curtains and paintings are stashed in a pile. Enola stuffs dry grass in the folds, sticking pieces anywhere they will stay.

I thank him and he shrugs. "Don't know if it'll light. I put the parts with the chains on the bottom. Figure that'll keep any of the damp in the sand from creeping up too high."

I shake the bottle of lighter fluid. "Hopefully it won't be a problem." His eyes gleam.

Crabs scuttle around us. Enola kicks at them, swearing. Yes, I remember walking into the water, how they crawled up me and it felt like an itch being scratched. And I remember her sitting back on the shore, knees pulled into her chin, petrified.

I will make things better.

I douse the wood and the curtains, squeezing until the bottle splutters out its last drop. The fumes are strong enough that even the crabs move back, forming a circle around us. I tear a page out, then tuck the book into the very top of the pile, nestling it between a curtain and a log. The page is ruined, an illegible muddle of brown and blue ink, unable to speak the names that were written on it. I roll it tightly and set Enola's lighter to it.

I only need to touch the burning paper to the curtains. A wall of heat pushes back as the pile becomes a Technicolor bright chemical blossom. Eyebrows and eyelashes singe and I fall. Enola and Doyle pull my shoulders, dragging me from the inferno. There is a putrid stink—smoke and rot together. The hair burned off my forearm and foul-smelling soot dusts my skin.

"Holy shit," Enola shouts. She repeats it like a mantra, *holyshitholyshitholyshit*. Soon it falls apart into laughter. The chemicals burn off and the fire settles to a slow roar as tinder smolders and logs catch fire. I watch a curse's touch turn to ash.

The crabs back away from the fire, retreating toward the water, and Enola and Doyle sit in the sand beside me. It looks like one of the fires Frank and my father built. If I leaned just to the other side I might see Alice, light hopping across her freckles. If I looked out to the water, I might see Mom swimming or hear her calling me. *Simon*.

"You burned the book," Enola says. She briefly touches her forehead to my shoulder. The gentle press is her thanks. Words she's always had trouble with.

"I burned everything. I got caught up in it because I lost my job."

"Good. Feel better?"

"Yes." My ankle hurts and my head still aches from where I hit it, my eyes are bloodshot, I'm gutted from destroying a priceless book, and I nearly incinerated myself. I feel remarkably good.

We watch the fire devour the last of the curtains, leaving nothing but the chains, glowing snakes in the sand. The wind picks up and carries sparks across the beach and into the water. Ashen remnants of Peabody's writing.

Doyle sniffs. A snap cuts through the air, a searing blue flash set upon by thunder. Then, then it begins to rain.

24

The wagon struck a stone, jostling Peabody and sending pages of correspondence fluttering to the floor. As troupe master, he eschewed driving in favor of minding the books, plotting routes, and managing the direction and composition of the acts comprising the show; the pitfall of the arrangement was suffering Nat's reckless hands at the reins. The previous day the strongman had driven over a large root, causing Peabody to spill a bottle of ink on the only cushion he'd not sacrificed to the Les Ferez act.

He was moving in the direction of sophistication. To see this progress he need look no further than Amos—from savage to mystic, to courtier with lovely wife—a remarkable transformation. The next step would be to get the troupe off the road. Peabody nipped at the end of a seagull-feather quill he'd acquired; the birds were unpleasant but made for excellent writing nibs, firm, yet flexible enough for sketching.

The ratio of days spent in each town versus the time in travel was disheartening. He lacked funds for anything approaching the arena he'd trained in. *Boats,* he mused. Were he to obtain a boat, they might float from city to city, alight for shows, and sleep aboard at night. The cart bounced as it hit a rut. A boat would mean no more impassable roads and no more of Nat's infernal driving.

He returned to his correspondence—a letter from his son. Zachary knew his father's routes and made a habit of sending word to towns he frequented, and the boardinghouse in Tanner's Ferry held his letters for months. The letter had come from Philadelphia. *June 1798.* Peabody grimaced. Had he known that Zachary had been in Philadelphia, he would have skipped New Castle if only to set eyes upon the boy again. *Man,* he corrected. Zachary was no longer the sprite he'd taught sleight of hand; he was grown.

Dearest Father,

I am certain this letter finds you well at Tanner's Ferry, and that you acquired an oilskin while in town. I recall your wagon being prone to leaks. Please do take care. You are not as young as you once were.

I have found employment at the hands of a wondrous fellow, Mr. John Bill Ricketts, and cannot help but think that you would find

his company enjoyable. (He is a spry
fellow and the most skilled equestrian
I have had the privilege to see. I
have witnessed him dance a hornpipe
on horseback, Father. Perhaps you
have met? Mr. Ricketts has said
that he trained with the Joneses in
London. While I know you threw
in firmly with Astley, it is not
so large a circle we move in. The
entertainments Mr. Ricketts presides
over are almost beyond believing. (He
has arenas in Philadelphia and New
York, each with a proper circus for
equestrian pantomimes and a stage for
entre-act diversions. A man called
Spinacuta—a silent type—has become
my instructor. Mr. Spinacuta performs
upon a tightened span of rope. In this
he is easily as skilled as Mr. Ricketts
is on horseback. Father, I've seen
Spinacuta perform a reel on his rope—
with baskets tied about his feet!

I am employed in the diversions, part of a comedic scene that requires me to tumble while bound in a flour sack. I am not yet so good as Mr. Spinacuta. Provided that I do not break my arms, I am confident I shall improve.

Mr. Ricketts is an excellent man to learn business from, Father. I believe all you lack is a proper venue, an arena of your own. I think too that Mr. Ricketts might benefit from your knowledge. (He is eloquent, but not half the speaker you are, and though he is confident and skilled in his performance, were he to fall, his enterprise would be unable to continue. You are wise to leave the entertainments to others when your mind is so keen with business matters.

I cannot say I am saddened to hear of Madame Ryzhkova's departure. While I am certain that you must be dispirited at the loss of her income, I must tell you that she was terrifying. Though it seems foolish to write, I am quite certain that she killed a little frog I once kept. Do not grieve her loss.

I must end this letter, as Mr. Spinacuta insists it is time to rehearse—endless rehearsals. I shall remain at this address until the fall, at which point I will travel to New York and Mr. Ricketts's second amphitheater. I shall take rooms at Larsten's Boardinghouse, as I have fond memories of our stay there. Be well, Father.

Your Loving Son,
Zachary

Peabody carefully tucked the letter inside his jacket. He missed his son, but envy stabbed him. Ricketts was the man he might have been had he not fallen at Astley's. Mindful of the wagon's rocking, he dipped his quill and began to sketch, first a curve and series of bumps, then a swift straight line. It was a moment before he realized that the thing he was drawing was the wicked-looking creature Benno had pulled from the dead river. He might easily call it a Sea Devil and display it. He toyed with the idea but decided against it, unable to shake the image of dying fish on the riverbank. A disturbing piece of business.

He blew the ink dry on the sketch. The world was changing. Fortunately, he was excellent with reinvention. *New potential,* he thought. *New things make us young again.* The Les Ferez idea had come along smartly. He found an empty spot of page and began sketching an elaborate water vessel, replete with rooms and stages, resplendent, yet light enough to float atop a shallow river.

While Peabody sketched and dreamt, the line of wagons followed the crooked road that ran the length of the Catawba. Axles whined and protested, cart doors swelled and stuck, and an uncommon damp settled over the procession as they moved blindly forward into the fog.

25

There is little to say about storms in Napawset other than they're never small, always dangerous, and any theater for the soul that accompanies thunder and lightning is replaced by fear of death by flood or falling tree.

Cursing and grunting, we climb the steps as rain pummels us. Water courses over the bluff, crushing the beach grass as it runs to the shore. Enola drags me by my arm while Doyle jogs behind. "Excellent stuff, man. Excellent," he crows.

A storm this strong means Hull Road has already flooded, the bend by the school is on its way to being impassable, and anyone who hasn't left Port is stuck; if they're bold enough to attempt to leave, the sea of floating cars on Main Street will stop them. We duck into the house.

"We can wait it out here," I say.

Enola disappears into the kitchen. "Where do you keep the hurricane candles?"

"Cabinets on top of the fridge." The last half of my answer is lost under a loud groaning. Doyle and I look up. Enola peers around the kitchen door. A dark oval on the living room ceiling pouches out like a pregnant belly, drips of water pooling at its bulging center.

"Shit," Enola grunts.

Seconds later a stream of rainwater hits the floor with such force that all three of us jump.

What follows is a dance of pots and pans, mixing bowls, mop buckets—things so long unused I'd forgotten they existed— emptying pots as they fill, and anticipating new leaks. We keep it up for an hour or so, rotating emptying and shuffling, until our hands are wrinkled and hair is soaked. Enola looks at me. "We can't stay here. The ceiling's going to come down. Simon, it's time to go."

In the past I might have gone to the McAvoys' house and asked to ride it out on their couch. That's off the table. I would go to the library, but I no longer have keys. Getting a room in Port is out of the question.

"We'll swing back by Rose's," Doyle says, touching Enola's arm. She pulls away as if stung.

She shakes her head. "Can't get there if Hull is flooded."

The roof creaks in earnest. "Get your stuff and get in the car," I say. "I think I know where we can go." I hope.

Doyle and Enola scramble outside. I grab my notebook and the stolen library books and dig through the closet for a bag to put it all in. Mom's coat is still here. I stared at that dark brown wool while she zipped me into a stiff red snowsuit, zip and snaps. I cried. It was too hot, too tight, the wrong color—not blue. She pulled a crumpled paper towel from her pocket and roughly wiped my nose. Yanked an itchy hat over my ears. *We can't have you freezing. If you keep crying you'll freeze your eyes shut.* I can almost remember her face just then, almost. Dad's coat is with hers, breast to breast.

I close the door behind me and hear a loud wet thump from inside. Don't look—it will still be there tomorrow. Now we need to leave.

Enola and Doyle wait in the car. She's put on a dark blue hoodie and has her hands stuffed deep in the pockets. Doyle is in the back, a duffel bag on the seat next to him. I ask what's in it. He says, "Stuff. Bulbs. Got to keep limber."

"Where are we going?" Enola asks.

"Alice's."

They both whistle.

"Think Frank told her?"

"Don't know. I hope not."

It's a slog to get to Woodland Heights. The roads are littered with downed branches and it's impossible to see anything but the rain on the windshield. No one says a word until we pull into the lot by Alice's apartment.

"We can crash in the car," Enola says. She's looking up at the lights in the apartments, the neat little balconies, glass doors, and porch lamps. I can't imagine what she sees.

"If you're with me there's a better chance she'll let me in." Alice might turn me down if she thinks I'm trying something—am I trying something?—but she wouldn't put three people out in a storm.

She doesn't answer when I ring the bell. We wait for a few minutes, rain soaking our clothes. Doyle rocks back and forth on his heels, his skin squirming.

"She's not here," Enola says.

"She might not be answering because, you know." Doyle shrugs. "Weird guy with tats ringing the doorbell in the middle of the night. I'm cool with staying in the car. Used to do it all the time," he says.

"She's not like that," Enola says.

"Wait, just wait." I knock, this time using my whole forearm. The dead bolt slides, the lock turns over.

Alice cracks the door. Swollen eyes, a red nose, face bruised from crying.

Frank told her everything. I'm sorry and wish we'd never come. The worst is she's a pretty crier and learning that is awful.

"Oh," she says. "Simon. What are you doing here?"

I tell her about the house leaking and not being able to get anywhere else. She opens the door a little wider, revealing a worn blue bathrobe, pajamas, and a pair of ugly gray socks with one of the toes out. She looks at Enola, then Doyle. Doyle waggles his fingers. Enola mumbles a greeting.

"I'll make coffee," Alice says.

"You don't have to."

"I've got to do something. I'll make coffee. It's what I do."

We stumble inside. Alice asks us to take off our shoes. We toss them into a pile by the door, sole meeting sole, sand mixed with carnival dirt. Did I do this last time? Despite having been here multiple times, I remember little of the apartment; I just remember her, leaning on a counter, falling on her bed, the refrigerator light and how she's the only person in the world who looks good in it.

Enola and Doyle hunker into an overstuffed love seat, brown birds huddling together. The taupe and peach apartment makes them look flat. I take the armchair beside them.

"Nice place," Enola says.

"It's good," he says.

"If you like this sort of thing."

"I'm not real big on leases."

"Me neither."

"I kind of like wheels," he says.

"Yes," she says. "Me too, me too."

Alice reappears with three cups on a white serving tray. Her shoulders hunch like she's been broken. She sets the tray on the coffee table, flops onto a peach chair, and curls her legs beneath her. "You can wait here for a little while for the roads to clear, but I don't think I can let you stay," she says. "I just need space tonight, okay? It's not you."

"You talked to your dad?" I say.

"Fuck him," she says, like a punch. She looks at some invisible point to the left of my shoulder. "He's like a wound that won't stop bleeding. Now that it's all come out he won't shut up. All those years he never said a thing, and now he has to tell us. Selfish bastard."

Her voice cracks and she sniffs and swallows, an awful sucking sound. "Why the hell don't people understand there are some things you don't talk about? You keep it to yourself so you hurt fewer people. You're supposed to pay with guilt. Guilt is penance," she says.

A soft ruffling to my right—Enola playing with cards. Doyle sips his coffee, holding the cup as though it's a delicate piece of glass.

"I'm sorry," I say.

"No," she says. "I'm sorry. I'm sorry he screwed up your family and I'm sorry he screwed up mine." Her chin starts to wrinkle up, tight little pits appearing.

"Hey," I start, but it's too hard to finish. I stare down at my coffee. It's undrinkable mud warmed over. Doyle has suffered through his entire cup. None of us has the heart not to. "I brought the books I borrowed." I dig them out and slide them across the small white table, toward her chair. "I'm sorry I got you in trouble."

"Oh," she says quietly. "Never mind that. Kupferman's an idiot. She's gone nuts about damaging materials and has Marci reshelving for three weeks because she was drinking a Coke outside the staff room."

"No."

"Seriously." Alice sniffles and rubs the ends of her hair between her fingers. I remember her sucking salt water from the tips of her pigtails. "Why did you take them?"

"My mom read to me from one." I shrug. "Ever love something so much you start to think it's yours?"

"It's good to have things that are yours. Keep them." She closes her eyes and locks her arms around her knees and I wonder if we're talking about books at all. She sniffs again, but says nothing. Silence blooms. Enola catches my eye. We should go. I set my cup down.

"I'll give you my library keys," Alice says suddenly.

"I'm sorry?"

She rubs her eyes and stands. "You can't go back to the house for more reasons than the leak. I'll lend you my keys. Go spend the night at the library." Then she's walking down the hall to her bedroom, where there's the mobile with a horseshoe crab, a creature she doesn't know why she likes, unless Frank told her that as well.

"She's drunk," Enola says.

"Probably," I say. "She's allowed."

Alice returns, leaning against the wall. Yes, tipsy. Good for you, Alice. I wish I'd thought of it myself.

"There's something I was supposed to tell you. What was it?" She waves the keys in my direction before tossing them to me. "The code is still the same. Kupferman says she's going to change it but hasn't gotten around to it yet."

"Thanks." We all get up. The storm is still beating down, rain slapping at windows and doors.

"Oh. Oh," Alice says. She pinches the top of her nose. The words come out in a great rush, "Liz Reed from North Isle called. Said she was trying to get in touch with you but your phone is out." She stops to take a breath. "That accident thing you were looking into checked out, she sent it to your email. What the heck was that name? It was something weird. Peabody and Sons Maritime Merriments." She scrunches her face. "Does that sound right?"

"Yeah, it does."

"Wow. Liz Reed. You called in the big guns. She also said that Raina found something for you on that Mullins name."

"Really?"

"Yeah, the last known relative is some guy in the Midwest. Churchwarry." I hear her, but she sounds like she's in another room. "Wait. That's your guy, isn't it?"

"Yeah," I answer.

Churchwarry is a Ryzhkov. A thousand ideas form and fade. Alice may have gotten it wrong; it would be understandable, she's worn out, buzzed. I need to talk to Raina, double check. I don't know what happens in the next seconds, when the door opens, why Enola and Doyle are standing by the car in the rain, or how it is that I'm alone with Alice on her step.

Alice leans forward and her hair falls down over her forehead. She shoves it back. "I'm sorry. I'm sorry I can't let you stay. I'm really ugly right now and I'm a little drunk and I need to be alone. I'll just look at you—"

"And see my mother."

"It won't always be this way," she says. "I need time. I need to be less angry."

"It's not you, it's me. It's always me." It's a thing people say, but it's true. If it hadn't been for me, her father never would have told her. "It's okay. I have a really terrible breakfast face."

A weak smile. "Don't. I know every one of your faces. Just put my keys in the book drop when you leave, okay? I'll get Marci to let me in tomorrow."

I could just lean in—a little kiss, nothing at all—but it wouldn't be right. She rubs her face, and I touch her hand. The hug is unexpected, but with her inside and me on the step below, we fit. And I should hold her for a little while. I want to. I could say something, but her cheek is on my shoulder and I can feel her body catching because she's crying again. Her lips brush my neck, light and awkward, but then she pulls away.

"Okay," she says.

"Okay."

She watches while I walk to the car, getting pelted by the rain. Even through sheets of water on the windshield, I see her in the doorway. She stays until we drive out of the lot.

"God damn," Enola whispers. "Alice McAvoy is in love with you."

I hope.

The car careens around the back roads, swerving around puddles, branches. Everything. "Pull over and let me drive." Enola's hand is on my arm.

"No." Hemlock Lane is flooded and the harbor is on the front lawns of the summer bungalows. A sharp left takes us inland, climbing up the hill toward the monastery where the brothers pray whatever prayers one says during storms. Churchwarry is Ryzhkova's descendant. He sought me out. "He must have known."

"Must have known what?" Enola asks.

"Nothing."

"The book guy?" she persists.

"Yeah," I say. "His relative, you tore pictures of her cards out of the book."

"Bullshit," she says, but there's no force behind it.

I don't have the energy to explain it to her. I assumed I'd find Frank at the end of the road, that his family had been passing down Ryzhkova's portraits, and that maybe my mother giving him her tarot cards had a certain poetic symmetry to it. It's nothing so easy as that. "Maybe you were right," I tell her. "Maybe he does want something from me. Damned if I know what it is, though." The road curves in hairpin turns—a nod to Robert Moses. Doyle's duffle slides across the seat and thumps into one of the doors.

"He could just want to latch on to you guys," Doyle says quietly. "You kind of have, like, a way of drawing people to you," he says.

I peer back at him through the mirror. "What do you mean?"

"I heard about you guys before I hooked up with Rose's. Didn't know it was your family for a while, but then Enola said some stuff, I saw you swimming, and things clicked. Your mom kinda sucked in your dad, and Mr. McAvoy." The way Doyle says Frank's last name is strangely respectful considering we just burned his belongings. He coughs. "And me. Enola just yanked at my guts, you know? Thom's half in love with her. You guys sort of have a pull."

Enola smacks the seat and screeches, "Yanked at your guts?"

"What exactly did you hear and from who?" I ask.

He stretches an arm across the backseat and drums his fingers; each tap spits a tiny nervous spark. "I was with a show that toured the Carolinas for a while. Had a high-dive guy who was real cool. Dave. We'd shoot the shit during downtime. He liked to talk old circus stuff. Told me about this family that called themselves mermaids because they could stay underwater forever, but eventually each one of them drowned." He shrugs. "He made you sound like the Flying Wallendas or something—long history, tragedy. Intense stuff."

Enola whips around in her seat. "Why the fuck didn't you say anything? Don't you think maybe you should have told me?"

The headlights hit something straddling the road—large, too vague to make out. There's no shoulder to go around, valley on one side, hill on the other. I slam the brakes. Flashing retinas. Deer. The wheels lock and skid. *Shit*. Water. We slide, the back end slips away, fishtailing. I turn the wheel hard. Enola shrieks. Doyle swears. The seat belt cuts into my stomach and we're spinning, spinning, watching rain roll over us and the lights from the town scream by. A loud crunch from the backseat. Something goes flying from Enola's hand. Her cards scatter across the dash, the floor, in the air around us.

Wheels grip, breaks kick in, we screech to a stop.

Gasping. Swearing, breathing. Whispered *Are you all right? Everybody okay? Shit, shit. We're fine. We're fine. We're in one piece.* Let the car gently roll the rest of the way down the hill. There's no body in the road, no deer. We pull over when there's a shoulder again. Shards of Doyle's lightbulbs cover the backseat. He sweeps them into a pile while Enola picks up her cards. Something's stuck to the inside of the windshield, held fast by a spot of water that got inside. A card. I pick it off with my thumbnail. A dark background, black maybe, hard to tell. Tall building. A lightning bolt. I know it. It's aged, but it's an exact image of a sketch in the book. Not a Marseille deck. Not a Waite deck. I trace my finger across the rocks.

"Give me that." Enola snatches the Tower from me.

26

Charlotte lay cloaked in the biting smoke of burning moss and deadwood. Though purported to be the next burgeoning place of industry, the town was barely more than a village built around two roads, Tryon and Trade. At their intersection was a courthouse, an impressive structure seated atop eight brick pillars that raised it ten feet above the ground. Below, a market buzzed, surrounded by a short stone wall. The people inside were stubborn, with a weedy toughness that had survived the war but not forgotten it.

"Chawbacons," Peabody called them. Expecting a cosmopolitan city, he was mightily disappointed by the town's lack in size and presentation. "The heart of industry, he told me. The finest minds in the South, why, they come from Charlotte, he said. And here we are in a veritable backwater. Mark my words, Amos, nothing but ill luck comes from trusting fellows in New Castle taverns. We ought to have pushed on to Charleston. Such time lost." He muttered and smacked a gloved hand against his wagon.

"We must make the best of it," he said as he addressed the troupe around the morning fire. "Culture is a balm to the soul. Here, friends," he said as he smoothed his coat. "Here is a town that is sorely in need of culture, the likes of such as we can provide." He declared that Amos and Evangeline were to be touted as beacons of learning and sophistication. "The Light of the World, you are, my good children. Be assured, should you have failings, this town will be none the wiser."

Haunted by the memory of suffocating fish, Amos and Evangeline wished to remain within the wagon rather than in town, but Peabody would hear none of it; M. et Mme. Les Ferez would keep rooms in a tavern run by the improbably named Captain Cook and his wife. They were to dine in costume and conduct themselves in what Peabody considered grand style. The job was well done. Hat shops, tailors, or taverns, wherever they went stares followed. At the end of the day when they retired to their room in Cook's, Amos and Evangeline closed their door and breathed in relief at the solitude.

Captain and Mrs. Cook were traveling to Charleston and had left the inn in the care of Louisa Tyghe, her son, and a harried kitchen maid. Mrs. Tyghe knocked too often, and her son trailed at Amos's heels, having never encountered a man who wore his hair in such a fashion.

"You'll be excellently looked after here, sir," Mrs. Tyghe said, straightening her starched red apron. "The bed in your room, Washington himself has slept in it. He liked us so well that he gifted us his hair powder. Should you need powder, we offer you the privilege of using some of the great man's own."

Amos found the idea of using another man's hair powder perplexing, but Evangeline had the grace to blush and thank Mrs. Tyghe before shutting the door in the woman's face. Amos did his best to rub the soreness from Evangeline's back and she began the ritual of combing and dressing his hair. At last they huddled on the mat-

tress, weary from the town's claustrophobic politeness—a politeness strangely at odds with the townsfolk themselves. Evangeline
fell asleep quickly, but Amos remained awake. In the quiet, he rested
his head against her stomach and listened.

On their second night the rains began.

Fine mist settled across the heart of Charlotte. Peabody ordered
a stage erected in front of an enormous rail house, but the ground
turned to mud and the platform sank under its own weight. Benno's hands and feet got stuck in the soggy red soil. Pins slipped from
Melina's hands and fire eating was rendered impossible. Sugar Nip
and the llama refused to be led from their wagon, forcing Nat to
carry the small horse in his arms.

Yet crowds lined up for M. et Mme. Les Ferez. Word of the menagerie had spread, drawing people from across Mecklenberg
County, people keen to be parted from their money for a moment
of gawking.

Shop owners waited, young women swooned. Children, never
had they seen so many children—little girls begging to touch Evangeline's sleeve, or to pull her hair. Boys were fascinated by her, but
also by Amos and the frilled attire that so differed from that of men
they knew. Young lovers, spinsters, the old and creaking, all sought
a glimpse into the beyond. Mrs. Tyghe visited and was rendered
breathless by the interior of their wagon.

"Oh, my," she whispered. "I daresay you are accustomed to finer
things than you'll find in Charlotte." Amos hid a smile. Mrs. Tyghe
would not have thought so had she seen his Wild Boy cage.

Exhausted at day's end, they fell to bed without a word.

On the third night in Charlotte the sky broke. The rain brought
mud from the hills and soot off the roofs in a ruddy deluge that
bathed the town in its offal. Benno and Melina did not leave their
wagons. Meixel stayed with the animals. The Catawba began to rise,
flooding the Sugar and Briar Creeks and surrounding the town,
yet Peabody insisted that Les Ferez work. A wondrous place, he'd
been told. Politicians came from here, men of learning—yet the town
was barely an outpost. Losses had to be recouped. If people wished
to give money to fortune-tellers, then the fortune-tellers must work.

Amos turned cards until his fingertips were raw. Evangeline spoke until her voice became a rasp. When her voice failed, Amos did his best to dance the cards to amuse the clients. He pocketed cards Evangeline should not see—not since the river, not since the rain had started.

On the fourth day Evangeline woke to a sharp pain. Her scream was soundless.

Amos and Evangeline had not left their room after the morning meal, causing Peabody to demand Mrs. Tyghe wake them. She called their names and rapped on the door until her hand ached with it. Amos appeared. At the sight of him—hair ratted and standing on end, half-clothed and gasping—Mrs. Tyghe shouted. Amos blocked the doorway with his body and fumbled for a card. After several failed attempts at communication, he gave up and allowed Mrs. Tyghe to enter.

The curtains were drawn. Trunks were in disarray with clothing strewn about—boots, shoes, brushes, combs tossed aside. In the heart of the disorder, on the great oak bed where George Washington had slept, Evangeline clutched her swollen stomach.

Mrs. Tyghe had birthed several children, both living and dead. Recognizing the condition, she said, "Monsieur, your child is coming. It is not proper for you to be here; I'll have the boy send for the doctor."

Despite Mrs. Tyghe's insistence, Amos would not be moved. He sat on the floor by the bed. When he reached to take Evangeline's hand, she batted it away. In silences between spasms, they listened to the rise of the rain. The storm grew heavier, but Evangeline found the pounding water a comforting reminder of the outside world.

When informed of the impending birth, Peabody clicked his boot heels and ordered the troupe to Mason's Tavern to celebrate, only to find it closed due to a flooded cask room. He settled for the parlor at Cook's, which sat on higher ground. The whitewashed walls and broad brown ceiling beams made a warm den for the performers. Ale flowed and the troupe claimed chairs, tested cushions, and watched as the streets turned to mud, then streams. They waited. Evangeline's child was in no rush to meet the day.

The doctor was sent for. Mrs. Tyghe's son made the trek down-river toward the Waxhaws and the doctor's home. When the boy arrived he was met by the doctor, who was well into sandbagging the house. The doctor's wife emptied washtubs filled with river water out the windows. The boy delivered his message.

"Women have carried about birthing for many a year without the aid of men, good son," said the doctor, wiping rain from his brow. "Sandbagging, however, is a different matter. Houses require man's intervention. Give us a strong back and lift."

The river continued rising. At midday the casks from Mason's Tavern floated past Cook's. The floor began taking water. The troupe lined the door with rags, sandbags, and tables to hold back the flood. Peabody took to a divan, reclining in relative safety while casting a suspicious eye to the rain. Benno and Melina balanced above the water on chairs. Melina asked if he would check on Amos.

"I believe I would not be welcome," Benno replied. "And what would I do?" Rocking on the balls of his feet, he frowned at the encroaching water.

By late afternoon Oren Mapother, the son of Charlotte's hatter, had drowned in the depths. The current would drag his body ten miles downriver toward Pineville.

Day wore into evening and Evangeline's body fell limp into the mattress, covered in sweat that smelled of iron and salt. She bit her lip until it was bloodied. Amos crawled into the bed and smoothed his fingers over her cheeks. Her mouth moved as she tried to thank him and he missed her voice. Evangeline contorted. Loneliness lurked within worry and made him grind his teeth. If she died and took the child with her, could he live? If she died and left the infant behind, could he raise it? It might have her eyes. It might be mute. Could he love the child that killed her?

In the night the Stavish farm livestock perished. The cows and pigs had crowded into the corner of the barn, trying to escape. Under the press of water and the weight of so many bodies, the structure gave way and crushed the animals. Those that survived made for a curious sight as heifers paddled down Sugar Creek, necks straining to keep above the tide.

In the creek, along with the cattle, floated the body of Eustace Wilder, a drunkard who had the day prior touched bloated lips to Evangeline's hand. He had stepped from his porch to shout at the storm, only to fall. The bald back of his head shone in the moonlight as the river coursed over it like a stone. The Presbyterian Church crashed down and pews piled against the courthouse walls like matchsticks. The streets of Charlotte were running over with scriptures.

On the second day of labor Evangeline took no food or drink. Melina was sent upstairs with bread but was turned away. The kitchen maid, fearing running through the dry flour, began to ration biscuits. The troupe became confined to tabletops. Peabody spread himself out over a stretch of the bar.

Amos dealt cards on the bed around Evangeline. What he read brought no peace, but he could not fight the slick rightness of a properly set card. He began to pick the trumps he desired, their words—happiness set beside her ear, home by her feet. He surrounded her with hope, each card a wish. He thought of life before her, the years in the wood and the running.

With night, the storm passed and the Catawba receded with the same swiftness as it had risen, pulling the creeks back with it. A last lightning crack signaled the birth of a girl, small, blinking, and silent. The father looked at the infant, red-faced and wrinkled with a dusting of hair as black as her mother's. Her wide animal eyes met his. Amos felt his heart begin to slow and still, finding the weight of the air, and the rhythm of his daughter's heart. On the crown of her head a circle of skin pulsed, shouting wonderful life, and terrifying him with her fragility. Had Evangeline been awake she might have seen Amos fade into the fabric of the room, vanishing into the gaze of their unnamed child. It was the first time he had ever vanished in joy.

The parlor of Cook's Tavern woke. Chairs that had rolled with the water came to rest once more. Benno climbed from a perch near the rafters. Peabody set booted foot to sodden board. With Meixel's help Mrs. Tyghe moved the rags, sandbags, and tables that had held back the water.

Into this slow-waking movement Evangeline descended, careful not to stir the child in the bend of her arm. Amos followed. One by one heads turned. Amos took the infant from Evangeline and handed her to Peabody. The girl yawned at the touch of Peabody's delicate hands. A smile crept from under the curled ends of his moustache. He'd not held a baby since his son.

"Dear little signet," he cooed. "Perfection, darling children. You have wrought perfection." He looked to Amos. "Shall we, my lad?"

Amos nodded and Peabody held the child aloft. All eyes fixed on the squirming baby. He began.

"Friends, children, grandest fellows. We are touched by the ethereal. From such loss as we have of late suffered, the gods have blessed us with a child of our children, a daughter of the menagerie as there has never been. Most precious friends, 'tis our solemn duty to grant this child a name."

Amos looked at his daughter and thought of the night he'd stood on a tree stump, when Ryzhkova had told him who he would be. His heart was tired.

"Ruth." Meixel began the calling of the names. Faces crowded around the wriggling child.

"Dorcas." This from Susanna, it being the name of a favorite aunt.

"Veronique."

From Nat, "Mariah."

"Danielle."

"Lucinda."

Names passed to and fro until Mrs. Tyghe emerged from the kitchen. "Bess," she said. The baby shrieked out a piercing wail. "My mother's name was Bess."

"It seems the whelp has chosen," Peabody said, returning the child to her mother with a soft pat on the back. "Bess she shall be. Quite well, for we must thank the goodly woman who has been kind in allowing our imposition." He flashed a smile to Mrs. Tyghe.

The warmth of beginning unfurled. With tenuous hope they set forth to greet the day, and Mrs. Tyghe went about the business of running the tavern. Stark, cold light filled the entry as they opened the door on the world left by the flood. A small wave rolled in over the threshold.

Charlotte had been stripped away.

"God in Heaven," Peabody whispered.

Gone were the tailors and the smiths. The grain mill lay in waste, destroyed. The courthouse had fallen to its brick-pillar knees. Trees lay like drunken men against hills and embankments. Bricks made pockmarks in shallow pools; there, the sign from Mason's; there a child's wooden horse half-hidden below the dark slurry. All that remained was encased in thick red silt. Mixed among the detritus were the same odd creatures that had been at the river. Dead, spidery legs in the air, their pointed tails stuck up from the mud like spikes. Though it lay far to the east, the air smelled of ocean salt.

Charlotte was no more. Cook's stood, the lone building that remained unharmed.

Mrs. Tyghe clenched her apron in her fists. "Should my son be—"

The kitchen maid took her by the shoulders and patted her gently. "Hush, Louisa. He may yet return."

Mrs. Tyghe lifted her head to survey the wreckage once more, and to search for her son. It was then that she spied, resting against the remains of a mounting block, the twisted filigree of the weather vane that had once sat proudly on the roof of the doctor's home. Any small hope she had was consumed by fury.

"You've killed him," she said. "You killed him sure as you stand here. Never have I met such cursed people. You brought this." She nodded at Evangeline. "You come here, saying you tell the future, things only the Lord would know, then lie up in my bed and bring the flood. You took my *son*," she shouted and turned to Amos. "You Devil, take you and your child. Leave here or I'll find who still lives and let them set their guns on you. Get."

Evangeline clutched Bess.

On the outskirts of what had been Charlotte, the menagerie's wagons were waterlogged yet functional, the llama and pig had been lost, but the horses remained dry, safe atop the hill past Sugar Creek.

They packed in haste. Peabody insisted that distance and time would remedy their misfortunes, though he found the words difficult to believe. Before the sun hit its peak they rolled onward.

"North," Peabody told them. "I find I am done with the South. Philadelphia," he said. "Philadelphia will welcome us."

Evangeline knew his words were empty. Looking over the destruction and at the strange peacefulness of her child's quiet face, she agreed with Mrs. Tyghe. Never had there been two such cursed beings.

27

We flee the rain, clinging to the library's walls. Blue security lights fix us flat like a photograph, burning everything away: Doyle, ink and skin; Enola, bones and a ravenous stare. She hasn't spoken to him since the car. Alice's key trips into the lock and turns with a satisfying crunch. The alarm squeals the moment the door opens. I find the keypad, punching in the numbers my hand has memorized the same way it knows to hold a pen or turn a page. The air is musky with paper, dust, and Grainger's unique redolence of disrepair. I move for the lights.

"No worries, man. I got it," says Doyle. He trots over to circulation and puts his hand to a desk lamp. One at a time, the fluorescents stutter on with percussive hisses, bathing books in cold green light. It's an uncanny thing to watch, but Doyle merely shakes out his hands when he's finished, as though this is as mundane as tying his shoes. Enola walks ahead, a visible shiver working its way up her spine.

"Little Bird," Doyle calls. She flips him the middle finger and disappears upstairs, heading toward the whaling archive. He starts to go after her but I stop him with a hand on his elbow.

"Don't. Let her go." Enola can sulk effortlessly for days. She once refused to speak to me when I brought Lisa Tamsen home after a shift at the Pump House. She shouted that Lisa smelled like old fry oil. I got seven days of silent treatment before she admitted that Lisa's sister had filled her locker with dissected grasshoppers from the biology lab. She'd glared at me as if I should have known what I'd done. I know what Doyle's done. "What do you know about us? I mean everything."

"Pretty much what I said." He shrugs and searches for somewhere to sit. He props his feet on one of the lounge chairs in periodicals and they land with a squish. "My friend collected circus stories so he'd have shit to talk about. He was big on accidents. Like, I bet you didn't know that they lynched an elephant in Tennessee, right?"

No. I did not. The wind has started clawing at the windows. Lights flicker.

"Yeah, this circus elephant snapped and killed somebody—trampled or strangled, I don't remember—so the town decides to put it down, but they can't figure how. They wind up using a crane to hang it. Anyway. He used to talk about train wrecks, fires, people breaking their necks on the high wire, trapeze stuff. Sometimes I think he was just waiting to see if I'd electrocute myself. I told him it doesn't work that way." He doesn't elaborate on how exactly it does work. "So, we're down somewhere around Atlanta and it's so unbelievably hot, and we'd just spent all day putting up tents. I guess I said something about wishing we had a dunk tank, and that starts him on a jag about mermaids. He says there are these women that pop up on the circuit every once in a while, they can hold their breath for an insanely long time and swim like they're half fish. They've been around forever. It's one family and they all look the same—black hair, and so skinny you could break them. Everybody takes them on, no matter what show, since a woman like that brings in cash like crazy, because you're watching the impossible, the actual impossible." He looks at me. Impossible meeting impossible. "The whole time I'm listening for the catch. His stories always had catches."

"They die."

"Yeah," he says. "They drown. Hardly any of them ever make it past thirty."

"Did you ask him how he knew about the women?"

"No. Dave had this way of picking up stories. I figure most of them were bullshit. I mean, drowning mermaids?"

"But you believe it now."

"The breath-holding? I've seen you swim." He grimaces, showing a slight snaggletooth. "The rest? A couple years later I'm working for Rose's. The first time I showed up with Enola, Thom took one look at her and I swear he nearly crapped his pants. He asked if I knew who I had with me. I told him she was the best damned tarot reader I ever saw. Thom kept asking if she swam or not. I said all I know is that she does cards. Pretty soon he tells me almost the same story Dave did."

"You know they drown." I won't say *we*. A question floats between us. Doyle nods.

"Enola doesn't swim. She reads cards," he says.

She hasn't shown him. She's said nothing of the breath-holding lessons, the hours I spent teaching her how to float on her stomach, how to push all the air out of her then fill up her belly, how to dive and listen to the water, or how we used to pretend that our mother was there in the deep. *She's out there past the rocks, plucking mussels from the boulders, eating scallops from the bay. She feels you holding your breath.* Enola's black bathing suit made her into a slick seal pup, a little selkie girl who trusted me when I held her face into the water. The trust is gone; she's been keeping secrets from Doyle, from me. "I'm worried about her."

"So why'd we burn that stuff? It wasn't about Frank, was it?"

"No."

Enola's footsteps pound down the stairs. Perhaps it won't be a long sulk this time. "It's freezing in here. I need a blanket or something." Her arms are hugged tight across her chest, her hoodie drenched. The whaling collection is kept cold; it's better for the books.

"There's always a coat or two in the lost and found. It's in the back of the kids' section, downstairs."

"I'll go," Doyle offers. He walks toward the steps, touching every outlet and computer plug as he goes.

"Does he pick up charge from that?"

"Don't know," Enola says. She curls up in the chair next to me. "He says it feels good."

"Strange guy."

"He's okay."

"You didn't tell him you can hold your breath."

"Why would I?" She stares down at her feet. Her red tennis shoes are wet all the way through. She peels them off, shivers, and tucks her feet beside her.

"Did anyone ever tell you about our family? If Doyle knows, someone must have told you. Thom Rose spotted me right away and I barely asked him anything. Did he tell you something?"

"No." A small tic in the upper lip.

"What did he tell you?"

"He asked me if I swim, the same as he asked you. I told him Mom was in a carnival. That's all." She takes the cards from her pocket and begins laying them out on the chair arm. A quick horizontal line of six, then clear. Repeat. Her fingers crab walk.

"Thom would have told you."

Quick six, clear, repeat. "I told Thom that I read cards, I don't swim. The same as I told Doyle. I said that if he bugs me, I leave and Doyle goes with me." A tap of the cards. Slide, shuffle, repeat. "Doyle would go, too. Nobody wants to lose him. He's special," she says. "I didn't know he knew about us." The cards slip against each other fiber against fiber, a little molecular exchange. Paper that old means the cards have bled into each other, becoming a single object, a single mind. "He should have told me."

"Why?"

The cards stop moving. "Because nobody tells me things. He doesn't. You don't. You think I don't know things, but I do." She resumes shuffling.

"You keep secrets. From me, from Doyle."

She shoots me a look. "Because it'd be good for him to know that I'm capable of carrying on in the footsteps of my suicidal mother. Who *drowned*."

Doyle nearly killed me trying to pull me up. Yes, it might be safer if he doesn't know. "Maybe."

"I wonder how long she was planning to do it. What if she woke up every morning for a year knowing it was one day closer? Maybe that made things seem more precious." She fans out the cards and then snaps them together into a neat pile.

"I don't think it works like that," I say.

"How would you know? Is there something you're keeping from me?"

"No." Silence stretches between us, filled only by quiet shuffling. She looks tired, washed out. "Are you sad?"

"I'm not like Mom," she says, softly. "I'm careful. I read cards, I don't swim. I don't tempt stuff. When you come with us, I don't want you saying anything to Thom or Doyle." She deals a perfectly balanced row on the chair arm. The Fool, the Eight of Swords, the Queen of Swords among them, startlingly familiar. They're faded, worn. Familiar is not even the word. I've seen these pictures before. This is a hand-drawn deck. Maybe it was hard to recognize because I'd seen them in brown ink, but I remember the curling shoe on the Fool, the tortured expression on the Eight of Swords.

"Found you a coat." Doyle jogs up the stairs holding an enormous black parka that looks like it's made from garbage bags. Enola stuffs the cards back in her pocket. He approaches and she hops up, letting him put the ugly thing around her shoulders.

"Simon?" she says.

"What?"

"There's water coming through the doors."

Underneath the rubber edge of the glass doors a dark puddle has formed, a black creeping stain on the green carpet. "Shit. Doyle, were there any more coats?"

"Sure."

"Get them. Coats, sweaters, shirts, whatever's there."

There are four exits to Grainger, the main doors, two fire exits, and a service door. Two of the exits are on the basement floor. The lost and found has only an armful of jackets and clothing, barely enough for one door. Doyle carries them all around his shoulders, a human coat rack.

"The rest's all bags and stuff. Umbrellas."

Downstairs is filled with children's books and newspapers, older local documents, and books in storage that no one uses except those writing theses, or me. Downstairs will flood quickly; there isn't a practical point in trying to save it if water from upstairs is going to rush down. Still. Ruined. Everything on the lower shelves, all those files. I can still feel the edges of each page.

"Simon?"

"Front door. We'll stop the bottom with coats and figure something else out from there."

A little boy's red winter jacket, a dark blue vest, a wool coat covered with cat hair, a stained sweater, a brilliant pink cardigan—I can picture it on Mrs. Wallace. They fill with water, soaking through. Doyle drags two chairs over to hold things in place.

Then comes the painful part.

Reference is sacrificed to the fire exit. A bottom shelf. An encyclopedia is opened and jammed into each crack in the door, volumes stacked upon volumes to make as close as we can to a seal. We tear out pages to fill in the gaps. Push back the water, don't think about the books. They would have gotten ruined anyway. Don't think about how tall the stacks felt when I first discovered Grainger. Don't think about how these shelves held the answers for me, to everything, to what I would be, how they were my own decimal code.

I feel Enola looking at me. "You're already fired," she says. "And you're probably saving books."

Doyle tears out a page covered in scrawl. "Somebody drew dicks all over it anyway."

That doesn't make it better.

When we can push no more paper, when there is no more to do, we climb the stairs to the second floor.

The whaling collection is cold, pristine. Plexiglas cases display scrimshaw, harpoon heads, and a blubber spade. The shelves have worn captain's logs, ship manifests, drawings, and letters in archival boxes. Sterile. A portrait of a young Philip Grainger hangs by the door; his round wire glasses and close-clipped brown beard convey both wealth and academia. There isn't a corner of the room that doesn't fall under his gaze. Alice likes to genuflect when she walks past him. The chairs here are softer than the ones in periodicals; this is where the money comes from and where it goes. If we're going to stay dry we'll do it here. Enola curls up in a chair. Doyle slides another chair beside her. She lays her head on his shoulder and tattooed arms snake around her. Somewhere between the car, the coats, and the water, he's been forgiven.

"Ever think," she says, "ever feel like the water is coming for you? The house, for sure. Your books."

"We're safe here." I watch her. Doyle's head begins tipping into the easy sleep of a child. Enola's eyes dart, eyeing the ceiling for leaks, I presume. "When I first started walking the buoys out, Frank told me that when we were born there were high tides each time, waves so big they washed over the bulkheads, right over the pilings. Everyone thought the docks would break, but they held. Good things can come with the tide."

She pulls her hood up and tucks her chin to her knees. "Frank is a liar."

She's right. I walk out to the stair rail and look over. A black circle has spread beneath the encyclopedias holding the back door.

She falls asleep against Doyle, his tentacles around her, skin embracing, ink embracing. I am out of places to go. Water has taken everything. The storm has even erased the pleasure of the fire. All I've done is burn our history and destroy a beautiful book. Then came the rain. Something's gone wrong.

I get up. The books downstairs may already be ruined but it's not right to let them go without a witness, and it's time to check on what Liz Reed found.

Doyle cracks an eyelid. "Where're you going?"

"Downstairs. I need to watch it go."

He nods slightly. Enola tosses in his arms, one hand darting out in a spastic thrust. "She's worried about you," he says. "That's why she came here."

"She didn't have to."

He looks around, lights sputter and blink—whether from him or the storm, it's difficult to say. "I don't know, man. Bad things have a way of happening around you. Just keep it together at Rose's, yeah? It's a good job and I don't want to have to find another." In his voice lurks the vaguest hint of a threat. His face remains calm, one eye half-open, nearly asleep. It should have been Dad's job to keep dangerous men away from her; now she's surrounded herself with an electric fence.

"I'm just going to the lower level. I won't be long."

The floor is wet, a thin layer of water gives the dark green carpet an enticing gloss, and a sucking sound follows each hobble. A deep ache sits in my ankle. I move books, put them on tables, but it isn't enough. It's hard to breathe; the room is thick with the stench of wet paper. I move everything I can from the children's books and lift them to higher ground—save the Thornton Burgess, the fairy tales, the Potter, empty the lower cabinets of any papers, everything I loved. I can't stomach watching books drown. A light hisses and pops, darkening the bank of microfiche machines. The tables fill too quickly and it becomes impossible to choose.

I wind through the rows of file cabinets—newspapers and journals stored on microfilm, microfiche, and paper yet to be digitized—unaware of what I'm looking for until I find it. *The Beacon*, for the week of my birth, then for Enola's. The Boater's Companion section with the tide tables and weather reports. High tides brought us, swells without the storm. The blame was laid on full moons. After the water rushed the land, the tide pulled the Sound back, emptying it nearly to Connecticut both times. For Enola there is a picture of a man standing out in the middle of a sand field where the harbor had gone dry. Boats ran aground. Fish died. Hundreds of bluefish and fluke drowned in the air. High tides brought us, and brought death. Under flickering blue fluorescents I look for my mother and find her storm. The week she died passed in a blur, leaving only the memory of being fed eggs and watching her leave, but there had been an event—a squall that came in fast, a red tide, and a beach filled with horseshoe crabs.

I go to my desk, what was my desk down here until a few weeks ago, it's still here, though it has changed. The book repair tools have been cleared away, the banker's lamp replaced with a fluorescent, the traces of me erased. All that remains is the computer.

It turns on with an alarming flash, but survives logging into my email. While it can't be safe to use electronics in a storm like this, time is of the essence. It's the twenty-third, and the relief that came from the bonfire vanished with the storm.

Liz's email is perfect, detailing an accident during the New Orleans flood of 1825, an entire showboat swallowed by the Mississippi River after days of rain. She found it in the *Louisiana State Gazette*. Most of the performers and animals perished with the boat's sinking. Among the five named survivors are Katerina Ryzhkova and her daughter, Greta. The child's father perished in the flood. The show's owner, Zachary Peabody, was taken to a hospital to recover. He later embarked on a long and disreputable career as a dance hall proprietor. As I suspected. Liz finishes her email with a small token: "Sanders-Beecher Archive is trying to get in touch with you. Your phone's out. Fix it. I think you might have a job."

Raina's email is next. Less eloquent than Liz's, Raina's message contains a list of names and abbreviations. Greta Mullins *m.* Jonathan Parsons. Three children: Jonathan Parsons, Jr.; Newton Parsons; Theresa Parsons. Jonathan Jr. died as a child, and Newton did not marry. Theresa Parsons, however, did. I read the line. Unsteady, I smash the print screen button. Seconds later an electrical pop comes from the printer. I stare at the screen. Theresa Mullins *m.* Lawrence Churchwarry. One child. Martin. I can supply the rest. Martin Churchwarry would spend an unremarkable life as a bookseller until one day stumbling across a fascinating book. Martin Churchwarry is a descendant of Madame Ryzhkova. Raina is brief, but her work is always thorough to the point of infallibility.

The computer blinks and the screen goes dark. My chest feels strange, hollow. Martin Churchwarry found the book and found me. He's a Ryzhkov. Is that why I kept talking to him? Was there a pull in the blood that kept me from hanging up on him? No, I called him. I did it. He sent the book, but I kept calling, pulling him to me. *Yanking at his guts.*

I rescue my notes from upstairs, where Enola is now fully asleep on Doyle's lap, her body stretched across two armchairs. I grab my bag and Doyle quirks an eyebrow. "Notes," I say. He says nothing.

I make the call from Alice's desk, because her chair is softer and it's farther away from the whaling collection than mine; it also smells like her, like salt and lemon. Her drawer is filled with purple pens, the caps ever so slightly chewed. Purple pens are for meeting notes. The receiver smells like her. Doyle stands at the stair rail, craning his neck, watching me, his head propped on one inky arm.

I don't wait for a greeting. "You're a Ryzhkov."

"Simon? I've been trying to get in touch with you. Where have you been?"

"My phones are out. You're a Ryzhkov. Did you know? The cards in the book, they were your family's."

He clears his throat. "I'm sorry, what?"

"I need to know why you sent me the book," I say. "It's important."

"It's just what I told you. There was something different about the book, wonderful, but it wasn't the sort of thing I could sell. Ryzhkova? Truly?"

"Libraries would have wanted it," I say. "A circus museum, maybe. There's always a demand for something that old, you just need to know where to look. You're a bookseller, it's your job to know where to look."

He sighs. "There's a circus museum in Sarasota might have been interested, yes. But haven't you ever felt connected to a book? My wife has a copy of *Treasure Island*. It's stained, missing pages, and it's in horrendous condition, but she won't part with it. I've given her others, beautiful printings, but she's not interested. That *Treasure Island* is *her* book." I hear chair legs drag across a floor as Churchwarry sits. "I went to the estate auction for *Moby-Dick,* but I saw that book in the lot and I needed a better look at it. I overbid terribly, but I needed to be certain I had it. Purely speculation, of course—nobody was allowed to get a good close look before bidding—but I thought there was a chance it was *my* book. The way *Treasure Island* is Marie's. But the moment I touched it I knew it wasn't mine. I knew it wasn't for selling, either, not at Churchwarry and Son. I can't explain it other than to say that it was begging to be given away. I kept it for a little while, looking through it to see if I could find where to send it. Then I saw that name. Verona Bonn."

"My grandmother," I say. "Martin, it was your book. Your great-great-grandmother was the fortune-teller in the menagerie, Madame Ryzhkova."

"You're absolutely certain?" He coughs for a few moments, not for sickness or age, but to gather his thoughts. "Extraordinary," he says. "The circumstances are so chance."

"I don't think it was chance. Books like this aren't supposed to leave a show or a family, but this one is different. Enola says she's never seen one like it. It found its way to you, and you found me. Like it was looking for us."

"How marvelous," he says, almost giddy with it. He's no longer listening to me, lost in his own thoughts. "To think of the time I spend procuring books . . . How fitting: a book procured me. Utterly fantastic," he murmurs. "I'd like to look at it again. Would you mind sending it back? Or better, could you bring it here? I'd like to meet you as well. It seems we should meet. It's as if we've been pulled together, haven't we?"

"I can't. I burned it."

"You *what*?" Behind me, the emergency door rattles, pushing against the encyclopedias. "What was that?" he asks.

"The library is flooding," I say. Churchwarry makes a startled sound before asking if I'm safe. "For the time being. I destroyed the book and everything from Frank's. I thought that would take care of it, like smashing a curse tablet—exorcism by fire, but then the storm came. Martin, something's very wrong. I'm worried."

"You think you've missed something," he says.

The water pushes forward and it's time to sacrifice another encyclopedia, and tear out another part of me. "I have to hang up, but I wanted you to know. You should know who your family was. I need to block the doors." I glance over to the chairs where Enola sleeps and Doyle sits, watching.

"Simon," he says, with a rasp in his voice that I haven't heard before. "Please be safe."

His words are heavy with rare things: care and possibility.

28

The menagerie fled Charlotte with a swiftness they had not used since a preacher had threatened Peabody with tar and feathers. They moved northeast, making no stops for as long as they could manage, camping at night on roadsides, away from towns, sending Benno or Nat ahead to purchase supplies rather than entering a city proper. They traveled this way until they ran along the Atlantic. "A restorative," Peabody called it, though all knew the break for what it was. They had been scarred by the drowned village.

With Bess's birth Evangeline's stomach rebelled against ripeness and carved itself anew. Her ribs stood out and it seemed each tug of the child's mouth at her breast sucked away life. She and Amos had spoken little since Charlotte. The cards became tools for divination only.

Peabody was the only buoyant soul. He sat Bess's tightly swaddled body on the high shelf of his belly, cooing and rumbling as he delighted in her. "Little starling, sweet Bess. Whatever shall I make of you? A fine mermaid like your mother? A gypsy as your father was? I think you will be far lovelier, my dear."

Had Amos not been consumed by the mother of his child, he would have recognized the profiteering gleam in Peabody's eyes. But Evangeline had begun to shrink away. When he laced her, the stomacher gapped no matter how tight he pulled.

"I will tell Peabody that I wish to take up swimming again," she told him one morning as they dressed. Amos flinched, breaking a lace. She sighed and searched for a replacement. "It's that or I will be a human skeleton. The water act always brought in money and we must be practical; the girl will need things." Wrapped tight in one of the velvet drapes from the Wild Boy act, Bess dozed in the costume trunk. Bess, whose birth had washed away a town.

Amos acquiesced. Though it cut him, if Evangeline wished to swim he would not stop her.

"Hush," she said. "I will still speak cards for you. I won't have you in a cage. Though," she added, "I would prefer if we begin to think of another act, another way."

Amos bit back his concerns. He worried at the nature of the water act in light of all that had happened. It had not escaped his notice that Susanna had ceased speaking to Evangeline and Melina barely murmured greetings. Benno had begun to subtly sneer as she passed. Once Amos lunged for him, but Evangeline had held him back with a hand to his chest.

"Stop," she'd said quietly. "He is afraid. If we give him nothing to fear, he'll come around." Nestled in her arms, Bess had cried out. Evangeline had looked at Benno. "I've known people like you." *I have killed a woman such as you.* Benno had walked away, but he'd shuddered; she'd felt it.

Evangeline had hardly slept since the flood. In candlelight she watched Amos's chest rise and fall, listened to her child's snores, and wondered what misfortune she'd brought upon them. Never had there been two such cursed people. While they dreamt, she spent hours with the tarot, asking questions and looking for meanings. *What will come of us? What will come of her?* A frightening pattern emerged.

The cards spoke of old wrongs, what had sent her running and what had happened since. The wasting death of her mother, Grandmother Visser dead, the disappearance of Ryzhkova, Amos's grief, the perished fish at the poisoned river, and Charlotte destroyed. She'd felt bold when Ryzhkova had confronted her, strong in Amos's affection and desirous of a portion of happiness, the same as when she'd met Will Aben by the Hudson. Ryzhkova had been right. Amos's life before Evangeline had been without worries; that was gone. Since their meeting, his face had gained hard, sad furrows. She touched the deck and her past and future spouted horrors, the paper recoiling from her. Amos need not know these things.

After a second week of clandestine prophesies, Evangeline asked Amos if she might avoid handling the cards during readings. Amos frowned but assented. The cards drove her to approach Peabody about the water act.

Peabody was delighted with the news of his mermaid's return. An extra half share of pay would be easily recouped by the additional gentlemen patrons that the act drew. The tub was repaired, varnished, and whitewashed. Peabody encouraged Evangeline to bring Bess with her as she practiced.

"We have no way of telling what our magnificent starling shall be." Peabody had taken to tickling the child's stomach when he spoke such things. Bess in return watched him, her yellowish eyes slow and unblinking like a rabbit's. "Broaden her horizons. Teach her cards, water, train her in contortion, juggling, anything she'll learn."

Amos abided the resurrection of the swimming tub, observing the sealing and painting from the Les Ferez wagon, but made no move to help. He blamed himself for Evangeline's apprehension of the cards. He understood fear, but he would not stand for the training of his daughter, not when he suspected that her birth had summoned a deluge and his readings spoke of water yet to come. Charlotte gnawed on their minds like a sickness.

Three months passed. Peabody kept them to a circuitous route toward Philadelphia and eventually New York, toward his son. On an evening before they were due to open in Millerston, Evangeline came to take Bess from Amos.

"Come now, little fish. It's time we teach you to swim." She brushed her hand over Bess's fine black hair.

Amos tucked the baby into his long coat, hiding her from Evangeline's reach. Fear made him tight.

"You know as well as I that Peabody will need her to work. We must teach her. If we begin now, she won't dread it the way I once did. I can make it safe for her."

He wrapped Bess more securely, gathering her into the folds of his shirt. Her grasping fist hooked on to a length of lace. He shook his head, silently cursing that he could not reach his cards.

"It will be years before she can read tarot," Evangeline reasoned. "And who would tell their secrets to a child? Most wouldn't want a child touching the cards at all."

He did not need her to say the rest. She did not want Bess near the cards. He would be unable to speak to his daughter.

Amos held Bess against the wall of the wagon, shuffling the infant into one arm. He removed the cards from their box and smacked the deck down onto a small table, hard enough to shake the legs. He meant to say no, that he was frightened—since the river, since Charlotte. He spread the cards across the table, each humming with his touch.

Evangeline reached for the cards. At the brush of her fingers a wind stirred in the wagon, blowing the deck across the table and to the floor, erasing Amos's words. New cards took their place, painting violence, a murdered woman, great floods, sorrow, and a map of desolation with her, the Queen of Swords, and him, the Fool, at its center. Evangeline bent to collect the cards, but he stayed her. He studied the placement, the layers of meaning. Bess squealed, the sound muffled by his body. He'd protected Evangeline from Ryzhkova's dread and the future she had read for him, but the cards on the floor told a different truth; he had been protecting himself. Evangeline had been keeping secrets.

The frail water girl he'd first met had killed. He saw it in the Swords and how they'd scattered, from Death falling across Judgment's face. Murder was a wearing sin. Each time Evangeline looked for solace, the unsettled spirit would draw misfortune to itself. Her expression held no surprise. He thought of all the cards he'd hidden, how there had been no need. He remembered the red mark that had marred her shoulder when he'd first seen it bared. The welt had torn at him, fascinated him, and his fingers had itched to trace it.

"Please," she begged. When he shielded Bess from her, Evangeline pressed her lips to his forehead. "I did not mean to kill her," she said. "I would take it back." Amos closed his eyes, but he did not let go of the child.

Evangeline had long since left the wagon when Bess began to scream.

Amos spent the remainder of the day in thought, running his fingers across the bed they shared, feeling the impression of her body. She curled up when she slept, a habit from when the tub had been her home. The baby tossed and kicked like her mother. It was good that Bess was not mute like him. He thought of Evangeline's sureness; she had chosen to swim and had sought out Peabody. The dead woman in the cards—Evangeline had done it.

He was not this way. From the moment he had encountered Peabody his life had not been his own. His name was not his own—whatever it had been lived in a house somewhere beyond his memory. He bundled Bess and put her to rest in the costume trunk. She shrieked, her face twisting and purpling with rage. They might begin again, without the cards or Peabody, in a house in Burlington, a place where they could live a solitary life. He would tell Evangeline he did not believe Ryzhkova, or that he would learn not to believe. It was that bruise that had let him love her, because she needed caring. She'd let him care, had chosen him, she had looked after him, learned for him, and kept him from the cage. A simple bruise.

Bess cried the way others bled, as though she might die from it.

He did what he could to comfort her, bouncing her, patting her, and at last turning to Susanna when he could think of nothing else. The contortionist rocked her and called Melina over to rub the child's belly. Nat popped his cheeks and gave the baby a sweet-smelling root to suckle on, but Bess howled until she choked. She needed her mother.

Amos waited.

Evening came. Evangeline did not return.

She'd walked to the ocean, past where the trees thinned into grass, and grass gave way to a strip of sand that beckoned like a smile to come into the water. In the past swimming and the stretch of her body brought her peace, but it did not now. Her breath came deeper than it had before the child; the baby changed her in unexpected ways. The troupe feared her. She could withstand it, but Amos's distrust cut deep. Her body had been reshaped by the baby, but it had changed too for him; the curve between her neck and shoulder had become a rest for his head, her spine had bent to fit to him, her heart slowed when his did.

They could leave. She could leave and take him with her.

The water smelled of salt rather than the sweet, rotting peat scent she'd come to know from rivers. She dove below and the familiar weight fell upon her, perplexing half-formed memories of being drowned by Grandmother Visser. In the water she was deaf to Bess's cries.

She set her feet to the ocean bottom. They came to rest on something smooth like a stone that scuttled under her step. Sharpness snapped her ankle, as though she'd been struck. She shifted her feet only to be smacked again by more lashes, dozens. A stream of breath escaped. The water tasted salt as well.

At the cold briny bottom she could not see the crawling legs or the tails that searched through her dress folds, climbing over her feet and up her calves, hooking into her stockings. She felt an ease she had not known since she was an infant. When her grandmother had held her under in the washtub it hadn't been fear that had caused her heart to race—it had been a sense of right. The hem of her dress sank into the sand, buried by scrambling legs. *Oh, but I belong here.*

When she left water she took lives. She killed grandmothers and sons, poisoned rivers. She washed towns away. But in the water she was whole, in the water she did no harm.

Evangeline let the creatures pile upon her, pulling down her arms, until she was shrouded in a living mantle. The shelled bodies swarmed her. When the weight became such that she could no longer stand, she sat. On the surface, bubbles burst and were lost among the waves.

When she could sit no more, she lay down. Legs and tails knotted in her hair until she became them and they her. Her back settled deep into the sand. Their bodies stole the last of her breath.

The cards were right in all things. She brought misfortune where she walked. She was a killer, though she had not meant to be. Evangeline thought of her girl, who in being born had caused so much misfortune. Amos, with his kind eyes and clever hands, would keep Bess away from the water. In this, she thought, her death would be a good thing. When the need for air came hard like hunger she opened her mouth. It filled with sand and ocean. Inside she became as much water as out. *Strange*, she thought. The mermaid could drown.

Amos did not sleep. He rocked the child against him until morning slipped between the wagon boards. He walked to the water to look for Evangeline, but there was no sign. He bounced Bess against his chest as she cried for milk, for her mother. He looked for footprints, for Evangeline's dress, but found only odd crab creatures on the shore. Swishing tails had swept away all trace of her.

Benno found Amos wandering, gasping, a harsh near-barking sound coming from him. He shook Amos's shoulder, shocked by the sound and his appearance. "What has she done? Are you hurt? Did she hurt the baby?"

Amos pulled free. Eyes narrowing, he looked at Benno, taking his measure from his worn shoes to the tear on his shirt, and finally his scar. He snarled and went to find Peabody.

Without mention of opening nights or traveling time, Peabody ordered a search party. He sent Meixel and Nat on horseback. Each packed a lantern in case they should not return before nightfall. Melina and Benno were to search on foot while Amos remained on the beach, waiting. Peabody came down to the sand with two cushions from his wagon; he dropped one beside Amos and sat, knees cracking like dry wood. "We'll wait."

They watched the ocean. When Bess's shrieks grew piercing, Peabody walked back to the camp and returned some time later with a cup of goat's milk. He dipped a finger into the warm cup, and without moving the infant from Amos's arms, he fed Bess, letting her suckle milk droplets from his fingertip.

Well into the night, after the crabs wandered back into the water, a spot of moonlight glimmered white on the ocean. Amos watched the light bob and dance before shooting to his feet. He jostled the dozing Peabody, who sputtered and coughed when Amos handed him the baby. When it was clear that Bess had not woken, Amos looked back to the water. He stepped in and it rose black and cold around him. The murky bottom sucked at his feet as he stumbled into territory that had previously belonged only to her. He waded to where a swift current ran. He'd not thought to remove his coat or shirt before walking in—she never had—and his clothing impeded progress. When he reached the glinting object, his legs ached and water lapped over his chin. He snatched blindly at the bobbing piece of light; the feel of it was at once familiar but he refused to think on it until he could see it properly. He was near to the shore before he dared look.

A piece of ribbon, white, from the waist of her dress; he knew its texture, the edges frayed from climbing in and out of the tub. His chest burst inside. She would not return. Evangeline was in the ocean.

"Come, let us see what you have," Peabody called from the beach.

Amos stared at the ribbon and caressed the ribs in the weave as he had each time she'd hung the dress to dry. He turned away from the shore and squeezed the scrap of fabric, rubbing at it until it rasped his skin. He moved toward the depths and the current. Peabody yelled to him, but Amos did not listen. The weight of the Les Ferez costume kept him so heavy that the water could not lift him. He disregarded the shout and did not hear the splash.

He was underwater when Peabody reached him. A sodden cotton-covered arm grabbed Amos from behind, pulling him back. Amos fought and kicked, but his clothing slowed him. Peabody hooked another arm under his shoulder and, with strength neither knew he possessed, hauled Amos back to shore.

"Do not fight me," Peabody gasped as Amos struggled. "If you fight me you will drown us both. Do you hear? You'll drown me, boy."

Amos surrendered and let himself be dragged. He let the water wash over him and clung to the ribbon. It smelled strongly of salt, the way her hair often had. When they came to rest on the sand, Peabody dropped him to his back.

"I will not have it. It will not do," he said between splutters. "Two of you gone at once, it is not to be borne." When Amos sat up, Peabody pounded him on the back until he coughed out water. "I have fed you, clothed you, given you all I ever possessed. And you would walk away from me."

A kitten cry rose up from the sand.

"I'd not taken you for a fool. Silent yes, but a fool, no." He extended an arm to Amos, waiting for him to take it. The crying continued. Amos grabbed the proffered hand. Peabody led him to where Bess lay wrapped in his burgundy velvet coat. Amos's hair was crusted with salt and sand, and Peabody's clothing hung like a wet sack. At the sight of them, Bess let out a delighted squeal. Amos stared at his daughter—small, round, with Evangeline's eyes. Painful to look upon.

For a moment he wished she'd drowned like Charlotte in the river, that if Bess had not been born Evangeline would be with him. He sickened at the thought and took the child.

"Good lad," said Peabody. "We'll make you a father."

It would be two more days before the menagerie moved on. Peabody was touched by a gray sadness and tried to attribute it to the downturn in accounts. He did not examine this feeling with a close eye, nor did he knock at Amos's door. He ordered food and goat's milk be left at the Les Ferez steps and kept vigil from his wagon to make sure it was taken.

Amos watched his daughter. Fed her. Slept little.

As days wore on it was decided that he must be coaxed out. Benno was sent to get him. When Amos refused to open the door, he resorted to the metal strips to open the lock. Amos's appearance stunned Benno into muttering a short oath.

The fabric that had once decorated the wagon's interior had been torn down, shredded and thrown about the room. Amos crouched over Bess. Hair wild, eyes sunken; his arms bore deep red scratches from where he'd clawed at himself.

"Oh," Benno murmured. "I am sorry. I am so sorry." He offered Amos his hand, but Amos pulled away. Benno leaned against the wall and slid down to sit on the floor. Amos gave him his back.

For the better part of an hour, they sat in silence. At last Benno spoke. "You would not remember how you were when you first came to us. Barely here. Mostly we did not see you, and when we did," he sliced his hand in the air and made a sound through his teeth. "*Fft.* Nothing. You were an empty glass. *Fragile,* I thought. Then I start to see you with the small horse, and you begin to remind me of my youngest brother. And you were kind to me. I am not one whom people are often kind to. I tell myself I will look after you. When Ryzhkova begins to teach you, I thought *good.*" Benno scratched the back of his head and then pounded it against the wall. "Then Evangeline." He felt Amos's eyes on him and a chill ran through his bones. "Ryzhkova feared her. She asked me to watch over you. Protect you." A dry laugh came from his chest. Amos tilted his head at the sound. "And I think to myself, what could be so fearsome that would drive Ryzhkova to leave? And so I watched. And then I saw Evangeline sneaking away. Then the river died, and then the town . . . I am sorry."

Silence spread between them. Amos gathered his daughter in his arms. They sat for hours until the small lines of sun that sliced through the gaps in the wagon walls stretched then faded into nothing. Bess coughed and sneezed once.

"The child," Benno muttered. "She has lost too much." He rose to his feet and opened the wagon door. "There have been lies, so many, and I have been a part of them. I am sorry, friend. I will find Ryzhkova for you. Her daughter, Katerina—Ryzhkova would go to her. I will find her and tell her what has happened. She will come back. You will work again and teach your girl. I will do this for you. You will not be alone." When he left he pulled the wagon door shut behind him. Benno was gone with the morning.

Amos's time was filled with secret work. Bess had become silent, had not uttered a sound since the night they'd returned from the ocean. For hours on end Amos sat in front of his daughter, trying to remember what Evangeline's voice had felt like when he'd pressed his ear against her breast. When he attempted sound all that emerged was a rough scratching. He held Bess to his chest in hope that the resonance of a beating heart might stir her to sound. It did not.

The cards slept in their box, untouched. They were marked by all that had passed between them—Ryzhkova, him, Evangeline. He would have to cleanse the cards repeatedly, how much he could not be certain, and to cleanse the cards would take the last of Evangeline away, the piece of her that still lived in them. It had been his mistake to not clear them once Ryzhkova had left. He'd only wanted to hold on to the woman who had taught him. The remainder, her lingering fear, had mixed with the cards and become a curse that twined with their fate like a braid. He kissed the top of Bess's head. He would not teach her to speak as he did.

The Wild Boy cage reappeared. Fall turned and they pushed north, hoping to make New York before the weather changed. The Les Ferez cart was painted green and adorned with depictions of a grotesque Wild Man.

In a clearing north of Burlington they made camp under the shelter of ancient oaks. The stop was unscheduled but the troupe was weary; being shorthanded made travel more difficult. Peabody approached Amos's door. It opened a scant crack. A single dark eye looked out.

"My boy, it is time you work. It will be good for your spirit and good for your girl to see you happier. The old act," here he coughed. "It will be as it was before. I think you will be fine at it." The door opened no further. Peabody chewed his bottom lip, causing his beard to bristle. "We got on well once, you and I. Please, let's do so again. We'll start anew."

The door slammed shut.

Hours after Peabody had knocked, Amos emerged from the wagon, child in arms. He was wiry like a stray dog and his clothing fell from him. He crossed the camp and eyes followed him, his every move of interest. He rapped at Peabody's door and was greeted at the first knock. Curly brimmed hat askew, Peabody smiled.

"Fine to see you out, good lad. And with our little girl looking every bit a beauty, she. Quite the—"

Amos thrust Bess at Peabody's chest. He looked a long moment at his daughter before turning on a rotted boot heel and walking back across the camp. Peabody took Bess in his arms and watched as Amos continued past the last wagon and toward the deep of the woods. By the time he thought to send Meixel after him, Amos had ventured far enough that Peabody lost sight of him. The infant looked up at his crinkled blue eyes, clenched a fist around the pointed tip of his beard, and cooed.

"Well, most wonderful girl," he said in the softest voice he could manage, "what have we here?"

In the wood among the branches, Amos divested himself of shoes. His bare feet welcomed the ground, toes digging into loam. His coat followed, discarded on a briar, then the tattered neck cloth and shirt were gone, until only skin separated Amos and the forest. It was curious to see how pale his body had grown under years of clothing. His deep brown hands looked like they belonged to another person. He walked for hours, scrambling and climbing. He held on to the piece of ribbon, winding it around his thumb, petting it. He picked his way over tree roots and stones, toe to heel, silent. Where three high rocks clustered, forming a small peak, he stopped. Rippling indicated a nearby stream, and in its sound he heard whispers of Evangeline. *You are home. I am your home.*

He scaled the boulders, feet digging for purchase in craggy ledges, fingertips hooking into crevasses until he perched atop the tallest rock. His breathing slowed as he came to rest. He sat as he had in the days before Evangeline, Ryzhkova, or Peabody, in the days when he'd crept into the house where he'd been born. The sun began its descent, making long shadows. A short huffing owl call echoed off the rocks. He sat. Amos's shadow mixed with the trees and bushes, shades black as her hair. His breath slowed further until it became that of the world around him—a low breeze, nothing more. He became a part of the woods and the air, and lines defining beginnings and ends softened. Then the sorrow stopped. One moment a young man sat atop an outcropping of boulders, the next he was gone.

In coming days Melina found Amos's clothing and the ribbon from Evangeline's dress. She offered them to Peabody, who abruptly ordered them destroyed. Though Melina told him it was done, she stowed them in a traveling trunk for Bess once she grew older. It should not be as if they had never been. Every child needed to know her parents.

Peabody cared for Bess as his own. He doted on her and began to think of her as the crowning achievement of his years of captaining the menagerie. He ensured that she was taught to swim. Bess took to the water as if made from it. He delighted to see that the girl had a remarkable capacity to hold her breath. In evenings he began sketching plans. Alongside columns of figures, a diving tank took shape in brown ink. Glass. If only they could manage glass. Bess's hair grew long and black like her mother's. Her eyes stayed wide like Amos's.

At her fifth birthday he presented her with a lacquered box adorned with intricately painted figures—a prince and a firebird.

"Bess, my little starling," he rumbled as she worked to open its lid. "These cards are most special; they belonged to your father, a wonderful man, and in them are the keys to all the world. It is time you were instructed. I've heard from my son, Zachary. Our friend Benno has found you a guide. Her name is Katya, and she is the daughter of your father's teacher."

Bess's soft fingers touched the orange deck, flipping over the first card. Lightning and flames—a broken sky. The Tower.

29

With morning comes pounding. We survived the night. Alice is at the front door, knocking on the glass with her forearm. She is in tall green rubber boots, practical as ever.

Enola rouses when I shake her. She smacks Doyle awake.

"Come on," I say. "Help me move the coats so we can let Alice in."

"She's here? I thought we were leaving her the keys."

"She probably just wanted to check in." We move the chairs and throw the coats and sweaters aside, each landing with a saturated thud on the wet carpet. Outside, Alice is bouncing on her toes. Something is very wrong. We open the door.

"Oh God," she says. "It flooded in here? How bad is it?"

The books. Of course, she's here for the books. I didn't know I'd wanted her worried about me until I'd been supplanted by books. "Downstairs got the worst of it. I kept whatever I could dry. I stopped the back door, but there wasn't much we could do. I'm sorry. The whaling archive is safe, though."

"Of course it is. In the archive we trust." The words are joyless. She looks me up and down. "Are you all right?"

"Sure," I say. Then her arms are around me in a quick hug, warm and good. She's still in her pajama bottoms. "Are you okay?"

She takes a breath and holds it. In middle school the girls used to have contests to see who could hold their breath the longest; Alice once held it until she fainted. Her words shoot out all at once. "You have to come with me. Your house is going over and you need to get whatever you can out of it now."

She says something else, but I can't hear it because Enola is saying, "Shit, shit, shit."

"It's bad?" I ask.

"It's bad. The roads are still flooded. My dad told me to get you. He kept calling and calling, and I didn't want to pick up but I thought it could be my mother." She tugs on her hair, wringing it out. "I'm really sorry. Look, I brought the truck. If you follow me I'll take you back where the roads are good. You can put anything from the house in the truck."

The water is more than ankle deep through the lot. We pile into my car and slowly move through the flooding, with Alice leading in Frank's flatbed. She must have picked it up from him, which means she's seen the house. She leads us nearly to the center of the island. Port must still be closed off.

Enola continues quietly swearing.

"You have a chance to get stuff," Doyle says. "That's good."

We follow Alice's taillights up Middle Country Road. Cars are stranded on either side—a ghost town of vehicles. She turns us toward the water, heading north, taking side roads around downed trees. When we reach Till Road, Enola starts to cry.

Alice pulls into Frank's driveway and I park alongside her. I tell myself not to look until we get out of the car and can stare it in the face.

The house is in silhouette, hanging off the cliff's edge, tilting like an Irishman's cap. We stand beside it, four tiny figures, no more than paper dolls, two huddled together, the smallest spark dancing between their bodies. Children at the gates of our history.

"Throw whatever you can get in the truck and come back to my place," Alice says. "You can stay with me."

"Thanks," I say. "It won't be forever."

"We'll work it out." She gives my hand a squeeze. "I need to talk to my mom." She walks toward the house where she grew up, and for a minute I don't know who has it worse, and then I do. It's Alice.

Enola tells Doyle to wait by the car. "This is excavation. Watsons only."

Though he says *cool,* he conveys *be careful.*

The door hangs off its hinges and the hole in the living room floor has become a pit. A wide split spiders up the wall between the kitchen and living room. I can see Mom's hand wrapping around the corner, laughing as she ran down the hallway. We walk around the edge of the room, balancing against things—the couch—I can remember Enola hiding behind it, giggling—my desk, anything that will take weight. Enola sees me limping and offers her shoulder.

"Get that picture," she says, pointing. "The one of me and Mom."

"Frank took that."

"Get over it." She yanks it from the wall. My grown sister hands me her child self. "You're going to want it."

"You don't want anything?"

She shakes her head. "You know I never asked you to stay, right? When it's gone I think you should just forget it was ever here. Be happy, okay?"

A sharp whining screams down the hallway. We tense. Her fingers dig into my shoulder. The sound deepens to a low howl, then crashing. I clap my hands over my ears, but it's too late. Enola mouths something—*what the fuck*. Plaster showers over us. I yell, "Run," as the floor begins to roll. I tuck my head to my knees. Tossed against the front wall, back slammed into the desk. A sucking spasm. Emptied out. A great tearing sound. A chair topples. Glass shatters. Papers and books tumble onto me. Air, air pushes up from under.

The sound dies and the floor stops moving. My ears buzz. The room is thick with dust. Enola is huddled in the corner by the sofa, covered in papers, shaking.

"Fuck! Are you all right? Everybody all right?" Doyle is in the doorway, streaming nervous chatter. Daylight comes from the hall through the dirt and debris. Tentacled arms lift Enola, me, pulling us onto what's left of the lawn and into the whipping grass; his grip has the bite of electricity.

We wind up on the hood of my car. The damage is incredible. The side of the house collapsed, spilling the contents of my parents' bedroom across the cliff, along with bits and pieces of the stone foundation. The bed traveled farthest, mattress hidden among the beach grass, headboard kissing the remnants of the bulkhead, and Dad's shoes toppled down the bluff until they bounced their way into the water. I wanted to throw them out, but I could never bring myself to.

The crabs are still here. They should be gone. They should have left after I'd burned Frank's things and the book. Or rolled out with the tide as the storm that took my house pulled back. It's stronger now, the feeling that I've missed something. Papers are scattered everywhere—leaves or snowflakes—pieces of my family thrown to the wind. Why are the crabs here? Was burning not enough?

"Is that Mom's typewriter?" Enola asks. It is, banked against a scrub pine along with what must be manuals. A piece of chimney falls. Down the cliff, Dad's tools dig themselves into the sand. It's gone. All of it.

Enola takes her cards from her pocket. In the light of day they're brown and worn, edges rounded out until there's almost nothing left at all. They're nearly pulp, worn by skin oils—hers, Mom's, other people's. They smell like dust, paper, and women. She sets them beside her on the hood of the car. Doyle hops down and begins pacing.

"Put those away, Little Bird."

"No." To me she says, "Cut."

"Fine," Doyle replies. "I've gotta walk. I need to walk." He twitches his hand in the air and heads up the street.

I touch the cards, these things that were my mother's. I try to feel her, but there is nothing except soft paper, fibers decayed beyond repair. I cut the deck deep. A thought takes root. It couldn't be. They can't be *the* cards.

"Three piles," she says. She watches intently, as if expecting something to happen, then moves fast, shuffling, flying through paper and setting cards on the hood.

It's a spread I haven't seen before, not the Cross or the Six Rows; it's seven cards in a V shape. Enola coughs and takes the cards before I can get a good look at them. "No good. Cut again." She shuffles and spreads the cards faster. Before she clears the spread away I glimpse swords, a sea of them, and what might have once been a woman. Enola sweeps up the cards, taps the deck. She twitches. "Again." I cut; she shuffles, spreads, then snatches the cards back. This time I catch a card that might have once been black. The Devil or the Tower, maybe. "It's always the same," she says and shuffles again, then sets the cards down to cut. I tell her to stop. She grabs my hand and forces me to cut the deck. When she tries to take the cards away again I catch her wrist.

I say, "Don't."

"Fuck," she says. A perfect V of seven cards. The Devil, the Tower, the Queen of Swords, Three of Swords, a Hanged Man, and a card too worn to read. She tells me it's the King of Swords. When

I ask what it means she shakes her head and picks each card up, returning it to the deck and finally to her skirt. She flops back on the car, flat like a dead man. "They're our cards," she says, almost too quiet to hear.

"What?"

"It's the same stuff over and over again." She digs her index finger hard into her forehead. "They keep coming up in places they have no reason to be. Like if I'm reading some woman about having kids—bang, there they are. Tower. Devil. Death. And water. Shit, there's water everywhere."

A sick feeling comes, followed by a shadow. Yes, these cards are *very* old. This is what Churchwarry and I missed, the cards themselves.

"What did Frank tell you about the cards?"

"They were Mom's and had been her mother's before. I don't know. It's been more than six years. I don't remember stuff like you do."

The satisfaction in solving a riddle is the flash of insight that triggers a tiny burst of dopamine. This does not happen. This is cold sweat. The pictures in the book were Madame Ryzhkova's cards, Amos's, Evangeline's. Enola tore them out because she'd seen them in her deck, Mom's deck. The book found Churchwarry, a Ryzhkova, as if leading her back to Amos. Bringing us together to undo it. And I burned it. "You tore pictures of these cards out of my book. *These cards*. Why?"

"I had to, okay?"

I ask why, but she stays silent. "Enola, put the cards away."

She won't look at me. "No."

"Give them to me."

"No." She gets to her feet. Enola with sea, sand, and shore. She's tight and fierce, with no excess to her sinew and muscle, bones and bright burning like Blake's tyger. She knows. Part of her believes she's going to die.

A dresser drawer slides down the cliff, smashing into a bulkhead. That one had Dad's watch that he wound long past the days when everyone else had switched to batteries. "I'll fix it. I'm fixing it," I say.

"There's nothing to fix. This is just what happens." Sick. Sick. Sick. A sour taste.

I hug her. She's too old to piggyback, but I want to take us both away. "We're going to leave. I'll go with you. Anywhere you want. I don't care. Let's go. Wherever. You, me, Doyle, and Alice."

"Brother mine, I love you some, but you're a very bad liar."

"I promise." Mom must have been trying to get rid of the cards and Frank didn't understand. A bookshelf careens down the bluff.

Enola looks out at the water. "It's pretty here. I forgot that."

"Can I see the cards?"

"Nope."

"We don't all die," I tell her. "There's me, and you don't swim anymore." I tell her we'll go somewhere else, anywhere she thinks is pretty. I tell her there are libraries all over. I can work anywhere. We'll be good again, she and I. I won't parent her, I promise. I say I can teach her about books and she laughs.

Somewhere a part of us does this, leaves and gets right. We climb into her car and let the tires roll, counting one-eyed cars. We toss the cards in a river and it's like Enola said, oysters up the sides like ruffles on panties. We rent a house, freshly painted and new. We start again.

This is not what happens.

There is a roaring sound when the foundation under the hallway breaks, followed by the kitchen, the refrigerator, cabinets, all toppling down. Frank runs out of his house, shouting. Shingles spring down the bluff. It is done. The house is destroyed.

Doyle jogs toward us from up the street. When he reaches us he picks up Enola in a hard, rocking squeeze. He puts her down when she smacks his side.

Frank has walked to the bluff. His hat lies behind him, discarded. He's smaller, empty.

I walk toward him.

"She did love this house," he says when I approach, as though it's his life spilling down the cliff, not mine. Creaking gives way to a sharp snap and Frank shoves me back. Enola's bed scrapes down the broken boards, coming to rest on a partially collapsed wall. "It's all my fault."

"I need to know about the cards you gave my sister. Did my mother tell you anything about them?"

"Your dad was going to move you. I told her it would kill me if she left. I couldn't help it. Then she gave me her cards and told me to hang on to them. They were her mother's and grandmother's. I figured if she gave me something like that she'd be back." He looks away from the rubble, back to me. Eyes bloodshot like beets, like my father's dead eyes. "They passed those things down like they were jewelry."

My skin feels too tight, like I might rupture. My mother must have read the end, the cards Enola keeps reading, the same thing Verona Bonn read, all the way back to Ryzhkova. They passed the cards to each other creating history, fingers touching paper, imbuing it with hope and fears, fear like a curse. Of course they wouldn't clear their cards, they were talking to their mothers, and isn't that part of why I've stayed here? The book noted a falling out between Ryzhkova and her apprentice, a falling out over the mermaid. Enola said that cards build history—what a perfect way to wound someone. The cards were hers, Ryzhkova's, then Amos and Evangeline's on down the line, each leaving themselves in the ink, each pulling from the deck, pulling in fears that work like poison.

The wind blows a sheet of paper across a split board. The only paper of consequence was never in my possession—it was in Enola's.

"I'm sorry," he says. He waits for me to answer.

"I'm sorry about the house," I tell him. I'm not.

I leave him at the bluff, grieving the house. I hear him shuffling through bits and pieces, looking for her in the rubble. He's lost her twice now. I only lost her once.

I see Enola dig her hand deep into her pocket, each shuffle working a hex into her skin. Doyle watches me, craning over the top of Enola's head. He asks after Frank and looks at me with wariness, too alert. He's touched the cards, Doyle who my sister lies to because she's scared, because she loves him.

Alice emerges from the McAvoy house and trudges toward her father. It hurts to watch her put a hand on his shoulder when she'd rather do anything but. But that's who she is—a daughter, a practical woman, the responsible kind. It hurts to see her pull him away from what was my house, toward the place I once wished I'd lived.

I ask Enola if she'll talk to Frank. "Alice shouldn't be alone with him and Leah won't kill him as long as you're there." The look she gives me is dark.

"Thought you'd be happy to see him dead."

"Alice wouldn't be. She's mad now, but she won't be forever."

Enola glances at the tattooed man beside her, then back at me. "What the hell am I supposed to say to him?"

Doyle rubs her hair, possessive, comforting. She chews her lower lip.

"Please," I say. "For me."

"Fine."

When Doyle starts to go with her, I ask him to hang around. He shrugs. We both watch her head toward Frank. With each step I whisper a refrain: *Be good. Be good. Please be good.*

"You put a lot on her, you know," Doyle says beside me.

"Maybe." I start for the bluff, a slow limp. He follows. Again the wary look. "They'll be fine. She'll be all right."

We walk to where the sand sharply dips, where Dad's nightstand emptied its contents: pill bottles, magazines, keys to locks that don't exist anymore. Off to the west a quiet horn signals the ferry's slow trek. I ask, "Where did you say your family's from?"

"Mom is out in Ohio."

Ohio is good. It sounds like somewhere I would never go. It sounds dry, like there might be dry places.

"Why did you come here? What did she tell you?"

He shoves his hands deep into the pockets of his cargo pants. They bulge out. He breathes in, then lets out a prolonged hiss. "She told me you're sick; she thinks you're going to do something, something maybe like your mom did. I thought she shouldn't be alone.

Man, I don't know. I heard about the mermaids and I saw you hold your breath, but I don't know."

"She lied."

He turns quiet. Thoughtful maybe. "Enola doesn't lie to me."

"Yes, she does. I taught Enola how to hold her breath. She's better than I am, or she was. Tell me, what's worse than her brother being sick? Worse to you. Something she would lie about."

His answer is pure reflex. "If she was sick."

I say nothing.

He grunts and drops his head down. He kicks a pebble with his bare foot and it caroms off a shattered mirror, vanishing into the crabs. The tentacle tattoo extends down, twisting around his ankles, stretching out to his toes. "Damn."

"You know some about my family. I'll tell you about some other things, about the cards, specifically the cards."

The sun is high, a bright bullet above the water. I tell him about the menagerie, about a Russian woman and a deck of orange cards, and how when you touch them you leave a piece of yourself behind, how these pieces work like a curse and the thoughts they contain seep into you like venom, how sometimes you hold on to things because you're searching for someone in them, someone you want desperately to love you. How the very best intentions kill us.

We watch as Enola and Alice take Frank back to his house. The tide moves out, thick with horseshoe crabs. After a long time he speaks.

"Do you want me to get the cards from her?"

"I should take them so you don't have to. I think we'll be fine once they're gone."

"I can pick her pocket," he says, quietly. "I used to, you know." Of course he did. "She's got this box for them. You want that, too?"

"Sure." I look at him, this boy. He twitches his fingers to imaginary music. "Can I ask you something?"

A shrug.

"Why the octopi?"

He blushes, a dark stain under the ink. "My pop was in the navy. It's an old sailor thing. Wards off evil."

"Can I ask you something else?"

"The electricity?"

I nod.

His mouth quirks up. "A doctor told me there's too much salt in me, that it makes me super conductive. I don't think he really knew what it was. Maybe I just touched a light switch and it lit me up instead of the lamp. Is it really important to know why?"

"You love my sister."

"I'm going to steal from her for you."

Across the water the ferry has passed the Middle Ground Light. The tide is past peak, the tops of boulders just breaking water. Doyle looks at me, squint-eyed, head tilted. He turns and jogs the distance to Frank's house and I watch his loose-limbed gait, the slow questing of tentacles. At the door he calls her name, then vanishes inside.

I wait, watching the remnants of the house. It's alive with crumbling plaster, blowing papers. It was a house before there was an *us*. After we die there will be nothing to say that we ever were, no house left to speak of us, we'll have all vanished into the water. But that will be later, much later. Not today.

Just now Doyle's hand must be reaching into a pocket, maybe as he brushes her back, maybe as he leans over her. When he lifts the cards it will be almost like the tentacles are sucking on them. I feel hope. With the cards gone, it will stop.

Not more than a quarter hour and he returns, bounding through the grass, box in hand. I ask if she noticed. He shakes his head no.

"She'll be pissed," he says. But she'll be alive to be angry.

"I'm sorry you had to touch them." He should go back to Enola before he's missed. Doyle cracks his neck. He wears guilt like another tattoo. Moments later he disappears back into the house across the street.

The box is smaller than I'd thought; I can hold it with one hand, rounded edges pressing into my palm. Dark red wood shows through layers of damaged paint. The top is covered with dulled illustrations—a man with a moustache, a faded bird with a tail made of flames. *Oh, I remember you.* I lift the lid and shock zips up my fingers. Maybe this is what it feels like when Doyle touches a light. Inside, the paper is orange faded to yellow, soft and ragged from my family's touch. I snap the lid closed.

My right foot hits the beach and a horseshoe crab walks over it. There is hardly a place to stand for the winding and writhing of the crabs.

Simon.

The crabs have dragged the buoys out, pulled them far below the water so that not even the anchor buoys show; I'd need to walk for hours to find them. I take the box from under my arm. I'll need sand, rocks, anything for weight. Quartz pebbles and ground-down bricks mark the high-tide line. As if knowing my intent, the crabs clear a path. I take as many rocks as I think will fit, but the box is so small that pebbles may not be enough. I'll need to bury it, to make sure that when I leave they won't come back. To give the Sound time to do its work.

The water is frigid, like April rather than July, and the first step strikes out cold. But even in the water the box feels hot like flame. Clawed feet swarm, and crab shells slow my walk to a shuffle. They circle, churning sand, tails switching and whipping my heels. As my bad foot moves forward they begin pushing, urging me along. Sharp feet pinch on my pant leg and the crabs begin to climb, clinging like a child to its parent, hanging on as if at any moment I might run. I dust off one and another grabs on.

As when taking out the anchors, I have to move slowly. With each step crabs grip higher, weighing me down. As the water reaches my chest, they've managed to dig into my shirt. I squeeze the box tight to my side. Now. Air out. A quick breath out that sucks in the stomach. Diaphragm up, like a tight drum. Navel to spine. One. Two. Three. Then in, quick breath, spread each rib. The trick is to breathe wide and not let go. The trick is to breathe like you're thirsty. A crab loses its grip, falls to the sandy bottom. I am under.

Simon.

My mother's voice lives in the waves as it always has, as though she never left. Each step is heavy, aching. The light from above fades, lost in the seaweed and the growing horde of crabs. If I look up I can see faint rays spiraling through the salt. I have to get farther out. I can't chance they'll wash up. A sharp tail pricks under my arm, tapping at the box. I pass a bicycle half buried in sand and rock, encased in barnacles and covered with crabs, now part of the Sound. My stomach flutters. A hiccup of air escapes. I walk.

A clawed leg digs at my neck then burrows into my hair. Skin crawls, electric. Stop. Hit it away. It scuttles down my back, clicking over others. More hooking, clawing. Twitch. Shake them off.

Simon, she whispers. Hush. Hush, I have work to do.

More scratching, pricking. The weight. Another hiccup. Pull them off. The box drops. One moment, falling slow to the ground, lid open. Cards scatter, drifting. Horseshoe crabs swarm the box. Prince Ivan clawed. Firebird drowned. A hiccup. More air gone. I reach for it, but my arms won't lift. Horseshoe crabs hang on my sleeves. Back up my neck they pile on. The Tower floats, then is flicked away by a crab. I kick. Scuffle them away. The bad ankle rolls. I fall, sag, to the bottom. Crabs move in. *Ah, god.* A thousand legs, a hundred tails. Onto my stomach, my rib cage, shoving me back. I look up. A beam of light, weak, clouded with algae and brine.

Simon. Sweetly, she says it, calling me home. I can hear her tell me I'm a good son, can feel the eggshells of that last morning beneath my fingernails.

My legs will not lift. My chest won't rise. More breath is pushed away under the weight. On the shore they might look for me. My fingers brush something smooth. A card. A small thing, simple. Water and salt will eat the ink, wipe away its face. Good. Burning was too quick. A slow curse demands slow breaking. The orange will bleed into the Sound. The oil from our fingers will wash away and the paper will soften and dissolve into the sand, into the water's mouth. As the cards break away, so will we.

Octopi for good luck. That's fine. They'll pull the trailer along to Ohio. Enola will lean an arm out the window, her hand flying over the wind. His family will be wide and warm.

I have saved her.

There is a woman with my sister's eyes, and hair long and black like ink—my mother, but not—a silent man beside her—then the mermaid girls, the diving queens, the fortune-tellers and magician's assistants, a sea of black-haired women with odd eyes, chests made wide for swimming and breath-holding, with laughs that sound like shattering plates. There are little girl hands, and scraped legs that I bandaged, knobby knees on my shoulders when I carried her down a cliff, the girl who left me because she wanted to live.

Ah, and now among the black hair and breath-holding, the fortunes and drowning, a single long red braid. Beside me, a pair of freckled hands digs into the beach with mine, French conjugations, cursing my family when I could not, the sweetest taste at the base of the neck, the curve of an arm reaching to the top of a library shelf. A life lived beside mine. I have not been alone. I can feel her now. I was never alone.

There. The last air. The crash of water around me. I am drowned, but it feels like being lifted—the sky's hands on me, pulled up from the sea as I am swallowed by it. Light. Brine. And here, a voice.

You are home.

The fingers on my wrists are hot, almost burning. Though it might be the fire from skin being cold. There's a tear in the black, a pinprick of light. It stabs deeper than the touch.

My name in a thousand voices.

A sharp electric snap, frigid. Bright.

Gagging.

Breath.

A soft voice. Two voices. Far back, distant smudges moving closer. My back hurts, itches, can't get warm. Louder. My name again. Two sounds, a hiss and a mumble. One voice now.

Simon.

My lungs, my guts, pushing out water—not coughing but turning—outside in and inside out, forcing me dry. Dry. Dry, just once I want to be dry. There are arms around my back, pounding my shoulders, beating my spine, clutching and holding. They're wet. Soaking.

A patch of skin worn hard and smooth by a fishing rod.

When light bleeds in again it's forgiving and comes as dots that fuzz and fade into more light, then grains of sand, then dots again, brownish pink. Alice's arms, pied like the shore.

I vomit a deluge onto the sand. Saltwater, algae. Once, as a child, I fell from the monkey bars on the elementary school playground and had the wind knocked from me. I lay on the pavement, diaphragm fluttering, gasping, waiting for the empty to fill. Undrowning is that in reverse. What's full is emptying to again take in life. My lips move. A word forms, a scratchy "Hey."

Enola answers, tiny, angry as I've ever heard her. "You asshole."

And then I'm smiling.

On the sofa in the McAvoys' living room I run my finger over the edge of Alice's thumbnail, though I know that drives her crazy. There's a solid sureness to fingernails, the shell over the tenderest parts of us. I tap on the tip of her nail and she flinches. Instead of pulling away, she tightens her hold. I stare at the scratches on my skin from the crabs' feet, and the fresh black bruises that line the inside of my arms. It wasn't easy to pull me up. I could tell her about her hands, and of all the women around me—all the water, the drowning, the voices—that it's been her hands, always. But it hurts to talk. The Sound has left my throat raw.

Doyle is talking, pacing, telling Enola and Alice what I told him. Littered with nuances and tipped phrasing, he makes my words sound a little like wind. I watch his long toes bend against the living room floor and remember the bite of a spark on my skin. At some point, when I was fresh from the water, he must have touched me.

"I didn't think he was gonna do that, Little Bird," he says. "I swear I thought he was gonna torch the cards or I wouldn't have swiped them."

"It's not your fault," she says. "He's always been like that."

I let them talk about me as if I'm not there. I'm tired. I look at the room from across Alice's shoulder, the slight bump of her vertebra,

330 · ERIKA SWYLER

the still damp weight of her braid. I can see Frank in the kitchen, hunched over, shaken. Leah moving about, making tea. She walks with purpose, calmly sliding a cup into my sister's hands, as though her entire world hasn't shattered. Enola might not even notice where the cup came from, but she drinks. I look up at Alice's mother, and catch the corner of a smile. Subtle, as if to say, *let them talk*.

Alice's voice is soft but forceful. The angry librarian. "He's worked himself to death for you, you know. Worried about you, wondered if you were ever coming back. Simon's been killing himself over you for years."

Enola says quietly, "Don't you think I know?"

It's Doyle who asks, "Shit, what's he gonna do? He can't swim at Rose's."

"Shit," Enola says.

The deepest shame is the one that comes from looking my family in the eye after having died and woken up. They've imagined me drowning again, dying three times nightly in Thom Rose's dunk tank. I can see them piecing together what to do with me, figuring out whether or not I need to be watched. I'm not used to being carried, but there are obligations that come with family, letting them care for you when they need to. Not one of them seems to notice that Enola's hands aren't twitching anymore, or that Doyle's stopped quietly checking in on her. The nervousness has leeched from her, leaving behind someone closer to the Enola I knew when she was a little girl. That lifts the shame. I won. Let them worry a little while. Watching me keeps them from noticing the shift in the air, in the way the salt smells, and the turning that has happened inside us.

"He can stay with me," Alice says. Enola starts asking questions about what I'm going to do, where I'll work. I stop listening. I picture the mobile in Alice's bedroom with its tiny horseshoe crab, and the photograph of her that her father took.

We carry our families like anchors, rooting us in storms, making sure we never drift from where and who we are. We carry our families within us the way we carry our breath underwater, keeping us afloat, keeping us alive. I've been lifting anchors since I was eighteen. I've been holding my breath since before I was born.

"No." No one hears me, so I say it a second time. When silence at last descends I say, "I'm not staying here. I have to be somewhere."

Enola's eyes get round. Alice lets go of my hand.

30

The sand is hot and riddled with stones, unbearable for a man his age. It would take a lifetime to build feet to walk on this sand—hard feet. His loneliness is unexpected, but it's been some time since he's traveled without his wife. Marie is minding the shop under the guise of indulging him. She saw how worried he was; it was kind of her to let him come. He would not have come at all were it not for her gentle push, her patient encouragement of his flights of fancy. He's been fortunate; true companionship is an elusive type of butterfly. He puts a foot in the water. *Good lord, that's cutting.* He misses his wife and the warm blanket that is an Iowa summer. This is the Northeast, he thinks, bitter and cold at the core. He wonders how anyone stands it.

A dilapidated staircase sprawls up the cliff's edge.

A man journeys down it, an older fellow by his pace, though younger than the man on the beach. The descending man is stout, wears a fishing cap, and has the look of a carpenter. He walks past a smattering of rubble, what remains of a house.

"This beach is private. Are you somebody's guest?" the hatted man calls as he nears.

"Are you by any chance Franklin McAvoy?" the man on the beach asks.

Confusion crosses the hatted man's face, but is followed by a terse nod.

"I'm Martin Churchwarry, a friend of Simon Watson. He's spoken of you fondly. Do you know if he's around?"

At the mention of Simon, Frank McAvoy's expression shutters.

Churchwarry's knees wobble, but he soon steadies himself. "Is he all right? I saw the house," Churchwarry says, motioning to the cliff.

"He's fine, he's just not here." Frank shakes his head slowly. "Damndest thing. That house has been around since the 1700s, then gone in one night. He's lucky he didn't go with it."

"Very." The relief Churchwarry feels is palpable. It's odd to feel protective over someone he's never met, but he's fond of Simon, almost unaccountably so. Both men put their feet in the water and stand next to each other, neither admitting to the cold.

"Churchwarry, you said?"

"Has he mentioned me?" Churchwarry's eyebrows snap up.

"Once or twice." Frank looks at the man beside him—a disheveled figure, pants rolled to the knees, a wild brush of gunmetal-gray hair, a long-ago-broken nose. "How do you know Simon?"

Churchwarry pushes his hands into the pockets of his threadbare trousers. He lets the wind blow at his back and wonders what on earth Simon might have said about him. He settles on something easy. "Our families were once close."

"You're the bookseller, aren't you? The one who sent him that book," Frank says.

"I thought he'd find it entertaining," Churchwarry replies. "It had a bit of family history in it. You knew his parents, I believe?"

"Yes," Frank says. At the mention of Daniel and Paulina, he winces. *I killed her. I am a killer.*

"Will Simon be back soon, do you think?"

"Doubt it. He left a letter for me to send you. Haven't gotten around to mailing it."

"A letter? How wonderful." Churchwarry nearly stumbles as a wave splashes his shins. The water is cold and of course he's not as young as he once was.

"I read it," Frank says.

"Of course you did," Churchwarry replies. "It's impossible to leave a letter unopened." Out in the water a bluefish jumps, twisting and splashing down.

"It's a thank-you, mostly, and an apology for losing your books. He wants your help on some kind of project. Didn't make much sense to me. Wasn't supposed to, I guess." He shrugs, not the least bit bashful. "It's back up at the house. You can come in, if you don't mind a walk up the stairs." He looks up the steps, thinking perhaps he should have checked with Leah first. He never would have in the past, but now he is learning his wife again, a process not unlike walking barefooted on the rocks.

"That would be fine." Churchwarry agrees. There's something pleasant about the idea of sitting down with Frank McAvoy. There's a familiarity to Frank that's more than just having one of those faces—a peculiar breed of déjà vu that Churchwarry finds himself reveling in.

"He doesn't have a phone right now, but he said he'll be in touch once they've settled. He's with his sister." The word *they* has a bitter sound to it.

"Oh, of course. He's moving. I should have assumed that after seeing the house." He scratches the back of his neck. "A fresh start can be a very good thing," Churchwarry says, looking back up at the house. Simon's sister is alive. A breath that he was unaware of holding escapes. He feels Frank surveying him, trying to puzzle him out. "You have a daughter, yes? I think Simon mentioned her."

Frank nods. "She left with him. Alice, Simon, Enola, all of them went together."

Churchwarry smiles. *Fitting,* he thinks. A small flash of white rolls at the top of a wave. Too far out to reach, Churchwarry waits for it to come in. "Simon's family, yours, mine, there's history there." The rest he does not know how to say. "In a strange way we know each other, Mr. McAvoy. You have grandparents a few generations back who went by the name of Peabody."

Here a murmur. "I do. And?"

"I was hoping to be able to tell Simon; I think he'd find it important. Does the name Ryzhkov mean anything to you? Ryzhkova, perhaps?"

Franks shakes his head.

"Ah, never mind then. Have you ever wondered why you're drawn to certain people?"

"Haven't thought much about it," Frank says, though he knows it is a lie.

Churchwarry inhales deeply. He's never understood the uninquisitive; but Frank McAvoy is a boatwright, so there must be a spark of art somewhere in him. A small white rectangle washes in on the tide, swaying with the waves. Churchwarry bends down for a closer look. A wave carries the flash of white close enough for him to snatch it. A bit of paper, soft, ruined. Out in the water another piece rolls in. Churchwarry's hands shake. A sharp pain runs through his chest, but it is soon chased by elation. He is touching history. His history.

"What's that?" Frank asks.

"A tarot card, I think," Churchwarry says. Across its face a blurred image, the faint outline of what was once a man's leg, with a small dog by its heel. The Fool. He watches the ink bleed and pool around his thumb until the last suggestion of what had been washes away.

"Oh, hell. Those were Paulina's," Frank mutters.

Churchwarry looks for cards in the waves. He thinks of all Simon told him and what little he remembers of the book. *Of course. It was the tarot cards.* There had been something more about the sketches, something outside the pleasure of old paper and fading ink. It makes sense, he thinks, that the family of mermaids would destroy a curse with water, far more sense than burning things. He chuckles. *More poetic.* He looks at the man next to him, then thinks of the young man he never met. Alive. Churchwarry knows it matters little how much of it he believes, only that Simon believed. And he'd like to as well. For all the wideness of the water, the town he is in feels closed, isolated. Perhaps the book opened a door; books have a way of causing ripples. He watches a card dip and vanish under a whitecap and sees in the water's spray a hope so bright it blisters.

At the shoreline a dark shape skitters near the sand. Churchwarry can make out the gentle movement of a sharp tail. He leans closer. "Horseshoe crab," he says softly. He turns to Frank, smiling at the descendant of the book's original author. "Magnificent creatures." He thinks on how they grow and shed shells, each new skin a soft and glistening beginning. Millennia of crawling, traveling, and clearing their tracks with swishing tails, patiently correcting. He smiles.

"Mr. McAvoy, I'd like to see that letter now. Then I think we should have a drink if you are so inclined. I suspect that we could become friends."

The car is the only noise for a hundred miles, even when passing through the city, as if the world has gone to sleep around them. The toll collectors make no remarks at the dented yellow trailer pulled by a car barely held together by rust.

"It looks like hell, but the engine is still good," Enola says.

Alice doesn't know whether to believe her, or whether to care. Being broken down in Delaware would still be preferable to being broken down in Napawset. She feels bad for leaving her mother, but knows that staying would have been worse. Impossible. Her mother needed her to go. *It's not good for children to see a parent grovel,* her mother told her on the porch. *Go for a while. When you call and both your father and I pick up the phone, come visit.* Alice knows her mother, how she can shame someone with a look. Her father will grovel. She almost feels sorry for him, but then it is easier to decide not to think about him at all.

When they drove past the reedy salt marshes and the clam diggers crouching in the loam and muck, she knew it was the last time she'd see them, and that she'd miss them. Now Alice stares down the highway, knowing that what she'll miss is the rhythm to her days—dawns spent fishing on the pier, looking at the playwright's house and wondering about the torrid affairs that took place inside it. She glances in the mirror at the two men sleeping in the backseat. Simon's shaggy black hair is pressed against the cracked vinyl. He sleeps as if making up for years of being awake. No, not beautiful, but hers. Doyle snores softly. Now and then a tiny snap of a blue spark dances off the end of a fingertip when it touches the window.

From the passenger's seat Enola turns to Alice and whispers, "It's like licking a penny." Alice does not reply and so Enola continues. "People wonder what kissing him is like. He's like a fresh penny."

Alice stays quiet. Thirty or forty miles of New Jersey later Enola says, "Thank you." Then much more softly, "I couldn't get to him. I just couldn't."

Alice takes her hand from the wheel. She finds Enola's thin fingers and squeezes them, because she's not good at explaining, other than to say that there are things you do for someone you've known your whole life, and that pulling them from the water is the very least.

They stop in Maryland. There is a shop with special paper, ragged edged, old feeling, the sort that likes a fountain pen but loves a quill. He wants leather, too, but there's no money for it. They pay in cash—Enola's money, crumpled twenties that Doyle had squirreled in one of his duffels, Alice's own, and the hundred dollars that Frank forced on her when she said they were leaving. The clerk's eyes bulge at the sum. Doyle has a difficult time lifting the reams.

At night, in scratchy motel beds on the way to Savannah, Simon stays awake to write. When his head starts to nod, Alice bends over him, kissing his arms on the bruises. Dark smudges from where she hung on to him as she dragged him from the Sound. Marks of living, she'd call them, and is grateful for the years of lifting volumes, of fishing, of being practical, for things that made her grip strong. Later, when he curls around her, when her spine curves to his stomach, he whispers, "I'm sorry, I'm sorry, I'm sorry." She hears, "Thank you."

He is building the book again. As they approach the bearded trees that mark the true Deep South, she wonders if this is just another obsession. She asks him why it matters when they're starting over, starting new. He answers, "I am this manuscript." The words hang heavy between them until she catches him drawing a rudimentary sketch of a black-haired child, and knows it is Enola. He's building his history, the menagerie at its start and everywhere after, all his notes on the forgotten women, the Ryzhkovas, the Peabodys, and her.

"What will you do if you can't find enough information?"

"Churchwarry will help," he answers. "Sometimes we'll make it up. The dirty secret about history is how much of it is conjecture." He shrugs. "And we'll fill in spaces. They were good at inventing themselves." He's referring to the women, the dead that have preoccupied him, but he means himself, too. He says *we* now. He didn't used to.

She knows that her name will find its way into his speculations. So will his. Because there are things you do for people you've known your whole life. You let them save you, you put them in your books, and you let each other begin again, clean.

A selection of questions posed to Erika Swyler by librarians.

The prize awarded for the winning question was a place on a bookbinding course.

1. **Have you had any feedback on the way you used tarot in the book?** – CAROLYN NICOLSON, NEWMAINS LIBRARY, NORTH LANARKSHIRE

   Yes! I was expecting quite a lot of negative feedback. I was afraid of tarot enthusiasts telling me I'd butchered what they love. The response I've received was very different from what I anticipated. By and large, people have been incredibly positive. One lovely woman said I've changed the way she reads tarot. It was important to me that the tarot cards be seen as a language. That seems to be an idea that people want to embrace.

2. *The Book of Speculation* **describes the power that a book has over the characters in the novel. What sort of power have books had over the author and is there a particular book that has had this power?** – WENDY BLOOMER, DEVON LIBRARIES

   Books have always been a safe place for me, not just to escape, but to connect. The books that have had the most profound impact on me have been Graham Swift's *Waterland*, and Katherine Dunn's *Geek Love*. *Waterland* changed how I view the place of an individual's story in world history. It's also a book I hated at first, but grew to love as I read it. It changed me as a reader. *Geek Love* is such a powerful and twisted book. You can't walk away from it without having an opinion. It's impossible. I've on occasion used it to choose my friends. If you can't have a good discussion about *Geek Love*, we can't be friends.

3. **With the relationships between Simon, Frank and Martin there is a belief in six degrees of separation. Was this your intention and do you think that is the case?** – DAWN VALLANCE, GLASGOW LIBRARIES

   Yes, it was my intent. There's unfinished business between the families in the book, the sort of things that would keep drawing them to each other across generations. Part of it is fate, but part of it is simply that the world is very small. I've found that once you develop a specific interest, be it in books, circus, or anything else, you start to notice that everybody involved with it knows each other, and quite a few people are related. Interests are both taught and inherited, and they make the world smaller.

4. **Do you believe that the characters in the book were capable of changing their fate, or, once the cards had been revealed did their message become self-fulfilling? Had they not known, could they have followed a different path?** – DENISE SPARROWHAWK, HARTLEPOOL BOROUGH LIBRARIES

I do think the characters were capable of changing their fate. To my mind, they did. The thing that ultimately changes fate is communication, between Churchwarry and Simon, Simon and Alice, Simon and Enola, between Enola and Doyle. Communication helps us recognize patterns. Recognizing patterns helps us break them. Had there been no communication, the curse would continue.

5. **Which chapter number did Stephanie Friedberg scream at you in the middle of the night?** – JANET WESTCOTT, POOLE LIBRARIES

Chapter 17. To date, nearly all of my friends have sent me an angry text upon finishing the chapter. Stephanie is a trendsetter.

6. **As the tale focuses on different generations of the same family, have you delved into your own family history and if so, how did this help you in the planning of your first novel?** – WENDY JEWITT, WAKEFIELD LIBRARIES

Years ago, my aunt had done research into my family tree and traced one side of the family back to the early 1700s. It was a list of names and nothing more. We knew dates, but nothing about the people. The other side of my family scattered during the Great Depression, so I have little to no information on anyone. I'm very familiar with the information walls that pop up due to lack of documentation, poverty, and time. In both instances, I wanted what wasn't there. For my "missing" family I wanted names. For the names I had, I wanted lives. To make up for my lack, I tried to give Simon both.

7. **Would you go swimming on July 24th confident that the curse has been broken?** – LIZ PARKES, BIRMINGHAM COMMUNITY LIBRARIES

I would and I have! I went swimming this July 24th and it was lovely. For me, much of the novel is about finding agency in situations where we feel powerless. So, yes, we all have to swim.

8. **You delved very deeply into the mysterious world of the circus and mermaids. Do you have any connection to circus life and do you believe in mermaids?** – LOUISE DOWELL, HMP LEICESTER LIBRARY

I have a very loose connection to circus life. I studied acting at university, and part of that entailed a semester of clowning, which I was terrible at. One of my professors was also a ringmaster in a small circus. Until that moment, I hadn't realized that running away with the circus was an option. Circus has always been fascinating to me. As for mermaids, my variety of mermaid *does* exist. There are free divers who can hold their breath for nearly nine minutes. While that's not quite as long as Simon or Evangeline, it's only a matter of time before someone does it.

9. **Your characterisation is so powerful; I could see the faces of the players in the story. As you develop your characters do their faces change for you?** – SORRELLE CLEMENTS, COVENTRY LIBRARIES

Yes, they do! Characters start out quite physically vague for me. As I get to know them better, they become more developed. I learn how they move in the world, how they're treated, and how they treat others because of their appearance. That's when faces really solidify for me.

10. **A Dilemma Question: Your favourite book banned and all copies burnt OR it's turned into a musical by Ben Elton? Which one would you choose?** – PETER HUGHES, PORTADOWN LIBRARY, NORTHERN IRELAND

(*This is my favorite question – the winner!*)

Oh! I'd have to pick the Ben Elton musical. My favorite book is Katherine Dunn's *Geek Love*. I push it on absolutely everyone, so I'd be beside myself if all the copies were gone. Also, there's something wonderfully twisted about having to make a musical that involves a large dance number about a cult focused on amputation.